Instinct or Learned?

Instinct or Learned?

E. Glenn Tickner

To order additional copies of this book, contact:
Xlibris
844-714-8691
www.Xlibris.com
Orders@Xlibris.com
807530

This novel is dedicated to my father, Ernest Tickner, and our mutual friend Christel Morris for their encouragement and thoughts during its creation.

Chapter 1: Oklahoma City

Employees in the Murrah Federal Building were beginning their day's activity on April 19, 1995. Abruptly and without warning, a yellow-and-crimson fireball, one hundred feet in diameter, surged up through the back of the building and headed towards the fleecy clouds. The fireball continued to grow in brightness and intensity as it expanded through the entire structure, consuming material and projecting fragments skyward. The earsplitting explosion temporarily deafened all in the neighborhood. Projectiles made of concrete pieces the size of an orange fell from the sky. The fireball continued to ascend into the morning sky, diminishing in color to form a white, mushroom-shaped cloud hundreds of feet above the building; the cloud began drifting eastward with the prevailing wind as white ashes continued to flutter to the ground.

Shortly thereafter, local authorities declared the event an emergency and notified local Community Medical Services and hospitals. Over the public address system within the Oklahoma University Medical Center, a broadcast echoed through all hospital rooms. "This is a medical emergency announcement. Our Hospital Disaster Plan has been declared by hospital management, code red. All HDP staff are ordered to the ER stat." The broadcast continued for several minutes, and staff HDP members ran toward the ER.

Dr. Jacob Gottlieb had just entered the building, when he heard the announcement, like others raced to the ER. He was among the first to arrive. He entered Dr. Campbell's office, who was on the phone and seated at his desk. Campbell looked up and saw Jacob leaning over it with both hands planted. "Jacob, we have a large medical problem ahead of us. There has been a giant explosion at the Murrah Federal Building."

"Yes, I actually heard it, even with my car radio playing."

"I am afraid there are many deaths and burned victims. I am so pleased that you are here to help us. Let's implement code red as developed in HDP. You take the lead, starting now as our triage physician. You will be assisted by nurse Conners from our ER staff."

Outside Campbell's office, medical staff were pouring into the ER. The two doctors exited Campbell's office to face the forming crowd, some breathing hard from their run. Gottlieb grabbed a straight-back chair and stepped up on it. In a loud voice, he said, "Quiet, please. I am Dr. Jacob Gottlieb. If you haven't heard, there has been a massive explosion at the Murrah Building. Ambulances are on site. We are expecting many causalities from the event, and they could be here within minutes. HDP has been ordered by management, and we are implementing code red."

Gottlieb turned his head as he spoke to the assemblage. "As you know, this means we are expecting a large percentage of burn victims. We also expect to receive the normal medical emergencies, except for orthopedic problems. The Community Medical Service director has assigned orthopedic problems to Integris Hospital. However, we will accept orthopedic patients with burns. Therefore, we will require orthopedic physicians to participate in at least three burn rooms."

Dr. Campbell interrupted. "Dr. Gottlieb was chief triage officer during Operation Desert Storm during the Iraq War in 1990. He has considerable experience in this regard."

Jacob continued, "Thank you, Dr. Campbell. Today I will be assisted by nurse Joanne Conners of the ER staff. Her job is to collect vital information from the patients, the paramedics, and me and log it onto the computer system. You will have our log and the CMS report on your ER network listed under both the patient's wristband number and name. We require one ER nurse in each treatment room. They have considerable experience with this system. Use them. Nurse Joanne will also assist me in preparing patients for the ER. I will place notes at the foot of each gurney with the patient's name and wristband number and identify the ER room for treatment. Further, I will also specify the medical priority from one to four. The higher the number, the greater the need for prompt medical care.

"Nurse Joanne and I will also be handling pain management of all untreated patients. Once we have completed our work outdoors, orderlies will move the injured into this room to await their turn for your services. I now ask the maintenance group to set up two tents for our triage work on the ambulance unloading dock outside those doors. Stat!" Gottlieb turned and pointed toward the emergency doors. "Each tent should accommodate six injured people placed on hospital gurneys."

The crowd was getting noisy, so Jacob hollered, "Quiet, please, listen up." He paused and wiped his lips on his coat sleeve as the room fell silent. "ER rooms one through six will be rooms for burn patients. ER rooms seven and eight deal with surgery. Rooms nine and ten are for cardiac, stroke, and pulmonary patients. ER rooms eleven and twelve are the catch-all rooms for noncommunicative patients and those suspected of drug overdose. All rooms will require one anesthesiologist or one immediately available. We expect four physicians, including anesthetists, and three nurses and one orderly in each treatment room."

There was motion in the crowd as Gottlieb's good friend, Dr. James Hanford, politely pushed his way through them and walked over to room twelve. It was easy to spot him because his six-foot, five-inch height and thick, bushy blond hair made him stand above the assemblage. "I got room twelve, Jacob," he said as he entered it.

"Okay, let's move!"

As taught during rehearsals, doctors and nurses began filling each treatment room and preparing their work areas. Gottlieb continued, "Excess personnel will remain until given the high sign to return to their normal work stations." Jacob stepped down from his chair and, as he did so, he heard a siren. Nurse Joanne, with long, brown hair flowing over her shoulders, grabbed his coat sleeve and pulled him through the double doors, tugging him outdoors on tiptoes.

The first ambulance was near. The dock was empty except for four gurneys and a few large wooden boxes. Joanne lugged her desktop computer out to the loading dock, placed it on an available wooden box, and logged into the emergency network through an external computer port. Jacob donned a white coat just handed him by an orderly as the nurse rolled her hair into netting. The maintenance group arrived and began assembly of the first tent.

The first ambulance backed up to the dock close to the edge, where tulips were in bloom and moving in the light breeze. The Paramedic and an Emergency Medical Technician hurried to the rear door of the ambulance and pulled out their gurney, carrying a woman, who was crying. The two pushed the gurney up to Gottlieb. The EMT handed their report to Joanne. The paramedic, EMT, Joanne, and Jacob grabbed a corner of the blanket the patient was lying on and transferred her onto a hospital gurney. The EMT and Paramedic returned to the ambulance for the second patient rolling their gurney behind. Joanne began entering the ambulance log data and the wristband number into the network.

Jacob started talking to the overweight woman, who was still sobbing even after delivery of Demerol through an iv. "Ma'am, I am Dr. Gottlieb, and I will be examining you. We will have to remove your clothing. Your clothes are badly burned." He could see some of the damaged skin through the hole in the burned dress. In an area on her left hip, her dress appeared welded to the underlying tissue. Rather than remove material affixed to her skin, Gottlieb decided to cut around it and leave it for the ER staff to handle.

"Joanne, do you have your nurses' sterilized utensil kit yet?"

"No! Not yet. It's on the way."

"When you are free, help me remove her clothing." Jacob was carefully removing her shoes and stockings when Joanne returned. An orderly, pushing a cart, barged through the double doors.

"Where do you want this cart with the sterilized utensils, nurse?" the orderly said.

"Leave it right here. Thanks."

"Ma'am, we are going to remove all of your clothing now. It might hurt a little. We are sorry if it does," Jacob spoke in a kindly voice. "Joanne, we are going to leave the portion of her dress fused to the skin. We will require bandage scissors for that when the time comes."

The two worked together, and much of the patient's attire was removed except around the hip area. The patient continued sobbing during the process.

"It's time to cut her dress," Jacob said. Instantly, the scissors were slapped into the palm of Jacob's right hand. "I am going to cut a circle around the badly burned area and leave the fabric. Then we can remove her clothing."

Gottlieb began cutting the dress into several large pieces, leaving a ten-inch piece over the worst burned area. As they removed the last of it, the woman began vomiting. Joanne grabbed a plastic container from the nurse's tray to collect the discharge, held it under the woman's mouth, and cleaned her face with a towel. "Do we have our drugs yet?"

"Yes, Doctor."

"Give her two ml of Zofran now please."

After the Zofran was delivered through the iv placed by the Paramedic, Jacob said to the weeping woman, "Ma'am, we are ready to administer some additional painkillers to numb the burned area." Following that injection, Jacob said, "I am going to lift her up. I want you to unsnap her bra and remove it." When the woman stopped sobbing, Joanne began cleaning the burned areas.

"Do we have any lidocaine for our muscle injection, Joanne?", Gottlieb asked. Instantly, a loaded hypodermic syringe with a needle was handed to Gottlieb. Jacob injected it into the muscle area around the hip through the fabric still attached to her skin. The patient winced a little when it occurred. Joanne logged the treatment on the computer.

"I am going to examine her now," he said. "Please make these entries in her file." The efficient nurse had already anticipated the next step and moved to her computer. Jacob turned his head toward her and began. "Third-degree burns on left hip and thigh. Second-degree burns on left ribcage, lower left thigh, and under left breast. First-degree burns on left ear, cheek, and calf. No bone breakage detected."

Joanne and Jacob placed a surgical gown on the woman and covered her with a blanket. Gottlieb wrote in large letters on an eight-and-a-half-by-eleven piece of paper "Janette Wallace, #4257, ER 3-6, grade 3." He motioned to an orderly to take the gurney into the ER. One of the tents had just been assembled, so the paramedic wheeled their second patient into it.

The Paramedic, EMT, Jacob, and Joanne transferred an unconscious male patient onto the hospital gurney. Jacob checked him for broken bones, stroke symptoms, insulin shock, and drug overdose; he found none. "What is his name, Nurse Joanne?"

"He had no wallet, Dr. Gottlieb."

"Well, that is strange. We'll call him 'Goldfish 1' for now." Jacob placed a note on the blanket. "Goldfish 1, #4258, ER 12 Grade 1."

In the distance, the outdoor medical staff heard more sirens. A few minutes later, six new patients arrived and were placed in the first triage tent. These were all burn victims, one having a possible broken tibia. A short while later, patients were wheeled directly into the open ER, to be rushed into a treatment room.

The stream of ambulances continued throughout the morning. The triage couple worked feverishly and efficiently to assess the problem and direct the patient to the proper treatment room.

Near one p.m., all patients were in the ER, awaiting treatments for their injuries or receiving treatments. Many of the patients had been treated and transferred upstairs to hospital rooms. Those with potential stokes were moved directly up to Dr, Chapman's ward for further examination. Jacob located a straight-back chair in the ER and carted it out to the loading dock; he collapsed onto it, causing it to groan. Out of nowhere, Joanne arrived at Jacob's side and handed him a turkey sandwich and a cold bottle of water.

Jacob just stared at his hands holding them. Perspiration dripped down his face. Joanne carried her own chair outside, sat next to him, and began munching on her sandwich. Jacob noticed she wasn't perspiring.

"You were great, Dr. Gottlieb."

"Thanks. I couldn't have done it without you. You are a fantastic young lady. Just fantastic! However, we are not done yet. I hear another siren off in the distance."

Gottlieb finally managed to take a gulp of water. His hand then slowly returned the bottle to his lap to join the sandwich and await the next ambulance. He craned his neck, looking to see it approach the ER entrance.

The tents were now vacated. Either tent would do. According to the Paramedic, this patient had to be dug out of the rubble. He could hardly speak, but he muttered, "John Keiper" and passed out. Jacob checked his vital signs. Miraculously, he was still alive. Since he was now unconscious, Jacob and Joanne quickly removed all his clothing. Jacob began his evaluation, and Joanne washed his abused body ravaged by flames and concrete.

Gottlieb turned to Joanne and said, "Not only does he have all of these burns, but he has multiple broken bones over his entire body. Make a note. His situation is dire." He placed a note on John Keiper's blanket, "ER 1 or 2 and grade 4," on a card placed on his gurney. He added an additional note. "Attend immediately."

Following a few minutes' pause without an ambulance, Gottlieb and Joanne went into the ER to check the pain levels experienced by the untreated patients still waiting for medical care. He looked for the last patient, Keiper, and didn't see him. He felt good that Keiper was in a treatment room.

Jacob heard the familiar tone of his good friend and business partner James Hanford as he approached him in the ER lobby. Jacob was leaning over an ER patient and straightened when he heard a familiar voice. "Are there any more victims, Jacob?"

"I believe we have all of them, Jim. I just came in to check on patients' pain levels." Jacob began rubbing his lower back with both hands.

"Did you have any major problems with your patients?"

"One of the druggies had to have his stomach pumped. I had another in insulin shock. I sent him up to Dr. Roosevelt in internal medicine. I feel certain that Dr. Campbell had serious problems with all of those burned victims. Wow, what a headache for ER staff."

"The last patient to come in is in Campbell's hands right now. He was dug out of the rubble. If anyone can pull him through, it's Campbell."

Jacob exhaled deeply and slowly. He scratched his nose and said, "That patient has deep burns and broken bones all over his body. I wouldn't know where to begin if I had to treat him. He was really in terrible condition. I hope they can save him, and if they do, he will have a difficult recovery."

Jacob raised his hands over his head and clasped them together in additional stretching. Then he headed outdoors, holding his lower back, and once outside sweat began to form on his forehead since the outdoor temperature had climbed. He slumped onto the straight-back chair and, while waiting, began munching on his turkey sandwich. Joanne plopped next to him.

"Joanne, do you know how to find out if further ambulances are underway?"

"Yeah. I can do that. I'll call the EMS director." She walked over to a temporary phone brought out by an orderly and called the director. She returned to Jacob's side, smiling. "The director doesn't expect any more survivors. Most ambulances have been sent back to their headquarters. One ambulance remains on site. We are waiting for problems elsewhere in the city other than the Murrah Building."

Jacob exhaled slowly. "Wow, what an experience! It reminds me of Iraq all over again."

About five minutes later, a sleezy-appearing man staggered up the stairs to confront Jacob. He had disheveled hair and dirt on his hair, hands, face, and clothing. His clothing was so dirty that it would be rejected by the county dump. He stared at Jacob for a long period before speaking. "Are you a doc?" he asked.

"Yes, what's your name?"

"My name is Jimbo. That's what everyone calls me."

"Do you have an emergency?"

"Yes! I've been puking for hours, and I can't stop. I got da dry heaves now." He leaned over and vomited, but nothing projected.

"What did you have for dinner last night?"

"Na, I don't have dinnar last night. It was today about three hours ago dat I had a problem. Ya see, I was walkin' by da drugstore, and I see a car with a half-full bottle of whiskey on the front seat. The door was unlocked, so I grabs it and runs around the corner and takes a big swig and swallowed. It wasn't whiskey. It was piss. I started puking, and I have been puking ever since. My stomack is all screwed up."

"Okay, I see," Jacob said, holding back a laugh. He ambled over to the drug tray and picked up a small jar of wafers. "Take one of these now and every half hour until the container is empty. They will calm your stomach.

"Orderly," Jacob called, and one showed up promptly. "Take Jimbo here to the bus stop and place him on the bus of his choice. Here is a dollar for the bus fare, and if he gets on the bus, hand him this twenty-dollar bill for his dinner."

The orderly and Jimbo walked down the stairs, by the tulips, and out of view. Then and only then did Jacob and Joanne laugh uncontrollably.

Between laughs, Joanne said, "That was nice of you to buy dinner for him, Dr. Gottlieb."

"The thought of you having to bathe him bothered me greatly. We just had to get rid of him."

Chapter 2: Hypnosis

Six weeks passed after the Murrah Building bombing. Erick Anderson, the man who had been unconscious in the triage tent, made his first appointment to see Dr. Jacob Gottlieb at the Oklahoma City Psychiatric Center. He was escorted into the treatment room by the nurse after she measured his weight and height.

Erick's eyes scanned the treatment room. The room was certainly different from any normal examination room he had ever seen. It was large with multi pastel-colored drapes around the four windows. Three windows faced an enclosed patio with flowers and a large olive tree in the middle. The fourth window opened to a floral, covered side yard. There was a professional desk, two comfortable stuffed chairs, a few rigid-back chairs with armrests, a large couch, a hall tree, and a silent wall clock. Two large-leaf plants adorned two corners.

The nurse led Erick to a stuffed chair and asked for his jacket. He gave it to her, and she hung it on the hall tree by the door. "Dr. Gottlieb will be in shortly," she said as she exited the room.

Gottlieb entered the room from another door, carrying Erick's papers. Erick stared at him for the first time, and noticed that Gottlieb was a striking thirty-five-year-old man and possessed the somewhat chiseled facial appearance of the Roman statue Apollo. However, unlike the famous statue, Jacob had a fawn-colored mustache, the same color as his thinning head of hair. The mustache was thickest directly under his nose and thinned out triangularly from there to the edge of his mouth. He appeared taller than him. He was wearing a comfortable pastel-colored shirt, which was adequate for the air-conditioned room.

After the obligatory greeting, Gottlieb asked Erick to be seated on the stuffed chair. "Erick, I understand from your forms and from a telephone call from your wife that you have a reoccurring nightmare. Further, she believes that it is associated with the Murrah bombing, because the nightmare started the night you returned home from the hospital."

"Yes, that's true, Doctor. I have the same dream about two times a night now, sometimes more, and I awaken her by thrashing under the covers. I kicked Abi hard enough to cause bruising once."

"Is Abi your wife?"

"Yes, Doctor. She is the one who demanded that I come and see you. She has been trying to get me here before, but I told her that I saw you when I hadn't. I should mention that her name is Sophia, but I call her Abi, short for Abigail, her middle name." Erick sat on his hands as he spoke to suddenly withdrawing them to sit on them again.

"Erick, do you remember the day of the bombing?"

"No-not really. That whole period of time before and after escapes my memory. I guess I have amnesia."

"You have an underlying cause for the nightmares. It is my job to help us find it and get you to face it. When we do that, the nightmares will go away. Sometimes the nightmares may not be directly associated with the actual trauma. The dream could be a secondary message and not the real message."

Erick watched Gottlieb's facial expression when he was talking, looking at him straight in the eyes. "I understand, Doctor."

"Erick, I want you to tell me your reoccurring dream in as much detail as you can. I am going to record your descriptions. I may from time to time interrupt you to clarify a point or situation. Okay?"

"Sure."

"All right then, you may begin. Please start at the first part of your dream. Oh yes, name people and what they are feeling or doing when you contact them in your dream."

Erick started, "It always begins with me waking up in the morning at the regular time and driving over to Mary's house. It's about seven thirty a.m. when I arrive."

"Who is Mary?"

"Mary is my baby sister. She is thirty-two years old, so she is almost three years younger than me."

"Are you close?" Jacob asked.

"Oh, yes, Doctor, Mary and I are—I mean were—as close as any two humans could be. We really love one another, and I am a good friend with her husband, Bart, too. Also, I really love their son, Sean."

"Erick, why did you change the word *are* to *were* a few seconds ago?"

"I sometimes forget. Mary was killed in the Oklahoma City bombing several weeks ago."

"That had to be just a dreadful experience for you."

"It certainly was, Dr. Gottlieb. It was awful. That memorial service was the worst day of my life by far. You see, I stop at Mary's home almost every morning on my way to work. When I arrive, Sean runs up and hugs me. You see, Doctor, Abi and I have been unable to have children, so Sean has been our surrogate son. We often kept him over a weekend so Mary and Bart could have some quiet time together."

Gottlieb asked, "Does Sophia enjoy Sean?"

"Oh yeah, you can't help it, because he is—was—so loving. Sophia—"

Gottlieb interrupted Erick. "Excuse me, Erick. Did Sean die in the disaster too?"

"Yes, Dr. Gottlieb. Abi told me that Sean was in the nursery when the blast occurred."

Gottlieb jotted something in his logbook. While he did that, Erick withdrew a hanky from a rear pocket and blotted his eyes of the forming tears.

"As I was saying, Doctor, Sophia sometimes picked Sean up at school and brought him home, and he spent time with us. She wouldn't do that unless she really loved him too. Sophia misses him as much as I do. I cannot imagine life without Mary and Sean. There has been a tremendous void since their passing." Erick changed positions in his seat as he revisited the dream. His back leaned against the seatback and quickly moved forward again.

"On this day in my dream, I had taken my wallet out to show Mary a new picture of Sean. It was a photo taken at a local park near my home. On that day, I had given Sean a chocolate ice cream cone, and he spread it all over his face, from his chin to just below his eyes. He had the biggest grin on his face that I had ever seen on a child. I was so proud of that picture, so utterly proud." Erick made a hard swallow, then continued.

"I overstayed my visit and rushed off to work, leaving my wallet behind. I had to drive to Dallas that day. When I was halfway to work, I missed my wallet and headed back to Mary's kitchen. Mary had gone to work, so I let myself in. But the wallet wasn't there. I assumed Mary must have taken the wallet with her. She also takes Sean, who stays there in the nursery, until Bart picks him up for school. I was certain Mary was planning on driving over to my office during her lunch hour to bring me the wallet. I couldn't wait because I had to drive to Texas for two days, so I headed downtown to the federal building where she worked.

"I was running late. I still had to go to work and pick up my materials for the trip. It was about nine a.m. as I neared the federal building. In fact, I was right there on the grounds, turning the corner at the back of the building, when a heavy blast from an explosion rocked my car, blinded me, and hurt my ears. It was terrible with fire and smoke everywhere in the building. I was still moving when I slammed on the brakes. I saw flames from the federal building, and pieces of concrete came flying. I stared in disbelief. I couldn't believe my eyes. I sat frozen in my car, viewing the building in flames."

"In my dream when the dust cleared and the debris stopped falling, for a second, I saw the missing portion of the building where the nursery/day care was located, and the floor directly above the nursery was where Mary's office used to be. When I saw that explosion, Dr. Gottlieb, I witnessed my sister's and nephew's deaths. They were gone instantly, just like that." Erick snapped his fingers. "I got out of my car, heading to the building to help Mary, when I staggered and fell. I remember crying, shouting, and cursing."

"What happened after that, Erick?"

"I don't know, because I always wake up."

"Erick, did this happen to you in real life or only in the dream?"

Erick twisted, turned, and finally managed a response. "I believe that it happened exactly, exactly as I had described in my dream. I know it—I just know it, but I cannot remember it. My memory and dream are all mixed up. I have no memory of anything for those few days surrounding the bombing."

"Why do you now believe you actually witnessed the bombing?"

"The police located my car in the roadway at the back of the federal building. It was completely coated with a white dust and had dents in it. The engine was still running. My car was brand new."

"Did you ever tell anyone about your dream?"

"No, Doctor! I could never get the courage to do so because I would always feel like crying."

"Erick, why did you not tell Sophia about this dream?"

"I don't know. It just messes me up inside. As I said a few minutes ago, I just couldn't let myself do it. I couldn't do it!" Erick's chin dropped to his chest, and his head moved sideways. "No, no, I couldn't do it."

Jacob began to talk to Erick. "Withholding these pent-up feelings isn't a good thing. I cannot overstate the importance of telling Sophia your dream as soon as possible. She must be made aware of the exact story, as you have told me. This will go a long way toward bringing her into the loop of understanding what you are going through. I want you to talk to her today and come back here next Wednesday. Okay?"

Erick nodded but said without conviction, "All right."

Shortly after his doctor's appointment, Erick parked in his driveway. Sophia saw him and opened the garage door. Erick entered the kitchen with chin on his chest, his stomach churning like a clothes washer. Seeing Sophia brought chills to his whole body. Gottlieb's words popped into his head. ***Tell Sophia the dream!***

Erick stumbled through the door with hands drooping by his sides. Sophia spoke first. "What did the doctor say?" she said with a tremble in her voice.

Erick mustered all his strength and said, "He ordered me to tell you the dream."

"Wait, Erick. Tell me after we have lunch. I have it prepared, and we can have it out in the patio. Do you want a beer?"

"No thanks. Alcoholic beverages just don't taste right to me lately."

They finished lunch with some innocuous conversation. Erick asked Sophia to sit quietly, listen, and not to say anything. "This was very difficult for me. First, I want you to know that I believe that the real event and the dream are one and the same. I believe my dream is exactly as it happened, but I cannot recall any of that day whatsoever, even the day before. The dream and real life are mixed together. I am conflicted. It's terrible."

Erick stood up and walked behind his chair while standing and staring at the fence. He began. His mind was still clear as he began the story. At the beginning, he smiled as he talked about Mary and Sean. Erick delivered his story of the actual day. When it unfolded near the disaster, Sophia leaned forward to hear every word without interrupting. Then the story came to the portion that always awakened him. She now understood. She reached out and grabbed his hand, and they both cried together for several minutes. Both of her hands wrapped around his right hand, and she squeezed it tightly.

Sophia now understood what Erick was going through. She also realized how difficult it must have been for him to tell her the story.

"Oh, Erick, I am so sorry for what you have gone through, so terribly sorry."

"Thanks, Abi. I know."

The following Wednesday, Erick arrived at Gottlieb's office on time. He was ushered into the treatment room and flopped onto the stuffed chair.

When Gottlieb arrived, he immediately noticed that Erick's brown eyes looked dull. He said nothing about it. He immediately asked, "What about the dreams, Erick?"

"I had one on Monday night, and two last night that woke me up. There may have been more. I don't know."

"Did you tell Sophia the dream?"

"Yes, I did, Doctor."

"Do you feel Sophia understands what you are going through?"

"I certainly do. She has been awesome."

"Okay then, Erick, let's talk about your feeling of all of this."

Erick remained silent for a while as he raced through his brain to grab the correct words to describe his current feelings. "Doctor, I know that I am an articulate person, and I have been around life a little. I know that there was nothing that I could have done to change anything. In fact, had I been a little earlier, I would have been in the building with Mary when it blew up too."

"Maybe that's your problem. You feel guilty about surviving."

"I really don't think so. I am certain that forgetting my wallet didn't affect Mary's arrival time at work whatsoever. Deep down inside, I know these things. Further, I have accepted the result. I have also talked to Bart, Mary's husband, and made my story known to him. This haunting dream still drives me crazy. I can't stop it. I feel so weak on the following morning that it is difficult to walk. I've lost weight since the disaster, and I am not overweight. I even skipped a couple of golf dates. I am no longer ultra-depressed, and my wife has been very supportive and understanding. Doctor, I know these things, but I find it difficult to think, let alone perform my daily duties. I am now actually having serious problems at work."

"Erick, many times a patient will say things like what you said, but deep down inside, they do not believe it. This is what we must work through together."

Gottlieb continued the discussion about these events for another forty minutes. Then he turned to Erick and said, "I believe you, Erick. There must be another explanation. Maybe there is something we don't know about yet. Next time, I will try hypnosis on you and see if we can uncover something new. I am going to give you a prescription." Gottlieb handed Erick a prescription, pressing it firmly in his right hand. "This prescription is habit forming, so I am limiting it to a ten-day period. That should give us time until we can calm things down."

After clearing his throat, Gottlieb continued, "Your dreams may continue, but you likely will not remember them or have them wake you. However, I strongly recommend that Sophia sleep in another room."

Erick nodded, said okay, and headed out to his car with the prescription in hand. He was to return on the following Tuesday. The prescription now gave Jacob Gottlieb time to further evaluate Erick's problem. He still had deep reservations about Erick and how to correct the problem. Erick seemed too well adjusted and wasn't responding correctly. This appeared as an abnormal situation.

Sophia was pleased that Erick had stopped procrastinating and visited Gottlieb. She had planned to retire in the guest bedroom, but that night was special. She would spend it with Erick. Two hours after making love, everything changed.

Suddenly, at about midnight, Erick began hollering louder than ever. His body shook violently and thrashed. Instinctively, Sophia sat up in bed and began to shake him. This did not awaken him. Erick was totally out of the conscious world from the new sleeping pill.

Abruptly, Erick's elbow came flying toward Sophia, striking her face and knocking her back onto her pillow. Stars flashed in her eyes for a few seconds; then came intense pain. Her nose throbbed, and she could feel copious amounts of blood running down her face onto the pillow and sheets.

She tried to wake Erick again, to no avail. The pill had done its job, and she had to deal with this problem herself. She looked at Erick. His thrashing was worse than ever.

Sophia scrambled out of bed, headed to the bathroom, and cupped her hands below her nose to catch the drops of blood before they reached the carpet. Erick was jumping under the covers in a violent manner and continued shouting incoherently. Finally, she heard a word she could identify, "Mary—Mary," and she knew for certain it was the dream. This time he might not remember.

She turned on the light in the bathroom. Blood was all over her face and still running out of her nose. She pinched her nostrils together to stop the bleeding, and they stung. More tears sprang from her eyes as she turned to look back at Erick, who became motionless. She believed her nose was broken.

She twisted together some pieces of toilet paper and pushed them up into both nostrils to stop the bleeding. Tears sprang from her eyes while doing so. Then she started washing the blood from her face.

Sophia looked back at the bed, and there was blood all over the pillowcase and sheets. She dressed hurriedly in work clothes to drive to the emergency room at Midwest Hospital.

When the doctor finally saw Sophia, her eyes were already beginning to swell and blacken. Her green eyes no longer sparkled, and her beautiful face was decorated with two bloody, wadded-up pieces of toilet paper sprouting from each nostril.

The doctor asked her how this happened. Sophia told the doctor the truth, but of course he didn't believe her. A stubby nurse brought in a wheelchair and asked her to sit. "You have a broken nose, but we will have to x-ray you to make certain it is nothing more than that," the doctor said. The nurse wheeled her off to the x-ray department.

When Sophia exited the treatment room with a bandaged face, she heard, "Mrs. Anderson?" It was a man's voice. She turned to locate the voice. There were two police officers standing there whom she didn't notice when returning to the treatment room with her x-rays. They introduced themselves as Buck and Jessica. "Mrs. Anderson," Buck said, "we are from the Spousal Abuse Squad, and we want to talk to you about what your husband did."

Sophia immediately responded, "Oh, he didn't mean to do it!"

"Mrs. Anderson," Buck said, "that's what they all say." As Sophia moved toward them in the empty waiting room, both officers studied her battered face. Sophia sat down near them and told them the abridged story of her husband's treatment following the Oklahoma City disaster. Naturally, they expressed disbelief. After all, it had been a couple of months since the disaster.

"Come with me," Sophia said. "I'll prove it to you. Come home with me right now before the effects of the knock-out pill wears off." It was now two a.m., so the drug would remain active for another four hours.

"Okay," said Buck. "Jessica will go with you in your car, and I will follow in my squad car. Why don't you let her drive? Jessica doesn't have tape all over her face."

Jessica and Sophia pulled into the driveway with Buck behind them. Sophia let them in, and all three went upstairs to the master bedroom. Sophia turned on the overhead light to expose Erick asleep in his bed. The covers were neatly pulled up around his neck since Sophia had tucked them in before departing to the emergency room. The lights didn't affect him. One pillowcase and the top sheet were bright red from the bloody nose.

Erick remained motionless as they talked freely. Sophia spoke to Erick in a rather loud voice, but he didn't respond.

Buck walked over to the bed to shake Erick, who was beginning to get tremors in his limbs. "It's happening again!" Sophia said. "His bad dream has started." Buck grabbed Erick's left arm and began to shake it to awaken him, but this had no noticeable effect. Suddenly, Erick's right fist came smashing into Buck's forehead.

Buck stumbled backward and fell to the floor, landing on his rump and knocking a glass table lamp onto the floor, which disintegrated upon impact without waking Erick.

"Are you all right, Buck?" asked Jessica.

"Yeah," said an embarrassed Buck as Erick continued to thrash about in bed but remained asleep.

Buck stood up and shook Erick again with no observable effect. Sophia was somewhere between many emotions and thoughts. She quickly handed Jessica the medication bottle, and she noted the previous day's date on the bottle.

Buck rubbed his forehead.

"Officer, are you sure you are okay?" Sophia asked.

Then with a somewhat silly voice, Buck said, "Yeah" as he rubbed his forehead again. "I should have seen it coming. He sucker-punched me." The two women chuckled with high-pitched voices joined by Buck's laughter with baritone overtones.

"Mrs. Anderson, what's the name of his doctor?" asked Jessica.

"It is Dr. Jacob Gottlieb at the Oklahoma City Psychiatric Center." She walked over to the dresser and grabbed his business card, handing it to Jessica.

"Mrs. Anderson, we believe you, but we will have to check this out tomorrow. You understand, don't you?"

Sophia nodded, and the two officers headed downstairs.

Sophia slept in short intervals. The ache of the broken nose kept waking her. She dragged herself out of bed at about five thirty a.m. and showered before going downstairs. She certainly wasn't going to work for a few days with tape on her face, a throbbing nose, and black eyes. Instead on this morning, she would stay home and prepare a hot breakfast.

Erick walked downstairs and saw Sophia standing near the sink with her back to him. He ambled up behind her. Sophia was preoccupied with cleaning the muffin pan and hadn't notice Erick approach.

"Good morning," said Erick with a pleasant, soft voice.

Sophia jumped a little and turned to face him. Erick lurched backward when her saw her bandaged face and black eyes. "What's— what's going on, Sophia? What happened?" he asked in a high-pitched voice.

"Oh, it's nothing Erick. I had an accident last night," she responded.

"How—what, where?"

"Sit down, Erick, and have a cup of coffee, and I'll tell you all about it." She poured both a cup and sat down next to him. "Erick, you struck me last night when I was trying to wake you up when you were having a bad dream."

"I didn't dream last night. Honest."

"Yes, you did, but the high-potency sleeping pill knocked you out. I tried to wake you to take me to the emergency room, but I couldn't."

"Oh, my God! I am so sorry. What did I do to you?"

"I know that you couldn't help it. Your elbow hit me across the bridge of my nose and fractured it. The doctor at the emergency room set it, and I will recover perfectly."

"Sophia, we won't be able to sleep together again until Dr. Gottlieb gets this problem under control."

"That's for sure. Ouch!" responded Sophia, pretending to give Erick a mock hit to the head with her right elbow. "Now Erick, stay put. Breakfast is ready." She hated to talk since the motion of the tape pulled on her nose and every spoken word made tears spurt from her eyes.

Erick got up from his chair as Sophia stood up to place breakfast on the table. He tugged gently on her arm, and she turned to face him. "I am so sorry, so sorry." They hugged for several seconds.

Sophia headed toward the stove. "Erick, you really pack a wallop. You knocked a cop on his ass last night too."

"I did what? A cop?" Erick bellowed from his chair.

Sophia told him about the entire episode as they ate breakfast. Erick stood up and wobbled. Sophia noticed his plight. "Erick, sit down before you fall down."

"What am I going to do?"

"See Dr. Gottlieb and make sure he knows what happened!"

Tuesday arrived, and it was time for Erick's appointment with Gottlieb, who greeted him by simply telling him the police officer had called. He presented Erick with a condensed version of his evening escapades, of which Erick had no direct memory. Erick appeared embarrassed to Gottlieb. "Well, Doctor, at least I am not being charged with spousal abuse or assaulting a police officer, and that's a relief."

When Erick was seated, Jacob handed him a cup of coffee. The cup rattled in its saucer.

"Erick, do you have any recollection of what happened that night?"

"None. I just know I had a great night's sleep. I know these events occurred because my hand is tender, and I believe all the stories. As far as I know, I slept well."

"I don't understand what's going on with the Oklahoma City disaster yet. You are dealing too well with it for it to be the root cause. I believe it is symptomatic of something else. As I said during your last visit, I would like to employ hypnosis today. It can therefore go past the conscious brain into the subconscious one. You are aware that I am talking about examining you under hypnosis."

Erick took a swallow of coffee and placed the cup on the small table. "Sure, Doctor, I understand, and go ahead. We need to get to the bottom of this as soon as possible."

Jacob paused a moment and stared out the window. "Erick, some people are more difficult to hypnotize than others, so it may take a few sessions. Sometimes I can do it immediately. It varies from patient to patient. In fact, there are patients I cannot hypnotize."

"What do I do?" Erick asked.

"I want you to relax completely in that chair, but do not fall asleep. Keep your eyes open and watch the pendulum. Listen to my words and let everything else go."

The countdown started with ten and then finally came to zero. Erick was hypnotized on the first attempt. Gottlieb realized this immediately.

"Erick, let your mind go back to the Oklahoma City disaster. Do you recall that day and what you told me?"

"Yes" was the response as Erick spoke slowly under hypnosis.

"Did anything else happen about that time that you haven't told me?"

"Yes," Erick said in a less-drawn-out fashion.

"What was that?"

Erick began to answer. "Just before the blast when I was driving." He stopped. His voice was without emotion as he continued.

Jacob listened intently. "What happened, Erick?"

"There was a voice in my car and a man looking at me."

"Where was this man?"

"He was in the car in the back seat, leaning forward, I guess."

"How do you know that?"

"I saw him in the rearview mirror."

"What did he say?"

"He spoke my name." Erick paused to catch his breath, since he seemed to quit breathing at this fearful moment he was reliving. He said, 'I am Lee. Today I want your mind; tomorrow I want your body! I'll give you a bad dream.' Fear raced through me. I drove a little further when the bomb hit."

Jacob was standing when he asked, "What happened to him?"

"He was just gone after that, but there was so much commotion."

"Please describe this man, Erick."

"He was Caucasian and had thin skin. His dark-colored eyes were beady and evil. His voice had—like a smirk in it. I didn't like him at all. I thought him evil. He frightened me!" Erick became very agitated, even in his trance. His hands began to flay, and his legs twitched. Jacob noticed facial tics.

"What happened next, Erick?"

"There was fire and thick smoke everywhere, especially around Mary's office. I was looking at the building when the blast hit. I was totally blinded, and I stopped the car. I couldn't see or hear anything for a while. When my eyesight returned, stuff was still flying everywhere. Then the air cleared for a moment, and I saw the hole at the back of the building—right where Mary's office was located." Erick began to weep, and the facial tics and his agitated state worsened. His hand struck a half-full cup of coffee, knocking it to the floor.

Gottlieb thought it best to get him out of the trance. He didn't want to overdo it on the first session. "Erick, when I count to five, you will wake up, and you will not recall our conversation. You will also feel good and refreshed."

At five, Erick opened his eyes. "Well, you couldn't hypnotize me. I didn't think you could."

"We will continue hypnosis on the next visit. Erick, can you recall anything more regarding your story, like seeing someone, something different inside or near the car? Stop and think about it. Place yourself in the front seat of your car."

Erick was agitated. His hands clasped each other to release and then clasp again. In an elevated voice, he said, "No, Doctor, no—I cannot think of anything at all for the entire day. It's all mixed up in my head, because of the dream. I can't tell the dream from reality. I am frustrated, upset, and—worried."

"Do you remember talking to anyone just before the blast?"

"No—why should I? There was no one in the car except me. I was alone." Then in an emphatic voice, he said, "I never talk to myself. It's just too boring."

Gottlieb chuckled and said, "That's the truth, Erick. Talking to yourself *is* boring."

Chapter 3: Lee

On this day, Jacob's fingernails were exceptionally clean, since he had spent some time the prior evening working on a car. He had a fetish about clean fingernails. Patients, particularly women, didn't like to see a physician with dirty fingernails, so Jacob always maintained them meticulously. Unlike most physicians, Jacob was an auto mechanic, and his specialty was restoring collectable cars. He truly took pleasure in this activity, perhaps because it was the antithesis of his work routine.

It was a profitable activity for him, if one discounted the personal labor involved, since he always sold restored automobiles that looked showroom new for a handsome price. The real joy came when he entered the car into a competition and won. Jacob was competitive, and he savored winning. Money was extra but nonetheless appreciated.

At lunch time, Jacob was in the cafeteria area, eating a peanut butter and jam sandwich and reading *Psychology Today*. Marilyn remained by the microwave, and Hazel stood patiently at the door, waiting for Marilyn. Jim Hanford squeezed by Hazel to enter the room. The microwave beeped, and the ladies exited the room, leaving the doctors alone.

Jim walked over to the table, sitting down next to Jacob. "Whatever happened to the comatose patient I saw at the emergency room saga a few weeks ago?"

"Nothing for a while, but recently he became my new patient. It seems that he has nightmares of the bombing, which he witnessed. Further, the explosion killed both his sister and nephew."

Wow! That's a heavy load for someone to take."

"You're right. The nightmares are becoming debilitating. Last week, while he was under hypnosis, I had him micro-step through the dream. I made a fascinating discovery. Erick, the patient, saw and talked to a heinous character, whom the patient claims is responsible for the bad dream, in his car with him. This character told Erick he wanted to take over his mind and body. Erick described him as evil. This character has a name, Lee. I scheduled a joint session with us to talk to Lee this Thursday if I can withdraw him. I wanted you present during that session."

Jim, who was swirling his half-empty coffee by rotating his wrist, stopped abruptly. "That's hard to believe. I look forward to Thursday. What else do we know about the patient?"

"The patient is well educated, responsible, married, and works for a marketing firm. He had no experiences with Lee prior to the bombing. No mental problems. He wasn't molested as a child, nor did he have any exceptional frightening experiences. He doesn't have schizophrenia—of that I am certain, nor does he get involved with alcohol or recreational drugs. He was raised with loving parents with his late sister. His sister, also adopted, felt loving about her parents, particularly her mother. It's a mystery. These conditions were verified during hypnosis too, another reason to get you involved."

At night, Jacob was preoccupied with a possible dissociative identity disorder (DID) formerly called Multiple Personality Disorder (MPD), as an explanation for Erick's case. Every psychiatrist wanted a case of DID, because of its rarity and the challenge. By Wednesday night, Jacob devoured nine DID case reports he had picked up at Bird Library. Although he had yet to talk to Lee, there were some similarities with DID cases, but major differences existed. In Erick's case, there was an underlying, hidden personality trying to get out unsuccessfully. Jacob suspected this character could be reached only by hypnosis, whereas in all DID case studies, the other personality could be reached in the conscious patient. Jacob was now certain the problem wasn't a psychosis of some type. It seemed reasonable that a second personality could be the exact reason why Erick was lashing out at night. Erick could be fighting Lee internally.

At 10 a.m. on Thursday, Erick was prompt as usual. When escorted into the treatment room, he hung his jacket on the hall tree and looked across the room to see a new face, that of Dr. James Hanford. "Erick, I want you to meet Dr. Hanford," Jacob said. "He is going to help me today if I cannot get you under hypnosis. Jim is better at it than I am."

The two men shook hands. Erick stood in front of the stuffed chair. "Sit down, Erick." Jim Hanford fetched a light, straight-legged chair and sat next to Gottlieb. Shortly, Erick was hypnotized. The two doctors had agreed ahead of time that only Gottlieb would communicate with Lee. Hanford had considerable experience with hypnotism, so Gottlieb depended upon him for suggestions should there be difficulties.

"Erick, I want your mind to go back to the time when you first heard Lee speak. Tell him that I want to talk to him."

"Lee—Lee, the doctors want to talk to you!" Erick said aloud, but there was no response. Gottlieb stared at every mannerism Erick made, his eyes remained closed.

Then Hanford whispered to Gottlieb, "Be more insistent."

"Erick, I need you to help me. In your head, I want you to tell Lee to talk to me. Please do that."

"Okay, Doctor."

"Let's try it again, Lee. I know that you are there. Talk to me." Gottlieb spoke in a quiet, positive manner but without any response from Lee. Jim tugged on Jacob's sleeve and whispered to him again. "Be more demanding."

Jacob changed his tone to become more assertive. "Lee, I know you are in there. It is time to defend yourself."

Gottlieb was very direct and forceful this time, even loud. There still was no answer. "Lee, we know that you like cowardly acts. That is why you enjoyed the Oklahoma City disaster! Isn't it? Come on, Lee; you're a coward!"

Jacob watched Erick intently to see how he'd react, noting that Jim was doing the same thing. Erick's face lost its relaxed nature, and a sneer formed around his mouth. The corner of his eyes began to twitch.

Jim tapped Jacob's leg without speaking. "Lee, you are a coward!" Gottlieb said in a much louder voice. With that statement, Erick's eyes opened and blinked twice. Jacob noticed he hadn't done that under hypnosis before. Erick squinted as if the room light were too bright. Wrinkles formed on his lips, and his lips became hard and thin.

Jacob looked at Jim, then quickly glanced back at Erick in amazement as the face before him contorted and the lips moved slightly. His tongue moistened them.

Then a robust voice came out. "What do you jerks want?"

"First of all, I want to introduce you to Dr. Hanford, my office mate, and I am Dr. Gottlieb."

"You guys are assholes, ya know!"

Ignoring the statement, Jacob asked, "Are you Lee?"

"What's it to you? You guys don't know nothing," said the voice. "Yeah, I am Lee. So what?"

"You are the one we want to talk to," Jacob said in a matter-of-fact manner.

"What if I don't want to talk to you?"

Ignoring his statement, Jacob asked, "Why do you torment Erick?"

"I have my reasons, and they're none of your damn business."

"I am trying to help Erick. That's why."

"I am trying to destroy him—so there."

"Do you control Erick?"

"No! I don't control him except late at night when he sleeps. He's stupid. I loathe him."

"Why do you torment him at night?"

"Ah—the moron is too strong during the day, so I get him at night. I will weaken him soon. I am biding my time, and I will win. Right now, I am doing a great job. That's why he is here doctors." Then the two doctors heard a fiendish laugh deep in his throat. Even though Gottlieb had considerable experience with difficult patients, Lee was different. Jacob's skin crawled when he laughed. Jacob whispered to Jim, "do you sense that we are possibly dealing with a homicidal personality." Jim nodded.

The dialogue between Lee and the doctors continued for ten minutes; Lee continued to spit out his venom while glaring into their eyes.

"You guys are real asses. I knew it was going to happen, ya know."

"What happened?" Gottlieb said without delay.

Lee began to shout at them and said, "The Oklahoma City bombing." He followed this with an insidious laugh. "Ha ha ha."

Jacob leaned forward and said, "Lee, I—"

"Ha ha ha," Lee interrupted Gottlieb.

Jacob tried to speak, but Lee's laughter kept interfering. Then total silence followed as the two doctors stared at each other and then at Lee. Lee's eyes penetrated each man as if he wanted to assassinate them. His head turned so his eyes could focus on theirs, as if laser directed. He peered inside them. Gottlieb felt uncomfortable. Further, there was an annoying smirk on his face.

After a few seconds, Jacob asked, "How did you know about the disaster ahead of time, Lee?"

The bellicose Lee said, "I know about all that shit."

"What do you want of Erick?" Gottlieb asked.

"I want his bo—" He never finished the sentence after cutting off the word.

"How long have you been trying to gain access to Erick?"

"A while! I will win. You cannot stop me, but I know you will try. I am almost there. Know I will win! I will win, and I'm getting close." His clamorous voice echoed in the room.

"What will you do if you win the battle?"

"It is none of your damn business, so why should I tell you?" Lee's words were interrupted by his heavy-handed pounding of the armrest. Lee became confrontational. He sat forward in his chair with his jaw resting on his chest and stared at the two doctors through his eyebrows.

"Because I am interested," Gottlieb said in a matter-of-fact manner to defuse the situation. "Lee, I want to—"

"I don't want to talk to you guys no more! You make me feel like puking."

"Lee, I need to talk to Erick now anyway. You will have to leave."

"That's okay. I don't like you no way!"

"Erick—Erick—I want to talk to you." Slowly the hideous, hate-filled face vanished, and the Erick's pleasant face reappeared before them. This time Erick's eyes remained open. "Erick, do you hear me?"

"Yes, Dr. Gottlieb. I hear you."

"How do you feel right now?"

"I feel a little apprehensive but okay." Erick was present but still under hypnosis.

Jacob started whispering to Hanford, and this continued back and forth for a couple of minutes. The subject was, should they make Erick aware of Lee at this time? Gottlieb decided to do so, because he was aware that Lee was trying to take over immediately. Erick needed to be in a position to fight him. It was, therefore, a high-risk situation for Erick.

"Erick, do you know what Lee wants of you?"

"Yes, Doctor. Lee wants to take over my body and kill me."

"How do you know that?"

"At this very moment, I can collect Lee's thoughts. He is telling me, and it is frightening. I normally cannot hear him."

"Thank you, Erick. You will feel good again, and you will not recall our conversation." Then Gottlieb started the countdown to "one, two, three. You are beginning to wake up—four, five."

"Well, Doctors, did you hypnotize me? How did I do?"

Gottlieb quickly followed up on Erick's question. "We succeeded in hypnotizing you, and you did just fine. Further, we discovered a second personality. I believe this personality is totally responsible for the nightmares. It is a matter of getting rid of this personality to make you whole again." Jacob looked at Jim and noticed his eyes rolling to the ceiling.

"Are you saying I'm crazy?"

"No. However, there is a possibility that a second personality exists within your brain. Do you remember the book *Three Faces of Eve*? It's a possibility that such a situation exists."

"Come on! You are putting me on! Right?"

"No, Erick. Both Dr. Hanford and I talked to Lee while you were under hypnosis."

Erick looked at both doctors, and Jim nodded his head up and down. Jacob continued with Erick, who was still uncomfortable with the statement. "Erick, I want to —"

Erick interrupted him. "What do you mean I have a second personality?"

Gottlieb responded, "It seems that your mind is trying to create a second personality."

"Do you really believe there is a second person inside my head?"

"In a way, I am beginning to think so. We even talked to him. The dreams are manifestations of his as he tries to take over." Gottlieb realized he had opened a tremendous bucket of lizards in full sunlight. "Erick, I want to see you next Wednesday. We will talk more about this problem and how we are going to solve it. That's it for today. Dr. Hanford must get back to his patients."

After Erick departed, Jim stayed to compare notes and said, "I am still uncertain that it is DID, but I don't know what it is. Further, I believe you will need to contact Lee in the future to find out more—what he wants and what this is all about. Lee is a heinous person. You must be careful, very careful. I believe you are in physical danger yourself."

"Right now, Jim, I also consider Lee dangerous, especially after he thought the Murrah bombing was child's play."

"In my opinion, you must be careful when you unleash a maniac."

Gottlieb was thinking about Lee's statements. Then he said aloud, "Maybe this isn't even a straightforward case of DID."

One week later, Jacob planned to collect information about Lee. Perhaps he could psychoanalyze Lee to solve the problem. At the bare minimum, he needed to know Lee. That would require Lee to cooperate, and based on the last session, that could be difficult.

"Okay, Erick, shall we begin?" Instead of the large stuffed chair, there was a large metal chair with a cushioned seat and back. The stuffed chair, normally in that position, decorated the corner.

Erick sat down in the new chair, and Jacob quickly hypnotized him. Then he wrapped Erick's wrists onto the chair's armrests with a secure belt often employed with dangerous psychotic patients. After turning on the video recorder, Gottlieb asked to speak to Lee. He watched as Erick's face contorted. The evil Lee appeared with open eyes, which fixated on Gottlieb. Then Lee spoke, "What in the hell do you want with me this time?" he asked.

Jacob used his easygoing way and answered, "I want to know more about you, like how old are you?"

"I am twenty-four years old."

"Are you—"

Lee interrupted him. "In 1959, I met my wife in Russia, and we were married there. In the following year, I brought her to the States." Lee was now relaxed as he continued his tale of time spent in the Marines. It just spewed out in continuous fashion without prompting. It was as if years of pent-up events were released. When he spoke of his wife, softer tones were used. Lee's story was so continuous that he didn't require prodding to keep him talking. Words, events, places, and times kept flowing throughout the session with English broken into gibberish. When Lee's dialogue broke into gibberish, Jacob let him continue for a while, hoping he would fall back to speaking English, and he did.

Lee sounded credible. Jacob constantly looked at the video recorder to make certain it was running. He didn't want to miss one word. The details of the cold war years in the Soviet Union were coherent and believable.

When questions got around to personal things, Lee spoke in English. He enjoyed fishing and hunting, good food, baseball, and betting. However, he became irritated when asked about what he disliked. "That's easy. I hate the USA and everything it stands for." Almost shouting, he said, "I hate it!" With the last statement, Lee's hands shook with rapid tremors. He tried to raise his hands and found them tied to the armrest. "Hey, what are you trying to do to me, Doc?"

"It's just precautionary, Lee. You can get a little exuberant!" Ignoring Lee, Gottlieb said, "Why do you hate the United States so much?" Jacob wanted to move past the arm wraps so Lee would forget them and continue his dialogue.

Lee leaned over to the armrest so his index finger could scratch his nose. Then he spoke. "Because they screwed me over when I was spying. That's why."

"Spying! Tell me more?"

Lee sneered and began to tell a bizarre story of double agents and intrigue. "It all started when I was a guard at the front gate of the embassy in Moscow. Then one day during a break, a guy in a suit called me into a back room. He showed me his badge. He was with the CIA. He asked me if I would consider being a CIA operative during my time off. I had a lot of time, and I was honored by the request. It meant extra money, so that was good too. I asked him why the CIA selected me, and he said, 'You speak very good Russian, and with proper attire, you would look Russian and become inconspicuous.' The next thing I know, I'm an agent."

Lee was calming down. His story was so believable that Gottlieb found himself mesmerized. Lee described the cities and local areas he visited, still breaking into gibberish on occasions. He also provided exact details of his CIA courier activities.

"Hey, you know what, Doc? I became a double agent too."

This statement was preposterous, unfathomable, and unexpected for Gottlieb, who uttered, "How?" Jacob looked up and saw an amber light in the corner, indicating that his new patient had arrived. Then, while looking at it and listening to Lee, a blue light went on, indicating that his time with Erick was overrunning. He looked at Lee and said, "Lee, I want to speak to Erick."

"What if I don't let you, Doc?"

"You will because you like talking to me. We will talk again."

"Okay," Lee said in a frisky manner, and with that his face started to mellow and soften gradually. Lee closed his eyes, and they remained closed as Erick took control. When Jacob was certain it was Erick to whom he was speaking, Jacob reached over, unfastened the wrist straps, and dropped them into his pocket.

"Okay, Erick, it is time to wake up on the count of five. Shortly, Erick was awake. "Are you current in recent world affairs, geography, and history?"

"No, Doctor. I can't say that I am. I do know a little about geography from my traveling around this country. World events are not my favorite. Why do you ask?"

"Do you read about it?" Jacob asked, ignoring Erick's question.

"Never. I have zero interest" was the answer. This statement shocked Gottlieb because of the details Lee had provided.

"Erick, your problem could be serious. You need to reduce your work stress. I—"

"I can't. We have a very important contract, and I am the focal point of that work. I need to be there. It will fail without me."

"Erick, we need to get your problem under control, or you may not get your work done anyway. Talk to your superiors and tell them you are on the verge of a nervous breakdown. I will provide a letter if you need one. Do as little as possible but keep the stress down. Do you understand me? I'll see you next Wednesday."

When Erick exited the treatment room, Jacob pondered what he had learned. Most of it had to do with the Soviet Union and the marines. These were difficult details to check. ***If I can get Lee to talk about his childhood, then I could judge whether all this is a figment of Erick's imagination.*** The detail in Lee's statement was totally believable yet it contained no supportive data.

Chapter 4: More Lee

On Saturday, Jacob wrestled with a dashboard from a 1940 Chevy. Both garage doors were open, and Jimmy, riding by on his bicycle, hollered, "Hi, Dr. Gottlieb." Jacob waved at Jimmy and continued searching through his loose tools for a special wrench he had designed years earlier to assist removing dashboard instruments.

The wall phone above the workbench rang, and Jacob answered it. It was Jim.

"Hi, Jacob, I just received a letter from Maury. They ran their innovative test on Erick's blood, and there is no indication of schizophrenia. You were right about that."

"Thanks, Jim, for closing the book on that possibility. Did you review the tape?"

"Yes, I did. You were correct to be surprised. I do not know what to make of it and all the nonsensical talk. It is fascinating material, however. The DID personality cannot know more than the patient himself. Clearly, Lee knows more than Erick. Maybe Erick knew these things once and has selective memory."

"It could be."

"Still that gibberish is a conundrum. Did Lee seem violent to you?"

"Yes, at first," Jacob answered. "Later Lee relaxed a lot, and he seemed fine."

"You were smart to bind his wrists. I cannot state more emphatically that I do not trust him. Keep me informed, Jacob." The two friends hung up. Gottlieb was after verification of his efforts to date, and he had received them.

Jacob was still standing and organizing the top of his workbench when the telephone rang again. It was Jerry, a longtime friend. "I called to see if you wanted to go fishing with me in Alaska in three weeks, just for the halibut." Then he chuckled. "I'll be there for a full week."

"Sounds wonderful, but my schedule is just too heavy for that now. Thanks for thinking of me. Maybe another time."

Jerry was a friend who always bordered on the edge, at least up to the time when he had purchased a furniture store with Jacob's financial assistance. He was a risk taker. Jacob sometimes went fishing with him for a weekend, but an entire week was out of the question.

Jacob's mind went back to Lee. The mystery seemed to swell and what this personality was doing in Erick's mind. Jacob didn't feel near closure. He kept thinking that Erick seemed well adjusted. This had to be a case of DID. It just had to be. Most conditions fit except the root cause, and that was big. Putting all pieces together, Gottlieb knew there was nothing like it in scientific literature. It was unique, mysterious, a little frightening, and potentially dangerous for Erick. Gottlieb was also concerned about Erick's wife; she could be in a risky situation if Lee took over. He would have to alert her.

On Wednesday, it was time for another appointment with Dr. Gottlieb, but this time things would be different. Having seen no progress in Erick's condition, Sophia was determined to sit in on the next session. She was a beautiful, slender woman with a hint-of-auburn hair and green eyes, a reflection of her Irish heritage. Erick's problem resulted in continuous and escalating friction between the two. Sophia wanted her family problem stopped and demanded resolution.

Driving with Erick near Gottlieb's office, Sophia remarked, "Hey, Erick, these buildings within this medical complex with all the flowers around them sure look nice. Don't you agree?"

Erick grunted.

Erick waited until Sophia was out of the car before pressing the door lock button. Then they walked to Gottlieb's office together. Sophia immediately made her presence known by telling the receptionist who she was and that she wasn't leaving until she had met with Dr. Gottlieb.

The message was relayed to Dr. Gottlieb before Erick entered the treatment room with Sophia beside him.

"Dr. Gottlieb," Sophia sputtered. "I am really concerned about Erick. We are not seeing any progress whatsoever. None!"

Gottlieb looked at her. "Mrs. Anderson, your nose is looking much better these days. Don't you agree, Erick? Mrs. Anderson, may I call you Sophia?"

"Certainly," she snapped.

"Sophia, we have made considerable progress. There is an inner conflict within Erick that is raging. We have identified a second personality. We call this Dissociative Identity Disorder or DID for short. It is a case where a second personality is attempting to control Erick."

She was still standing and felt her knees weaken. "What?" she bellowed in a voluble voice.

"Do you remember the book *Three faces of Eve*?" Sophia nodded.

"His condition is somewhat analogous to that situation, except there are only two personalities in this case. As I said, we are certain the second personality is causing the nightmares, but he is challenging our understanding of DID."

Sophia listened in total disbelief as Dr. Gottlieb gestured for them to sit down. "These things cannot be solved overnight. Folks, please sit down."

After sitting, Sophia spoke with a mellow voice. "Dr. Gottlieb, why now after so many years? There has been no indication of it before now, so why now?"

"That's a good question. I wish I could answer it with certainty, but it will have to wait until I collect more information from Lee."

"Lee! Lee who?" Sophia quickly asked in a surprised voice.

"Lee is the name of the second personality in Erick."

"What? You're kidding me!"

"I am afraid not. Lee is there. Dr. Hanford has met him too."

"Are there more personalities?" she said in a controlled voice.

"So far, Lee is the only one to appear, but to answer your question directly, I do not know for sure. Sometimes another personality may surface. We will have to wait and see." Jacob continued, "I am working with Dr. Hanford on this matter, and I believe that we have made great progress toward our understanding of what's going on."

An agitated Sophia interrupted by saying, "What about curing him? Isn't that what you are supposed to be doing?"

"Yes, but we must first diagnose the problem."

She said in a high-pitched, piercing voice, "I do not see improvements. It is sickening, Dr. Gottlieb. Why don't you do your job? I thought you just told me that you had diagnosed the problem."

"You are correct, Sophia; that is the first step. Now in our therapy sessions, I am trying to determine the cause. There must be a reason for Lee's appearance, and I do not know what it is. I suspect that the emotional trauma surrounding the Murrah bombing has played an important role. It was after that event that Lee made his appearance."

Sophia shook her head. She looked at Dr. Gottlieb and said, "I'm sitting in today."

"I am afraid that request is impossible."

"I insist."

"Then I cannot treat Erick today," Gottlieb said. Seconds passed. He stood and turned to walk to the door. Sophia rose from her chair, stomped to the entry door, and glared at Gottlieb over her shoulder as she reached the door. Gottlieb looked at her, smiled, and said, "Thank you for coming in, Sophia."

"Have it your way, Dr. Gottlieb."

After Sophia's departure, Gottlieb collected his thoughts. "Erick, it is common practice not to let family members into the treatment room. It always causes more problems than it cures. This has nothing to do with Sophia other than that she is a family member."

Jacob wanted Erick to understand that patients' wives and psychiatry don't mix. He regretted what he had done to Sophia, but he had no other choice. To ease Erick's mind, he said, "Erick, I will keep Sophia informed in the future."

Having cleared the air, Jacob got down to business. "Erick, I want to continue to deal with Lee, because Lee is the source of your nightmares. Dr. Hanford and I both agree on this point. Further, Lee told me that he causes them. To do this, I must deal with Lee to understand what's taking place. If I can find out what Lee needs of you, then we can set out to get rid of him."

"Dr. Gottlieb, Sophia was correct and made some good points. You haven't kept her in the loop at all. That cannot continue. You must keep us informed."

"You are correct, and I promise that I will do a better job of it in the future. Now, let's begin."

It was time to hypnotize Erick. Within seconds, he was under and sat there with his eyes shut. Gottlieb didn't feel it was necessary to go through the preliminaries as he had in the past, so he simply said, "Lee, I want to talk to you." Erick's mind and body wrestled with the metamorphosis as Lee made his appearance with wrapped wrists.

"Do you like donuts, Lee?"

"Yeah."

Jacob placed a glazed donut on a paper plate near Lee's left wrist. Lee picked up the donut and smiled. "Hey, Doc, you ain't goin' to get rid of me. I heard what you said to Erick. I am in the process of gaining control. I'm getting rid of Erick!"

Lee glared at Gottlieb. His minacious voice still sent chills down Jacob's spine. Jacob, having considerable experience with difficult patients, disguised his inner emotions.

Lee glared at Gottlieb for a while, then said, "What are we going to do today, Doc?"

"Today, Lee, I want to learn more about you."

"Me?"

"Yes, you, Lee."

Lee responded, "Doc, I already told you a lot of stuff about me. As you could see, I know hellava lot more than Erick."

Gottlieb ignored his statement. "Where is your home, Lee?"

"My home is in Erick's head." He laughed mockingly.

"You know what I mean," Gottlieb prodded.

"As I told you last time, I have lived in the US and the Soviet Union."

"Where have you lived in the US? Where were you born? What are the names of your parents?" Gottlieb asked in rapid-fire succession.

Lee appeared to be relaxing as Gottlieb questioned him. His body language, which Gottlieb continually monitored, revealed that he liked the attention. "I was born in New Orleans, Louisiana, at the Old French Hospital on October 18, 1939, but I do not remember New Orleans. My father, Robert Oswald, died before I was born, so I never met him, and Mom never talked about him either. My mother's married name was Marguerite Ekdahl. She married Edwin Ekdahl before I was in kindergarten, and I went by that name, Lee Ekdahl."

Lee continued to deliver a plethora of information about his early life, including places, schools, descriptions, and even a few names. Lee had two brothers, Robert and John, who had spent much of their time away from the family in a military boarding school. He stopped talking for a minute to bend over and take a bite of his donut.

When asked where he had grown up, Lee responded, "Guess that I would have to say Covington, Louisiana. Yep, that's it, and I remember my first school there too. It was a big elementary school, real big. I also lived in Dallas and New York City. Mom was a restless type, and we moved a lot. I mean a lot." Jacob noted in his logbook that there was a smile on Lee's face.

Now Jacob was transfixed by the testimony. He was beginning to collect usable data, which he could check. "Where is Covington?"

"It's close to New Orleans."

Now to collect something he could check, Jacob asked whether Lee could remember his home street address, but he could only remember only that the street had a number like Ninth Street. However, he described areas in detail as well as the grocery store that he frequented. All Lee's answers were without gibberish. Jacob smiled as he collected an abundance of data.

Gottlieb noted in his logbook that Lee's attitude certainly was different now that he was thinking about his youth. He was not hostile as earlier. Once in a while, Lee glared at Gottlieb with beady eyes. However, he was answering questions.

"Are your parents still married?"

"No. They divorced when we were still in Covington."

"When did you leave Louisiana?"

"When I was in the second grade, Mom met a man that lived in Texas, and we moved near him."

"Where in Texas, Lee?"

"He lived on a ranch outside of Wichita Falls. Mom bought a small ranch there."

"Tell me about this place."

Lee looked at the ceiling as if imagining the ranch there. "I can remember an older ranch house with a screened-in front-porch and a long driveway. There were a few outbuildings—a barn and a large tank house. Oh yeah—a fishpond in the front yard."

"What's a tank house?"

"Ya know, a building with a water tank on top. There were two floors up to the water tank. The water tank had a big Folgers Coffee sign painted on it that faced the highway. The ranch was located a few miles out of town on—on—on Highway 79 South."

"What town?"

"Wichita Falls. The ranch was between that town and Archer City." Lee's eyes finally quit staring at Gottlieb and darted around the room with quick, direction-oriented glances as he answered questions. His hands and feet moved continuously.

"Thank you, Lee. You were very helpful." After extracting Erick, the session ended.

Jacob sauntered into his office, still mulling over Lee. Although he was treating Erick by the limited book as psychiatry knew it, there was no real book on his presumed diagnosis. The problem was exacerbated by Erick's new sleep habits. Gottlieb had almost run the gamut of sleeping pills.

Jacob was concerned about Sophia, who must be made aware of the latest findings. With that in mind, he called her at home. When she answered the phone, he said, "Hi, Mrs. Anderson, this is Dr. Gottlieb."

"Dr. Gottlieb?" she uttered with a question in her voice.

"I am calling you because I want to talk to you in private about Erick's worsening problem. Could we have lunch together this Friday?"

"I guess so."

"Great. How about meeting me at Marco's on Second Street at noon?"

"Okay. You're on."

"By the way, it is probably best not to say anything to Erick about the lunch."

"Yes, I quite agree, and I'll see you at noon on Friday at Marco's."

Jacob opened his lower desk drawer and withdrew his bagged lunch as he waited for his computer to boot. As he unwrapped his tuna sandwich, there was a light knock on his door. Jacob looked up to see Jim standing there.

"What happened today, Jacob?" Jim said while leaning against the open door.

"I started a new line of inquiry with Lee. I asked him about his childhood, and there was a surprise. He had one. He gave me a detailed account of his youth and the many places where he lived. Things that he did as a child and the names of people and places."

"No," uttered Jim.

"I have all of this detail now, and it is something I can at least check out, whereas I was stuck with the Soviet Union information. Furthermore, I inquired of Erick while still under hypnosis about his childhood. It wasn't the same as Lee's." Jim was leaning forward not to miss anything. Jacob continued, "Erick and Lee act as different people with different thoughts and recollections. This is downright unexpected."

"Wow" was his only reply. The conversation continued until all pertinent information was exchanged.

Jacob continued, "I am having trouble planning the next step in Erick's treatment. According to the book, I—"

Jim interrupted by stepping into Jacob's office and quietly shutting the door. "I cannot believe Erick has DID. Every case I have studied has another personality in the conscious mode. Lee is only present in the hypnotized mode. It must be something else, but what?"

"We cannot dismiss that diagnosis so glibly. There are just not enough cases to say for sure."

"You are right about that. What is the diagnosis, Jacob?"

"I don't know—damn it, I just do not know. I am frustrated about it too."

"See—something else can be the cause."

Jacob reluctantly nodded.

"What are you going to do about it?"

Jacob straightened. "I have collected considerable material from Lee today. Much of it can be examined. I intend to check these out over upcoming weekends. I will become a detective and go to these places because I still need to know if Lee is credible."

"Jacob, you won't find anything. You are just wasting your time and money." Jim hesitated for a few seconds. Then, looking at Jacob, he asked, "Is Lee a sociopath?"

"Oh, yes, Jim, probably worse. I still believe that to be the case. Lee is dangerous."

Friday finally arrived, and Sophia was genuinely excited about lunch. She had noticed earlier that Gottlieb was a handsome man and, as expected, with good upbringing. She had forgiven him for kicking her out of the session and hoped he had forgiven her. Maybe now she could obtain some answers.

That morning she dressed in one of her nicer dresses, which showed off her womanly features that men notice, maybe even doctors. She also took some extra time preparing her face. The makeup covered the slight but lingering darkening under one eye.

Her morning work passed in normal fashion, and no one commented on her attire. Before her lunch appointment, she quietly slipped out of the office. She arrived before Jacob, so she waited at the bar, sipping a gin and tonic. Jacob arrived five minutes late and apologized immediately. He had requested a corner table, and his request was honored. They were escorted to the table immediately.

He began the conversation by apologizing. "Sophia, about my office problem, I have a standing rule that family and treatment don't go together. After our talk today, perhaps you will better understand the reason."

"I understand that I was out of line, but I really wanted to see improvement in Erick, and I saw none. Just the opposite—he was getting worse."

Jacob scooted closer to her in the curved seat, because he didn't want to broadcast a medical problem over the entire restaurant. He took a second glance at this attractive woman.

After they placed their order, they would get down to business, but for now the conversation concerned pleasant issues. The conversation got light enough that there were a few chuckles.

When lunch arrived, Jacob got down to business. Now, talking between bites of a hot pastrami sandwich, Jacob discussed the situation in a serious manner. In his most professional voice, he said, "As I mentioned during your visit, it appears that Erick has DID. There are no more than a hundred cases documented in history, and of those reported, many psychiatrists dispute the findings. There is no clear-cut way of dealing with it either.

"Erick has a second personality within his brain, trying to take over Erick's mind and body. If successful, it could be a terrible thing for both you and Erick too. That other personality is not nice."

Sophia stared at Jacob when she heard these words.

"Sophia, this other personality is an insidious person. We cannot let him take over." His voice dropped to a lower register when finishing the sentence.

When Sophia heard these words and the tone of his voice, chills ran down her spine; she reached over to grasp Jacob's hand to receive some solace. She was now transfixed by Jacob's words and listened more intently than she had in her entire life. Jacob continued, "One reason for meeting with you, Sophia, is to warn you that this second personality, Lee, could be very, very dangerous to you and even the world."

Sophia's mouth gaped; she hesitatingly managed, "What do you mean?"

"Lee is capable of almost anything if he gains control. What I know is that the dream is Lee's way of destroying Erick by breaking his will and wearing him out. I have talked to Lee on several occasions. This is no joke. Lee is a bad person. I believe you should sleep in another room and have a deadbolt on your bedroom door as a precautionary measure. I am serious!"

Sophia began sipping water.

"There is always a reason the mind creates a second personality, but so far I have been unable to locate it. The personality is quite real. I now have several hours of video tape of him. I just cannot discover the reason for it. The scariest thing of all is that Lee knows things Erick doesn't, and further Erick doesn't know anything about Lee other than what I tell him or Lee tells him."

"You don't mean that Erick is possessed by the devil, do you?"

"I do not believe that, but I suppose we cannot discount that possibility."

Sophia's hand grasped Jacob's hands so hard that her knuckles turned white, and Jacob tried to extricate himself from the grip.

"What are we going to do?"

"I am communicating with experts around the world to see if this world body has any experience in these matters. So far, no one has. I am flying blindfolded. I am going by the book, as best that I know, and trying to get to know Lee. Maybe I can work backwards from Lee to Erick rather than vice versa. I am an expert in schizophrenia, and that medical problem isn't the case. By knowing Lee, maybe I can get rid of him, but right now I do not know how."

"Maybe we need another expert."

"I have talked to some, but no one in the world knows more than me right now. Please understand, Lee is very dangerous—Erick is not!"

Sophia found herself squeezing Jacob's hand again. "Wow, what a bombshell!"

"Sophia, it is even more complicated. Erick is a kind man, who is currently depressed, as you know. Lee is the antithesis of him. I am concerned for you should Lee take over. I am trying to determine why this occurred in the first place. There must be a reason, but neither Dr. Hanford nor I have come up with it yet. My current position is to treat Erick like I would any other DID patient, and that means working with Lee."

Sophia interjected, "But it is not working! You have to do something else."

"I agree, and right now I am trying to learn as much about Lee as I can."

"What is the danger of that?"

"In my opinion, there is more danger for Erick if I do nothing and let the two fight it out. Remember, Lee has been there for a while, and Erick has fought him off."

"Doctor!"

"Please, call me Jacob. You are not my patient."

After a pause, Sophia said, "Jacob, can the second personality really take over?"

"The school of conventional knowledge on that remains open. Some say never and some say yes. The answer is that we do not know. It is entirely possible that Lee will never surface other than through hypnosis. I'm frustrated. I just don't know!— However, my gut feeling is that he will. That is why we are having lunch today."

Sophia noticed a serious look on Jacob's face. "That's terrifying," she spouted. She just couldn't imagine her husband sinister. Devious, yes, but not sinister.

"What should I do?" she asked.

"One, keep Erick as happy and contented as humanly possible, and that is both of our jobs. Two, keep yourself as safe as possible. And three, get him to sleep well enough so Lee doesn't cause more problems. That is my job. I have no way of knowing what Lee's will do to you if he takes over. He may do nothing, or he may become mean spirited." Then Jacob volunteered, "Sometime I should let you see a video of Lee so you can identify him should he appear. Remember, so far he only appears under hypnosis. That video is time for another lunch if you are willing."

Chapter 5: Louisiana

It was now 9:30 a.m. on Saturday, July 22 when Jacob entered Covington. Jacob drove in the slow lane of an elevated highway in his rental car, looking for Highway 21 or Tyler Street, whatever it was called. He saw it just in time and dropped down to the city street level. He moved along Tyler, reading the street signs on the right-hand side. Then a street sign appeared for Eighth Avenue. He drove by Saint Tammany Parish Hospital and knew he was getting close because he remembered seeing it on the map as an unmistakable landmark. Finally, there it was—Seventeenth Avenue.

Jacob turned left and pulled over to the side of the street to examine his Covington map. He had only a few more blocks to go to reach the first target, Covington Elementary School. If that was the correct school, a grocery store would be located nearby. The traffic was light on this Saturday morning as he moved east. Then to his left, he saw two different large schools, but he appeared to be on the backside of them. He continued down the street, examining the homes alongside. He stopped occasionally to photograph a home or school. The entire area appeared to have large trees all around them—sycamores, he guessed. He continued towards the two schools and went a few blocks past them. He turned left to move over to Eighteenth Avenue. He continued seeking a rock archway without success.

The map showed that Eighteenth Avenue ended at Covington School. He turned left onto Jackson that fronted it, and across the street was the entrance to Covington Elementary School. The school covered a couple of city blocks. It was not a small, inconsequential school. He stopped across the street to better examine what he saw. Yes, it was old enough to have been here in the forties. He continued driving on Jackson to the intersection with Nineteenth Avenue. Straight ahead of him and across the street, tucked under trees, was a grocery store. He pulled into the parking lot.

The store was larger than it appeared from the street. He entered and walked to the back of the store, where there was a fresh meat counter. Two customers stood there, being attended to by their own butcher. The floor of the entire store was wood, black, and coated with penetrating oil for years. He looked back toward the entrance. A high school girl was working the cash register, so his eyes searched the store for help. Not far from the girl checker was an elderly man with white hair and a thin, white beard. The old man sat in a rocking chair positioned to talk to anyone. Jacob approached him as he completed his conversation with Mrs. White concerning her son Bobby.

The alert old man looked at Jacob and said, "You are new around here, aren't ya?"

"Yes, that's true, and I need help. Perhaps you can help me."

"Maybe I can, and maybe I can't—but I will try," the old man said with a gleam in his eye and a smile crossing his lips. The old man immediately put Jacob at ease. He reached out his hand in greeting. "Hi! I'm Emit Stall, the owner of this store."

Jacob shook hands and introduced himself. "Sir, I am seeking information about a family that lived in this area many years ago now. Their name was Ekdahl. They apparently lived someplace around Nineteenth Avenue."

"When was that, sir?" responded the old man.

This question caught Jacob off guard because he hadn't considered that request. His mind raced; he would guess Lee had been twenty-four or so in the 1960s; therefore, he had been born in the forties. Then Lee was about six or seven years old when he was here, so it must have been between 1946 and 47. "The war years, sir."

"Okay," said the old man in between quick chews of his tobacco. His spittoon was placed on the floor next to him. "I remember two Ekdahl families over the years. One family was long after the forties, so it can't be them. I do indeed remember a family in the mid-forties," old man Stall said in a rather slow, deliberate manner with a hint of a southern drawl.

"Ekdahl. I remember that name, sir." This was followed by a healthy spit of tobacco juice.

"Did they have a son?"

There was a long pause as the old man raced through his mind to locate the information. Jacob moved forward, waiting for an answer. He had his notepad and pen handy.

"Just a minute, sonny. I am still trying to remember. No, they didn't have a son." Jacob felt a wave of disappointment caress his mind. "They had three sons. But two of them stayed in a boarding school out of state. I remember the youngest son was skinny and liked licorice candy."

"Do you recall his name?"

"Do I remember it? That's another question. Let me think a minute; that was a long time ago." The room was quiet for a while, and then Emit spoke. "Well, that's a hard question because it has been a lot of years since then. It was a short name, but I can't remember it right now."

Gottlieb prompted, "Was it, Lee?"

"Yes! I remember," said the old man. "He had a sister about one year younger than him too. That was a real shame about the little girl."

"Why?" asked Gottlieb.

"She was killed right across the street on Nineteenth Avenue. Right out there in the crosswalk." Stall pointed toward the front window. "It made the mother distraught." The old man smacked his lips together, followed by a healthy spit into the spittoon. He pushed the wad of tobacco higher up into his cheek and waited for Jacob's next question.

"Do you remember the girl's name by any chance?"

"Not right now, but maybe it will come to me as we talk."

"Do you recall where they lived?" asked Gottlieb.

"Down the street by five to ten blocks. I can't tell you, but I can likely find it if we drive by it," he said, again smacking his lips together.

"Can you show me the home? It is very important. I'll make it worth your while."

"Okay," said Stall. "But y'all have to do the driving. I don't drive anymo."

"Is now convenient for you?" asked Jacob.

"Sure."

Jacob could see the old man struggling to get out of his chair and offered him his hand. The old man grabbed it and rose out of his rocking chair. He headed for the door in a labored walk and looked over his shoulder, saying, "Come on, young fellow, we have some work to do."

They proceeded to the parking lot exit. Jacob looked up and saw the market's sign, Nineteenth Avenue Market. He reached into his raincoat pocket and pulled out a notebook and pen; he scribbled the store name and Stall's name in his logbook before entering his car.

A couple of minutes later, they headed east. "Now, go slow here, young fellow, until I get my bearings. I got to look around, ya know." Jacob pulled over to the side of the road to let a car pass and allow Stall time. They continued slowly down the street.

"Stop here," the old man said. His eyes focused on the two homes on the opposite side of the street. "I used to deliver groceries to them," he said, "so you would think that I could remember. Neither home had a rock fence.

"Nope! Continue ahead and turn right on Vermont Street."

Jacob turned the corner and stopped near the curb. "Did the home have a rock fence and archway?"

"Yeah," said the old man. "That one over there." The old man pointed to the home directly across the street. "The new owners tore down the archway a few years ago. They were afraid someone could be injured. But as you can see, they still have a stone fence."

"Is that the home there, with the number 311 near the front door?" he said as he pointed to the house behind the rock fence.

"Yeah," the old man said with considerable pride. "That was the Ekdahls' home all right. I used to take groceries in the side door over there on the left and place them on the kitchen table. Then I put the perishables in the refrigerator."

"Are you certain?" asked Jacob.

"I am certain" was the rejoinder. "I delivered groceries and meat there, hundreds of times. Of course, I am certain," he barked.

Instinct or Learned? | 51

"Thanks," Gottlieb said as he made a U-turn in mid-street. He took the old man back to the store, reached in his wallet, and handed the old man a fifty-dollar bill before they got out of the car. Then Gottlieb stepped out and went over to the passenger door to assist him. He applied constant hand pressure, and slowly Emit Stall vacated the car.

The old man was still squeezing the money when Jacob asked him one more question. Pointing diagonally across the street, he asked, "Is that the school Lee attended?"

"Yep!"

"I'll be back after I drive over to the school and take a few photographs."

Jacob's mind was abuzz with the new information; he breathed rapidly. It happened so quickly.

The quick trip to the school yielded exactly what Lee had described. After taking a few pictures with his Minolta SLR camera, Jacob headed down Nineteenth Avenue and drove back to 311 Vermont Street; he snapped a few more photographs from his car. There was no swing in the front yard but certainly large trees that could have accommodated one years ago.

Jacob stepped out of his car and photographed the home from several different locations along the street and the house directly across the street. Further, he observed that indeed there was a solitary window facing Vermont Street. The home was on a corner, so he drove to the side of the home on Nineteenth and a little behind the home. There was no fence, so he took additional photos from the sidewalk. From his position he could see the back of the house and a single rear upstairs window, just as Lee had described. His excitement almost overwhelmed him as he headed back to the store to meet Stall.

Emit Stall sat in the rocking chair, waiting for Jacob's return. His eyes were fixed on the front door, so when Jacob walked in, his eyes met those of the smiling old man. "Everything okay?" asked Stall.

"It sure is," answered Gottlieb while taking his notepad out of raincoat pocket. The old man motioned Jacob around the counter and pointed to a straight-back chair next to him. Jacob complied and sat down with the pen ready.

The old man looked at Gottlieb, then almost shouted, "Elsa." Jacob was startled by the intensity of his voice and had no idea what else the old man was talking about. "Elsa," he said again. "That's the little girl's name. Elsa!"

"Oh, I see," said Gottlieb and followed that statement with a quick thank-you.

"You can verify that from the newspaper office. There sure was a lot of commotion here when it happened. She was walking to preschool at the time."

Jacob scribbled Elsa's name down in his notebook. The old man looked Gottlieb directly in the eye. His eyes twinkled, and his browning teeth revealed his mood.

"Why are you asking?" said the old man.

"I am a doctor, and I have a patient related to Ekdahl. I am trying to collect some background information to assist his memory."

"What kind of doctor are ya, may I ask?" There was a brief pause, and then he asked, "Are ya a shrink?" Then the old man stared at him, not blinking.

Gottlieb was transfixed for a moment, watching the unblinking pair of blue eyes amid a wrinkled face. "Yes, I am a psychiatrist." Jacob began questioning the old man and getting more facts, but the years had taken their toll, and the old man had lost a lot of the information.

"Do you recall what Lee's parents did to make a living?"

The old man stared across the store. "Let's see, his mother—can't rightly remember her name now. I just used to call her 'Mrs. Ekdahl.' She ran a dress shop downtown. Oh, heavens, let's see, her husband———he was an engineer. Yeah, a consultant. He traveled a lot, as I remember. It seemed to bother Lee that he was gone so much, because when he was around, Edwin paid a lot of attention to him."

Jacob thanked Emit Stall and headed to the airport near New Orleans. He had time to fly home and drive to Texas.

During his return drive on Sunday to Oklahoma City from north Texas, where he had discovered Lee's ranch home, Jacob pieced together the collected facts. The bottom line was that Lee had spoken what appeared to be the truth, at least about his youth. Many of his recollections were corroborated, still awaiting Lee's verification. Now there would be an opportunity to test Lee further. *I may be able to determine when Lee turned into a sociopath. This could be important in extricating him from Erick's mind.*

Erick would come in Wednesday afternoon, so Jacob had time to talk to Jim, make follow-up telephone calls, get films developed, and make new plans. He wanted to see whether Lee could recognize the Covington home and the farmhouse Lee had described during an earlier session.

On Monday morning, Jacob placed a call to Bradley Tucker, a private investigator he knew in town. They had worked together two years earlier on a joint project. Jacob asked Bradley to check newspapers in Covington, Louisiana, regarding the details of Elsa's death and get back to him as soon as possible.

They hung up, and Jacob turned to another item on his 'to-do' list regarding Erick. He made a note to talk to Erick during his Wednesday visit about his parents, who had adopted him. Maybe that would shed some light on the subject too.

Marilyn walked into Jacob's office and handed him a note that Sophia Anderson had called and requested a call back. Jacob called her immediately. "Hi, Sophia, this is Jacob."

"Thank you for calling back, Jacob. I wanted to let you know that Erick is experiencing that bad dream during his daytime naps now. Last Saturday, I was working in the kitchen while Erick was in the living room watching a baseball game. He dozed off during the game. I walked into the living room to decrease the volume of the television, since Erick was asleep, when he had another of the bad dream. I knew better than to awaken him from the front, so I walked around behind the chair and started shaking him. After several hard shakes, he awoke and realized what was happening. He apologized, and there were tears in his eyes. I felt terrible for him and walked around to the front of the chair. Erick stood up to greet me, and as we embraced, he began to sob. All I could do was hold him." She paused before continuing.

"There are moments like this, but there are so many more when he was confrontational and just mean and nasty, like he wanted to bop me in the nose, and I sure didn't want that again. However, this was the first time I was aware that Erick was experiencing the dream during the daytime. I thought you should be aware of this. I know he often doesn't tell you things he should."

"Do you sleep together, Sophia?"

"I no longer sleep with him, so I haven't seen him at night. Oh yes, I took your advice, and I got a carpenter install a solid, painted wooden door with a deadbolt lock when Erick was out playing golf. I don't believe Erick has noticed it yet."

"Good going, Sophia. I'm proud of you. That makes a lot of sense and removes a major concern I have."

During the noon hour the following day, Jacob was microwaving some soup when a call came in from Bradley Tucker. Tucker told Jacob he had collected the information he requested. He had located it in the newspaper, the ***Covington Times***, and had printed an online copy of the most complete article concerning the death of Elsa Ekdahl. Elsa had been killed by an automobile while walking in the crosswalk to her kindergarten class at Covington Elementary School. She was one of several children in the crosswalk, but she was the only one killed. She was almost six years old at the time of the accident. The driver was cited for vehicular manslaughter. The accident occurred on March 27, 1946. Her obituary provided the names of the parents.

This new fact further confirmed the statements of Emit Stall. Stall must be credible too. However, Lee had never mentioned having a sister, only two brothers.

Shortly thereafter, Jim sat down in the near-empty lunchroom. Jim was unaware of the results of the weekend trip, since he had been off on Monday, and Jim was eager to hear more information about this unusual case.

The two talked over soup. "Jim, I located a school and grocery store described by Lee in Covington. An old man who owned a store the Ekdahls frequented remembers delivering groceries to them. He showed me the house, and it fits the verbal description Lee gave me. Emit Stall told me about an accident in front of the store that killed Lee's sister, but Lee hasn't mentioned his sister. I will ask him next time."

All Jim could say in the now-empty room was, "Jacob, that is simply impossible, implausible, and hard to believe."

Jacob continued, "Lee described his mother's property near Archer City, southwest of Wichita Falls Texas, and I located it. Lee told me there was a Folgers sign on the tank house. I found it. I further talked to a neighbor, who remembered young Lee and his mother, and everything Lee told me corresponds to what he said, and that includes Lee's fishing hole, which I located. The neighbor told me Lee loved fishing. The child Lee appears credible. I have yet to talk to Lee about these findings."

Jim continued to shake his head in disbelief as Jacob delivered his narrative. All he could say was, "This cannot be, Jacob. It just can't! I am proud of you. I didn't believe you would discover anything at all. I now believe you are about to discover something big, but I don't know what."

"Jim, I am prepared to show slides I took to both Lee and Erick's next visit. Half of the photos will be unknown to Lee. It will be fascinating to see if Lee recognizes any of those places I visited. I drove around and took photos of other locations in the area as well, and I will mix those in with the others."

The two friends walked out of the lunchroom with Jim's hand on Jacob's shoulder as a way of condoning his successful effort. Just before the door, Jim said, "Jacob, I am so proud of you. Keep up the great work. I don't know what you got, but don't let go of its tail. Watch the head; it can swing around and bite you. I think Lee can bite pretty hard."

On Wednesday evening, Jacob listened to Mozart. It soothed his mind but didn't alter his excitement over his Covington experience. It was miraculous to say the least. He confirmed Lee's grammar school years recollections. It was nothing short of amazing. A miracle! Jacob's insides still quivered like a porcupine threatening a predictor by rattling his quills.

He agonized over how he was going to handle Lee. If he tied his wrists to the chair, Lee could just refuse to acknowledge the photos. If he didn't, he risked releasing a mad man in a darkened room. Then he had an idea and walked to his phone, calling the Cedar Ridge Psychiatric Center. "Hi, this is Dr. Gottlieb. Is Mike in?"

There was an affirmative answer in response. "Great, may I talk to him?"

A minute later, Jacob heard Mike's generous voice on the phone.

"Mike, this is Dr. Gottlieb speaking. By any chance, are you free tomorrow at ten a.m.?

"Yes, I am, Dr. Gottlieb. It's my day off. Why?"

"How would you like to earn a hundred dollars for an hour's work being my nurse here at the office?"

"Sure, Dr. Gottlieb. Doing what?"

"Actually, I wanted you to sit in on a session with one of my patients. I believe this patient could be dangerous. I will be hypnotizing him, and I want you there to control him if necessary. I do not anticipate any problem. I have been binding his wrists, but tomorrow I will be doing a lengthy slide show with him in a darkened room with wrists untied. I am concerned to do this with his hands free without you present. I think the hypnosis part of it would be valuable experience for you too."

"Sure, Dr. Gottlieb. It sounds interesting. I will be there at ten a.m. at your office."

Mike could be an intimidating individual; he weighed 260 pounds and was muscular, literally standing head and shoulders above most men. Jacob breathed a sigh of relief.

Chapter 6: Practice Makes Perfect

"What's going on, Dr. Gottlieb?"

"First, Erick, I want you to meet Mike Garland. Mike is going to be sitting in today and observing. He is a specialist nurse, and we work together. He is studying hypnosis, and I thought that this would be a learning experience for him. When you are under hypnosis, I will also be instructing Mike. Is this all right with you?"

Erick shook Mike's hand but couldn't get a full grip because of its massive size. He stared at Mike with his mouth gaping.

Mike was first to speak. "I am pleased to meet you, Erick."

"Good luck with the hypnosis study today, Mike," Erick volunteered.

"Sure, Dr. Gottlieb. It is fine with me. What's the projector all about?"

Jacob spoke again as Erick eyed the gentle giant. "I will be showing both you and Lee some slides and see if either of you can identify any of the photos. I do not expect either of you to identify many of them. It may be only an exercise in watching slides."

"Okay, Dr. Gottlieb. Thanks for filling me in. Before we begin, I need to tell you that for the first time I have experienced the dream during the daytime while I was snoozing."

Gottlieb listened to every word but didn't tell him Sophia had already mentioned this. If he increased the dosage of his medication again, it wouldn't help. On the other hand, he could switch him to Popodine. Popodine had more of a tranquilizing effect on patients.

While Erick was talking, Gottlieb wrote out a new prescription and handed it to him. "Erick, I am switching your sleeping pills to see if this one works a little better for you. Give it a week. Follow the directions. Okay?"

"Sure, Doctor," answered Erick as he relaxed in the upright, straight-back chair.

"Erick, before I forget to ask you again, I recall that you were adopted. It might be important that I contact your parents. Do they live around here?"

"My father is deceased, but my mother, Margret, is still alive and well. She lives outside Amarillo, Texas."

"Erick, I would like to call her regarding background information. Before I do, would you call her and let her know I will be contacting her so she is comfortable with the call? Just tell her I am treating you for recurring dreams, dealing with Mary and Sean's deaths."

"Certainly, Dr. Gottlieb. I will do it today."

Mike sat behind Erick, slightly to one side and within arm's reach.

Mike looked away so as not to watch the pendulum swing and plugged his ears with his index fingers. Within minutes, Erick was hypnotized, and Gottlieb called on Lee to make an appearance. There was the usual fidgeting, and then Lee said, "Who is the creep behind me?"

"His name is Mike Garland, and he is a nurse learning about hypnosis. Lee, today I want to show you some slides and see if you can identify any of them."

Jacob stood and handed Lee and Mike each a glazed donut on a paper plate before he turned off the lights.

Lee sat in the chair, looking around the darkened room and at Mike too. Mike scooted his chair a little closer to Lee when he noticed Lee was searching the room. Jacob had the projector ready and turned on the switch. The screen was mounted on the wall. Jacob placed a mirror behind Lee so he could see the projections.

"Lee, I want you to look at these slides and see if you can identify any of them. Tell me what you think and feel."

"All right, Doc," he said with arms crossed and remained calm during the initial process. The first picture brightened the room, and their eyes adjusted to the projector light. Jacob checked the video recorder to make certain it was still running.

The first image flashed on the screen. Lee studied it.

"Do you recognize this photo?" Jacob said.

"Yes. It is the front of this building."

"That is correct. How about this next photo?"

Lee looked at it and said, "Yes, that is Erick and Sophia's home here in Oklahoma City."

"Very good, Lee. Now I am going through several slides of homes, most of these photos you won't be able to recognize. Just tell me you don't recognize it, and I will move on. If you do recognize one, tell me, and we will talk about it."

Lee, now calm and controlled, said, "Okay, Doc, just before taking his first bite of donut."

The next slide lit up the screen, and Lee smiled for the first time. Jacob eyes were fixed on Lee and not on the screen. Lee said, "Yeah, Doc, I recognize it. It is my home in Covington, but the rock archway is missing."

"Good memory, Lee." Then Gottlieb showed him a picture of the home across the street.

Lee said, "That's the Clements' place across the street."

"That's correct, Lee. Very good memory!" Jacob jotted Lee's comments in his logbook, including the statement about the missing stone archway. Jacob hadn't given Lee any indication of where the homes were located. He also showed Lee some locations he likely wouldn't recognize, and he didn't.

Next came some slides Lee found puzzling. "I do not recognize that photo." Lee seemed to be enjoying this experience. Gottlieb made note of it.

During the ensuing photos, Lee identified the store and the school. However, he failed to recognize Emit Stall, the old man who owned the store. Jacob understood this was because Emit Stall had aged a great deal since then. Jacob next engaged Lee in more discussions about his youth. He was particularly interested in Wichita Fall or Archer City, because he believed Lee had begun his antisocial demeanor around that time.

When pressed by Gottlieb, Lee discussed the death of his sister, Elsa, and how it upset his mother, so much so that it probably led to his parents' divorce.

He showed a few slides taken of the Texas trip but not in crucial areas. Lee didn't recognize them. Then Jacob dropped in a wide-angle view of an Archer City home.

"Wow," said Lee. "That's the Archer City ranch." Lee stood up, while Mike watched him closely.

"You are correct."

The next photograph was of the ponds. Seeing this, Lee said, "That's my fishing hole. I used to catch crappie and bluegill there."

Next came a close-up photograph of the tank house. "See," Lee spouted as he stood up again, "I told you it had a Folgers Coffee sign on it. You don't believe nothing, do you, Doc?" he said as he sat down. Mike stood behind Lee.

"Did your mother find another boyfriend after the divorce?"

"Yeah, that's why we moved. Adam Johnson was his name, and he had a ranch near Archer City."

"Did you see a lot of him, Lee?"

"He was around, helping Mom a lot at first, but then he kind of vanished."

The conversations continued for another thirty minutes about life in Archer City, Texas. It didn't appear that Lee was mistreated as a child by his stepfather, mother, or her boyfriend. So far, Jacob hadn't uncovered a reason for Lee's antisocial behavior.

Lee's testimony verified Jacob's findings from his trip. Lee was credible. How could Erick come upon this information? Jacob couldn't understand any of it, because Erick couldn't know this information.

Jacob woke Erick and showed him the slides. Erick couldn't identify any of them except for the first two.

Later that afternoon, Jacob placed a call to Margaret Anderson. He found, as expected, that Erick and his sister's parents hadn't mistreated them. Although annoyed by Jacob's probing questions, his mother answered all of them. She said she would send a copy of Erick's adoption papers. Jacob felt uncomfortable with the call, but she verified all Erick had stated.

Jacob's second call was to the grocery store in Covington to speak to Emit Stall. A woman answered the call and informed him that Mr. Stall was in and would be with him shortly. Jacob could hear her calling Mr. Stall for the call. About a minute, Stall came to the phone. "Hello," he said. "This is Emit Stall speaking."

"Mr. Stall, this is Dr. Gottlieb speaking. I had a couple of follow-up questions concerning the Ekdahl family, which we spoke about over the weekend. Do you recall our conversation?"

"Sure, I do; I am not senile," Emit said, raising his voice. "What's your question?"

Gottlieb found himself feeling defensive. "Is now a good time to talk?"

"Certainly!" Emit snorted.

"As far as you can recall, did Lee's parents have any major problems there in Covington?"

"No. They were just regular folks until the little girl's death. The mother took it real hard. I heard said that she started ignoring Lee at the time and then divorced Ekdahl. But I know nothing about any of them after they moved. Wait, don't hang up. I have been thinking about Lee, and I know something else about Lee that I didn't tell you."

"What's that?

"Oh, not much, except when he growed up, he changed his name back to his birth name, Oswald. You have heard of him. He's the man who assassinated President John Kennedy. You know—Lee Harvey Oswald." There was complete silence from Jacob Gottlieb before he managed a thank-you and hung up.

Lee Harvey Oswald! It was incredible, impossible, and unrealistic. Jacob Gottlieb's head spun like a child's top as he conjured the possibilities of Lee Harvey Oswald being there inside Erick's head. He also thought about his patient, what this was doing to him, and the fact that he, Jacob Gottlieb, hadn't helped his patient one bit. Erick was going backward fast, and an assassin was taking over. In thinking about the issue, he realized Lee Harvey Oswald may not have been the same person who assassinated the president. After all, it was only the accusation of an old man who knew only the name of a boy who was seven years old, and then many years before. Clearly, Gottlieb had to talk to Lee about this new revelation at the next session.

The alarming change in Erick's daytime habits had exacerbated his unstable condition and greatly concerned Gottlieb. It could mean Lee was about to break out. Jacob had to warn Sophia in some way; he must protect her. He fetched reading glasses from the desk drawer, and searched his phone directory for her phone number. Jacob scratched his nose and poked out the numbers on his phone.

"Good morning, Sophia. This is Jacob. I wanted to take some time to go over part of a video of one session so you can clearly understand what we are dealing with in Erick's case. I will also give you a general update on where things stand. I would like you to come by the office at eleven thirty today, and then we'll follow it up with lunch, where you can ask questions. Oh, by the way, there is no charge for my time. I am doing this as a courtesy to you."

After the call, Jacob was seated at his desk. Marilyn had just brought in the mail. Before opening it, he thumbed through it to see whether there was anything of importance. He found two pieces of mail that intrigued him. One, a large envelope, was from Erick's mother; and the second letter was from Dr. Albert Becher, from the medical school at the University of Bonn in Germany. Dr. Becher had studied more cases of DID than anyone in the world, and Jacob had written him a letter concerning Erick's problem.

He unfolded the letter and snapped it with his fingers to straighten out the creases. It was a letter from the world's foremost authority on DID. Dr. Becher admitted that Jacob's case was somewhat different from most. However, he also had a patient, through whom he had accidentally discovered the key to unlocking the analysis, and he encouraged Gottlieb not to give up and to continue searching for the key.

Lying almost crumpled under his hand lay a large envelope from Erick's mother, which, he guessed contained the copies of the adoption papers. She had done as she promised. Jacob read through the papers, but of course there was no record of the actual parents. However, there were court document numbers that might help track down the actual parents. Clearly the Andersons had picked up the infant directly from the hospital as a released newborn, and he had the name of the hospital. That was a start.

He placed a telephone call to a private investigator, Robert Darwin, referred to him as one who had handled things like the adoption in the greater Dallas area. When they made telephone contact later that morning, Jacob asked Robert whether he could uncover the birth parents of Erick Andrew Anderson. Robert didn't promise and stated that he perhaps had a 50 percent chance of obtaining that information. However, he would try. Gottlieb assured him that it wasn't a rush situation but rather important background information to assist him in treating Mr. Anderson. Darwin said he would get back to Gottlieb within two weeks and report where he stood on the case.

Friday arrived, and Jacob awaited Sophia. He had the video recorder set to the point where Lee had made his first appearance into the heinous Lee. His receptionist announced the arrival of Mrs. Anderson and escorted her into the treatment room.

They approached each other with a handshake, and Sophia wondered what would happen next. Her emotions were magnified by ongoing events and her home life with Erick.

Now in the treatment room, Gottlieb spoke first. "Sophia, how are you personally handling this situation at home?"

Sophia was direct and honest. "Erick is like a time bomb waiting to explode. I can say small, innocuous things, and Erick reacts way out of proportion. I am afraid to even speak. The more he sits at home with nothing to do, the more he becomes emotionally distressed and depressed. I am at my wit's end. If I speak, he bites my head off. If I don't speak, he bites my head off. It is a terrible way to live. I don't know what to do. I hate it! I would like to run away—far away. I can't win or even calm it down, and it bothers me greatly."

"Have you had any encounters with Lee yet?"

Sophia didn't understand and said, "Lee who?"

"Oh, I am sorry. I will introduce you to Lee shortly. "Remember, Lee is the other occupant in Erick's mind, who is trying to take over. His name is Lee Ekdahl."

"Oh yes," responded Sophia. "I had forgotten the name. As far as I know, I haven't had that experience, and I am glad."

"Good, Sophia! I record my treatment sessions with my patients. I am not recording us now because you are not a patient. I make these recordings for many reasons, but the most important reason is that it enables me to review the session and pick up little things I may have missed. This is a tape where Erick is under hypnosis, and I am attempting to bring out the second and hidden personality, named Lee. Dr. Hanford was with me when this was recorded. I was unable to bring Lee out on my first attempt, but on the second attempt, I withdrew Lee. I do this routinely now.

"As I said, Dr. Hanford sat in on this session, so sometimes you will see us whispering together. But as you will notice, I did the communicating with Erick. Please understand that there are only about one hundred documented cases of DID ever recorded, so what you are about to see is extremely rare. I am not going to show you the entire tape but only the beginning. I want you to see the metamorphosis of Erick to Lee. Further understand that this metamorphosis is attempting to take place daily within Erick by Lee. Do you have any questions before we begin?"

"Yes. Why are you doing this?"

Jacob looked her straight in the eyes. "I am doing this to protect you. Lee can be very dangerous. If he takes over, I believe you could be in physical danger. I still need to know Lee better before I understand him. Understanding him and what caused this problem is imperative to eliminate Lee from Erick's mind."

"Erick would never intentionally hurt me in a million years, Jacob. Never!"

"I believe that, but Lee is not Erick. Lee could." Gottlieb had dropped his voice down at the end of the sentence to demonstrate the serious nature Sophia was facing. Hearing these words brought a chill across her entire body as the words fell on her ears.

"Please understand something before we begin. This experience won't be pleasant, but it could possibly save your life. It is *that* serious! Do you understand?"

"Thank you, Jacob. I do realize that you are doing this for me."

They both sat in the comfortable stuffed chairs side by side as Gottlieb reached for the remote control. Sophia squirmed in her chair.

"I believe you should see this, so if it happens in real life and you are around, you can react to help yourself. Make no mistake about it—Lee is dangerous."

Sophia nodded and said, "Okay. Let's do it!"

Jacob flipped on the recorder. The audio and video quality were quite clear, since Jacob had wasted no money on good equipment, so Sophia had no problem seeing the event and hearing the spoken words.

It started with Erick in his hypnotic state, and Gottlieb was now asking for Lee. Then she saw Erick's eyes open in the form of a squint. Erick began opening them a little more, like he was trying to get used to a bright light in the room. In the next few seconds, Sophia couldn't believe her eyes. Erick's face began to contort, and his upper lips curled in a devilish manner. His lips thinned as if being driven by another force. The face—yes, Erick's face—became evil, and chills ran up her back. His eyes stared at the doctor's in a piercing manner. She wanted to hide as the face contorted with a plethora of wrinkles around the mouth.

"For God's sake, what's happening? Lee is crazy!" Sophia shouted.

Jacob stopped the video.

Sophia stood up, shaking her head and uttering, "No—no."

"Are you okay?"

Sophia began shaking over her entire body. Her throat had a lump in it, and she couldn't swallow. Jacob went over to his desk, poured her a glass of water, and returned with it. After drinking a few swallows, she reached out to hold both of Jacob's hands as she began to sob.

"It gets a lot worse," Jacob said. "I think you have seen enough."

"That cannot be Erick," she said. "Erick is kind."

"That wasn't Erick. That was Lee. At that moment, Lee controlled Erick's body."

Sophia sat down and said, "I need to see a little more Jacob. Just hold my hand, please."

Jacob reached for the remote controller and turned it on again; he offered his hand, which she readily accepted. She watched as the lips moved slowly at first.

"'You guys are jerks.'"

"'Are you Lee?'"

"'I am Lee. What's it to you? You guys don't know nothing.'"

Sophia watched for a few more minutes, then said, "That's enough; I can't take any more."

Jacob hit the rewind button and stood up. "Come on, let's get out of here and go to lunch."

Fifteen minutes later, Jacob and Sophia were seated immediately at Marco's. Jacob ordered drinks. Sophia was unable to focus. Seeing Erick that way was unnatural—it couldn't be him. Yet there he was. She finally managed to speak. "Why does this happen, Jacob?"

"That's the million-dollar question in Erick's case. I don't know the answer yet."

Just then, the waitress walked up with the drinks. "I can sure use this," offered Sophia.

After placing their order, Jacob started the dialogue by apologizing to Sophia. "You can see now why I didn't want to get involved in a conversation with Erick around, also why I didn't want you to participate in a therapy session dealing with Lee. Sessions can get testy—much, much worse than what you witnessed. I must strap Lee's hands to the chair.

"Erick only knows that there is another personality trying to take over, and this person is not nice. Lee is a sociopath and probably worse. I am still working on Lee's diagnosis. I need more time."

"Erick is not and never has been evil," she said. "Lee seemed evil to me. How can that identity come out of Erick's mind?"

"You got me—I do not know. I have discovered that Erick is everything you said he is. One cannot imagine evil coming from good, but there it is." Jacob looked directly into Sophia's green eyes. "I must tell you that, later in that session, it gets worse. I will never show it to you."

"You showed me enough. I don't think I can ever get close to Erick again after that experience."

"Sure you can, and you will."

Sophia squeezed Jacob's hand hard. Jacob noticed a faraway look in her eyes.

"Sophia, please listen to me. I showed you this video so you would know what to look for should Lee ever take over Erick's body. Remember his eyes and mouth. I cannot promise you that it will not happen," Jacob said in an emphatic manner. "I just don't know."

"What should I do if Lee takes over?"

"Call me immediately and stay out of his way. Memorize my office and home phone numbers." He withdrew a business card from his coat pocket and popped open a pen, scribbling his home phone number on the back of it. "I just wrote my home phone number on the back for you. Memorize both. Program these numbers into your phone. If it occurs, lock yourself in your room or drive away from him fast."

After swallowing a sip of his Scotch, Jacob began again, "I believe that showing you that tape was necessary to forewarn you should that terrible event occur, so that you would recognize it. It is unmistakable once you have seen it."

"Jacob, should we place Erick in a hospital now?"

"We can't do that legally. The takeover may never occur other than through hypnosis. We are damned if we do and damned if we don't, since it may never happen. There is no legal precedence for hospitalization. No judge would authorize it."

Jacob needed to change the conversation to a more civil but related one. "Sophia, did you care for Mary and Sean?"

"Oh yes, Jacob. Sean was almost my son. I loved him so much. Erick and I have been unable to have children. I so badly wanted to be a mother. Sean became our son, and we shared him with Mary and Bart. Sometimes the husbands would go golfing, and Mary, Sean, and I would spend the day together. We had a wonderful time." Sophia continued to relate her pleasant experiences with Mary and Sean. She loved both.

The lunch was completed with Sophia still shaken. Jacob rose, but Sophia made no move to leave. She just sat there, obviously thinking about what she had just become aware. Jacob implored Sophia to continue. He needed more time to learn about Lee so he could get rid of him.

Jacob changed the conversation as she stood to leave. His kindness showed through as well as his caring for her by what he had done earlier. She felt strangely attracted to him. Perhaps it was only because of the Erick situation, which was driving her away.

Gottlieb fretfully awaited Erick's next office visit. This was the day when he would discuss Lee Harvey Oswald with Lee. Jacob's attitude changed to unadulterated excitement as the time grew near. Finally, Erick was ushered into the session room, and Jacob was waiting for him, almost unable to breath. Before Erick crossed the room, Jacob asked, "How did the Popodine work for you, Erick?"

"Much better, Dr. Gottlieb," Erick said as he sat in the straight-back chair with armrests. "I do not recall dreaming once since I started taking it, and I have been sleeping well. I don't feel like I've been knocked out in the morning."

"Great news. Erick! That is a major step forward. That will give us more time. Popodine is habit forming. Let's keep up the medication at the same dosage."

Gottlieb quickly changed into his session mode and said, "Erick, relax, and I will speak with Lee." Erick knew the routine and was instantly hypnotized.

"Yeah, Doc! What do you want this time?" Lee said.

"I want to talk to you."

"About what?"

"The first question that I have for you is, what is your entire name?" Lee responded, "Lee Harvey Oswald."

"You mentioned the name Ekdahl. What was that all about?"

"When I was a kid, Mom married a man named Ekdahl, and I went by that name as a child. It was her idea. Later, I took back my birth name Oswald."

"Lee, are you the same man who assassinated President John Kennedy?" Lee remained silent. Then Gottlieb asked again with an elevated voice, "Lee, are you the man who assassinated President John Fitzgerald Kennedy?"

Lee twisted and turned a little but didn't offer an answer.

"Lee, I am talking to you, damn it. Did you assassinate President Kennedy?"

Then Lee's sneer spread across his face, and he looked Gottlieb directly in the eye. "Did you shoot President Kennedy?"

"Yes! I did, and I am proud of it." Lee spoke in an elevated voice as he made the pronouncement. His beady eyes stared at Gottlieb to check for a weakness.

Gottlieb made a hard swallow, then calmly said, "I want you to talk about it."

"Sure, Doc; it's okay with me. I got time." Then Lee let out a fiendish laugh. "Ha ha ha!" Lee glared but said nothing more.

"Did you perform the assassination on your own, with somebody else, or for somebody else?"

"I already told you I was an operative for the CIA, but you, being so stupid, don't believe me." Then Lee shouted, "I did it for them! I was paid to do it!"

"Are you telling me the CIA paid you to assassinate the president?"

"I don't know for sure."

"What do you mean that you don't know for sure?"

"I already told you I was a KGB operative. It could have been them."

"Why do you say that?"

"The guy I dealt with didn't tell me, so it could have been either of them. I don't know for sure. They both operate exactly the same way."

"If you had to guess, which one do you think ordered you to do the deed?"

"I believe it was the CIA."

Gottlieb, again using a subdued voice, said, "Go back to the time when you first learned about the assassination."

"Give me a minute to think about it." After a pause, Lee said, "Yeah! My contact was Vince Williams. The time was about six months before Kennedy visited Dallas, May of 1963. He called me at home and he asked if I was up for an assignment.

"I answered yes."

Three days after I received another brief phone call from Vince. He said, "I'll see you at the meeting place on Thursday at 4 p.m.' The meeting place was at Marsalis Park near the playground. I arrived two hours early and walked the perimeter around the playground area three times in very wide circles, in and out of the trees, checking the faces, stopping frequently. I made sure each woman's face had a child associated with her; otherwise I wouldn't sit down. Everything seemed okay, so I sat on the bench facing the kids. About four thirty, Vince sat down beside me. Most of the kids and mothers had gone by then. He had a piece of paper curled up under his hand, but he didn't offer it to me.

"I hadn't been with him very long when Vince said, 'Would you have trouble killing someone?'"

"'No, not at all. Why?'"

"'I have an assignment for you. You will need training on a special rifle. You must become an expert with it. Further, I want you to maintain your job at the Texas School Depository." While seated, Vince slid me a folded piece of paper cupped in the palm of his hand, flattened against the bench seat. Then out of the side of his mouth, he said, 'Your directions and the time are on the paper. They are quite explicit. Goodbye.' Vince stood up, walked around behind the bench. and departed.

"We are trained not to look. I waited my customary five minutes without turning around. Since no one was near me or looking at me, I placed the paper in a magazine I was reading. The note consisted of directions and a time to be at a specific location out of town I didn't know. That date was in two days. Two days later, I drove out in the county in north Texas. It was out in nowhere, and no houses around. I remember the rolling hills near State Highway 81. The site was an abandoned gravel quarry.

"I can't remember the name of the quarry now. It began with the letter *J*, maybe a letter *K*, but it doesn't come to me—it's like Johnson but a shorter word than that. There were 'Keep Out' signs at the front. I crept down a gravel road around some small mounds until I came to a sturdy cyclone fence and a locked gate. I stopped and got out of the car and waited. A man wearing blue jeans and a polo shirt walked toward me from around a little mound.

"'Lee, I am your instructor Joe. I am going to be teaching you this special new rifle. You must become an expert using it.'"

"We drove into the quarry and walked into the smallest building there, a rickety single-wall construction with gaps between the side-boards. There was a box that had just been opened. Blue metal parts lay in the box. 'Okay,' he said, 'here is how you assemble the rifle.'

"He grabbed the various pieces and put them together to form a very unusual-appearing rifle. Joe then disassembled it, handed me the pieces, and said, 'Now you do it.' After several attempts, I finally got it. It was blue and looked peculiar. The barrel appeared larger in diameter than most rifles, but the bore seemed normal. The rifle butt looked more like a heavy-gauge wire with rubber padding where the butt is placed against the shoulder. The essential elements were there. On the floor lay boxes of bullets."

Lee then discussed the quarry, shooting range, and targets in exact details. He remembered that the main bunker was slightly tipped to the north. There were three targets. One target was fixed, and the other two moved. "After each practice, I left the rifle in the shed, and someone else cleaned it before the next practice." Jacob logged many of the details Lee provided.

Gottlieb remained in complete silence and looked at the video camera to make certain it was on and rolling. Lee continued to talk and still seemed gleeful in telling his story. He never talked in gibberish. "For the next several practices, I continued as ordered, and I shot at both moving and fixed targets. The weapon and I were one. The next order was rapid fire, and I concentrated on that. After several weeks, I considered myself an expert, and I could place ninety-six-plus percent of my shots within a four-inch diameter circle, even if the target was moving."

Gottlieb continued to let him speak just in case he said anything that could be checked out. Lee was quiet for a minute as he seemed to be thinking. "Yeah," he said. "I remember. Weeks later, when I was finished, I walked into the shed, and Joe was in there waiting for me. He handed me a dull blue bicycle—a girl's bike. 'What's this for?' I asked.

"'It's your new bicycle,' he answered.

"'It's a girl's bike!'

"'No, it is not.' I should have known better. Joe grabbed the rifle I was still holding and dismantled it into the original pieces. He then placed the barrel between the seat and front steering column and turned it into a male's bicycle. The unusual shoulder brace then formed the water bottle holder on the column supporting the seat. The barrel grip was placed on the column from the handlebars to the drive sprocket, making it look like one piece. The bike had two gears up front, six in the rear, and skinny tires. The trigger assembly, some pins, and the front and back sights were placed in a leather bag that hung from the saddle. When Joe was done, the weapon totally vanished from view, yet it was in plain view. It was amazing. The blue colors matched the bicycle, and all pieces locked into position. Then Joe made me disassemble and reassemble the bike several times. I was astounded each time. I could take a weapon down a main street, and no one would know it, even if they touched it. Of course, if they looked in the saddlebag, they would see the trigger assembly and sights."

Gottlieb listened with utter fascination, but there was nothing said to check facts. Then he asked, "Lee, can you give me directions to the rifle range?"

"No, Doc, not anymore. All I remember was taking Highway 79 North from Dallas, about two hours of driving."

"Think about it. I will ask you again in another session."

Now the stark reality of what Lee was saying hit home. Lee was saying he was an operative for the CIA and the assassin of President Jack Kennedy.

Gottlieb's mind raced as he pondered the possible repercussions of what he was hearing. If it indeed verified the events surrounding the Kennedy assassination mystery, then he himself was sitting on a bomb. He began worrying about the CIA. *What would the CIA do if they found out about Lee.*

As he further thought about this event, he decided this information would remain secret from everyone until such a time that he was certain of where he was going with it. His mind came back to Lee. "Lee, please continue. How and when did you receive orders for the assassination?"

"I was at the shooting range when Joe approached me. It was mid-November.

"'The time has come,' he said. We were in the shed. We walked outside. Joe said, 'The target is President John Kennedy tomorrow.' He handed me a paper and asked me to memorize it and then burn it. 'Ride the bicycle to work with the rifle integrated into the bicycle. You will shoot from the attic of the Texas School Depository building. The presidential caravan will pass directly in front of your building, moving toward you initially. When they get in front of your building, the caravan will turn to their left, your right. They will be traveling about ten miles per hour. The president will be in a convertible. The distance is the same as you have been practicing.'"

"At first, my knees shook a little, but then I had a duty to fulfill. After all, I am a marine. Once a marine, always a marine. I had forgiven the CIA, and I believed in them. My whole body quieted down after a minute as Joe detailed the plan. 'Take a bus from home to work and ride your bicycle for the last four blocks. After the shooting, the cops won't be looking for a bicyclist without a rifle. Then take a city bus with your bicycle out to Mesquite and get off at the Sunnyvale stop, taking your bicycle with you. The bicycle with rifle is designed to handle the rough ride on the racks on the front of the bus. The rifle barrel is securely locked into place and will not release. Next, ride the bicycle to Lake Ray Hubbard onto Rockwell Forney Dam. Go out to the middle of the spillway on the far side and throw the bicycle as far into the water as you can without being seen. This is the deepest part of the lake. This part of the lake is not highly attended, so it is a safe place to go. Next, take a bus home, call work, and say that you became ill. Then meet me at the Texas Theater. Don't let anyone follow you. Do you understand?'

"'Yep!' I repeated what he told me.

"'Now, go and check out the lake and dam this afternoon. I'll contact you at home tonight.' Joe mounted his motorcycle and left quietly. When I got to the shed, there were six bullets sitting on the floor next to the bicycle. I placed the bullets in the saddlebag and assembled the rifle into the bicycle. I walked outside, wheeling the bicycle to my pickup. Then I drove to the park."

Gottlieb was fascinated by what he had heard. He tried not to interrupt to keep everything flowing. Lee continued spontaneously. "That afternoon, I rode my bicycle over to the spillway. I could see that it was possible to throw everything into the water without anyone noticing because of the surrounding trees and the remoteness of the area, so my problems were solved. Next, I rode back to my pickup.

"Of course, when I got home, I said nothing to Marina. She immediately noticed my new bicycle. I told her it was an experimental bike that I was trying out. I placed it in the bathtub so the girls wouldn't mess with it.

"That night, I remember the two of us watching television. About nine p.m., there was a call, and I answered. I expected some last-minute instructions. The caller didn't identify himself. He said, 'Lee, be ready at eleven thirty a.m. The caravan is expected at about twelve thirty. There is an old rifle on the top floor behind a tarp. Make sure that you fire it once at anything and leave it there.' He hung up, and I went to bed."

"Tell me about the next day, Lee."

"I took the bus to work about seven a.m. and placed the bicycle on the rack up front. I sat in the front seat to make certain no one would steal it. I got out of the bus on Seventh Street and rode it to work."

"How far was that, Lee?"

"It was four blocks. Then I entered the building and placed the bicycle in my office—if you want to call it that—near the maintenance room. I had a large trash cart in there with wheels on it. I placed the rifle parts in it and six bullets, stuffed trash on top of it, and took the elevator to the seventh floor. I unlocked the door and wheeled everything in. I remember walking over to the windows and opening the center window. It was a perfect spot. I had a great view. I left things the way they were and returned to do my normal work. I didn't want to arouse any suspicion. I then went downstairs to get Eddie and have my cup of coffee. Eddie and I generally have a cup every morning."

Gottlieb interrupted Lee. "Lee, what is Eddie's entire name?"

"Eddie Montana!"

"How old is he, and where does he live?"

"I have no idea of where he lives, but he was between twenty-one to twenty-three years old at the time. Yeah, sometimes we would go outside to have our coffee, and on that day we did too. I made Eddie go out front, because I wanted to study the terrain. Eddie commented on my new bicycle, but I told him that I borrowed it from a friend for the day. I was glad that he didn't want to look at it closely. After our coffee, we went back to work."

"What did you talk about, Lee?" Gottlieb wanted to get some inside information so he could corroborate Lee's story.

"I don't remember, Doc. I just can't remember, but I do recall laughing a lot.

"For the next couple of hours, I did my normal job, and then at about eleven thirty, I headed upstairs to the seventh floor by taking the elevator. I placed a pencil in the elevator door so it wouldn't completely close. There was a second elevator, so people would never notice that one wasn't working. Then I entered the room and locked the door behind me. The room was never used. I was comfortable that no one would show up except Eddie, and he had no reason to be there, and he didn't have a key either. Once in the room, I located the other rifle that was behind the tarp, and it had a couple of bullets ready for use. I set it down near the window and assembled the blue rifle. It was time."

Lee's eyes got a gleam in them as he pondered the next hour. He was looking forward to the assassination. "Yeah, ya know, Doc, I never talked to anyone about this before.

"Everything was ready. I even had a small radio there, and I was listening to a local radio station that was conveniently announcing the status of the presidential motorcade from an overhead helicopter."

"Lee, did you ever wonder or did the CIA fellow, Joe, ever say why they wanted the president assassinated?"

"No, in my business, you never ask questions. I sat there for a while, and a cat that I befriended a year earlier came up to me. I feed her up there, and she catches mice for me. I sat on the floor, stroking the cat, when I heard on the radio that the presidential motorcade was nearing me. It was after noon when the caravan was within a few blocks of me. I was ready. I knew what I had to do, and my hands were steady. The cat kept rubbing my leg, so I kicked her. I needed to concentrate. The cat ran away and hid behind some boxes."

Jacob asked, "Lee, have you ever killed anyone else before?"

"No, but I knew that I could do it. I had both rifles leaning against the wall. The center window was open, and I was standing back out of view. There were a lot of people standing everywhere, but they didn't block my view because I was up so high. The first thing that I noticed was a bunch cops on motorcycles coming toward me and clearing the streets as I was pulling on my latex gloves. They stopped cars and made them do a U-turn in the street.

"Then in the distance, I saw the convertible with people jogging along beside it and cops up front and behind. I thought, *Whoever figured this assassination thing out was really smart.* I had the perfect position. The president was coming toward me and turning right on a slow-speed corner, so I had a lot of time to shoot. Further, they were moving at jogging or fast- walking pace, so speed wasn't a factor. The weather was clear. People began to stand on the bluff overlooking the turn in the road to wave at the president, so I couldn't shoot right at the turn. I would have to wait after the turn. A secret service man stopped on the corner and got out and was looking around. I stepped back from the open window. He didn't notice me. The convertible was now two blocks away. I kissed ole 'Blue,' as I called her, and prepared myself.

"The cat got close to me again, so I stepped on her tail to keep it out of the way. She screamed and ran away.

"Since the secret service man was still there, I backed up about three feet so the rifle barrel didn't protrude through the window. The convertible got closer."

Even as Lee told the story, his voice rose in intensity as the excitement of the moment overcame him. Tiny beads of perspiration formed on his forehead. Then Lee spontaneously continued. "My eyes are exceptionally good, so I didn't need a telephoto scope. I could see the president and his wife and other people too. I picked up ole Blue and began to follow the convertible, staying focused on the president. They were just about ready to make the turn. Now was the time, but people standing on the lawn obscured the target. I was ready. When the car cleared the corner, I fired off three shots in rapid-fire sequence at the back of the president's head. I saw the president lunge forward after the first high-powered bullet struck. The second bullet struck him too. I then grabbed the old rifle, not caring if it hit anything or not, and just shot it, not really aiming at anything, and laid it down on the floor. I picked up an empty cartridge and placed it in my pocket. I quickly disassembled ole Blue and within seconds threw it in the garbage cart I had used earlier, covered it up, and wheeled out to the elevator. I was excited!

"I got in the elevator with the trash container and pushed the down button. The elevator stopped on the third floor, and Mrs. Pringle got on, and we smiled. I hid my hands because I still had the latex gloves on, and they were shaking. We said nothing to one another. She exited on the first floor, and I continued down to the basement. I went directly to my office and locked the door behind me. Within thirty seconds, I had the rifle installed on the bicycle, and it looked fantastic. I pulled off the latex gloves. I wanted to hear what had happened, but I needed to leave. I carried the bicycle up the stairs and out of the back door. I was wheeling the bicycle when a Dallas police officer stopped me, but the building manager, who was standing next to him, told him that I worked there, and he let me pass. Once outside, I rode away from the hectic scene taking place out front. I could hear sirens screaming in the distance."

"Lee, did you see or hear anything unusual at this point or see anyone?"

"There was the same ole stuff as always there, like slingshot tree."

Instantly, Jacob asked, "Lee, what is slingshot tree?"

"Oh, it is a tree with a trunk about six inches in diameter that comes up about five feet from the ground and has two branches bent out and up, shaped like a slingshot. You get a clear view of it when you walk by it from the building."

Gottlieb asked, "Did you see any people?"

Lee was silent for a while as his mind raced to recall. "Yeah, Doc, I saw lots of people, but they were running toward the front of the building, and they ran past me. I rode a few blocks to the bus stop, being careful not to attract attention, and waited for the bus. The bus was late. I placed my bike on the front rack and got on. I sat in the front seat. When we were a few blocks away, I got off, because with all the traffic, the bus wasn't moving. I collected the blue bicycle from the bike rack up front and rode off.

"I peddled to Lake Hubbard and up the trail to the dam. I got off the bike and looked around. There were two people walking away from the spillway. Otherwise it was clear. After they walked out of sight, I rode the bike up to the middle of the spillway and threw it as far as I could into the deepest part of the lake. I watched it go all the way down into the water and saw it sink. I also threw the casing I had collected from the floor. I then walked back to catch a bus home."

"What happened next, Lee?"

"I was getting excited over this whole thing, very excited. Marina was home, and the girls were in the other room. Marina wanted to know what I was doing home so early. I told her that I was horny. She wasn't in the mood for sex, but I grabbed her wrist and pulled her into the bedroom. She was stunned. I had never done that before. I disrobed her. She wasn't cooperating, plus my attitude wasn't good. I was in a hurry, because I still had to meet someone at the Texas Theater, and further I couldn't explain any of this or the intense need for her body. I almost raped her. She gave in at the very end. Here I was having sex, and I had a million things on my mind and someplace to go. The excitement of the day hit me."

"What happened next, Lee?"

"I don't know, Doc. I remember Marina crying, but that could have been during sex. I cannot remember any more. I have no further memory of the day."

"Surely you must remember something."

"I tell you, Doc; my mind is totally blank after that point."

"Tell me about the theater."

"What theater? What are you talking about?"

"The Texas Theater, where you were supposed to meet an agent."

"I don't remember, Doc."

Gottlieb was stunned in hearing the details of the assassination. They were consistent with everything he knew. He wondered how Erick could come by this information if it were true. "Lee, I need to talk to Erick now."

"Okay," said Lee, and he shut his eyes, and the transformation took place again.

"Erick, I want to talk to you." There was a slow yes response as Erick's mental faculties took over his mind. Gottlieb asked again, "Erick, are you with us?"

"Yes, Doctor" was the reply.

Jacob removed the arm straps. "Erick, I want you to think carefully about this question. What do you know about the Kennedy assassination?"

"Do you mean, what do I think about it?"

"No, Erick, I am talking about the facts and details of the assassination."

"I don't even recall the year, let alone anything else. Kennedy was assassinated by somebody named Oswald, but I cannot remember anything else." Erick was still under hypnosis, so he had to be telling the truth. *Maybe Dr. Becker was correct, and he put it out of his mind.* If that were the case, then he, Gottlieb, could stimulate Erick's recollection.

"Erick, do any of these words mean anything to you: Texas School Depository, slingshot tree, ole Blue, bicycle, motorcade, and CIA? Think about them individually. Let's start with Texas School Depository."

"It means nothing to me," Erick responded with a rather slow pattern to his speech.

"What about a slingshot tree?"

"I don't know what you are talking about."

"Ole Blue."

"Do you mean ole Blue Eyes, Frank Sinatra?"

He answered the remaining questions by knowing a little. Erick had no recollection pertaining to the assassination except he remembered President Kennedy had been in a convertible when he was assassinated. Gottlieb was doubtful that Erick was ever aware of the Kennedy assassination facts. ***How then can Lee know these things?*** It was clear to Jacob that a trip to Dallas would be necessary.

Jacob reflected on the testimony and thought that if this were proved true, he, Jacob, and anyone knowing this information could be in danger. He thought ***I wonder how long the CIA holds a grudge.***

Chapter 7: Dallas

Jacob realized he needed more information about several issues, and the location for this information was around Dallas. He discovered online that there was a tour bus that followed the route of President Kennedy on that fateful day. This tour included a visit to the museum located in the Texas School Book Depository building. Further, this was also an opportunity to meet Eddie Montana and obtain inside information about Lee, if Eddie still worked there. Since he would have a car, he could travel to Hubbard Lake and Rockwell Forney Dam. Last but not least, he wanted to locate the site where Lee did his target practice.

On Friday morning, August 4, 1995, Jacob took the tour on a half-filled bus on the Kennedy route and museum. While at the museum, he purchased a couple of books on the Kennedy assassination. He further took indoor photographs, without use of his flashbulb, mounted in a display case and from the now-famous window.

The bus tour stopped at the Dallas Police Department, where an officer briefly talked to the assemblage about the assassination of Oswald. It turned out that he was the officer who had questioned Oswald. Jacob managed to corner him for a few minutes to personally ask him questions about Lee Harvey Oswald. It was a beginning.

About two p.m., Jacob entered the parking lot at the School Depository. He walked to the elevator, and this time he pushed the button for the basement. The elevator door opened into the maintenance room. He stumbled around obstacles, looking for someone, but no one was there. He thought he had better make his inquiries upstairs when he heard the elevator groan. He waited, but no one appeared. Then the second elevator made sounds, so Jacob waited in front of the door. The elevator door opened, and a large man with a triple chin walked out. They exchanged glances, and Gottlieb said, "Hello, are you Eddie Montana?"

"I'd be him," was the response. "What can I do for y'all?"

"I am glad that you are still here. I heard that you were retiring."

"Not yet, next month."

Gottlieb pulled out a business card and handed it to Eddie. "I have a patient who believes he is Lee Harvey Oswald. I am trying to obtain inside information to prove to him to be otherwise."

"Okay, Doctor, I understand. Let's go!" Eddie motioned with his head to follow him, so Gottlieb stayed close behind as Eddie waddled into a 'kind of' office. There were two chairs in there, and Eddie was anxious to sit down, exhausted from his walk from the elevator. He took several deep breaths and said, "Ask away, Doctor."

Eddie lit up a cigarette and blew a smoke ring, which lingered in the still room.

"Okay, did you know Lee well, and what was your working relationship like?"

"Lee and I were buddies." Raising his voice, he said, "I could never believe that he could assassinate anybody, let alone the president of the United States. We ate lunch together nearly every noon, and we took our breaks together. I can remember us sittin' out on the front lawn on that day, and he was funny. You couldn't be laughin' like that if you were plannin' on killin' a president."

"Like, what did he say that was funny?"

"Oh, I can't remember that now, but I can remember laughin.'"

"How did Lee get to work on the day of the assassination?" Gottlieb asked.

"Ya know, on the day of the assassination, he had a borrowed bike, looked brand new too. It was a special make."

"Did you and Lee talk about the bike?"

"Yeah, but it wasn't his. As I remember, it belonged to a friend."

"What kind of bike was it, and what happened to it?"

"I don't know the make. I guess he took it home."

"What did it look like?"

"Like a bike, except it was a blue color. Beautiful, that I remember. Oh yeah, it had narrow tires and gears up front and back. Ya could shift gears on it."

Gottlieb stopped a minute to examine his notes. "What was Lee's relationship to Marina?"

"I guess it was all right. He didn't talk about her much."

"What were his hobbies?"

"He loved to hunt. A good shot too. I went with him once, and he shot four pheasants. I missed every bird, so he gave me two."

"Did Lee have any major dislikes—for example, the president of the United States?"

"If he did, he never mentioned it."

"What was the story about the slingshot tree?" questioned Gottlieb.

"How'd ya know about that?" asked Eddie while raising his bushy eyebrows.

"I heard about it upstairs."

"That's real strange, ya know. It used to grow out back, but it died after Lee did. It had a trunk that came up and ..." There was a pause as Eddie rolled his chair over to his desk and fumbled through some papers in his desk drawer. "Here it is. I took a picture of it years ago." He passed the photo to Gottlieb and then used his finger to point out the fork in the tree on the black-and-white photo he held in his hand. "After it died, they cut it down and replaced it."

"May I have that picture for a while?" asked Jacob.

"Ah—go ahead and keep it. I was gonna throw it out."

Jacob's mind raced a mile a minute. Here again was positive proof that Lee was indeed the same Lee Harvey Oswald. How else would he know about this? What a windfall!

"Did Lee keep any animals up in the top floor?"

"Yeah, how'd you know? He had a female cat that caught mice."

"Eddie, is there anything different about the top floor now than when the event took place?"

"Other than a heater, it is still the same."

"How tall was Lee, and how much did he weigh?"

"I would guess he was about the same size as me, five eight tall, and he weighed about 150 pounds. Of course, I was a lot thinner in those days too." With that last statement, Eddie let out a big belly laugh, which made his entire body shake like an elephant seal exiting the ocean.

Gottlieb continued the conversation to collect personal information about Lee. He continued down his list, asking one question after another until he came to the bottom of his list.

Eddie blew another smoke ring as Gottlieb rechecked his list.

Jacob handed Eddie his business card. "If something new occurs to you, give me a collect call, and I'll get back to you as soon as I can. How can I get ahold of you after you retire next month?" Eddie grabbed a piece of paper and wrote down his name, address, and phone number. He handed it to Jacob. Gottlieb placed it on top of the photo of "slingshot tree" inside his notebook. He had many notes from Eddie's comments, and many of them seemed germane. "Thanks, Eddie. I must leave now. I appreciate your help."

At four thirty a.m. on Saturday, the screeching alarm awoke Jacob in his Hampton Inn room in Denton, Texas. He had to get to the Jefferson Quarry to query truckers about the location of an old, abandoned quarry. When Jacob reached the quarry, 18-wheelers were parked alongside the road, awaiting the opening of the gate. Jacob pulled ahead of them on the other side of the entrance, and with his notepad in hand, he started toward the first truck. The driver saw him coming toward him and rolled down his window.

"Hi," said Jacob. "I am looking for the directions to an old, maybe abandoned quarry north of here. All I know is that the name began with the letter *J*, maybe *K*. I was hoping that one of you truckers might be able to help me."

The driver, in his mid-thirties, just shook his head. "Sorry, man. I can't help you."

There were about twelve trucks lined up, so Jacob methodically went down the line. All the answers were the same. When Jacob came to the last truck, he looked at the driver. The driver was near sixty. Maybe he could help. He asked the same questions, but this driver, like all the others, said he couldn't help. "Go inside and talk to Pete. You'll find him in the office near where we stop to be loaded. Pete has been around here for a long time. Maybe he can help you."

Having gotten no help from Pete, Jacob waited for a couple of hours, and not one truck entered the quarry. Jacob was still in deep thought when a trucker blasted his air horn just after entering the yard. The very loud acoustic blast startled Jacob back to reality. The driver motioned to him, and Jacob jogged toward him, forming a dust cloud behind him; now his newly polished shoes were totally coated. Gottlieb jumped up on one of the steps. "Hey," said the driver, "I talked to my dad, and he remembers an old, beat-out quarry north of here named Jett & Son. It's difficult to find."

"Can you give me directions?" Jacob had his notebook and pen ready.

"Yeah, take Highway 81 north to Bowie. Then there is a gravel and asphalt road northeast to Montague. He said the quarry is about halfway between the two towns. It is very desolate country."

"Thank you and your dad very much for your help. I will check it out. I really appreciate your thoughtfulness."

Gottlieb stayed there until noon, but no more trucks showed up. It was closing time on Saturday. He had the only lead he was going to get. He thanked Pete again and headed back toward Denton. It was time to eat, and, having missed breakfast, he was hungry. He would spend the evening in Dallas. He planned to visit Hubbard Lake in the afternoon, but a fast-food lunch came first.

Two and a half hours later, Jacob pulled onto a narrow street near Hubbard Lake Park and parked. Jacob was thinking. *According to Lee, he rode his bicycle from the bus stop to where I am standing. He therefore must have entered the park at the entrance ahead. Lee then rode on this trail to the spillway.*

Jacob walked through the entrance gate. The trees overhead were eighty feet tall, and he heard the rustling of leaves as the wind blew. It was muggy and uncomfortable. The sky remained cloudless as the day earlier but obstructed from view by trees. His steps carried him along a trail wider than eight feet and paved. He snapped a couple of pictures before proceeding. With purposeful steps, he continued toward the dam.

Trees were in great abundance around him as the trail began to climb. In about an eighth of a mile, the trail leveled off. The tree density decreased, and now splashes of blue sky materialized through their canopy.

In another twenty yards, the reservoir, blue with a hint of aqua green, became visible. The trail forked near the lake's edge. The portion leading to the left followed the shoreline, while the other fork headed toward to the dam. Jacob walked directly to the dam.

Tall trees completely encircled the lake. Jacob's shutter clicked away. As he neared the dam, he could see that the trail passed directly over it. From his vantage point, no one was in sight. He continued walking to the spillway of the dam. At the dam, the walkway was about twenty feet wide with railings on both sides. Jacob looked down into the water. The wind caused small waves, which harmlessly splashed against the nearly vertical face of the dam. He continued his journey to the middle of the spillway. He could picture Lee throwing a bicycle off the dam. *He probably would have done it where I am standing and threw it out to the deepest part.*

His mind's eye pictured a bicycle airborne in front of him and splashing into the water below, causing waves to issue from the splashdown point. *It would be possible to throw a bicycle from here.* Again, he snapped pictures with the camera from several angles before heading back to his rental car. He next thought, *Maybe I could search the lake at a later time, but I would require scuba gear. The water is pretty deep here.*

Chapter 8: The Appearance

Sophia completed her shower, made up her face, and struggled into her tight-fitting jeans. She never ran around the house in anything scanty ever since learning of Lee. She unlocked the deadbolt and opened her bedroom door to head downstairs to the kitchen, peeked out first. The light in the hallway bathroom let her know Erick was awake.

She started walking to the stairs when she heard a strange voice from the hallway bathroom. "Erick—Erick, I am talking to you! Erick, damn it—I am talking to you." She crept close to the open bathroom door to get a closer look, since the voice was loud and unfamiliar. She observed Erick's reflection in the mirror. He hadn't seen her.

"Damn it, Erick, I am talking to you! Look in the mirror, stupid!" Erick's mouth was moving, but it seemed another power was controlling it. It appeared that Erick couldn't stop it from moving. The voice said in a loud, harsh manner, "Erick, I want to use your body now."

Erick became angry. "You can't have it!" he shouted back in the eerie verbal exchange with himself. "It's my body, so get out of it!" His voice was loud and exhibited what Sophia sensed as frightened tones. "Now, I order you to get out of my body!"

"Ha ha ha, you stupid ass. You can't get rid of me. I'm goin' get rid of you," Lee said in a sinister manner. "Shut your eyes, stupid, and I will move in! Damn it, I mean now!"

"You bastard. Leave me alone."

Sophia was frozen in time and place, staring in disbelief. The voices now shouted at full volume, cursing at one another. Erick shook his toothbrush, and the lather from it spattered around the bathroom. He appeared frightened.

When Sophia looked in the mirror again, the second voice said, "Erick, I am goin' to use your body whether you like it or not!" Sophia should have known it was Lee but was bewildered. Further, now frightened, she remained fixed in that spot. Fear instantly washed over her entire body.

Erick screamed back, "No, damn it! You can't have my body. You son of a bitch, get out now."

The face that said those words looked and sounded like Erick, but then the contorted face in the mirror hollered back, "I want it now!" That face looked like Lee, whom she saw in the video.

"Why do you want it?" shouted Erick.

"I need that pretty, little wife of yours, and I'll take her the hard way if I have to!"

"I won't let you," shouted Erick. "Get out of my body! I order you."

Then Lee's face appeared, and he began to laugh a fiendish chuckle, which grew in intensity and vibrato. The laughter continued in a heinous manner. Sophia put the pieces together. It was Erick and Lee fighting over Erick's body, and further, they were fighting over her.

Oh my God; Lee intends to rape me. I must get out of here.

Seldom does a woman get a warning of impending rape, but here it was. Now total unadulterated fear swept over her body, and her knees became weak, with her feet cemented to the floor. They hadn't yet seen her.

I must get to the bedroom, lock my door, and call Jacob.

However, Sophia couldn't move. She tried to turn, but her feet wouldn't cooperate. Finally, she turned and crept back toward her bedroom, but her body weight made the floor squeak.

Lee had just taken control of Erick's body. Sophia began to run to her bedroom as Lee exited the bathroom and raced after her. She dashed into her room and slammed the deadbolt into place just as Lee arrived at the door.

He turned the doorknob slowly and pressed against the door. The deadbolt held.

He began kicking the door, but it was made of solid wood. The door withstood Lee's kicks.

Next, Lee slammed his shoulder against it. Each time, the door and frame withstood the collision.

Sophia stood facing the door, terrified and frozen in place.

Suddenly, Sophia remembered the phone and grabbed it to call Gottlieb's office. She pushed the programmed button for Gottlieb and heard the ring. She didn't expect to get him but rather to leave a message. The recording began, and she waited an interminable time as Lee pounded the door with his body. Finally, she left the message.

Sophia called 911 to get the local police involved, but they may not get there in time to save her. On the second ring, the operator answered.

The panic-stricken Sophia shouted, "Lee is threatening to rape me, and I have locked myself in my room. He is kicking down the door." In response to the operator's question, Sophia provided her name and address.

"Stay with me, Sophia. We have officers on the way right now."

Suddenly there was total silence outside the door. She was unaware that Lee had departed and headed downstairs.

She waited as the 911 operator seemed to be babbling and saying, "Stay with me." Next, she heard heavy footsteps of Lee running up the stairs. Unexpectedly silence followed, then she heard Lee say with abrasive overtones, "This is your last chance, Sophia. Open the damn door."

Sophia was drawn to the door, as if compelled by another force much greater than her, and felt compelled to open it.

Then in a kindly manner, she heard, "Please, Sophia! Open the door." It was Erick's voice this time.

"Erick, is that you?"

"Yes, dear. I know what's happening, and I want to help you."

"What happened to Lee?" she asked through the still-closed door.

"He's gone, Sophia. He left as quickly as he arrived. Please, Sophia, open the door. It's okay now."

Sophia placed her hand on the deadbolt. Her trembling hand gripped it. She was ready to slide the bolt back and open the door when she heard, "Damn it, Sophia; open the damn door, - please."

Erick never said "damn it" to her. It was Lee out there. She dropped her hand from the dead bolt and stepped back. She thought, *Maybe I could delay him until the police arrive.*

"Erick, dear, I have to think about this for a while, so I cannot open the door just yet. I am so frightened! Please forgive me. Please give me a few minutes to compose myself; then I'll open the door."

Next she heard another sound, a high-frequency buzzing of an engine in the hallway. She did not know what it meant. Then the door began to rattle, and momentarily wood chips started flying around the room. Lee had Erick's fourteen-inch chainsaw and was cutting through the door. She saw the tip of the blade rotating pass through the door.

She grabbed the phone and shouted, "Lee has a chainsaw. He's going to cut me up with it. I cannot stay. I am on the second floor. I'll have to jump!"

Sophia remembered there was an emergency rope ladder in her closet. She ran over to the closet, found the box, opened it, and dragged the rope ladder over to the window as the saw's blade made its way through the door.

Leaving the ladder on the floor, she opened the window and kicked out the screen. She looked back. Lee had already cut down one side of an opening.

Oh my God. He's getting close to entering my bedroom.

Having completed his downward cut, Lee was now cutting his way across the bottom.

Sophia attached one end of the ladder to the sill and threw the remainder out of the window. *Good Lord. In a few minutes, he will have cut an opening. I must leave now.*

The rope ladder twisted and turned in unimaginable directions as Sophia attempted to descend. It acted as if it had a mind of its own and tried to toss her to the ground. Each step was difficult to establish a proper foothold as the flimsy ladder swung wildly.

When she was near the bottom, there was a loud thump. She instantly knew the cut area of the door had fallen into the room. Lee was in her room.

Sophia disengaged herself from the ladder and looked up to see Lee's head sticking out the window. He screamed at her, "Get the hell back here!" His eyes were beady and evil, and blood vessels in his neck protruded.

Lee stared out the window on the ladder, cussing at her. Sophia in total fear headed toward the street. She pulled open the side gate, ran toward her Chevy Malibu parked in the driveway, entered it, and locked the door behind her.

Frantically, she tried to withdraw her car key out of her tight-fitting jeans, but the sharp angle had pinched off the pocked; she could touch but not grasp the key. Sophia continued to fumble for her key, sometimes touching it.

Lee arrived at the car and yanked on the driver's door. It was locked. He began beating on the driver's side window with the heel of his hand. He screeched, "Open the damn door and get out of this car now before I tear it apart." He continued hollering obscenities.

He ran to the passenger door, which was still unlocked, opened it, and leaped in. Her left hand pushed the driver's door open, and she jumped from the car as Lee's hand touched her wrist. She was free.

Lee slid after her across the front seat, to be held up by the steering wheel, as Sophia raced toward the rear of the car.

Now in total unequivocal fear, Sophia saw Lee's left leg as he departed the driver's door. She sprinted around the rear of the car as he headed in her direction. She headed to the open passenger door.

Lee stumbled near the trunk. She slipped inside, locking the door behind her, and reached across the seat. She pulled the driver's door shut and locked it too.

Lee righted himself and ran over to the garden area to pick up a large rock.

Sophia straightened her leg enough to withdraw her key from her jeans, thrust the key into the ignition, and turned it to start the engine. The engine roared to life.

Lee threw down the rock and ran back into the house, leaving the front door open behind him. Sophia knew Lee was going to get his keys to the Mercedes parked inside the garage. She threw the automatic transmission into reverse.

She headed down the long block to the first cross street and turned left. Just as she turned, she looked back over her shoulder and saw the rear end on the Mercedes backing out onto the street. Lee was after her and probably saw her car turn too. She turned right at the next cross street and accelerated down the street at speeds of nearly fifty miles per hour, then a left turn and another right.

Oh my God, she thought, *I hope the kids are still indoors.* She continued zigzagging through the residential streets for several blocks. There was no sign of Erick's Black Beauty.

Sophia began to sob to the point that the tears were blurring her vision. Now with some comfort that Lee wasn't around, she took self-inventory, tried to decide what to do next, and slowed down to a safe city street speed.

I must get out of here. I can't wait for the police to arrive. Lee will catch me. At least, he doesn't have the chainsaw.

Sophia almost stopped at every intersection, looking in all directions for a black Mercedes. She hadn't noticed it before, but the low-fuel light stopped blinking and showed continuous red. The gas tank registered empty. That sight rattled her brain. *I need gas.*

She reached over for her purse. It wasn't there. "Oh my God!" she shouted. *My purse is in the backyard. I forgot it. I've got to go back and get it. What if Lee is there waiting for me? I have no choice. I must go back.*

As she headed home, she made a plan. *If there is no sign of the Mercedes, I will leave my car running and run into the backyard, grab my purse, and run back to the street. I won't park in the driveway to be trapped by Lee.* Lee undoubtedly was nearby.

There was no traffic on this Sunday morning. She slipped in behind the Wilsons' old Buick, parked on the street. *Maybe I could get them to take me in until the police arrive. No, they were late sleepers. Lee could catch her trying to awake them. No, it's better to get the purse and get away.*

Sophia was lucky. Lee wasn't home, and she located her purse in the oleander shrubbery. Further, she made it to Speedy Mart unseen and added gas to the tank.

Sophia slipped into the front seat of the Malibu, ready to exit the Speedy Mart. She looked around carefully; everything appeared clear. Finally, after several attempts, her engine started. Then, about a block away, she saw it—a black Mercedes.

Oh no. It can't be Lee.

The car sped toward her. It *was* Lee.

The adrenaline rush hit her as she started to accelerate; a tingle passed through her hands and toes. *It's Black Beauty. Lee's seen me!*

She again started zigzagging through the residential district, but Lee was too close to duck this time, and every second he was getting closer. Wheels squealed as both cars took corners at high speeds. She didn't know exactly where she was. On the previous corner, Lee lost a little control of his car, allowing her to increase the distance between them. She now had about half of a block lead ahead of him. *If I knew where I was, I could drive to the police station, but I don't know this area.*

Lee started closing the distance between the two cars again. Sophia created a daring plan if Lee got close again. It likely would happen because of the faster Mercedes. *I will slow down a little while Lee is traveling fast, and at the last second, I will make a right-hand turn.*

Lee was accelerating as they headed southeast in the southern part of the city. She was ready to boldly implement her escape at the next block. Lee was still accelerating, and she dropped her speed down to 40 mph.

At the next street is when I'll do it.

Lee was speeding at 70 mph and closing fast. Black Beauty was now seven car lengths behind her. The street where she would turn drew near, and she readied herself for the last second right-hand turn. *Good, there is no car coming.* She didn't want to touch the brakes to give away her plan until she started the turn.

The street was just in front of her.

Sophia took her foot off the accelerator pedal.

She started through the intersection, then jammed on the brakes and turned.

The Malibu's two passenger side tires lifted up off the pavement on the passenger side as if it were going to roll over, but the sedan settled down again with a bounce as she completed the turn but in the wrong lane. She swerved over to get in the correct lane and hit the accelerator again.

Her high velocity caused some momentary careening down the street until she slowed down. She saw Lee go by in her rearview mirror. She turned right at the next street and then took a left as before. *Maybe I can ditch him again.*

Sophia began zigzagging through city streets. Unfortunately, this time she outsmarted herself and inadvertently drove into a cul-de-sac. She slammed on her brakes and stopped just before hitting a parked car. She made a U-turn and drove back to the intersection as Lee drove by, so she turned the opposite direction he was traveling and accelerated to the intersection.

Fear washed over her entire body again. In her rearview mirror, she saw Lee turning around. Sophia turned left again and then right. The street widened, but she didn't pay attention as to why. She watched her rearview mirror. Sophia wasn't reading the street signs, and before she knew what was happening, she had made an ingress onto Highway 35 South. She hoped Lee hadn't seen her make the transition, but a quick check of her mirrors proved otherwise. There he was, behind her and entering the freeway. She couldn't stay ahead of the Mercedes with the Malibu; she felt doomed.

I have no choice. I must speed up.

The freeway was largely deserted on this Sunday morning. Now she possessed a substantial lead on Lee, but it meant nothing on the freeway with miles between off-ramps. "It's too bad that I wasted that nice trick on him," she cried aloud. "He won't fall for it again."

With the Malibu accelerator pedal pressed to the floor, her speed was over 90 mph, and she could still see Black Beauty behind her. She had never driven at such speeds before, so the experience alone terrified her, let alone a crazy driver pursuing her. Her insides quivered. Her mind screamed in anguish.

Lee closed the distance between them, exacerbating her fear. She didn't know what to do, so she urged the Malibu onward by accelerating. The distance between cars shortened. Now, like the bad dream, the Mercedes grew near, and she could do nothing about it. There was an off-ramp one mile ahead. *Maybe I could do something there*, she thought. Lee was now twenty car lengths behind her. While she was attaining a maximum speed of 95 to 100 mph, Lee was moving faster. The distance between them decreased.

Lee moved over one lane. This would certainly prevent her from turning down the upcoming ramp of the elevated freeway. Seeing this, Sophia moved to the innermost lane. A cyclone wire fence separated the north and southbound directions, but there were openings in it for the highway patrol to turn around. She would look for one.

Lee was now only four car lengths behind and in fact had to slow down to avoid hitting her. As he drew closer, she observed his agitated face in her rearview mirror.

As Sophia approached an off-ramp, she continued to seek a fence opening. Her mouth was dry, and chills pervaded her exterior. She found breathing difficult. Her fingertips and toes tingled as the effects of adrenaline expressed themselves.

They both moved over the overpass, doing over 100 mph. An Oklahoma highway patrolman was entering the freeway and observed two speeding cars. He gave chase with red lights flashing. The Mercedes was close to striking the Chevy. The officer flipped on his siren and accelerated to catch up to the two speeders.

Sophia sought a break in the fence between the north- and south-bound traffic lanes, unaware of the police car or siren. Ahead, she saw a break in the center fence and slowed even more. Lee was too close and struck the rear end of her car, sending it fishtailing.

The impact caused her body to slam backward, whipping her head back against the headrest. She almost lost control of her car. Chills shot through her body, and her fingers could hardly hold the steering wheel.

Her coasting slowed the Malibu as the break in the fence appeared before her. At the last minute, she hit the brakes hard and swerved into the opening. Dust flew everywhere as her car hit the dirt median and ricocheted off the fencepost.

Sophia gained distance as she sped north and watched her mirrors. Lee made it through the opening. Then and only then did Sophia see the OHP vehicle with red lights flashing. She was saved.

She slowed down on the right-hand side of the road and came to a complete stop as both Lee and the officer approached her. Lee pulled up behind her and jumped out of his car. She checked all locks to make certain Lee couldn't get in.

Lee began beating on her window as he had earlier. In her mirror, she saw the officer sprinting toward them. He was breathing hard when he reached them alongside the Malibu. "What's going on?" he asked.

"Oh, it nothing, officer," said Lee. "It is just a family problem."

"The way you two were driving wasn't nothing," he said with a firm voice, still breathing in gulps. "It looks more serious to me."

Sophia rolled down her window about four inches and screamed, "Officer, he is trying to rape me!" Then she began to cry.

Looking at Lee, the officer said, "You had better come with me, sir, until we get to the bottom of this." He pushed Lee, but Lee resisted and remained in place, and hollered, "go to hell." The officer, now directly behind Lee, pushed him with force between the shoulder blades toward his patrol car. Lee moved in spurts as he resisted each push.

At the police car, the officer said, "Okay, sir, lean against the hood of my car and spread your legs."

Lee complied as the officer checked him for weapons.

"I can explain everything officer," Lee said in a civil, now relaxed tone.

"I am sure you can," said the officer. "Okay sir, I want you to walk to the back door of my car."

"Sure, officer. Whatever you say," Lee said in a lighthearted manner, putting the officer at ease. Lee noticed that Sophia got out of her car and followed at a respectable distance.

The officer opened the door and told Lee to duck his head and get in. As customary, the officer placed his left hand on Lee's head. Then, as quick as an ocelot, Lee reversed positions with the officer, and the struggle began. The officer was partially in the back seat with Lee holding his right arm behind him.

Sophia observed this event in disbelief. Lee unsnapped the pistol cover and removed the pistol. The officer kicked backward and struck Lee in the groin. Lee dropped the pistol as he recoiled in pain. During the altercation, Lee inadvertently kicked the pistol under the patrol car. Then with a quick push and a slam of the door, the officer was locked in the back seat of his own car as Lee bent over in pain.

Sophia began running toward the Malibu, and Lee raced after her. Although Lee still in pain from the groin kick, he managed to sprint. Sophia ran on the gravel side of the road and slipped, enabling Lee to close the distance.

She was getting close to her car. Her hand grabbed the passenger door handle. As she tried to open it, Lee stretched out, and with a thumb and two fingers he latched onto her right wrist and dislodged her grip.

Both tumbled backward, falling down the steep embankment. Sophia and Lee started rolling and sliding down the incline of the elevated roadside. The impact of the landing dislodged Lee's grip, and they slid separately. Sharp rocks littered the embankment and dug into both Sophia's and Lee's hands and face. Sophia didn't slide as far as Lee. Lee skidded all the way to the bottom, and his right leg slid under a cyclone fence, temporally locking him in place. Lee looked up and watched as Sophia navigated the embankment while he attempted to extricate himself.

Chapter 9: Jacob Returns

While Sophia was being chased, Jacob was returning to Oklahoma City in a chartered private plane. All the gravel quarries Jacob was interested in were located between Dallas and Oklahoma City. Jacob had the pilot fly over them in a circular pattern so he could take photographs from the air. Just maybe one of these was Lee's practice area.

After disembarking the plane in Oklahoma City, Jacob headed toward his office. On the way, he stopped at a local drugstore and dropped off the film at a one-hour developer. He would pick up the prints on his way home.

At the office, Jacob checked his telephone. He had eleven messages, but he had time to listen. Lee filled his mind with questions. His trip was successful, because he had located proof of the slingshot tree's existence, and that was partial verification of Lee's story. Additional verification required Lee. Now he had to bring himself back to reality and deal with his other world.

He flipped on the message recorder and jotted down the date and time of the message on a notepad. The first several messages were inconsequential and dealt with meetings he was supposed to attend. Then there was a message from Jim detailing one of Jacob's cases, which Jim had handled while he was away.

Next came the Sunday calls. There were only three. The first call was from Sophia, and it sent him reeling. "Jacob, this is Sophia. Help me! Lee has taken over Erick's body, and he is planning on raping me. I am locked in my bedroom, and he is breaking down the door."

He couldn't believe this could happen. He listened intently to the remaining part of the call. He heard Sophia crying and someone banging on the door. The call had come at 8:08 a.m. that morning, and that was hours earlier.

The second call was from Sophia. "Jacob, I escaped. Lee chased me with a running chainsaw. I am so frightened. I am okay now, and my wounds are only superficial. I am all right and staying at the Norman Motel. I am registered under the name of Sophia Gottlieb. Please give me a call if you get back here on Sunday. I am not going home or to work until I talk to you. Please call!"

Jacob wanted to hear the last message. It too could have been from Sophia. The last message, however, was from Erick at 1:15 p.m. "Lee took possession of my body, and Sophia is missing. I have no idea where she is. I am back home, and Lee is gone. I have a very bad, deep gash on my leg. It required nine stitches at the emergency clinic. Dr. Gottlieb, I am really frightened. Will you help me?"

Jacob put in a call to Sophia's room. "Hello?" she said with a shaken voice.

"Sophia, are you okay?"

"Yes. I am physically fine, but you cannot imagine what I went through this morning. Never in a million years can you imagine. I witnessed Erick turn into the heinous Lee right before my eyes." She began to cry. Between tears, she said, "I am still frightened by what I saw and went through. Jacob, I cannot go home with Erick there."

"I understand, Sophia, and you shouldn't. Erick is there. Why don't you stay at my place tonight? I have three bedrooms, and you can tell me what happened."

"I would like that, Jacob, but I don't want to drive there alone."

"I will come and get you, and we will drive together."

Fifty minutes later, Sophia heard the car door slam and peeked through the curtains to see Jacob walking toward her room. When Jacob arrived at the door, Sophia opened it to greet him. The two fell into a long, warm embrace. Her arm clenched around his neck, her hands trembling.

"Oh Jacob, I was so frightened. You cannot believe it. If you hadn't shown me that video of Lee, I could even be dead by now." She started to thank him again, but she couldn't finish since her voice broke and tears gushed from her eyes. Jacob held her, wrapping his arms around her shoulders.

"It is going to be all right, Sophia. You are going to be okay. Sit down for a minute." They both sat down around a small table. Jacob scooted his chair close to hers. He placed her head on his shoulder and she wept intermittently.

After a few minutes, Sophia regained her composure.

Jacob examined her wounds and observed that none were serious but likely painful. After treating the wounds, Jacob said, "The traffic is very light today, so if you like, you could follow me in your car, and then you would have a car when you need it. What do you think? Say yes."

A half hour later, Jacob and Sophia arrived at his home. The city street was lined with large elm trees. Jacob's home was a fully landscaped, two-story, Tudor-style house in the swanky areas of the city. The lawn was thick, plush, and dark green. Jacob waited for the two-car garage door to open. As it was opening, he walked over to Sophia's car. "Sophia, you may park in the garage if you like, or you can leave it out here. It is your choice." He returned to his car, drove in, and parked. Sophia followed.

They entered his home through the garage, and Jacob immediately went to the air-conditioner controller and turned it on. "It will take about twenty minutes to get comfortable in here, Sophia. I'll be back in a minute," Jacob said as he lugged his suitcase and camera up the stairs.

Sophia used the time to check out the downstairs. It was well appointed by somebody who knew what she was doing. While Sophia was admiring some artwork, Jacob had picked up in South America, Jacob walked up and said, "I bought that in Chile about three years ago. Do you like it?"

"Yes! I cannot decide what the paint material is. It seems to be a mixture between acrylic and standard paint."

"That's a good description, because it is the Chilean's medium. That's how I would describe it too." Jacob looked at Sophia. "When did you last eat?"

"Last night."

"Well then, before we get started, maybe we ought to consider dinner. I can run down to the grocery store and pick up one of those rotisserie chickens. With that and rice and veggies, we can have an easy dinner. That will give us more time to talk."

"Sure, Jacob. May I go with you?"

After jointly doing the dishes after dinner, they adjourned to Jacob's office. He had two soft chairs for such occasions. "Sophia, I would like to record our conversation if you don't mind. Is that all right with you?"

"Sure."

"I would like you to start at the beginning and proceed through the whole experience. I still need this information to treat Erick."

"It started when I left my bedroom to prepare breakfast. I began to walk downstairs when I heard some shouting from the hall bathroom." Sophia told Jacob about the terrifying events in exacting detail.

"Wow, Sophia, what a story. You are a brave and lucky lady."

"What are we going to do, Jacob? I cannot live with Erick."

"I know. We will have to institutionalize him until I solve the problem."

"You mean, place him in a mental hospital?"

"Yes, that's exactly what I mean. I still believe I can cure Erick, and this transformation will never occur again. Lee cannot be allowed to take over Erick's body. You and other people, including the officer, could have been killed today."

Upon hearing these words from Jacob, Sophia felt chills covering her body and tears dripping down her cheeks.

"Sophia, you don't have a choice. You must. Lee is dangerous, as you found out. Lives are at stake, including yours. I can no longer ensure your safety. Of course, I will know more when I talk to Lee and Erick. Maybe I can get an answer for why it occurred, but for now Erick/Lee must be placed in a safe and secure environment."

Sophia was thinking about what Jacob had said. It had been a terrifying day, and she never wanted to go through it again. While she was mulling over the situation, Jacob reached into his desk drawer, removed some papers, and began filling them out.

Sophia's eyes wandered around the room while she was deep in thought. "How can I do that to Erick? Jacob, what if you solve the problem and Erick is all right? Won't the hospital stay ruin his career?"

"This is an emergency mental hospitalization for Erick. We will place him in a seventy-two-hour hold. That will give us time before making it permanent, and it will not show up on his record. To answer your question, EMS will not cause a problem. However, a permanent hospitalization could, and it is something he will have to work through. On the other hand, I will place on the form that he suffers from extreme epilepsy seizures and is a danger to himself until a cure can be developed. This will give us time, and when we cure him, Erick's medical record will show that he has a common medical problem." He placed the completed form in front of Sophia and asked her to sign it. He handed her a ballpoint pen. Then she thought about the issue and put down the pen.

"Sophia, you cannot live your life in fear."

"I know. It is so difficult to do. Shaking her head and with a shaking hand, she picked up the pen and signed below Jacob's signature.

"Sophia, before I pick up Erick, I need to confirm your story."

"I know. It's okay." Jacob called the Oklahoma City Police Department. After getting shuttled to several people, he contacted Officer Greg, who confirmed the story."

"Please add to the record that Mrs. Sophia Anderson is here with me now, and she is in good physical condition. I know where my patient is located, and I plan to pick him up shortly and take him to Cedar Ridge Hospital on a seventy-two-hour hold. I may need your assistance and a court order later. However, I believe I can convince him to go voluntarily tonight.

"Okay, Sophia. The police were at your home and confirm your story That is sufficient independent confirmation for the affidavit. I will pick up Erick immediately. We cannot let this continue." He looked at Sophia and asked, "What's your home phone number?"

Erick answered the phone on the second ring.

"Hi, Erick. This is Dr. Gottlieb speaking. Sorry I didn't get back to you sooner, but I have been out of state. I got your message, and I am—"

"Something terrible has happened to Sophia. Lee took over my body, and there are bad signs here."

"Erick, I received a phone call from Sophia, and she is fine, although very frightened. You need not worry about her. Do you understand me? Sophia is fine."

"Oh, thank God. I have been worried sick."

"Sophia will not be home tonight, so don't worry!"

"Okay, Doctor, I understand."

"Erick, I want you to stay there. Do not leave. I will be there shortly, and we can talk about what occurred."

Jacob immediately called a service that picks up psychiatric patients. Sophia overheard some of the conversation. "I want you to come by my home, which is on your way, and collect the pickup order. Then we'll go together to pick up the patient."

"I know what you are thinking, Sophia. These people are kindly and extremely skilled in handling difficult patients. Erick is in good hands with experienced people."

Sophia listened but sat there, shaking her head. "What if Erick will not go voluntarily?"

"I believe I can talk him into it, but if he is unwilling, I will implement a provisional seventy-two-hour hold."

While they waited, Gottlieb made copies of the pickup order and the seventy-two-hour hold order. Jacob switched his attention to Sophia.

"Do you really know what Erick's problem is yet?" she asked.

"I feel certain that it is DID. However, I still am uncertain as to how to treat it. There is no other like it in documented history. I have been in contact with some great experts in the field. My diagnosis is shared by all of them. Unfortunately, there is not a definitive cure yet. But do not give up. I will find one for Erick. You can count on it."

"Jacob, I am not certain that I can ever feel loving toward Erick again after today. I honestly saw Lee so angry that I thought he would kill me by the way he beat on the car window and screamed at me. I know my marriage to Erick is over."

"Don't give up on him yet, Sophia. We could cure him, and this will all become a bad memory."

"What will you do when you get to my home?"

"I will talk to Erick and convince him that it is best for all concerned to be at Cedar Ridge. I suspect that Erick will comply without incident."

"Oh, that sounds a lot better than what I was imagining."

The ringing of the front doorbell interrupted their quiet time. "I'll be back in about an hour. Feel free to watch TV and make yourself comfortable." Jacob picked up the forms and notes, and walked to the front door.

About an hour later, Sophia heard the garage door opener making sounds. When Jacob appeared, Sophia asked about Erick. Erick had understood what was happening, Jacob said, and went voluntarily.

"I will be called when Erick is registered in the hospital," he said. "You will have to go over there tomorrow and fill out some forms. It will also be safe for you to go home tonight if you like. I am not trying to chase you away. I'm giving you options."

"Thank you, Jacob. If you don't mind, I would like to stay here tonight. I need a safe spot for the night."

"Good, then it is settled."

Sophia continued talking about her morning experience for some time.

To change the subject, Jacob asked, "Sophia, what do you want in life? Have you achieved it?"

"No, Jacob. I desperately want to be a mother, but Erick doesn't want children. I am conflicted. When Sean was alive, I could take my mothering out on him. He was so—"

The telephone rang, interrupting her. It was the hospital. Erick was registered as a patient.

Jacob turned to face Sophia. "You will always be safe at the hospital. There are professionals that can handle any situation. Go there relaxed with the frame of mind that you care about Erick, and you want to help him. Okay?"

"Okay, Jacob. I will go visit Erick in the late morning." She was staring at Jacob with soft eyes when he turned toward her. Her eyes darted away.

Jacob yawned. The hour was getting late. He escorted Sophia upstairs and gave her a choice of two rooms. "The bathroom is right across the hall. Sophia. There are towels in there and a shower too."

He handed her pajamas with a pull-string at the waist and exited to his bedroom. Looking back, Jacob said, "Hey Sophia; the pajamas maybe too big for you, but you can roll up the cuffs and tighten the waist string. It'll have to do for tonight unless you get bigger instantly."

Sophia crawled into bed. She lay down and tried to relax, but the events of the day flashed continuously through her mind. She felt safe. About twenty minutes later, she drifted off to sleep.

Jacob woke near his normal time. After a shave and shower, he ate a light breakfast. Before he headed to work, he checked to see whether he still had the Dallas pictures and his notes. He placed them in his soft briefcase and went up to the guest bedroom. He hoped Sophia would be awake, but Sleeping Beauty was still gone to the world.

Sophia awoke two hours later. Jacob was nowhere to be found. She showered and bandaged her wounds. Before leaving, she wrote Jacob a note and placed it on the kitchen table.

> My Dearest Jacob,
>
> Yesterday was like a terrible nightmare that will never leave my memory. NEVER! Several times, I believed that Lee was going to kill me, one time with a chainsaw, so I experienced anxiety coupled with extreme fear. The hectic high-speed car chase was equally dreadful. Further, I cannot imagine that heinous person was Erick, who triggered additional emotions.

Somehow and strangely, it all seemed worth it by being with you last night. You were a wonderful gentleman and an inspiration to me. I can <u>never</u> express to you such that you would truly understand how wonderful it was to spend the night. I felt so safe! God bless you. Thanks for your wisdom, kindness, and hospitality.

Love, Sophia

Chapter 10: Cedar Ridge

When Erick woke, he noticed his male roommate was still asleep. The Popodine had worked again, and Erick had no recollection of the dream; perhaps he didn't dream. He dressed himself, stopping to look at the stitched-up gash on his lower-right leg. He opened his door and walked into the hallway. A number of people were in the dining room, so he walked over to a table with a breakfast buffet.

"Are you hungry?" asked a female attendant.

"Sure," responded Erick.

"It's buffet style today, so get what you want and eat what you take."

Erick filled his plate, then collected another piece of bacon and sat down at a table. He looked across the table, and a man roughly his age was staring at him. "Don't I know you?" the man said.

"I don't think so," responded Erick. "My name is Erick Anderson. What's yours?"

The man said in a slow, drawn-out fashion, "I don't remember." The conversation ended.

Following breakfast, Erick walked around the room. There was an outdoor garden, cyclone fenced including the top, should he want to go out there. He observed patients out there smoking.

The main room was bright in colors with a few male and female attendants. It was easy to spot them; they were all dressed in white. After a while, they became part of the room. Small offices with windows were located along one wall. When Erick asked an attendant about them, she told him they were examination rooms used by the doctors and therapists. "You can look in there if you like," said a friendly Hispanic attendant.

Erick opened the door and saw a table with three chairs. There were two paintings hanging on the wall. Both landscapes featured a wild river scene. The room interior was beige with no other distinguishing features.

He left the side room and continued his inspection. He guessed there were forty or more patients, both sexes. Some patients talked to themselves incessantly. Others appeared deep in thought, while still others existed like zombies. A few, such as himself, appeared normal.

In an adjoining room, Erick found some exercise equipment: treadmills, exercise bicycles, and weight-training equipment. He wandered back into the main room and discovered a library in one corner. The library contained some current magazines and popular novels. A television and VCR player decorated another corner. Two patients were watching a movie, but he couldn't determine which one it was. He picked up the cassette holder. The title was **Black Magic**. He had never heard of that one.

He decided to wait for Sophia in the library. Just after he sat down, a giant of a man approached him. "Hi, Erick. Do you remember me? I am Nurse Mike." He held out his hand, and Erick complied immediately by shaking it.

"Yeah, I remember you from Dr. Gottlieb's office."

"Good memory, Erick. I am the head nurse here today. I wanted to find out if you have any allergies and that type of thing."

"As far as I know, I have none."

"Your doctor is still Jacob Gottlieb. Is that correct?"

"Yes, that's correct."

"We are pretty open here. We want your life to be as comfortable as possible while you are visiting us. You can read, play the piano, exercise, or walk outside, but you cannot leave the building without a doctor's approval. You cannot enter the nursing station. Do you understand?"

"Yes. I understand."

"There will be no fighting, arguing, sex, stealing, drugs, harassing, and smoking indoors whatsoever. If you feel compelled to smoke, you must go outdoors through that door over there. Do you understand?"

"Yes, I understand, but I do not smoke."

"Erick, I have to tell you this: if these rules are violated, you will be moved to a more austere and ascetic quarters. Do you understand?"

"Yes. I understand," responded a now-grumpy Erick.

"I am sorry to tell you those things, but I am legally obligated to do so. On a more pleasant subject, I just talked to your wife, and she will be here shortly. She will bring you some clothing and toiletries. I'll see you later," Mike said with a smile as he departed.

Mike meandered toward the nursing station. Erick's eyes followed him. He was astonished by the huge size of this man, who had towered over Erick like a giraffe among zebras. Mike didn't have a neck. His skull came straight down to his shoulders. Further, there was not an ounce of fat on him. He was pure muscle neck to toe. His hair was short, blond, and combed neatly with a part on the left side. Mike seemed stern. Erick wondered whether he was friendly. He couldn't tell from that first meeting; but after all, Mike was performing an obligatory task.

Sophia arrived at the hospital a little later with two large bags of clothing and a smaller bag containing toiletries. She walked up to the registration desk and sat down in a chair until a young woman appeared at the window. She started the registration process involving insurance and other forms including a medical history of the patient. Gottlieb had warned her about saying too much regarding Jacob's decision to hospitalize Erick, so she wrote, "Talk to Dr. Gottlieb. She then handed the woman three bags and sat down again until called."

After hearing her name, Sophia went to the door. The door opened, and a young man in white attire approached her and said, "Please follow me, Mrs. Anderson. Nurse Nancy will check you. In the future when you enter the hospital, ring this bell, and someone will fetch you." The young man was holding all three bags, and as they passed through the door, a pleasant, middle-aged woman approached her.

Nurse Nancy asked, "What patient are you visiting?"

"Erick Anderson."

Nurse Nancy went to her patient list and looked at the top. "Erick is first on the list. That was easy. I need to check your body for unauthorized materials." She began to pat Sophia's body, including the cleavage area. After the pat-down, Sophia and the male attendant walked together in search of Erick.

Erick was in the far corner, reading. Sophia spotted him first.

"You may go ahead. Tell Erick that we placed your bags on his bed."

Suddenly, when Sophia saw Erick, she started to feel the trauma of yesterday. She knew it wasn't Erick's fault. It didn't change the fact of what she had experienced; nor did it change the way her body had reacted. She walked toward Erick tentatively, not knowing exactly what to say. She remembered that Jacob had told her to fill Erick in on everything that happened should he ask. She thought about these things as the distance narrowed.

Erick was still reading when he heard a "Hi, Erick."

Erick stood. "Sophia! Are you okay?"

"Well, I have a lot of cuts and scrapes as you can see, but I am fine. How about you, Erick?"

"I had to have nine stitches to close the wound in my leg, but I am physically all right. Sophia, please understand something. I would never, never harm you or scare you."

"I know that. Dr. Gottlieb explained that to me." She almost said "last night" and thought better of saying it. "How did it start, Erick?"

"Lee never took control before. I believe that it was because I forgot to take my Popodine Saturday night after the dinner party, and of course I was awakened by the dream. I just couldn't let myself go back to sleep, so I was fatigued in the morning." Erick reached out to hold her with a trembling hand, and Sophia obliged him, However, chills ran through her body. She hated them.

The next hour passed by with Erick asking her to provide the details of what Lee had done to her. She complied as Gottlieb had requested. However, the more she talked about the event, the more internalized it became.

"Sophia, I do not understand why Lee would run into you while you both were traveling at speeds of over a hundred miles per hour. It just doesn't make any sense. It could have killed both of you."

"It doesn't make any sense to me either, Erick, but it happened. I could see his face in the rearview mirror, and he was madder than hell. He looked livid!"

Erick continued to ask Sophia questions to uncover a missing part of his life—a part he didn't like. Erick's eyes held tears from what Sophia had said. The creepy feeling Sophia felt by being around Erick pervaded her body. She had to leave. She stood up and said, "I have to leave now, Erick. I still have a lot to do. I'll see you tomorrow night."

She turned and left without even hugging or kissing him. She walked to the entry door, and the attendant let her out. The door had a small glass window. As she exited the room, she turned and looked through it. Erick was still watching her, so she waved and walked away. Tears welled up in her eyes, and her stomach churned. She desperately needed to get away. She mused to herself, *Next week Jacob will be treating me.*

When Jacob arrived at Cedar Ridge Hospital, Erick was waiting. The first thing Erick said was, "How much longer must I remain in here, Doctor?"

"For a while, Erick. We need to know what triggered Lee to make his appearance. Lee isn't a very nice guy, so we cannot let him loose on Sophia or the world, for that matter. He fought with a highway patrol officer and controlled the officer's weapon. Lee has done some despicable things. We cannot let him loose. "You understand that, don't you?"

"Yes, Doctor! I understand, but it seems unfair."

"Yes, it is unfair. Let's go over to a side room, and we will talk about it. Meet me there. It'll be in room C."

Jacob noticed Mike at the nursing station. He was alone, and Jacob filled him in on yesterday's events. "I will be talking to Lee in a few minutes. Please watch the monitor and rescue me, if required."

"I will be pleased to help, Dr. Gottlieb. Would you rather have me wait outside the door?"

"I think you will have sufficient time from here. You may listen to our conversation, but let's not allow others to hear, so please use earphones. Remember, what you hear is patient-doctor privileged information."

Gottlieb walked directly to room C, and as he entered, he looked at the monitor to see whether the light was on. When he sat down, he said, "Okay, Erick, what happened yesterday that was different that led to Lee's appearance?"

"Sophia and I had a party on Saturday night. I was so tired after the party that I forgot to take my Popodine. Count them. I brought them along—I have one extra. Anyway, the dream woke me, and I couldn't go back to sleep. I lay awake for hours, and when I got up, I was really fatigued. While I was brushing my teeth, it happened. Lee started to make an appearance, we verbally argued, and then he took over. It happened because I was too tired."

"Erick, you haven't been on Popodine very long. You had those bad dreams before without Lee making his entrance. I can't believe that scenario. Relax, I want to talk to Lee. Maybe he'll tell me."

There was a pause as the metamorphosis took place, and then Lee appeared. "Hi, Doc!"

"You really did it this time, didn't you, Lee?"

"I guess I got a little excited, but I haven't had a body for a while, so it was nice having one."

"Lee, why did you make an appearance yesterday morning?"

"I told you before that I was getting stronger. It was just a matter of time. That morning was my time. Erick was tired. It was easy. Furthermore, I know how to do it."

"Was Erick' being very tired the primary reason?"

"It was a partial reason, but it was going to happen at some time."

"Lee, do you know where you are?"

"Yeah, I am in a mental hospital."

"Do you know what is going to happen to you if you do it again in here?"

"No."

"You won't stay in here. We will put you and Erick in a padded cell for the rest of his life. Is that what you want?"

"No! I want to be free," Lee shouted.

Without warning, Lee jumped up and reached across the table separating him from Gottlieb and grabbed his shirt, pulling Gottlieb to his feet so their heads were almost touching. Lee looked menacing. "Just who do you think you are talking to, Doc? I am one of the important men in history. I could kill you right now."

While this was happening, Mike was monitoring the situation; as Gottlieb had asked, Mike raced to the room. When Mike arrived, Lee held Jacob by the shirt collar and began to tighten his grip choking Jacob. Jacob was fighting him by trying to pry his hands off. Lee turned around, not releasing Jacob, and glared at Mike for invading his privacy.

With his powerful hands, Mike reached over Lee's shoulder, placing his thumbs on the topside of Lee's wrists, and four fingers wrapped around with his fingertips driving to the bone of Lee's wrists. Then, with amazing strength, he clamped down and rotated and twisted Lee's wrists so forcibly that he caused Lee to release his grip. He then pulled Lee back into his straight-back chair, made Lee clasp his own hands on his lap, and patted Lee on the shoulders. A stunned Lee sat quietly in his chair with hands folded.

"Do you want me to take him to the room, Dr. Gottlieb?"

"No! Wait a minute, Mike. Lee, are you going to be cooperative or not?"

Lee uttered a quiet "Yes."

"We are okay, Mike, and thanks. However, continue to watch the monitor."

When Mike stepped out of the room and shut the door, Lee still exhibited a scowl. Gottlieb was somewhat shaken by the suddenness of the encounter but tried not to show it. "Lee, you are pushing your safety zone. That behavior was unacceptable and will not be tolerated. Am I making myself clear? Lee, are you or are you not going to work with me?"

Lee nodded but didn't speak. Jacob took that gesture as a yes.

"Now, let's go back to yesterday. Tell me everything that happened."

Lee looked at Gottlieb and nodded. For the next fifteen minutes, Lee detailed the whole story in a manner that was in total agreement with Sophia's version.

When he completed his detailed explanation, Gottlieb asked Lee, "Why did you want to rape Sophia?"

"Originally, I didn't want to rape her. I just wanted sex with her. She's a good-looking chick. You must have noticed that. But Sophia didn't want to have anything to do with me and ran away to her room and locked the door. So I was going to get it the other way. It was something I had to do. They can't convict Erick for raping his wife, can they? Ha ha ha ha."

Jacob now understood what had happened, and the three stories were all in agreement. "Were you planning on cutting her up with the chainsaw?"

"Hell no! How could I screw her if she was cut into pieces? Think about it, stupid. She was in a room with a bed with the door locked. If I cut open the door with a chainsaw, she was mine!"

"Why did you chase her car?"

"I am not sure, but once it started, it was happening, and nobody could stop it."

"What about hitting her on the freeway? You could have killed both of you."

"I didn't mean to hit her. We were both driving fast, over one hundred miles an hour, and the stupid bitch slammed on the brakes right in front of me. What was I supposed to do—she didn't signal, ya know?" Lee laughed fiendishly. Gottlieb now had a complete understanding of what had occurred on Sunday. At that moment, Lee was mellowing as he moved past the confrontation.

"Lee, when you were in jail, do you recall any of the police or FBI detectives who interviewed you?"

"No! I don't remember being in jail. In fact, I have never been in a jail," he said emphatically.

"What about a Dallas officer with red hair? Think about it a little."

"I don't remember him at all."

"I talked to him last week. He told me a few things. He said that he thought that you were a very intelligent individual. Another thing he told me was that every time someone new came into the cell block, you ran up to the bars. Inmates do not do that. Why did you?"

"I do not remember doing it, but I can tell you why. Remember, I was a CIA operative, and I was expecting someone from the CIA or a lawyer to talk to me."

"The officer also told me that Marina was pregnant."

"Really, are you shittin' me? A boy or girl?"

"The officer said that they don't know. Marina went back to Russia after all the commotion was over and probably before the baby was born. Nobody knows. The FBI made her stay around for a while, because they felt that she might have been involved, but they concluded that she had absolutely nothing to do with the assassination. They withdrew their stay order. After that, Marina vanished. Did she have anything to do with the assassination, Lee?"

"Hell, no, Doc—none whatsoever!"

"You have two daughters, don't you?"

"Yes, June and Rachael. They are both small."

"Where were they at the time of the assassination?"

"With their mother." Lee stopped talking and stared at the ceiling for a while. Then he began again. "That's too bad that Marina went home. She was the only one I ever cared about. At least now she can speak Russian all the time, and that will make her happy. She hated English.

"She sure understood gambling though. Remember when I told you that Eddie Montana, Marina, and I went to St Louis? We stayed on one of those gaming riverboats that go up and down the Mississippi. It was great fun, and Marina loved it."

Lee's attitude had changed. There was a pleasant look on his face and even a hint of a smile.

Jacob didn't collect any information to confirm O'Malley story. He questioned Lee again, but Lee wouldn't provide any further information about his jail time. As far as Lee was concerned, it never occurred. Jacob also had an understanding for Lee's pacing and looking toward the door. That was helpful and made sense. Jacob felt that Lee fully expected the CIA to save him, probably through some counterfeited eyewitness testimony.

"Lee, there is a grassy knoll across the street from the shooting site. Some claim that a shot came from there. Was that CIA activity?"

"I don't know squat about that, Doc. If it was, I don't know nothin' about it."

"Lee, I have some color prints to show you. I want you to tell me if you recognize anything. Most of them were taken from an airplane, and you may not be able to identify any of them." Lee now seemed friendly and cooperative. The antisocial behavior Lee had exhibited minutes earlier was gone.

"Okay, Doc, let's give it a whirl," he said in a casual manner. Gottlieb had written the location or nearby locations on the back of each picture. Then he grouped them together. They appeared in the time sequence as he had taken the photos. The first set of pictures was of the Texas School Book Depository building, starting with those taken from the bus. He handed these to Lee in one batch. "Well," said Jacob, "do you recognize the building?"

"Sure do, Doc. I worked there."

"What is the name of this building then, Lee?"

"It is the Texas School Book Depository building!" Lee moved the photos from front to back after examining them for several seconds each. "Where is the slingshot tree? I don't see it—it should be right here." Gottlieb noted that Lee pointed to the correct position based on the photo taken from the back of the building.

Lee thumbed through the pictures. The last one was a black-and-white photo of the slingshot tree, that Eddie had provided. "Hey, Doc! There it is. I told you there was a slingshot tree. What happened to the tree?"

"Eddie told me it died and had to be replaced."

"See, I told you there was such a tree. You really are a doubter, Doc, a bad skeptic."

Next, Gottlieb had a series of pictures taken inside the museum, but he hadn't given them to Lee yet. "Lee, exactly where were you standing when you shot President Kennedy?"

"Now let me think. I was standing back and to the left side of the center window. I did that because I am right-handed, so I was nearly hidden, but I still could see my target."

"I want you to look carefully at the following pictures. I know they are a little blurry. Can you recognize anything?"

Lee looked carefully at the pictures. He didn't recognize anything until he came to the photo of the assassin in the window.

"What window were you standing behind?" Gottlieb asked again.

"The center window! Look, there I am, and I am standing to the left side just like I said. You must believe me now. This photo is proof!"

Lee discussed his relationship with Eddie, and it seemed normal to Jacob.

The next collection of color prints was of Lake Hubbard and Rockwell Forney Dam. Lee looked at the first three pictures. "This doesn't look familiar to me. Of course, the trees had grown considerably since the time Lee was there years earlier. Then he looked at additional photos. When Lee saw a photo showing the lake, Lee said, "Lake Hubbard!"

"You are correct, Lee. This picture that you are looking at was taken near the dam when the entrance trail splits. Most people go to the left, but I went to the right. Continue looking, Lee."

Lee held several pictures and smiled a little. "Yeah," he said. "Here is the damn dam." He chuckled at his witty remark.

"Where were you standing when you threw the bicycle off the dam?"

"Right in the middle, Doc—right in the middle of the spillway." He pointed to the position. "Doc, see the trail over there?" Lee pointed to a trail on the far side of the Lake. "That is where those people were walking just before I threw the bike into the lake. They never saw a thing. Then I left on that side of the dam too, because it was a lot shorter walk to the bus stop."

"What type of bike was it, and how many gears did it have?"

"It was a special make, so there was no brand name on it, and it had twelve gears. The front sprocket had two gear clusters, and the rear had six. The tires were skinny. They weren't the fat tires that most bicycles had." Lee remained quiet, so Jacob handed him the next batch of photos.

The next batch was divided into groups based on the suspected quarry sites. Jacob handed Lee the first group, which consisted of the Jefferson Quarry. Lee looked through them.

"Do you recognize anything, Lee?"

"No, nothing. But there are some pretty nice trucks down there."

Next came the airplane photos taken of Johnson Quarry, Kaiser Quarry, Jett & Son, a poultry farm. "Lee, all of the remaining photographs were taken from an airplane, so the view will be different than what you may have seen on foot. Look at them carefully and tell me if you recognize any of them."

Lee snatched the six photos of the Johnson Quarry and thumbed through them, putting the first to the last until he had seen all six. "Nothing here, Doc."

The next batch was of the Kaiser Quarry. Again, there were six photos, and Lee repeated the process. "No, Doc, but the terrain is starting to look familiar."

Next came the Jett & Son photographs. Jacob handed Lee eight photographs. Lee started staring at the first one, and he moved it to obtain better light. That photo was placed at the bottom of the stack. Lee stared further at the top picture. "Doc, I recognize this place. This is where the CIA trained me. See this flattened building laying on the ground?" Jacob leaned forward and looked at the spot where Lee pointed. Then Lee said, "This was the building where we assembled and disassembled the rifle. It was standing then. See, there is the cyclone fence with a lot of grass around it. There is the little mound the guy hid behind near the front gate." Jacob had missed the fence when he looked at the pictures because of the dead grass.

"Lee, what about that bunker there? You never mentioned it."

"It was there, Doc. It just wasn't important, and it's still not important. Doc, look over here. See this rectangular building? I practiced my shooting next to it. It was at my back. It is a little hard to tell from this picture, but there was a big hill over the entire length of the cleared area. Look, Doc, you can still make it out. Yeah, this grassy area between the hill and building was where that machine returned my target to me, but I do not see that equipment now."

Gottlieb remembered seeing the hill, and now he was ecstatic about the revelations. Had not Lee pointed out these items, he would have missed them. Further, Jacob had thought there was nothing of value in the photos. Right now, he was thankful for truckers' CB radios.

Lee wasn't ready to return the pictures and continued to examine them. Then he laid all eight on the table in front of him. His attitude changed. He'd had an undercurrent of hostility when Jacob came in, especially after Jacob had threatened him regarding his behavior. Now Lee looked at every detail in each photo, and he continually babbled out new material, which Gottlieb took down in his notebook and collected on the video. Lee felt he had just proved he was Lee Harvey Oswald. Gottlieb thought, *Lee Harvey Oswald has been dead for many years now. How can this be possible?*

Jacob's hands started shaking—not so Lee could notice. His weekend trip had been a total success. The inner excitement was building, and he had come to the logical conclusion to this whole phenomenon when there was no logic to be found. *Lee is credible.* He still had a few i's to dot and t's to cross, but overall, he was firmly convinced that the Lee inside Erick's head knew things no one in the world could know except Lee Harvey Oswald. Jacob was euphoric with these revelations.

Now he had another important item in mind. He needed to have Lee remain under control so he could effect a cure. It was time to turn Lee's thoughts back to Erick. "Lee, we can talk about these findings at another time. However, it is now time to collect your wits about what is happening here. If you take over Erick one more time, I will have to change your location, and you will never get out of here.

"Lee, I need to talk to Erick now." A minute later, Erick returned to the body, and in a natural state.

"Why did Lee do those things to Sophia, Doctor?"

"I think he wanted female companionship, Erick, and with his terrible attitude about life, his lust for sex got out of control. When that happened, he had to have her. Lee wouldn't take no for an answer."

"What about me, Doctor? How are you going to cure me?"

"I am working on it, Erick. You will just have to have faith in me. I haven't given up, and you shouldn't either." They both stood up, and Gottlieb opened the door. "Erick, for your information, Lee got out of hand earlier, and Mike had to restrain him. Lee is still around."

Chapter 11: The Lion

About an hour later, there was a lot of commotion around the television at Cedar Ridge. It seems that a rerun of a World Wrestling Association (WWA) bout between The Lion and Black Bart was beginning. The viewers were getting excited even before it started.

Erick never paid any attention to wrestling matches, but this time he walked over to watch from the rear of the assemblage. The viewers became excited as the beginning unfolded. The entry aisles were wide to enable the villain to enter without being pummeled by old ladies' purses. Bart entered, avoiding the purses, slid between the ropes into the ring, and flexed for the clamorous crowd.

Shortly thereafter, the world champion, Mike, The Lion, Garland would enter the arena. Background music played before he entered, and the crowd noise built to deafening levels. The crowd in the large arena turned into almost synchrony toward the eastern door. A bright spotlight illuminated that door as two trumpeters walked through the door, carrying ultra-long trumpets, which were reminiscent of Roman days long gone. They blared the arrival of The Lion, the world champion. The Lion's long, blond hair hung over his shoulders like his namesake, the African lion. After the fanfare, the noise in the auditorium continued to escalate.

Through the open doors, a metal band marched, announcing the arrival of The Lion. Promenading behind the band, The Lion pranced, waving to the crowd. Fifteen thousand paying spectators stood up and cheered wildly. When he became visible on the overhead monitors, the crazed crowd began chanting, "Lion, Lion, Lion!" The noise level was deafening, the band inaudible.

The Lion stopped frequently to accept the adulation of fans and acknowledge the love of the crowd. The Lion was the most beloved of all WWA wrestlers. His body was as massive as was his hair, all six foot eight inches of him; he had no fat. He was just muscle and bone. He wore a cardinal-red robe with gold and charcoal-black trim. The extra-large sleeves looked like wings hanging from his massive shoulders. His opponent, Black Bart, stood in the ring wrapped in his black cape, showing his disdain for the proceedings and verbally taunting The Lion.

Erick stared at The Lion, and when The Lion turned and the camera caught a frontal view, Erick smiled. Erick turned to Mike, who was standing next to him. "That's you, Mike, right?"

Mike nodded. "Why did you get out of the business?"

"I had no choice, Erick. I was injured."

"What happened?"

"On the very next match after this one, there was an accident. Angry Art accidentally broke my back when he jumped off of the ropes. I was paralyzed for a while, but a wonderful neurologist saved my back. While in the hospital, they placed me in an ice bath for a while to keep the swelling down. I was knocked out, so I don't remember it. I will forever be indebted to Dr. Gillette. I am fine now, but I can no longer wrestle."

"Francis, my wife—bless her heart—was with me much of the time while in the hospital. She protected me from the onslaught of ambulance chasers, who approached me. I couldn't do much. I was depressed and paralyzed from the waist down. After a few days following the ice bath, Francis was seated near the foot of the bed. I looked at her and said, 'Honey, would you pick up the sheet and look at my feet please?'

"As Fran looked, I moved my right big toe, then my left, and back and forth. Fran started crying, 'Mike, Mike, your toes are moving. Are you making this happen?'"

"'Yes, beautiful.'"

"Fran and I were hugging one another and crying together. Fran ran off to get the floor nurse, and when the nurse arrived, I had tears of joy flowing down my cheeks.

"On the following morning, Dr. Gillette came in to see me. I clearly remember Dr. Gillette telling me that this was exceptionally good news.

He followed up these words with a few tests on the lower extremities. He reiterated that this was very good news. He told me I would make a full recovery if I followed his instructions explicitly. However, I would have to find a new vocation. Wrestling was out."

"So, what did you do?"

"While I was still hospitalized, a lawyer from the WWA came to see me. He told me the WWA was paying all hospital, doctors', and therapists' expenses. They wanted me to recover, but I told them that wrestling in the future was out. The WWA wanted to help me develop a new occupation. The WWA paid for all my four-year college expenses and provided me with a modest income during those college years.

"The recovery and therapeutic time were most difficult, but I completed them to regain nearly full strength and use of my back."

"Why did you become a nurse, Mike?"

"First, I decided that if I could recover, I wanted to do something to help mankind. I started eliminating various occupations. I got my list down to two. I considered being either a nurse or a therapist. My final decision was to become a nurse. I completed my education at the University of Oklahoma Nursing School four years later."

When the patients in front of Erick began shouting as The Lion defeated Black Bart, Mike departed. Most viewers never realized The Lion was their own beloved nurse, Mike.

Jacob still had serious concerns about the CIA-sponsored activity. If that information was correct, anyone knowing about Lee was in potential danger. *I could be a target. After all, I am no one compared to a president of the United States.* If the CIA could assassinate a president, an unknown doctor was nothing. Furthermore, the CIA could easily make it appear that one of his patients did it. Now, many years had passed since the Kennedy assassination. The question was, *would the CIA still be willing to assassinate a doctor after many years? Does the CIA hold a grudge?* Gottlieb didn't know the answer to that question.

Although Jacob now believed that Lee was intimately knowledgeable of Lee Harvey Oswald, others might not. Many people witnessed the death of Oswald and further many in authority saw the body of Oswald. He thought, *Oswald had to be dead. Further, I need a real Oswald expert, who could deal with the historical issues and the CIA questions, so Jim and I could deal with the medical issues.* He decided he should at least make a token attempt to locate such an expert. Jacob looked through his Dallas notes and located the phone number of the John Fitzgerald Kennedy Museum. He placed the call to speak to the head curator. His inquiry was rewarded by locating an expert right there at the University of Oklahoma, Dr. Hunter Tripp.

Later that afternoon, Jacob dropped in to see Jim in his office. "Jim, I'm really pleased that you are here. I require your assistance on the Anderson case. I now have definitive information concerning this case, and I need your input." Jacob reached back and closed the door. Then he leaned over toward Jim and spoke in barely audible tones. "I must tell you this first. When I pass on the information to you, your life is potentially at risk, just as mine is right now."

"What do you mean by my life is at risk?" Jim said in a near whisper too.

"Exactly that. Someone may try to kill us if I pass along this information." Jacob never played games, so Jim took him seriously.

"My God, man, what did you uncover?"

"Nothing that I planned on or wanted. I'll tell you that."

Jim still couldn't take the potential death threat seriously. Then Jacob looked at him and said, "I cannot set any probabilities on this possibility. If the word never gets out, then there is zero risk, but if it leaks out, we could be in trouble."

"I am still in this to help you, Jacob. When do you want to meet? It will take me three hours or more to go through the video tapes. Then there is time required to go through the photographs. I will draw my most objective conclusions, and then we can talk."

"It sounds like a four-hour deal, doesn't it?"

"I am afraid so. When that concludes, we need to discuss future steps and potential medical treatment. I suggest that we do it in two parts here at the office after work. I am free Tuesday and Wednesday night."

"Jim, I am thinking of bringing in an expert and have him sit in with us. Do you have a problem with that?"

"It is highly unusual. Does he know the seriousness of the discovery should information leak out?"

"I haven't talked with him yet because I first wanted to discuss it with you. I assure you that he will know the potential dangers far better than us."

On the following Tuesday evening, Jacob heard the door alarm and headed out to greet Professor Tripp. After pleasantries, he walked Tripp into the lunchroom with an assortment of aromas filling the room. Shortly thereafter, Jim Hanford walked into the room, sniffing the aroma of hot Chinese food. "Jim, Dr. Tripp is professor emeritus of history at the University of Oklahoma and quite knowledgeable of the era of Lee." As the two shook hands, Jacob said, "Gentlemen, we will start in this room as I go through the preliminaries while we are eating, and then we will move into my treatment room to view half of the videos."

"Before we begin, Professor, I have here two identical confidentiality disclosure forms, which basically tell you that you must treat this information as proprietary and confidential. Sign both and keep one. I have already signed both." He placed the papers on the table. Tripp signed two copies and slipped one into his briefcase.

"Hunter, we are dealing with a very fragile patient, and the situation was exacerbated last weekend. Dr. Hanford will assist me in the medical aspects of this work, and I would like you, Professor, to deal with the social and historical elements of the situation. I assure you, Professor, that you will find it fascinating. You may not agree with me, but you will find it interesting. I am looking for you to separate the wheat from the chaff."

"I look forward to the challenge, Dr. Gottlieb."

"Only I know all of the contents here, and I have come to some definitive and improbable conclusions that, if broadcast outside of this room, would have people suggesting that I see a psychiatrist. Fortunately, I need only need to go to the next office." Jacob smiled, and the other two men chuckled when they heard the statement. Jacob continued, "Dr. Hanford participated in a treatment involving hypnosis and encountered Lee.

"The patient's name is Erick. Erick is now a resident at Cedar Ridge Hospital, a local mental hospital. Professor, to complete your assessment of Lee, you will first need access to him, and you will get that through me and only me. To reach Lee, we must do it through hypnosis at the hospital. Lee is a sociopath and over the weekend performed some very dangerous stunts, like breaking into Erick's wife's bedroom using a chainsaw and chasing her in his car at speeds in excess of one hundred miles per hour after she escaped. You will be safe at the hospital should you decide to continue in this investigation."

Jim, hearing this for the first time, blinked.

Jacob continued, "It would be very helpful to know who the personality, Lee, is, if he is not a figment of Erick's imagination, the usual case. If the personality Lee is who he claims to be, there is potential danger for us here in this room. Professor, you are in an excellent position to state how serious this potential threat is as a member of your committee. Dr. Hanford and I would definitely want to hear from you. Is that okay with you?"

Tripp looked at each man and said, "If this personality is who you believe, I will assess our joint safety and promise to give my honest opinion."

"Professor, if after tonight or both nights you are still interested, I will make the patient available to you on Saturday and/or Sunday. I want to get down to the bottom of this as soon as possible before Lee destroys Erick's life. The patient is going downhill fast. Further, if my treatments are successful, I intend to erase Lee from Erick's mind. Hence, this personality will no longer be available to you as a historical personage."

"Do you have any questions, doctors?"

"Yes," asked Tripp. "Why are we in danger?"

"Lee claims he was an assassin for the CIA, so we are in potential danger from them should they hear of this and if it is true." Hanford shuddered upon hearing this.

"This is the first tape when Lee made an appearance. As you will see, Dr. Hanford was with me at the time. The name of the second personality is Lee, and note his antisocial behavior immediately.

"After it ended, the next session was on the same tape. Again, Lee made his appearance, and he wasn't kind. He spewed venom and anti-USA slogans as he entered his sociopath state. Then Lee went into exacting details of his time in Russia, and during his discussion, Lee began speaking gibberish."

Jacob and Jim began talking during the gibberish, and Hunter barked, "Hush up! Replay that section and be quiet!" Jacob backed up the tape and replayed it, ignoring Hunter's barking. "No, go back further." Jacob did and started the player again.

"Amazing," explained Hunter. "Erick speaks very good Russian."

"What?" spouted Gottlieb.

"I know. I teach Russian here at the university. I was born in Russia and immigrated to the United States with my parents when I was eleven."

Gottlieb asked, "What did Lee say during that sequence?"

"He said he enjoyed the preliminary dealings with the KGB more than with the CIA."

"How would Erick know how to speak Russian that well? You have to spend years of conversational Russian to speak like that," Hunter remarked. "He speaks very good Russian."

"Erick cannot speak a word of Russian," volunteered Gottlieb. "I have asked him under hypnosis, where patients do not lie. Erick can only speak English."

When that session was over, Gottlieb looked at the others, who were shaking their heads.

"If you noted, there was little that I could check out based on that last interview, even if I could understand Russian. Therefore, I decided in the next interview to cover areas where I had a chance to verify the credibility of what Lee was saying. That will be shown on the next tape. It's break time while I rewind the tape. Help yourself to more Chinese food too."

When everyone returned with full plates, Jacob continued, "On this tape, you will see a softer side of Lee as he discusses his childhood. Listen to his voice tones particularly when he talks about his childhood."

Erick seemed just the same. This time when Gottlieb called out Lee, Lee came willingly, as if he wanted to talk. "Professor, what do you know about Lee's siblings?" asked Gottlieb.

"Nothing at all except their names."

"Well then, you will discover something on this tape," said Jacob. Jim looked at Gottlieb in a peculiar manner. As they watched, a different Lee emerged, a kinder and gentler Lee. Jim and Hunter watched in utter fascination as Lee profiled his childhood in Covington, Louisiana, and Wichita Falls, Texas. Hunter was writing down his notes from the tape since Jacob had warned him that the tapes wouldn't leave his possession. Lee became mellow as he talked. It was almost as if he had put himself back into his childhood, a good time for him. He went on to describe his neighborhood and friend, Wesley. His voice was serene, and he sounded much like Erick. He gave copious details about his street and neighborhood. He also gave exact details of the farm they had lived on in Wichita Falls, Texas. Then, of course, Lee had tears in his eyes when he discussed the death of his sister. All three men saw a kinder, softer side of Lee, and there was a multitude of details about the homes and neighborhoods that could be checked out in detail.

When that session ended, Jacob stopped the tape and turned on the light. Then he spoke. "Gentlemen, I now had some kind of data to check the validity of what Lee was telling me, so over the following weekend, I spent time in Covington and Wichita Falls. Amazingly, I found Lee's home in Covington, the grocery store, and school. I also talked to the grocery store owner, who recalled the Ekdahls and the tragic death of Lee's sister, Elsa."

"Wait a minute," Hunter uttered. "I heard that on the tape. Lee didn't have a sister. Got ya!"

"That is not true, Hunter. Here is a copy of a newspaper article detailing her death by a hit and run driver, and here is a copy of her birth certificate. I hired a private investigator, who uncovered this story about her death and confirms both Lee's and the store owner's version." Jacob withdrew from a folder a clipping from a newspaper concerning Elsa's death.

"I can't believe it," Hunter uttered.

"On that weekend excursion, I took pictures, not only of the suspected home of Lee but also of others in the area. To my amazement, Lee told us of a rock archway in the front yard and identified the store, his home, his neighbor's home, and the school. The store owner remembers a rock archway, now removed. I went to Wichita Falls, Texas, and located the ranch Lee described. On the upcoming tape, you see me showing Lee those photographs I had taken. Remember, half of the photos had nothing to do with Lee."

Hunter spoke up. "Doctor, that is some pretty impressive detective work."

"Thanks, and I believe so too. You see, I couldn't believe Lee could be in Erick's head. Further—and Jim can verify this—patients will not lie under hypnosis."

"Gentlemen," said Jacob, "I will close our topic for the evening by telling you one more story. I still had a couple of questions for the old store owner, who recalled the Ekdahl family. A few days later when I had him on the phone, I asked him if he had ever heard of Lee after he moved away from Covington.

"He told me Lee made the national news. 'What news?' I asked.

"'You know, when Lee Harvey Oswald assassinated President Kennedy.'" Hunter expected that statement, but Jim didn't. Jim's mouth flew open, and for the first time in years, he couldn't find the words to speak.

Finally, he stammered and said, "You mean, the man who assassinated President Kennedy is supposedly the same person inside Erick's head."

"Yes! Further, tomorrow night, Lee is going to tell us exactly how he did it."

"My God," said Jim. "Was the CIA behind it?"

"According to Lee, yes. Professor, you will have to assess our personal risks in this matter. If you believe they are too high for your comfort, you may leave." The men stood up and adjourned for the evening.

"Tomorrow night, I'll have Mexican food for us. We will meet here at six p.m."

Chapter 12: The Assassination

On the following evening, all three men munched on burritos, enchiladas, rice, and salad in the lunchroom. Naturally, the conversation was totally fixated on Lee. "Jacob," asked Hunter, "when I talk to Lee, may I use those same photos and repeat your interview process?"

"Absolutely. I will bring them."

"What about talking to him in Russian?"

"Yes to all of those questions, Hunter. I want the truth to come out. Remember, Lee may be available to us only for a short time, or it may be around twenty or more years. I just don't know. But understand, I intend to remove Lee and give Erick's life back to him, if possible, and when I do, Lee will be gone."

Hunter raised his eyebrows and nodded, acknowledging his understanding.

The participants moved to Jacob's treatment room with Hunter balancing a Coke while each doctor carried his Carta Blanca beer and half-filled plate of Mexican cuisine. Jacob had preset the tape so it began with Erick turning into Lee. Shortly thereafter, they heard Gottlieb force Lee to admit he had assassinated President Kennedy. Lee then began to discuss the details of his training on a weapon that was integrated into a bicycle.

"Bicycle—what bicycle?" asked Hunter. "No one of authority could believe Lee could walk out of the building normally with a weapon, then dispose it later. I am an expert. The FBI proved conclusively that the old rifle found in the top floor of the Texas School Book Depository building did not kill the president. In fact, it wasn't even the same caliber. Furthermore, many witnesses told police that Lee didn't walk stiff legged as if he had the rifle strapped to his leg. A thorough search of the building and surroundings never uncovered the weapon. Therefore, some people didn't believe Lee Harvey Oswald could have killed the president. This bicycle story offers an explanation not heretofore known or even surmised. It does explain how a man could ride away from the assassination site with a rifle in view, but how could Lee get rid of a bicycle? How could he hide a rifle in a bicycle? I want to learn more. This is fascinating, absolutely fascinating!"

Jacob and Jim stopped to listen to Hunter, who now was approaching the tapes with less skepticism. "Gentlemen, yesterday's session ended because of time constraints. The following tape goes into the details of the assassination."

The new tape began as the past one, but Jacob asked Erick whether he had spent time in Texas as a child. The answer was no. "At that time, I was convinced that Erick, alert or hypnotized, was unaware of the details of the Kennedy assassination. When Lee arrived, he painted in grizzly details the preparation for the assassination and the act itself. Lee sat on the lawn at morning break time laughing with Eddie."

"How do you know they were laughing?"

"Both Lee and Eddie discussed it."

"Imagine laughing when you are in preparation for a presidential assassination," said Jim in a rather emphatic manner. "Lee has no moral fiber."

During the next video, Hunter took rapid-fire notes. This was his area of expertise and the easiest way of tripping Lee as an imposter. Lee acknowledged the slingshot tree. He also discussed the details of preparing the elevator doors and how he had disassembled his bicycle to obtain the weapon and then smuggled it upstairs in a portable wastebasket. It actually made sense to Hunter, and several times Jacob noted Hunter was nodding in agreement with what Lee was saying. Jim and Hunter were taken aback by Lee's callused and hardened nature. Lee then described the assassination in meticulous detail. Hunter twice asked Jacob to rewind a few minutes so he could collect additional information.

As the tape was rewinding, Jacob pulled out the photos he had taken. "I chartered a small private plane to search for the quarry where Lee trained. According to Lee, I located it near Bowie, North Texas."

The lights dimmed, and video began the latest drama. Jacob watched both men throughout. Both had probably thought Jacob was a little off center when this started, but both became less skeptical as more evidence accumulated. Lee detailed the assassination in an almost matter-of-fact mentality. As Lee was speaking, Jacob interrupted, "Note Lee's sociopathic attitude coming up." Then Lee discussed executing the rapid-fire sequence, integrating the rifle into the bicycle, and leaving the building with the blue rifle in plain view but invisible to the eye. Jacob surmised Hunter was fascinated by the concept based on the rapid writing Hunter was doing.

Next Lee discussed his escape from the scene by taking public transit. He bicycled to Hubbard Lake. The three men listened as Lee discussed pedaling through the park to the spillway of Rockwell Forney Dam.

"'I was mid-spillway when I dismounted my bike. Some people were on the far side with their backs to me, so I did as instructed and threw the bicycle as far as I could. Then I went home for a while.'"

"Does anyone want another Carta Blanca or Coke?" Jacob asked.

"I'll take one," responded Jim, but Hunter shook his head.

"That cannot be," said Tripp. "What evidence do you have to support this bicycle theory?"

"At that time very little except Eddie, a building manager, and a police officer all saw Lee holding a blue bike. However, I have been able to confirm several important points." Gottlieb took out his notebook and proceeded to go through the evidence collected from Eddie, the Dallas PD, the Texas School Book Depository building, and Rockwell Dam.

"On the next tape, I show prints to Lee and ask him questions about them. Lee identified these places, although Erick has never been there. Lee was one hundred percent correct. Almost everything has been confirmed to my satisfaction, and Erick couldn't identify one photo except for his home and the front of this building."

As before, Gottlieb projected video on the screen. Many of the pictures evoked no response from Lee. Then when he saw the first photo of the Texas School Book Depository building, Lee said, "'Yeah, I remember that place. I used to work there.'"

"Watch carefully," commented Gottlieb. "Lee is about to see the back of the building and the area where the slingshot tree used to grow. That tree died many years ago."

On the tape, all three men heard Lee say, "'Hey, where's the slingshot tree?'"

Jacob stopped the tape again and said, "Here is a black-and-white photo Eddie gave me of the slingshot tree. Notice the building angle in the background."

The tape started again. Lee was speaking. "'What happened to the tree, Doc?'"

On tape Gottlieb spoke to him and said, "Eddie told me that it died and had to be replaced, so they planted another tree in the same place. Notice now that Lee knew immediately that the tree was missing and its location. That is extraordinary coincidence, wouldn't you say? No one else could know that or even think about it, except for Eddie Montana." Jacob stopped the video. "Here is a photo I took and showed to Lee, and here is the photo of the slingshot tree. Look carefully at the building in the background. That replacement tree was planted at the exact location. There is no question about it."

"How long has Erick known Eddie?" asked Hunter.

"Erick and Eddie have never met. They just do not run in the same circles," Gottlieb replied. "Erick is a marketing expert, and Eddie is a janitor. Erick hasn't been in Dallas often, but he has done some business dealing there and has changed planes at the Dallas/Fort Worth airport. Erick has never been to the museum and was unaware of its existence."

Jacob took a few swallows of his beer and said, "Now I want you to recall what Lee told us about the CIA training outside Dallas. I chartered a small plane and flew over all of the existing quarries north of Dallas and took about eight pictures of each quarry. On the next video, I show these photos to Lee, and Lee recognizes only one set as being the target-practice area. Now let's watch."

Jacob turned on the video, and they witnessed all the proceedings that transpired. Hunter moved forward in his chair. They heard Lee identify the quarry and even point out the hill behind the shooting range, the rifle/bicycle assembly shed, and the overgrown fence. Gottlieb spoke up. "Gentlemen, to be honest with you, I didn't believe the quarry Lee selected was the correct one because Lee had mentioned the cyclone fencing, and I didn't notice it while flying around because it was so overgrown with weeds and brush, but Lee noticed it right away."

When the video showings had concluded, Jacob looked at the two guests and said, "Gentlemen, that concludes the video. That is not all of the data but most of it. What do you think?"

Hunter spoke first. "Assuming that people cannot lie under hypnosis, it is very convincing. However, I would independently need to verify your evidence and talk to Lee. The most amazing part of it all is that for the first time we have an explanation of how Lee did it. That sounds pretty far out and unbelievable but possible."

Jim spoke up and said, "The key definitive evidence is still missing, and that is the bicycle. I remain a skeptic until we have that bike and confirm that it converts into a rifle of the correct caliber. Also, I believe the slingshot tree was very convincing. No person or agency has ever speculated about a bicycle, have they, Professor?"

"No, Doctor, no one has advanced a hypothesis regarding such a bicycle."

Jim continued, "If indeed the CIA sponsored this assassination, they probably had divers in the lake to remove the bicycle as soon as the climate cleared in Dallas."

"No, I disagree," said Hunter in a confident voice. "Lakes are sometimes never drained, and there is no swimming in that portion of Hubbard Lake, because of the high current going over the spillway. There is no reason for anyone to discover that bike. Further, the water is very deep there, so it would have to be located using scuba gear." Since the professor was an expert on the CIA, Jim and Jacob listened intently to what he had to say. Jacob sported a big grin.

Jim spoke up, "We need to find that bicycle. That will prove or disprove your hypothesis."

"You are right, gentlemen, I will be right back." Jacob exited the room. Jim and Hunter wondered what Jacob was up to. A minute later Jacob returned, holding a dull, blue bicycle.

"Last Sunday, I went scuba diving in Hubbard Lake. I sneaked into the lake at sunrise wearing a wetsuit. Look what I found."

"That can't be Lee's bicycle," Jim asked with a question in his voice.

"Yes, it is, Jim. I assumed Lee did exactly as ordered by the CIA, and I went into the lake at the center of the spillway to do the search. A rope was tied to the center-most post above the spillway. I started my search about five feet from the wall with the rope tied to my weight belt, and I swam in a semicircular path toward the opposite face of the dam waving my metal detector as I swam. Then I increased the rope length by about five feet and swam in an arc to the originating side, repeating the trip in the opposite direction at the increased distance.

"I located the bike in silt about eighteen feet out from the spillway in dead center. One handlebar protruded from the mud. I didn't need the metal detector. Lee couldn't have thrown it any better. The first thing I did was feel a tire to determine whether they were wide or narrow because visibility was poor down there. When I was convinced the tires were narrow, I worked the bike out of the silt, being careful not to create muddy water. I remained still for a while, and the current swept it away. Next, I rubbed the mud off the horizontal bar and saw it turn blue. Then I began pawing through the silt for a leather pouch. I located it, and it held a heavy, metallic object within. I placed the pouch inside my scuba suit. I was convinced that I held the correct bike. The final thing to do was to get the hell out of there."

Jacob unfolded a red shop rag, and it held a fused metal object that appeared like a trigger assembly. Jacob handed it to Hunter.

"My God, Jacob, this is a trigger assembly. There is no question about it," bellowed Hunter, who quivered with emotion. "Look, you can see the trigger and the chamber."

"You are correct, Hunter," Jim volunteered.

"I have the sites and pins too, but I didn't bring them. They are just too tiny. I was afraid that I might lose them."

Jim asked, "Did anyone help you?"

"Yes, I had a personal friend to act as a lookout on the dam. He steered a ranger away from the lakeside of the spillway, as I worked underwater. He saw a ranger walking toward the dam, so he gave me a couple of yanks on the rope to warn me and moved to the opposite side of the dam. He told me that his insides were quivering.

"The ranger asked, 'Kind of early to be out here. Isn't it?'"

"'I am waiting for a friend. We planned this walk around the lake a few weeks ago in the morning before it got too hot, but he hasn't shown up yet. I guess this drizzle scared him off. I'll wait a little longer and then go home if he doesn't arrive.'"

"'We don't like people to hang out on the dam, you know.'"

"'I didn't see any signs to that effect.'"

"'No, it's just park policy.'"

"'Well, since we're walking to the western side, I'll wait over there.'"

"The ranger never noticed the bubbles from the scuba gear. Jerry said that his toes tingled for an hour."

Jim and Hunter stood and applauded, and Jacob bowed in response.

"Since getting the bike home, I performed a power wash of the bicycle and soaked key junctions in WD-40. I will begin to disassemble the bike at my place in two weeks, and you guys are invited. Hopefully, the penetrating oil will loosen up the frozen parts by then."

Jim spoke up. "Wow, Jacob, that was a high-risk activity you guys undertook. I am dumbfounded. This information cannot be real. This whole story is too unbelievable to be true. I just can't comprehend what I just learned. Amazing, simply amazing, stunning! I am flabbergasted."

"Why didn't you ask one of us to assist?" Hunter asked.

"I thought about it, but because it was high risk involved, I didn't want either of you to get into trouble if we were caught. My anonymous friend owes me big time, and he has had legal problems before and I bailed him out. He owed me. We were lucky, very lucky. Based on the way things have been going with Erick lately, it was time for my luck to change."

"Jacob, did you have anyone else come by during the dive?"

"Yes, two bicyclists came by, but my friend didn't warn me because they disappeared as quickly as they arrived."

The three men kept patting the others on the back. When they departed, Jacob flopped into his chair. He stared at the bike leaning against a wall, and his mind drifted back before the weekend.

Jacob called his close personal friend, Jerry and asked him whether he would join him in Dallas over the weekend. He'd needed his assistance. "What do you need me for?" Jerry asked.

"I am going scuba diving next Sunday in Lake Hubbard, and I need a lookout."

"You're kidding!"

"No, Jerry, I have been thinking about it, and I believe it is relatively safe to do it, particularly at sunup. I will be looking for an old bicycle that has been under water for years. My major concern is a roving ranger. I am willing to risk it with your assistance. I would like you to drive your pickup, just in case I get lucky."

On the way to the dam, I reminded Jerry of what I had planned. I will walk up the trail on the eastern side of the lake and place my gear near the lakeshore hidden under a tree. I will change into my wetsuit there, slip into the water, and swim back to the dam. I want you to tie the rope to the center post at the spillway. I will swim up below you east of the spillway, and you will throw me the end of the rope. Then, I'll dive to the bottom to start my search a few feet from the dam on the eastern side. My major concern is a ranger walking the trail around the lake. If you see one, give two strong pulls on the rope. I will stop what I am doing until I feel two strong pulls again. After you warn me the first time, go to the opposite side of the dam and walk slowly away from the spillway. Engage the ranger in conversation, if he catches up to you, as you walk him away from the spillway to distract him from seeing my bubbles. They may not even be visible because of the high surface current.

"How do I know that you have located the bike?"

"When and if I locate the bicycle, I will surface and show you the bike. That is the time to remove the rope. I will swim back to my starting point and change into my clothes under the tree. I will wave when I am ready to walk out with the bicycle and gear. Wave back when the trail is free of pedestrians."

Jacob continued thinking about the dive. He expected strong currents at the bottom, but the current was low, especially compared to the surface. However, the current was sufficient to remove the silt my flippers stirred up. Once it cleared, visibility was adequate. *I drove my hand into the silt on the bottom and found it about six inches deep. I hoped I could see the handlebars sticking up from the bottom, and I did. The discovery of the bicycle and leather pouch was one of the more exhilarating moments in my life.*

I can't wait to show the bike to Hunter and Jim.

Chapter 13: Jett & Son

Saturday experienced the arrival of a summer thunderstorm. Hunter and Jacob entered Cedar Ridge Hospital with umbrellas over their heads; they dashed into the building at the same time as lightning flashed nearby. A man walked over to Hunter with a Polaroid camera and snapped a picture to have on record for future visits without Gottlieb's presence. Then both doctors entered the ward.

Jacob looked around for Erick and found him in the library, and the two men walked towards him side by side. Erick looked up to see Jacob and Hunter approaching and walked in their direction. They met in middle of the room. "Erick, I would like you to meet Dr. Tripp. He will be assisting me today in our session. He is going to improve our understanding of Lee."

They walked towards one of the side rooms. Gottlieb tugged at Erick's arm and said, "How are you sleeping, Erick?"

"Just fine, Doctor. In fact, I feel so good I would like to get out of here."

"We are not ready for that yet, Erick. You and Dr. Tripp go ahead to room C while I talk to Nurse Mike for a minute." Mike informed Gottlieb that Erick had been acting unusual lately and appearing very depressed.

Erick, I asked Dr. Tripp to join us today, because he has an interesting perspective on Lee, and I am confident that he can help me. You don't mind, do you?"

"Oh no, Doctor, anything—anything to get over this DID."

"Very good, Erick. I want you to sit there, and we will begin."

After the hypnosis, the baton was passed to Hunter, Jacob sat back in his chair. All went well except for the start. Lee didn't like Hunter at the beginning and became antagonistic toward him until Hunter began speaking in Russian, which changed the remainder of the session with a compliant Lee. Hunter verified all Jacob had discussed during the two video sessions.

"Lee is totally credible. Every minute detail of which I am aware is consistent with things I know. I work with a handwriting expert, and I will have her analyze Lee's signature that I obtained. Can you get a set of fingerprints for me? I can get an expert to check them against the real Oswald prints." They exited the room and walked to the nurses' station.

"Well, what did you think, Hunter?"

"I am fascinated how you can use hypnosis like that. It amazes me. You are doing your detective work in someone's head, and that astounds me. I enjoyed the entire experience today except for the beginning. As far as Lee is of concern, like you, I feel like he is Lee Harvey Oswald although we know that it impossible. Lee is credible. However, I am certain that Lee was assassinated, and I was present when they exhumed the body. There were too many witnesses, even at the hospital, to say otherwise. The hospital made all staff members that had anything to do with Lee available to the press. Lee Harvey Oswald was DOA. There is no question about that."

Gottlieb broke in. "Hunter, as a physician I want you to know that Erick is indeed Erick Anderson. His physiologic age is the same as Erick and inconsistent with Lee, who would be thirty-plus years older. I cannot explain this whole thing. I am at a total loss to explain it."

On the way home, Hunter decided to locate Jett & Son Quarry the following day. The four a.m. screaming alarm clock awoke him. He was off to North Texas. He'd loaded his pickup the night before; all he had to do was fill his thermos with hot coffee and grab his prepared lunch.

Hunter had lived alone ever since his wife passed from cancer, so the Oswald situation engaged his mind totally. He personally believed that, even had the CIA cleared the quarry, there would have been a lot of casings lying around for him to discover, at least one. He also believed that if he could locate the hill behind the target area, thousands of bullets would be buried therein. The CIA would never try to remove them. Hunter pondered, *If I found one, I could check it against the bullet found during the autopsy. Can I locate the quarry?* That's my major question?

Since Lee had mentioned the chain-link fence, he also loaded two five-foot aluminum ladders in his Ford Ranger pickup bed. He wanted to be ready for any eventuality.

On Sunday, August 20 when the coffee was ready and the thermos filled, Hunter headed out to his Ranger. He poured a cup of coffee in his spill-proof cup and started driving in the light summer drizzle. Minutes later, he was headed south on Highway 77, heading for Gainesville, Texas. The radio played soft music, and Hunter's mind recalled in vivid detail the day earlier when he had talked to Lee. Jacob had been correct about one thing, and it was an experience he would always remember. It was impossible to describe the hatred Lee had first exuded when he met Hunter, and he was grateful for his good fortune of talking in Russian. *If I talk to Lee again, I will always start the conversation in Russian.*

A scraggy coyote scampered across the road in Hunter's headlights to vanish in the tall grass alongside the road. The miles passed by in the darkness as the telephone and power poles flicked by in his headlights. Hunter wondered, *Lee Harvey Oswald has been dead many years. How can this be possible? How could Erick's mind house Lee's mind? It is impossible, but so many improbable elements of the scenario have been proven correct. It is up to me to prove otherwise. This is something Jacob can't do.*

The skies didn't appear to lighten until he was just north of Gainesville, Texas. The weather forecast on the radio announced light rain for the entire day. He slowed and drove deliberately, looking for Highway 82 West or a sign saying "St. Jo." In the rain, the sign appeared before him, and Hunter turned west. About ten minutes later, he saw the Highway 69 sign and Montague too. As he turned, he guessed the quarry was on this road about four miles ahead. He noted his odometer and jotted down a mileage number. The drizzle persisted, which kept the dust down on the broken-down road paved in a few locations. His shocks on the pickup required replacement, and occasionally a tire hit a chuckhole and slammed his teeth together.

The roadside area was becoming desolate without homes or buildings. The early-morning sun was trying to make its way through the clouds, but although it was unsuccessful, it was illuminating the area. Ahead on his right, he saw the old bunker from a quarry in the filtered light. A check of the odometer let him know this was likely the quarry he was seeking.

He excitedly turned onto a long driveway; the buildings were several hundred yards in from the road. He noticed a fallen-down sign of Jett & Son. His pickup moved slowly across a cattle guard.

Hunter drove forward until he came to a cyclone fence and steel gate. All the visible structures appeared dilapidated. A gate with a chain and lock closing it appeared in his headlights. A large sign saying "Keep Out, Violators will be prosecuted" and another sign, which said, "Beware, Property Patrolled" were nailed to a post ahead.

He backed his four-wheel-drive pickup to the county road. He noticed an old, scraggy chestnut tree with branches touching the ground. He maneuvered his pickup under it so the truck was hidden from the road. It didn't matter whether the branches scratched his truck; he was at Jett & Son Quarry.

Hunter leaned one of the aluminum ladders against the cyclone fence at an acute angle. Then, climbing the ladder, he hoisted the second ladder over the barbed wire at the top and dropped it down against the fence on the other side. Carrying his lunch, notepad, a sack of tools, and his camera, he climbed to the top of one ladder and stepped over the fence and onto the second ladder without a single tug from the barbed wire. After stepping down and placing his supplies on the ground, he climbed the second ladder and hoisted the first ladder over the fence, tossing both in the weeds. He walked through the weeds to the driveway and went down the unused road for another hundred yards, carrying his supplies.

The bunker to his left stood tall and leaned a little to the north. He walked toward a small building to the right of the bunker, which

Lee claimed was where the rifle had been assembled. That crumbling building was almost on the ground now with the roof falling to the rear with the backside touching the ground. The only door was facing skyward. It would take some time to tear that building apart to find anything. *I'll check out this building later.* Hunter lugged his supplies out to the area where Lee had reported a rifle range.

When he arrived, he asked himself, *could this have been a rifle range?* It was flat and level as Lee had said. He pulled out his notebook, protecting it from the drizzle, sketched the area as he saw it, and paced off distances.

After a few photos, it was time to look for casings. As he walked around, he saw none along the entire candidate shooting areas. He grabbed a trowel from his tool bag just in case he found something worth digging. The grounds appeared to be cleared, or there were no casings. At least, he saw nothing except an endless supply of dead weeds with new grass beginning to grow through them. He simply couldn't see any exposed ground.

He made a wider search area from where he guessed Lee would have been standing when practicing. High-power rifles can eject casings some distance, so Hunter expanded his search area. As he walked back to the long, rectangular metal building, he noticed a different metal color wedged under the corrugated siding. He located a screwdriver in his bag, wrapped tape around the tip, and pried out the metal cylinder. It was indeed a casing of a bullet in reasonably good condition, protected by the siding. He dropped it into a plastic collection bag he had brought along and continued his search.

The rectangular building was located on a concrete pad. He examined the crack between the siding and the pad by running the stick along the crack starting at the closest end. If the stick contacted something, he stopped and used the stick to pry out something, generally a rock. Then, not too far from the suspected practice area, the stick kicked something out. He leaned over to examine it and found a metal cylinder. His fingernail verified that it was a cartridge, and he dropped it into the collection bag.

Hunter spent twenty minutes searching the general area. Having found nothing more, he moved down to the far end, where Lee said he had practiced shooting at a moving target. Again, he tried using the stick and forcing it along the edge of the concrete pad and the dirt. This time the stick kicked up another casing. All three appeared to be the same caliber.

It then occurred to him that the weeds had been building up and composting for years. Any casings would likely be under the newly formed soil. He reached down with both hands, grabbed a large handful of dead grass, and pulled upward. Begrudgingly, the grass came up with a huge dirt ball attached around the roots, exposing the rocky subsoil below. Perhaps an inch of dirt was removed. He then looked at the hole just made. The ground was covered with crushed rock without a casing. He began pulling more weeds and throwing them away. On one of his throws, he took time to examine the root ball and saw a casing. He removed it and added it to the collection bag. Hunter continued the process until he had thirteen casings.

His heavy-duty tool bag provided him with a collapsible shovel. Turning toward the open area, he unfolded the shovel into form as he walked toward the mound supposedly behind the target area. *If Lee had been shooting his rifle here, then bullets were in this mound.*

The moist ground was packed sand and free of the base rock and/ or clay. He pulled the weed clumps and feverishly threw them aside, continuing to pull weeds until he cleared a ten-foot area about mid-height of the hill. Then he began digging and making a mound beside him.

Shoveling was made easy by the sandhill. His hole would be three to four feet deep before he guessed he would find any bullets. His hole was getting larger as was the mound he had created.

An hour later, the hole depth was achieved. He now removed dirt in thin layers to spot by sight or feel of the shovel tip any bullets he may find. Methodically, he worked inward in an area. Now using a trowel, he felt a hard, small object. He got down on his knees and felt the area. He removed the dirt, and indeed it was a bullet. He walked back to the concrete slab and picked up the plastic bag, returning it to the dig. As he walked, he cleaned the exterior with his fingernail and inserted the bullet into a casing.

It was a perfect match. He was euphoric.

Hey, don't get too excited, you old fool. It may be the wrong bullet. I won't know that until I examine the casings at the museum and more importantly, the bullet that killed President Kennedy.

Hunter continued his deliberate task and slowly dug up another ten bullets. They too were the same caliber. As he was digging, he became worried about the CIA. Did they still monitor this site anymore? He decided to play it safe and fill in his hole. Before he did that, he walked over to his tool bag and removed his camera; he began shooting photos of the general area including where he had pulled up the grass balls. Then he grabbed his shovel and filled in the newly dug hole, throwing dead grass back over the top and stamping it down. It was now lunchtime, and he was anxious to get out of the drizzle, so he collected his lunch pail and sat under the eaves of the metal building, feeling proud of himself.

After lunch, Hunter decided to leave that area and examine the fallen-down shack. The backside of the building was rotted and lay on the ground. Part of the roof laid on top of it. The building was a single-wall construction, which explained why it had collapsed along with rotten boards while all other buildings stood upright. The front side faced skyward but wasn't horizontal. The highest point of the roof, at the front of the small building, was perhaps two feet above the ground.

Hunter pushed on the siding to see whether it would be safe to crawl inside. After several pushes, he decided that crawling in a short distance was okay. He opened the door and peered at the floor, seeing nothing. It was awkward opening the door at that angle. Hunter removed a long four-battery flashlight out of his tool bag, bent down, and crawled in one body length. It was difficult to see anything in the far corner, even with the bright light. The floor was covered with thirty years of dust. The old building creaked as he slithered to the right side of the room. The siding had pulled away from the foundation a little in its decaying state. Using the backside of his pocketknife blade, he scraped the gap between the floor and the siding, if the gap existed. He inched sideways and tried again without success. Then he backed toward the open door and repeated the process on the left-hand side, working his way toward the side of the collapsed building. The knife scraped along without anything being discovered except rusty nails until he was at the far end of the room. With the aid of the bright flashlight, his eye spotted a shiny surface. It couldn't be a nail. It was too large. He tried to remove it using the knife, but it was wedged in too tightly.

Hunter slithered out of the building and went to his tool bag, returning to the interior with a tape measure. He measured the distance from the object to the doorframe and maneuvered out of the building. Next, he measured the same distance on the outside of the building and marked the board. He reached into the bag and removed a hammer and a claw-foot nail puller. He didn't want to break the board, so he carefully freed two nailheads and pried them away from the foundation. They moved begrudgingly, providing a loud squeak until there was a gap between the board and frame. He reentered the shack and reached in with his hand to see whether he could feel the metallic object detected earlier. He couldn't see anything, but his fingers felt a cylinder. Using his other hand, he grabbed it with two index fingers and withdrew it, an intact bullet. He pulled out a casing from the plastic collection bag. The casing of the intact bullet appeared to be identical to the casings uncovered.

Hunter was euphoric. It was time to head home. He hammered down the siding with a small hammer. Around the corner of the metal building, he heard human voices. "Over here."

Hunter had no place to hide, and his pickup was too far away to make it. He opened the door of the flattened building and threw his supplies inside, crawled in, and closed the door. He slithered away from the door and positioned himself such that he could see through a half-inch gap in the rotted siding.

Two officers wearing dark-blue uniforms came jogging around the building toward him. Hunter looked down at the ground, where his footprints were discernible. The officers slowed their pace to a walk and began trying to open all the doors of the long, metal building, door by door, still heading in his direction. Yanking the last doorknob, one said, "This one is locked too."

The second officer spoke, and the first officer reached into his pocket and withdrew something; he began fidgeting with the door, which opened. They looked around and brushed cobwebs away. They began to check other doors." They knew what they were doing, which concerned Hunter.

The sky continued to weep. When he looked down, his shoes depressed the soil, leaving a distinct trap for rain. Now the shoe print was filling with water and leaving a water trail aimed directly at his hideaway. ***Keep going guys—keep going***, he thought.

They were now at the far end of the rectangular building, and Hunter breathed a sigh of relief. They were talking, but he couldn't make out what they said. Then one walked around the corner, and the second officer headed his direction. The second man turned and hollered when he was fifty feet from Hunter.

The officer who went around the corner returned into view. "Yep," he shouted, "it came from about there, Tom." They headed off to a small building near what used to be the rifle range.

Hunter heard a squeaking sound within the collapsed building. His head turned in time to see a rat scamper across the corner, then another. Hunter thought this was the time to escape and get the hell out of Texas, so he started sliding forward. But he couldn't move; his shirt was caught on a nail. He would have to back up and try again. He slid backward and pushed up on the siding to create some additional space. One rat ran across his leg. He kicked at it, and it scampered out of sight.

Having moved sideways a little, he slid forward, but minutes had passed. He couldn't see the area where the officers headed. When he got to the entry door, he lifted it just enough to peek out. The door even opened toward the rifle range. He looked in that direction and saw nothing. If he ran, he could be caught, maybe by a bullet, remembering the CIA involvement.

Before he decided what to do, the two officers walked around the corner and were walking directly toward him. He lowered the door and began slithering backward as fast and far as possible given the circumstances. He looked out a crack and noticed that the now-heavy rain overflowed the footprints. The officers were standing on his footprints. He could hear them talking.

Seeing the fallen building, one said to the other, "He can't be in there. It is almost flat."

Hunter's heart raced. A rat scampered across his leg again.

"You're right; maybe we should head over to the bunker."

"Wait a minute, Fred. Let me look inside."

Hunter gasped.

"Don't bother, Tom. I'll flatten the building by jumping on it."

Hunter felt the claws of a rat crawling up his calf under his pant leg. His skin crawled. He reached down and pressed against the bulge.

Then Fred, who was well over two hundred pounds, ran and jumped on the siding, smashing Hunter head between the siding and floor. He thought to cover his mouth and nose with his left hand and withstood the impact without uttering a sound, but the building groaned. The frightened rat scampered away.

"Come on, Tom, you can't do it by yourself? Let me help." Both men starting running toward the collapsed building and jumped, sandwiching Hunter's head between the siding and flooring. It hurt, but Hunter made no sound. "Hey, Fred," said one of them. "Look at the two rats running away. We scared the shit out of them. Look at them go." They both chuckled as they walk away. "Let's go to the bunker."

Hunter waited for some time and thought how fortunate he was that no nails were protruding over his head. In total silence, he listened for the sound of an engine starting. He had no idea whether they had seen his hidden vehicle. If they had, they certainly would write down his license plate number. He worked his way back to the door and opened it a small amount at a time, inspecting the surroundings for the officers. Then and only then did he open the door fully and crawl out of the building with his bounty.

He crept over to the fence, threw the tools over it, leaned a ladder up against the fence, and climbed over as he had entered. He examined the ground to see whether he could see footprints. He saw none and generated a smile of relief. He looked at his watch and noted the time of nearly three p.m. *Oh my God, that was close. It's time to leave Jett & Son.*

Chapter 14: The Blue Bicycle

Jacob answered the ringing phone. "Jacob, are you free to talk right now?"

"Yes! What's wrong, Sophia?"

"Today at lunch with you, Mike, and Erick, I realized I no longer love Erick, and I am uncertain that I can continue this charade. Whenever Erick touches me, my skin crawls. A couple of weeks ago when I was near him, I vomited. I can't control these things. My body is just reacting. I hate it, just hate it. I do feel sorry for Erick because he cannot help what's happening."

"Sophia, I know the problem. If you could erase that bad memory, would you feel any different?"

"I suppose I would. But why should I? It really happened once and could happen again. In fact, it could even be worse! Imagine getting cut up by a chainsaw."

"I am not going to let Erick out of the hospital until I believe it will not happen again. It is not only you that I am concerned about but also society in general. Lee could have killed you and others on the highway and city streets, and that includes the highway patrol officer. I cannot let that happen. On the other hand, I cannot lock Erick up for life for something that may never happen. Psychiatry isn't a perfect science, and we do make mistakes. But we try to err on the side of caution. Erick is a kind, wonderful man. Lee is the antithesis of that. Thus, Erick's personality is a veritable Dr. Jekyll and Mr. Hyde."

"Jacob, maybe I should be out of the equation because that is the way I feel inside right now. I have to deal with a husband who is depressed and institutionalized, a terrible, mean-spirited second personality that may appear at any minute and wants to kill me, and you, a doctor who wants me to stay with both of them when everything in my body screams run away."

"I understand that, Sophia, but without you, I do not believe Erick has a chance. See him as you have and offer him encouragement. Bring along a jigsaw puzzle you can both work on together without much dialogue. All that I ask, at least for a few more months, is to continue a little longer, please."

"I'll think about it, Jacob, but you should know ahead of time that I absolutely hate it."

"I understand, Sophia. I am working hard trying to solve the puzzle, and I will."

"Okay Jacob. I'll try a little longer, but I do not know how much more I can take."

"Sophia, do you believe it would do you any good if you saw my partner, Dr. Hanford? He is a wonderful doctor."

"Not now, Jacob."

When she hung up, Jacob knew time had run out on that marriage. That meant time was also running out on Erick. Right then and there, he wanted to make Erick well in the worst way, but he still had no explanation for the phenomenon called Lee. Further, he didn't know the trigger that had caused it. Jacob was frustrated.

He turned to his reading when the phone rang again. It was a male voice he didn't quite recognize. "Jacob, this is Hunter Tripp speaking."

"Professor, how are you?"

"I am exceedingly well tonight and very excited, very excited."

"About what?"

"I went to the Jett & Son Quarry early this morning and spent most of the day there."

"No! You did? Did you uncover anything?"

"Yes, I did. I uncovered many casings, and I also found about ten bullets in the hill located behind the target area. Further, the bullets and casings match. The casings appear very much like the one found in the attic of the depository building."

"Wow," muttered Jacob. "That is exciting news."

"Guess what, Jacob? I also located an intact, unused bullet."

"Amazing work, Hunter. You didn't tell me you were going."

"I didn't know I was going when I left you yesterday, but on the way home, I said to myself, *Why not?* I saw what you did, and I wanted to contribute in the worst way. I know how you feel, Jacob. My hands are trembling. There were armed guards at the quarry, and I almost got caught. It was frightening."

"Who were they?"

"I do not know for sure, but they weren't county sheriffs, and they weren't private police either. They were armed and very professional, and they wore dark-blue uniforms, so I am guessing they were federal police or marshals."

"Wow, Hunter, I am pleased that you are safe."

"I will be at the Kennedy Museum this Thursday, and I can discreetly compare the actual bullet that killed President Kennedy with a few of my samples. Since I have hands-on authority in the museum, I can also compare my casings with the one found on the floor of the attic. I should have an opinion by Friday night."

"Please let me know!"

"You can count on it. I promise."

"How come you have access to those bullets?"

"The museum has selected a group of us for accreditation. I am one of those people. This means I have keys to all of the various files and exhibits. I also have a study room there at the museum, so I can do my comparison in complete privacy—even lock the door. I will bring along my own high-caliber zoom microscope. I have a camera mount built into it, so I can photograph the two bullets and casings side by side."

"Wow! Hunter, fantastic work! What a blessing for me to find you."

"Jacob, it would be extremely valuable to have the bicycle dismantling process pass standard accreditation procedures. This means have an expert, besides me, witness the process and document it. Maybe let the FBI do it."

"You are asking me to commit suicide, Hunter. The answer is no." Jacob spoke with a resolute voice.

"We are dealing with an extremely important moment in our history."

"I don't give a damn, Hunter. I am doing this to save a man's life from a killer and not get killed in the process. I am doing this to learn who Lee is in order to treat my patient. History doesn't enter my decision process—the Hippocratic oath does."

"Maybe it should, Jacob. History repeats itself, so it could happen again. The more we learn, the less likely for it to repeat. I am only asking for another committee member to witness the bicycle dismantling. Please consider what I am asking."

There was a pause in the conversation as Jacob mulled over Hunter's request. "Okay, Hunter, but here are my conditions. One, Jim and my names, occupations, and my home address will not be divulged to this person. Two, Jim and my face will not be photographed. Three, this person will be blindfolded between your home and my home until I close my garage door and during the return trip too. Four, this person must sign a confidentiality disclosure form with you regarding releasing this guarded information. And five, the exposed film will be given to me, and I will see that prints are provided."

"I would like more freedom, Jacob, to use my discretion."

"I am extremely concerned about the CIA disposing of me. I can't, Hunter. Take it or leave it!"

"Okay, Jacob, I'll take it."

After some grumbling, Hunter hung up the call.

Jacob dialed Jim immediately and passed along Hunter's report and the new witness, giving Jim the option of staying home.

Saturday morning arrived with Jacob stimulated about the upcoming event, the attempted dismantling of the bicycle to form the intact rifle that assassinated President John Fitzgerald Kennedy. At eight o'clock, he was out in the garage, arranging his workbench.

Jacob's hobby was restoring classic cars, so he accepted the bicycle as his latest challenge. As a consequence of his experiences with damaged and corroded mechanical parts, he possessed a plethora of special purpose tools, and it was these tools he was readying for use on the workbench. The bicycle was placed in a bicycle stand Jacob had purchased for the situation. With the stand, they could work on the bicycle in the middle of the garage floor, but the bench-mounted vice was still available if needed.

Jim Hanford was the first to arrive, and as they waited for Hunter, Jacob showed him color prints taken by Jerry of Jacob in the water, holding a muddy bicycle over his head.

Jim walked up to the bike stand. He passed his left index finger across the blue horizontal bar, which was believed to be the rifle barrel.

"Jim, notice that there are six rear gears and two front gears, just like Lee said."

"Jacob, this horizontal bar sure looks as if it is part of the bicycle and not a rifle barrel. Look at the junction of the horizontal bar. They look as if they are one. I can't see how you can separate these pieces."

"Look closely, Jim!" said Jacob, pointing at the slight rust buildup at the junction. "If these were welded together and then painted, this union would still be blue like this horizontal bar, but it's not. This means they are separate pieces and note that the rusting is the same at the other end of the horizontal bar." Jim nodded as he heard Jacob's explanation.

"It should be interesting to see, if we can remove it," Jacob said as Hunter and his blindfolded colleague walked in the open garage.

"Hi, gentlemen!" Hunter said as he walked through the open garage door, leading his guest by the elbow. Jacob pushed the button to close the garage door as Hunter began removing the blindfold.

"Gentlemen, may I introduce you to Dr. Anthony Chester of the University of Texas."

Jim walked over to greet him with an extended hand. Jacob followed, and the greetings concluded. Jim slapped Hunter on his back and said, "Congratulations for your discovery of Jett & Son and the bullets."

Following social dialogue, Jacob wheeled over a bright lamp mounted on a portable stand and began pointing out the features of the bicycle. "I was able to remove the seat, and it is located on the workbench." Jacob grabbed a strangely shaped but symmetrically bent piece attached to the bar joining the drive sprocket to the handlebars. "This piece is called the 'stock' of the rifle and also serves as a water bottle holder when mounted on the bike. Note, this piece here," he said as he moved his hand over to the bar connecting the saddle to the drive sprocket. "This is the cushion for the shoulder end of the stock, and this metal piece here attaches to this piece over there." He pointed to part of the stock.

"I have been soaking these critical points in WD-40 for about two weeks. Hopefully, it will make life a little easier today. Let's remove these first because they will be easiest to get off, and second, this rubber piece is water damaged, and we don't want to damage it further. Both pieces are held on by wing nuts, so I will first brush the threads off with this fine-gauge wire brush."

Jacob wrapped a cloth around the bar to avoid scratching the paint when he brushed the treads. After a couple of minutes, he clamped a vice grip onto the bottom wing nut, painted blue, and began turning. At first, the nut held tight, but the WD40 did its job, and with continuing pressure an expert mechanic knows how to apply, the wing nut loosened and came off. Next Jacob moved up to the top wing nut and repeated the process with the same results. He then tapped the screws inward to loosen them with a light hammer and a metal punch removed them from the opposite side. Using the same hammer and special curved tool, something like a curved screwdriver, he drove it between the rubbery piece and the vertical bar with light taps of the hammer. The rubber moved away without cracking further.

"I believe that the rubber was bonded originally to a metal piece I am now tapping. The screws holding it are gone, so I only have to break loose the corrosion bond. Hunter, would you catch the piece when it comes loose?"

Hunter moved up, and Jacob rapped it hard a few more times, moving vertically upward with each rap until the metal pieces separated and fell into Hunter's waiting hands. During the procedure, Anthony, who was listening intently to what Jacob was saying, snapped photos.

"We need to talk about the rifle barrel assembly before I start," stated Jacob, looking each man in the eyes in turn. "Now look over here on the column passing up to the seat. There is a painted hex-head nut located here protruding from the backside, indicating that this junction is active. Now look at the junction under the handlebars. Do you see this round blue knob facing forward with a reflector mounted to it? This assembly must be active too. I believe it is threaded, and by unscrewing them, we will withdraw a solid, smooth shaft that enters into the rifle barrel at each end. "What do you guys think?"

Jim wasn't mechanically inclined and stepped back. Hunter started toward the bike and remained silent as he studied the bike and pondered Jacob's question. "We need to get the handlebars off first to know for sure."

"You are correct, Hunter. Then we can look down the tube and see the assembly—after we clean it, of course."

"Good idea, Jacob! Let's do it."

Jacob walked over to his tools, removed a fabric-strapping wrench, and returned with it and a roll of black electrical tape. Both men stared at him as he started wrapping the stainless-steel collar that tightened the handlebar shaft within the tube multiple times with the electrical tape. Then he opened the wrench, adjusted it, and placed it over the tape. "Okay, this is probably going to take a lot of force, so I need someone to hold the bike and bike stand."

Jim stepped forward since he needed to be part of the discovery. With both hands on the end of the one-foot handle of the wrench, Jacob began pulling mightily, but the contrary unit remained fixed. He walked over to his workbench and returned with a three-foot-long steel pipe and slid it over the handle of the wrench to lengthen it. Now, with both hands on the end of the pipe, he began again. "This is going to loosen it or twist the metal," he said as he slowly increased his force. Slowly and begrudgingly, the cantankerous collar began to turn.

"It's moving, Jacob," Jim offered.

Jacob then removed the three-foot-long galvanized pipe from the wrench and began removing the collar with only the strap wrench. He added more WD-40 between the collar and tube. "Let's give it a few minutes to penetrate before we try to remove the handlebars."

Jacob motioned the men to join him at the workbench as he walked over to it. He reached into the plastic cup that contained the trigger assembly and removed it, placing it on several red shop rags. Rusty WD-40 liquid ran off the surface into the rags as they all looked at the red-rust-colored surface. After several more wipes with clean rags, the assembly began to look more like a trigger. He pulled out his electric wire brush, placed the device into the vice, and began wire-brushing the surface. A few minutes later, the exterior trigger assembly was shiny and clean but remained fused internally.

After a thorough external cleaning, Jacob laid it down on a clean rag. "Hunter, may I have the bullet now?" Hunter handed it to him, and Jacob laid it on the rag, just below the magazine portion of the trigger assembly. He reached up on the shelf and picked up his camera. The flashes popped as he took four photos of the two items lying on the clean rag from different angles, as did Anthony. When Jacob finished, he turned to his accomplices, saying, "The interior of the magazine is too dirty right now to insert the bullet, but we can see that the chamber and magazine are the correct length for this bullet. Also note that the magazine is designed into the trigger assembly, further indicating that the weapon was a special design for one purpose—killing someone— maybe a president."

Hunter nodded in agreement as Jacob reached down, retrieved the bullet, and returned it to Hunter. "I believe that the trigger assembly is sufficiently cleaned to integrate it mechanically into the other rifle parts, if we are able to separate them from this rusty bike, to determine whether they form the blue rifle."

Jacob continued, "Okay, let's see if we can remove the handlebars." Jacob stood at the front of the bike with his two hands gripping the handlebars and his two legs straddling the front wheel. He planned to remove the bar by rotating the handlebars back and forth while pulling upward, thereby freeing them from the fused enclosure. The first twist and pull on the bars yielded nothing. "Okay, how about some more manpower?"

The three men began the disassembly technique of freeing the handlebars using high torque to do it. "I think it moved a little," Jacob said. After another drop of WD-40, the continuation began again. Jacob now rotated the handlebars about thirty degrees back and forth. He continued the rotation until the handlebars rotated a full circle, and while he pulled upward, the handlebars popped free, almost smacking him in the mouth.

Jacob walked over to his bench and returned with an empty coffee can. "What's that for?" asked Jim.

"I am going to drain the dirty water inside the tubes. Professor, will you hold the can while Jim and I pick up the bike and pour the water into the can?"

The column was filled with perhaps a cup of water, which flowed into the can with a copious quantity of rust. Jim replaced the bicycle in the stand, and Jacob returned from his bench with a bright flashlight.

"Everything is too dirty to see much down there." He grabbed one of the rags and twisted it into a cylinder with a pointed end. He pushed it into the open column, rotating it continuously while pushing it in. Upon removal, Jacob said, "look, there's something down there, and perhaps our rag cleaned things up a bit. He was correct, and when the light beam entered the column, a threaded bolt became visible.

"Now this is going to be tricky removing the reflector/bolt assembly." Jacob grabbed another clean rag and wiped the backside of the reflector. "I could start to unscrew it here." Jacob went over to a specialty drawer with two wrenches. The first one fit the bolt head under the reflector, so he placed it carefully on the bolt and began a counterclockwise rotation. No movement occurred. Jacob then returned from the work bench with a propane torch. "Let's give this bolt a little heat. Maybe we can loosen the corrosion bond."

Jacob waited for the bolt to cool down, and then he tried the wrench again. With the same force, the bolt turned a little. Begrudgingly, the bolt turned. The process continued until the bolt, with the reflector still attached, was removed, leaving a smooth, threadless end with a hemispherical tip. "This smooth end goes inside the rifle barrel and holds the end of the rifle barrel securely in place," Jacob commented. "The head is hemispherical end is shaped that way so as not to damage the rifling when the bolt is threaded into place. Now we will continue the process with the bolt on the opposite side." After comparable effort, that bolt was removed.

"Okay, now we are left with the rifle barrel. It will be necessary to break the corrosion bond with force. We will use the rubber hammer for that by pounding it upward a little at one end and then the other.

Jim, you hold the bicycle, and I will tap it." There was a squeak as he struck it. Millimeter by millimeter, the barrel lifted until it popped out in Jacob's hand. Jacob handed it to Hunter.

Hunter held up the barrel to his eye, aiming at the overhead light. "Jacob, I can't see through this thing." Jacob went over to another closet and returned with a rifle cleaning kit. "I have never had occasion to use this before, but there is always a first time for everything." He ran the rod with an oiled rag through the entire length of the barrel without any physical obstruction. Next, he changed rags saturated with fresh cleaning oil and repeated the process. "Here, Professor, do your thing. He handed the barrel and cleaning equipment to Tripp. Okay, guys, all the rifle parts are free."

Anthony began photographing the bicycle still mounted in the stand as the others eyed the barrel after Hunter laid it on the workbench.

"Did you look through it Hunter," Jacob asked.

"Yes, you can see the rifling."

Jacob departed into the house and returned with freshly brewed pot of coffee. "Time out, gents," he said as he handed each a cup of French roast coffee.

Jacob wiped the trigger assembly with clean towels from the workbench, and placed all the key pieces in a correct physical position for assembly but without touching one another. The next step was to determine whether the pieces would assemble into a rifle. Camera bulbs flashed.

"The way I see it, gents, the barrel attaches to the trigger here by slipping the barrel into this hole like thus. It locks into place with these two pins placed horizontally. I located these pins in the leather pouch and cleaned them earlier."

These pins would slide horizontally across the trigger assembly, into these two holes locking the assembly. "That's why the barrel is thicker than normal. It must accommodate these two pins while maintaining structural integrity during discharge. We won't slide them in now because the holes have not been cleaned,"

These two tiny pieces I found in the decaying leather saddlebag must be the sights on the barrel, and he pushed them partially into a tiny hole in the barrel. The holes were still plugged, and the sights wouldn't bottom out, but clearly the parts were correctly deployed.

Anthony cast a discerning eye on the leather pouch, then asked, "Why didn't the leather pouch rot away underwater?"

Jim volunteered an answer. "When organic materials remain free of oxygen, organic things won't rot. The answer is, there was insufficient oxygen in the mud at the bottom to cause substantial decay."

"Oh, I see," Anthony said.

Jacob continued, "The stock has to assemble into the trigger assembly here, but we still need to clean up this area first." Jacob grabbed his Dremel tool kit from the shelf and plugged it into the wall socket. Next, he inserted a soft wire brush into the tool and began brushing the stock assembly. He continued brushing for several minutes as Hunter and Jim looked over his shoulder and sipped coffee. Jacob set the Dremel aside and brought the stock up to the trigger assembly again. "The trigger should drop into this channel slide." He pressed downward, and the stock snapped into the assembly. The cushioned shoulder piece dropped into the stock. After he said these words, the intact rifle took form. "I won't insert the two pins now, but you can see where they go and why the assembly requires them."

"There you are, doctors, just like Lee said," spoke a beaming Jacob.

Anthony, Hunter, and Jim were astonished at the sight. "Imagine all of this on that bicycle in public view," volunteered Jim Hanford. Everyone snapped pictures of the assembled rifle. Flashes brightened the garage.

"Some serious engineering went into the design of this weapon," Hunter remarked. "Gentlemen, I would like to restore this rifle to usable state if possible. I would do so at my expense and knowing that it is your property, but it is a valuable piece of history. May I take it piece by piece, starting with the trigger assembly? I have a good friend who believes he can restore the trigger. If he can, we can verify the imprint on the shell casing caused by the hammer with those found at the assassination site. That is the last piece of the puzzle to test your hypothesis that Lee assassinated the president using this rifle."

Anthony jumped in, saying, "That is a great idea, Hunter. Please Jacob and Jim consider Hunter's request carefully."

"Hunter, let Jim and me talk first for a minute." Jim and Jacob walked to the corner of the garage and conferred. Jacob returned to Hunter, reached into the sack, and handed him the trigger assembly. "Okay, Hunter, here you are. Take good care of it. I am going to work on the rest of the bicycle."

"Thanks, Jacob. You won't regret it."

Chapter 15: The Key

On the following Tuesday evening, a white Malibu moved through the streets of Oklahoma City on a blustery, sticky summer evening, heading to a restaurant near the town center. Sophia anxiously passed the time after work at a beauty parlor and waited for the eight p.m. dinner. Now the time for dinner arrived. She justified having dinner with Jacob by knowing it was the only way she could get an accurate assessment of Erick's condition, but now her mind had reached a new stage—she didn't care. She also hoped Jacob wouldn't pursue that point as he had in the past few weeks by pressuring her to continue the course and visiting Erick daily. Dinner at a swank restaurant like La Forét added luster to the evening and increased her interest. It was an offer she couldn't refuse.

She also justified the dinner engagement as a means of getting back some of the money she had invested in Erick's treatments. However, there was the other side of the coin, and that was that she wanted to be with Jacob. Ever since the afternoon at the motel when she felt Jacob had rescued her from the heinous Lee and doctored her wounds, she was unquestionably drawn to him—not just casually but in a deep-down visceral attraction. She thought about the awkwardness of the situation: herself, her husband, her husband's doctor, and obviously Lee. She found her mind involved with a very complicated foursome, and only part of it was appealing.

The events as they unfolded for her were unreal. Jacob was all those things Erick wasn't: bright, witty, good with his hands so he said. He demonstrated deep caring for people, whereas Erick was superficial and cared only about people when it suited him, with the exceptions of herself, Mary, and Sean. She had badgered him to spend some time with Mary's husband, Bart, after Mary's and Sean's deaths, but Erick simply procrastinated and did nothing except call Bart one time. Imagine losing a wife and son like that. There was no question in her mind that Erick had been good to her during their marriage until the dream, which changed everything. Now she had been considering how far was far enough for their marriage.

Sophia was contemplating divorce. Certainly, some of the kind folks at Wednesday night church group therapy had encouraged her to follow the course during Erick's treatments. The stark reality of her situation hit her. Jacob would ask her to stay the course too. She would never know about his feelings, and she suspected that Jacob would do only those things to encourage her to continue onward to assist Erick. The dinner would be a waste of time except for the wonderful gourmet delights. Somehow, she had to make it fun.

Sophia pulled into the parking lot, fashionably late, and walked into the restaurant, looking for Jacob. It was easy to spot him. Jacob was now sipping his warm cognac in the corner while deep in deliberation. She sauntered to the table and said, "Hi! A penny for your thoughts, stranger." Her voice startled Jacob from his thoughts, and he rose to greet her with a smile on his freshly shaved face. Jacob walked around the table to greet her, and they embraced with a bear hug. As they ended the hug, Jacob kissed her on the cheek and pulled out her chair to seat her. He helped her remove her coat and hung it over the unoccupied chair.

Jacob, in a temporary loss for words, found himself staring at her. "Sophia, you look—fabulous. You didn't go to work looking like that, did you?"

"No, Jacob. Today happened to be my day at the beauty parlor. I am pleased that you approve, however. How nice of you to notice. How are you?"

"I am fine, Sophia, just fine." The obligatory beginning started along with a waitress asking Sophia whether she cared for a cocktail. She ordered a vodka and tonic, and the preliminaries were underway.

"Jacob, you must first tell me about Erick and how he is progressing." *I want to get all conversation about Erick out of the way immediately*, she thought.

Jacob gave her a sorrowful look. "Sophia, I am afraid that I have bad news for you, because the answer is still the same. The nightmares continue according to the night nurses, not Erick. Erick believes he is well over the malady, but it's not true. Lee is still there, and unfortunately Lee is doing well. He is getting stronger every day. In fact, Mike believes he saw an unsuccessful attempt by Lee to take over Erick during daytime hours."

"What are you going to do about it?" she asked in a monotonic voice.

"I have recently made several important discoveries, but unfortunately they are about Lee, not Erick. The worse news of all is that I have yet to uncover the key. If I can find the key, I believe I can get rid of Lee. I originally thought the key lay with Lee, but after extensive interviews with experts about Lee, I have discovered nothing more about the malady. I now have Drs. Hanford and Tripp assisting me on occasion, but the key eludes us." Then Jacob quickly added, "These experts were at no cost to you, Sophia." Then he continued on with the original thought. "We have learned a great deal about Lee, and that ultimately will teach us how to get rid of him. At this moment, I have only minimal good news."

There was a pause in the conversation before Jacob spoke again as a means of changing the subject. "How are you dealing with your situation?"

"I have started the therapy class at my church as I told you, but it is too early in the two meetings to say anything about its possible success. The good part of it as you know is to discover that I am not alone in having an impossible problem. People have so many problems that I am now uncertain how we can operate a civilized society. Some people in political power must have comparable problems too."

Jacob spoke up. "Of course, they do, Sophia, and the continued success of our country puzzles me too."

"Let's decide on our dinner."

The obligatory social dialogue continued, since both were still uncomfortable in this situation. Finally, the roasted Guinea fowl and sautéed scallops were served.

The candlelight flickered, and the background music played, and softness surrounded the two. They were becoming comfortable with one another. Their voices became quiet and mellifluous as if someone were listening to their conversation, although the room was now entirely void of diners. They looked directly into each other's eyes, and there was a continual smile on both faces. Their fingertips met, with Jacob's hands on the bottom. Jacob said something humorous, and Sophia patted his hand.

Sophia asked Jacob about his interests. "Do you have any hobbies, Jacob?"

"Yes, I do. I restore classic cars."

"Really, a doctor doing that! I would have never guessed. Where do you keep them? I do not remember seeing any in your garage."

"I generally do the work in my garage. I am in the process of locating my new chassis."

"Where do you find them?" asked the interested woman with sparkling, green eyes.

"It really depends on a lot of variables. Sometimes they are wrecks, other times just used cars, and often a car someone started and didn't complete."

"Where do you get parts for older cars?" she asked.

"One can order them from a club, but mostly I get them from an auto-wrecking yard."

"Really, I can't imagine you in a wrecking yard."

"I have spent many hours in wrecking yards fetching parts. I enjoy it."

"I just can't picture a psychiatrist as an auto mechanic."

"It is the antithesis of my everyday activity, so I find enjoyment in it. It is also very enriching to turn a wreck into a showpiece. Two years ago, my restored 1950 Cadillac Seville was judged the best of show."

"Do you keep them, Jacob, or do you sell them after you have restored them?"

"I am not a Jay Leno, so I generally sell them and buy new tools with my profits. Right now, I keep one car I have restored. It's a 1930 Alpha Romeo. I keep it because it was my first restored car. Do you have a favorite older car, Sophia?"

"Yes, I like the looks of the Thunderbird with the porthole windows on the sides."

"That is the 1957 model, where they dropped the grill down into the front bumper and added a circular back window. They are very popular now, Sophia, and if you had one, it would be a very good investment."

Conversation about cars continued though much of the dinner. Then Jacob asked her about her hobbies.

"On winter days, I like to crochet. I have made all of our bedspreads in the house and most of the doilies."

"That's a terrific and useful hobby. I always wished I had a beautiful, crocheted bedspread. Nowadays, one cannot even find a nice bedspread in the better stores. I was going to ask my mother to make me one, but she passed away before I had a chance."

The waitress arrived with the bill, and Jacob tossed a credit card on the platter.

There was silence for a few moments, so Sophia filled it with a question. "Do you have a girlfriend, Jacob?"

"No," said Jacob.

"Why? Are you gay?"

Without thinking it through, Jacob uttered a rather loud, noisy, and instantaneous, "No—no." When he looked up, Sophia was laughing, and the laughter got a little louder all the time and carried through the empty restaurant.

She held up her pointed right index finger and drew an imaginary one in the air, about six inches long. She reached across the table, grabbed his hand in both of hers, leaned over toward him, and whispered, "Got you!" Jacob saw the humor in the situation, and he too began to laugh as she outwitted him and made fun of him at his own expense. People generally didn't do that with a sophisticated physician. His smile warmed Sophia heart. He had always been so serious. She liked a man who could laugh at himself, and Jacob had just demonstrated that he could.

When the time came to depart as they were walking out of the restaurant, Jacob looked at her and said, "I hope we can do this again. I so enjoy being around you, Sophia. I truly do."

"I enjoyed myself too, Jacob, but we both are caught in a complicated situation that seems to be unsolvable. I wish circumstances were different. Please know that I consider you the finest, most lovable man I have ever known."

Jacob walked her to the Malibu. Neither wanted to speak. She unlocked the door, opened it, and before entering, turned and kissed him softly on the cheek. She backed into her car.

"Good night, Jacob, and thank you for the dinner and the laughs."

Jacob stood there in the light wind, watching Sophia drive away.

On the following night, Jacob answered a telephone call. "Jacob, my friend was able to separate the trigger assembly and polish the parts. The assembly is slightly pockmarked but looks terrific."

"How did he do it, Hunter?"

"The rusted assembly spent forty-eight hours in an ultrasonic bath in the solvent AquaKlean. He had to change the solvent four times, twice on the first day. The ultrasonic cleaner was particularly effective on the rusted parts. He showed me the unit this afternoon, and you cannot believe it is the same device. He is putting it through a special bluing process now, and that will be done next week. I placed the bullet in it without him seeing me do it, and it slips into the chamber perfectly too."

Jacob responded, "That's terrific, Hunter. I am anxious to see it. I've been cleaning up some of the remaining parts here too, and they now look better. I had an exact copy leather saddle pouch made by a leather shop. I needed to replace the rubber pieces. I haven't gotten around to that yet, but I purchased bulk rubber. Also, I picked up a bicycle seat from a used bike shop, which looks almost identical to the damaged one, and I purchased a replacement chain, two new tires and tubes, and two used rims. Last night, I cleaned the used rims, replaced a few spokes, and mounted the new tubes and tires. The wheels look like new, if I don't mind saying so myself. I have yet to locate the set of front and rear gears derailleur/cable assembly, but I'll try another shop this weekend. My goal is to restore the bicycle to as near to original as possible and ride it around the block, carrying a concealed weapon too, just like Lee." Hunter chuckled.

"I am still concerned about the rifling in the barrel. I have been cleaning the barrel earlier this evening. It looks okay, but the water damage seems to have eroded a portion of the rifling more than anything else. That was expected because of the surface-to-volume principle in corrosion. I was surprised that the interior of the barrel is as good as I found it. I believe the tight fit at each end where it joins the bicycle frame minimized the oxygen level within the barrel and limited corrosion. Overall, I can't believe how good it appears. Oh yeah, Hunter, I purchased another reflector and mounted a bolt to it, so we can attach the rifle barrel to the bike. I believe it is coming together just great."

"Can you give me the rifle barrel and I'll get it blued."

"We do not want to do that Hunter because I'll paint it. The purpose of bluing is to protect it from weather, but paint does that too."

"Oh!—Jacob, I am anxious to put it all back together again in a restored fashion."

"Me too, Hunter! When we do, don't forget your camera. Did you guys pull the trigger on the trigger assembly?"

"Yes, we did Jacob, and it is working just fine, although it seems slightly loose. Of course, we didn't try to fire a live bullet yet, and I am not certain that we want to do that. But we can trigger one of the spent casings and look at the impact marks and compare those with the one collected at the shooting site. I am selecting one that has minimal damage, and I will pull the trigger on it over the weekend. I should get a good contact and indentation for comparison. Then the next time I am in Dallas, I will do a microscopic comparison of the just-impacted one to the shell recovered in the attic and photograph the results."

"That is hard to believe that you could even get it to operate based on the damage incurred underwater," Jacob sputtered.

"Jacob, this whole affair of dealing with Erick and Lee has been so exciting to me. I have been in the doldrums ever since my wife passed away, and now I anxiously anticipate each new day."

After a brief pause Jacob surrendered, "I too have become involved with this discovery."

Tripp spoke again. "This whole thing, Jacob, is like the culmination of my lifetime work. I can't thank you enough."

"I needed your help, Hunter, and I got infinitely more than I even hoped. It's been my pleasure and good fortune."

"Have you had any further success with Erick/Lee?"

"I have had a couple of sessions with Erick, but for now I am leaving Lee alone. I am trying to get Erick to tune into Lee in his head. So far, no luck! I am still trying to find the key that keeps evading me. Originally, I believed the key lay with Lee, but I no longer believe that to be the case. I am now concentrating on Erick. I know there is one; there has to be. We know from the ongoing nightmares that Lee is still there doing his thing. I am really upset with myself for not finding the key. I'm very exasperated about it too."

"I understand just how frustrating it is for you, Jacob. You are almost there, but miles away or millimeters, and you don't know." The curmudgeon Hunter Tripp's understanding warmed Jacob. *Hunter has been a better part of this whole problem with Lee.*

Friday afternoon rolled around, and Jacob had just finished his last patient. Rich missed McCarty; she just wanted someone to listen to her, and it was easy money that didn't involve insurance forms. She had to leave early, which was fine with Jacob because he would charge her for the full hour.

Jacob called the front desk. "Marilyn, is Dr. Hanford with his last patient today?"

"No, Dr. Gottlieb. He has a five thirty patient today."

Jacob wanted to talk to Jim, but that would have to wait. "Did I receive any mail today?"

"Yes, it's on your desk."

"Oh, I see it now. Thank you." He would have to wait until six thirty p.m. to talk to Jim.

Jacob was almost asleep, and he was opening and reading mail like a robot. He now stood up and continued examining his mail while standing. The long hours of the day found him sitting, so he used this opportunity to stretch a few unused muscles.

His letter opener slashed open the tops of all the letters before reading and then the ten-by-thirteen manila envelope. The letters were all perfunctory, except for an inquiry for a talk at the upcoming conference, which he dismissed, having nothing to report on the Erick/Lee case. He then opened and withdrew the contents of the envelope. It contained a letter, a bill, and legal papers.

His eyes scanned down the letter. He couldn't believe what he was reading. His heart rate jumped, and he began taking deep breaths; perspiration flowed instantly from his body. Jacob's eyes opened wide—then wider. His hands trembled so badly that he couldn't hold the letter any longer. It fluttered to the floor like a butterfly descending on a flower. *I can't believe it, the key.* He reached over and picked up the papers, and they fell to the floor again, slipping through his shaking fingers. *This just cannot be!*

His entire body began trembling as the excitement grew within like an erupting volcano. He picked up the paper in his feeble fingers. Then he began jumping in the air and bellowed, "I've got it! I got it! I have the key," Jacob shouted.

Marilyn heard the noise and knocked on his door. Jacob opened the door. Marilyn asked, "Dr. Gottlieb, are you all right?"

Jacob grabbed her and pulled her into the room, whirling her around and around with her feet off the floor like in a waltz, and taking in air in labored gulps. He then placed her down and said, "I am fine, and I've got it. I've got it."

Marilyn stared at him. "Dr. Gottlieb, what are you talking about?"

"The Erick Anderson case I have working on for several months now. I have been unable to discover the key in order to treat him. I am not certain, but I just discovered the key. I am so pleased!"

"That is wonderful news for the Andersons. They both are lovely people," she said as she exited the room.

Jacob reread the letter and examined the paper. *It's true—it's true. There is another category other than DID. I need to talk to Jim about this one. What a surprise, and it was right in front of my nose almost from the very beginning. Erick and Sophia are sure going to be upset with me over the late diagnosis, but how can they know—how could I know—Erick is the first patient in history?*

He desperately wanted to share his diagnosis with Jim, but Jim was busy with patients for another hour and a half. *Maybe I should get organized first and think through this whole matter before I speak to him. I'll call him tonight and see if he is free tomorrow.*

Jacob left the office, feeling very proud of himself with a twinkle in his eye and a skip in his step. As he walked, he thought, *I have the key. Why couldn't I see it before?* He strolled to his car, carrying a single piece of legal-size paper. Leaning against his car, he read the birth certificate of Erick Anthony Anderson.

Father: Lee Harvey Oswald.
Mother: Marina Natasha Oswald.

Chapter 16: The Advocacy Document

Earlier during the summer, Jim and Jacob had attended a talk at the medical school by Dr. Nicolas van Kaathoven, a renowned ornithologist. Van Kaathoven had performed definitive experiments, showing that migrating geese were guided in flight by stars and concluded that instinct was only learned behavior passed on genetically from one generation to the next. Other researchers had studied whales for the same reason. Gottlieb now was convinced that selected memory could be passed on genetically, and Erick was his example. His current question was, would Jim agree? Jacob needed Jim's agreement to approach the Neurology Department at the medical school to examine his hypothesis.

Jacob kept his morning appointment with Hunter at Cedar Ridge on Saturday, and Hunter was in the lobby waiting. "Do you have all of your questions ready Hunter?"

"Yeah, I think so."

"Mike is bringing Erick over here now. What are you planning on learning today?"

"For historical reasons, I would like to learn more about this double agent thing, if it exists, and, if so, how extensive. There is nothing I know of that is direct proof of Lee being associated with the CIA or the KGB. People have wondered how he could get Marina out of the Soviet Union without their assistance. It now appears they assisted."

Mike walked in with Erick at his shoulder, except at the door since it was only wide enough for Mike, so Erick entered first. "Hello, Doctors," offered Erick.

"How are you doing these days, Erick?"

"Not very good. I am becoming confused by what's going on. Sophia is withdrawing, and I seem to be spinning in a circle. I want off the merry-go-round. I sometimes feel sick to my stomach. Lee is scaring me. I want out of here. I want to go home."

"Unfortunately, your bad dreams continue, so that is out of the question."

Erick's chin dropped to his chest.

"Today, Dr. Tripp needs more clarification from Lee."

In a short time, Lee was present, looking at Hunter. Hunter, having learned from past experience, began their conversation in Russian to relax Lee. Lee didn't exhibit any hostility, so Jacob gave Mike a sign to leave, which he did in an almost invisible manner.

"Today, Lee, I would like to know how you became a CIA operative."

Lee began the tale Hunter saw on the video tape. However, as time went on, it expanded into discussions of the various document exchanges Lee made during his trips. One found the KGB chasing him on a moving train, whereupon Lee escaped by jumping into trackside bush from a moving train.

Regarding the KGB, Hunter discovered that Lee did play a role as an operative, but it had barely started when it ended.

"Lee, thank you. I want to talk to Erick now."

Erick returned with eyes closed. Jacob turned to Hunter and said, "Our joint session is through, Hunter. However, I am doing something else with Erick, and I may need your services. Can you hang around for another ten minutes?"

"Sure, Jacob. I can do that."

"Great, Hunter, but you will have to step out of the room for a while. I will come and get you if I need you."

Jacob had been mulling over since Lee, Erick's father, was present in his brain; perhaps his mother was there too. After all, it was a genetically inherited mutation. *I must check this out. I will see if I can withdraw Marina.*

"Erick, is Marina in your head?"

"Yes, Dr. Gottlieb. She is here."

Jacob's head popped back in surprise. "Ask her to talk to me. Marina, this is Dr. Gottlieb. I want to talk to you. Please talk to me." Jacob remembered that it had been difficult to get Lee to respond on the first attempt, so he spoke again. "Marina, I need to talk to you." He examined Erick's face, but there was no change.

Now using a kindly voice, Jacob asked, "Marina, I want talk to you, please."

Erick's mouth began to move. Then the lips parted, and a voice said as the eyes opened, "You wanted to talk to me, Doctor?" The voice exhibited a thick Russian accent and used Erick's falsetto voice.

"Yes. What is your name?"

"My name is Marina Natasha Oswald."

Jacob had difficulty understanding her. "Are you married to Lee?"

"Yes."

"What was your maiden name?"

"It was Prusakova."

"Marina, I want you to meet someone who speaks Russian. Let me get him."

Jacob stepped out of the room and motioned Hunter forward. When he arrived, Jacob said, "Hunter, I have another surprise for you. Please join me and meet Lee's wife, Marina Oswald. Talk to her in Russian and ask some imposing questions."

Hunter looked at Jacob as if Jacob had lost his mind. However, he sat down in front of Erick. He saw Erick sitting there with his eyes open. "Marina, I want you to meet Dr. Tripp."

"Hello, Doctor," Marina said.

Jacob motioned Hunter to begin. "Marina, I am pleased to meet you. Where do you currently live?"

"I live in Dallas."

"Where were you born?" Her head tipped sideways as if she didn't understand. Then Hunter began talking Russian, and Marina's smile widened. In Russian, Hunter asked, "Where were you born?"

Now in Russian, Marina said, "Oh—sorry. I didn't understand a minute ago. I was born in Minsk, Soviet Union." The dialogue continued for fifteen minutes. Tripp asked all the questions and got Marina to answer both in Russian and English.

"How did you meet Lee?"

Marina repeated the story Lee had told in almost identical form. Then Jacob interrupted. "Marina, I want to talk to Erick now."

"Okay, Doctor." She shut her eyes, and Erick appeared with eyes open.

"Wait here, Erick, I will be right back." Jacob and Hunter stepped out of the room. "Well, Hunter, what do you think?"

"Jacob, I am in such a state of shock that I am uncertain that I can answer. She speaks very good Russian and poor English. She was born in Minsk. Her maiden name was Prusakova, and I know both of those answers are correct. This is unbelievable. I asked her specific questions about the Soviet Union and Minsk, and her answers were correct. I can't believe it!"

"Thanks, Hunter. I am through." Jacob motioned to Mike to let Hunter go. Mike walked toward them as Jacob shook Hunter's hand and thanked him for his assistance. Jacob stepped back into the room to wake Erick.

Rather than leaving, Hunter waited in the lobby. As he and Jacob exited the lobby, Hunter stammered, "Jacob, what just happened. First, it was Lee. Now his wife. Will tomorrow be the grandmother?"

"No, Hunter. In this case of DID, there are three personalities. Erick, Lee, and Marina. However, only Lee is a threat to Erick's survival."

Hunter, changing the subject said, "Jacob, I wanted to let you know that bluing on the trigger components is complete, and the trigger reassembled. I was able to run an impact test on it and compared it to the casing found at the assassination site. They are identical. There is no doubt in my mind that we have the rifle used to assassinate the president. Since my tests are complete, I present to you this small gift. Oh yeah, I almost forgot. Lee's signature is identical to Lee Harvey Oswald, but his fingerprints are not."

"That is what we both expected."

Walking to the parking lot, Jacob opened the box and removed the trigger assembly carefully and examined it, turning it in his hands and pulling the trigger a few times. "Wow, Hunter, it's beautiful. It can't be that old rusty piece without moving parts that I gave you."

"Yes, that's it, Jacob. I assure you that it is the one and same."

"Thank you. Wow, what a bonanza for us."

Saturday afternoon arrived, and Jacob anxiously approached Jim's front door. Marge answered the door and took him into Jim's office. "I'll get Jim. May I bring you a cup of fresh-brewed coffee?"

Jacob nodded. He was still standing when Jim entered. "Sit down a minute, Jacob, and tell me about the breakthrough. I heard about your behavior last Friday. Is this related?"

"Yes! I believe I found the key in the Erick Anderson case, and I want to discuss it with you. This is something that can be charged to the patient. We can do it now. Lee is about to take over Erick, perhaps permanently, so I have a rush to get to the treatment phase. In fact, I have a report from Mike that he saw Erick and Lee arguing during the daytime, but Erick won that time. This is getting very serious." Handing Jim a copy of the advocacy document, Jacob said, "The first step is to go over my findings and the Advocacy Document, then discuss the results and answer all of your questions.

"Last Friday, I received a legal document that, when combined with that advocacy document, presents my case for a new psychiatric disorder. I will show you that document later and wait to see if you come to the same conclusion.

"With this advocacy document, I cease my detective activity and become a physician again. Following our evaluation, I want to discuss our conclusions and a next step for the 'new' disorder. Okay?"

"That sounds like a great start to me, Jacob, but a little annoying." Jacob handed Jim the advocacy paper, and they began at the top. Jim was familiar with many facts, so he rapidly read through the beginning.

Jim read down the document until he came to the Oklahoma City bombing; then he turned to Jacob and said, "Why do you believe the bombing is still not the stimulus to trigger the disorder?"

"I did believe that seeing such a horrifying event to be an explainable cause of the continuing dreams initially. I thought it to be a straightforward trauma-related problem that could be controlled by facing the outcome. However, upon hypnosis, I discovered Lee in the picture, and Lee spoke to Erick before the bombing. Neither Erick nor Lee has changed this fact after repeated hypnotic sessions. Thus, Lee made his first appearance before the bombing."

"If that is the case, I still do not understand why the trauma didn't trigger Lee in Erick's mind."

"It could have, and I thought that too for the longest time. It was only after Lee possessed special knowledge that I changed my mind."

Jim continued reading down the list, looked up, and asked, "Why do you believe Lee overtook Erick's body at that time in front of the mirror in the early morning?"

"Erick seemed to have the answer, although for obvious reasons I never acknowledged that he was correct. It seems that Erick forgot to take his Popodine the night before, so he couldn't return to sleep after the dream awoke him. It kept him awake for the remainder of the night, and as a consequence, Erick was in a very weakened emotional state in the morning. Lee took control and remained in control for five hours. Thus, Erick was in a weak emotional state when the takeover occurred. Further, Lee acknowledged that it was a partial reason."

"That's very interesting. I didn't know that, but I certainly accept your description. It makes sense. Being the person Lee is, I can understand why he did the things to Erick's wife that he did."

"What do you mean—that Lee can tune into Erick's mind and thinking?"

"I tested this point by posing suggestions or situations of Erick while he was alert, but he did not give me the answers until after the session. Then during the session and while dealing with Lee, I asked Lee what Erick was thinking. Lee knew the answer most of the time but not always. It appears that Lee can access Erick's thinking on most occasions, whereas Erick can never access Lee thinking unless Lee tells him. He just feels Lee's presence."

Jim's eyes scanned the page and offered, "I believe that the strangest piece of evidence of all of the data is that Lee can read, write, and speak Russian—and that Erick can do none of these."

"You are very observant, Jim, and I felt the same way, and that is exactly why I believe I now have the answer."

"How did you test for short-term and long-term memory, Jacob?"

"I used the Morgan test for both."

Jim's head bobbed up and down in agreement with Jacob's remarks. "Jacob, on section B dealing with Lee Harvey Oswald, did you go over these with Hunter?"

"Yes, I did this morning. In fact, I went over the entire list with Hunter to see if there was an area I missed. Hunter is in total agreement with section B, except he does have to take Lee's word that he was a CIA operative. This morning Lee admitted that he was only a small-time player for both the CIA and KGB. In fact, the KGB activity went nowhere."

"I would agree with everything here except for the last item. How do you apply the Morgan test for Lee?"

"I was uncertain also, so all that I could do is assume that Lee is Lee Harvey Oswald and then apply the test. When I did that with help from Hunter, I found that Lee had a score of fifteen, whereas Erick had a fifty-seven. This is a remarkable difference and certainly shows that Lee's long-term memory is relatively poor with the exception of selected events, and those events are lucid, clear, and exact."

Jim asked, "Do you have an explanation?"

"Yes, I do, and I will give it to you shortly."

Jim continued through the remaining sections without comment until he finished with, "I guess I am confused as to why Lee took over without an external input."

"As you know, in the chronicled cases of DID, this phenomenon goes on all of the time and is still unexplained. I believe the same cause is implemented here, but we do not know what it is.

"Okay, Jacob, I have completed the advocacy document, and I have *no* problems with it. The whole thing is totally unexplainable to me, and I do not see a psychiatric cause. I am stumped!"

"As you know, I have been stumped, embarrassed, and humbled by this case. I could never put my arms around it. Then I remembered what you told me several months ago. You said something to the effect of 'Think out of the box, be different, and be creative.' I have, and as I believe as I said earlier, there is a creative answer. The key was this legal document I received last Friday that got me excited." Jacob reached across Jim's desk and slid a single-page legal document under his shaking hands. This was the defining moment, and Jacob was quivering within.

"Jim, please read this legal document carefully. I will remain silent."

Jim was shaking his head, and Jacob delayed the answer. Jacob on the other hand wanted Jim to reach the same conclusion independent of his prompting.

Jim started to read carefully as Jacob had requested. Then he said, "I'll be God damned. I do not believe it." Then with a raised voice, he said again, "I do not believe it. Jacob, is this correct?"

"Yes, Erick is Lee Harvey and Marina Oswald's son. He was adopted directly from the hospital nine months after the Kennedy assassination. Remember the talk we attended last summer at the medical school? I vaguely remember that professor what's-his-name from Holland, the ornithologist who believed that some long-term memory was transferred genetically, but that doesn't imply to personality. Oh yeah, Van Kaathoven was his name."

"That's it exactly. Lee knows this information because it was transferred genetically. Lee had intercourse with Marina on the afternoon after the assassination just before he departed for the theater, and conception occurred. I have checked this point, and Lee confirmed it during hypnosis. He almost raped Marina. You see, they had separated for a while, so this was a big deal for her. Lee has no memory after that sexual act. He doesn't remember the jail time, the people there, or his own assassination. Under hypnosis, Lee has never lied to me, never. There are two parts to this problem: first, the diagnosis; and two, the potential cure."

Jacob watched Jim's face intently. Jim's mouth was still open as he thought about it. "This explains his attitude when he took over Erick's body and tried to rape Sophia, if indeed the complex personality aspect of humanity was transferred. Lee needed to do what he last did, and that was to rape his wife on assassination day and then attempt it with Sophia as Lee. This is amazing, Jacob, stunning, awesome, unbelievable!"

There now was silence in the room. Jim grabbed the advocacy document and reread it with a new mindset. "Jacob, you are a damn genius and lucky too. Everything you did on this case was unbelievably wonderful. The diagnosis all makes sense. Yes, it does, Jacob; it all makes sense! Imagine that memory is transferred genetically but also personality. The probability of both being transferred together is improbable. Therefore, it doesn't occur in most cases. It is absolutely amazing. Wow, Jacob, do you know what this means for psychiatry?"

"Yes! I also know what will happen to you and me if the word gets out. Look at my hands Jim." He held up his hands, and they trembled dramatically as if he had Parkinson's disease.

"One more thing, Jim. I discovered a second personality in Erick's brain."

"You what?"

"I discovered a second personality this morning. If Lee could exist there as one parent, why not the other? I discovered Marina is there too!"

"No! It can't be. This is getting out of hand."

"Not really. If one parent can be there genetically, why not the other? Both speak exquisite Russian, and Hunter talked to both yesterday. He had visited her birthplace several years ago and verified most of the things she said."

"You are pulling my leg. Right?"

"No, Jim. What I said is true and was also witnessed by both Hunter and Mike. Further, I have it on tape."

Jim shook his head in disbelief.

Jacob felt Jim would be a proponent for his new theory. "Jim, we need a name for the effect too."

"That will come. How do you propose to cure Erick Anderson?"

"That is precisely why I need your total, one hundred percent backing on this case. First, I see no way of disposing of Lee in Erick's head through therapy, unless you have a new brainstorm. I have tried everything at my disposal, and Lee continues to gain strength and is taking over Erick. Lee must be stopped immediately."

"I agree, Jacob, but how?"

"Do you remember what Dr. Van Kaathoven did in his goose migration study? He created a cerebral infection in the area of long-term memory, which triggered memory loss, and the geese couldn't fly to the north at night."

"You don't mean to say that we give Erick a cerebral infection, do you?"

"No, not at all. There are other ways of damaging or destroying brain cells that are better suited than an infection. First, we have to determine if Lee's memory is localized—and particularly the cognitive center. If it's not localized and removed physically from Erick's cognitive center, there would appear to be no practical means of destroying those cells. However, Lee's selected long-term memory is quite specific, and I believe it is localized, just as the solar map was localized in the brain of the wild goose. The technical procedures available to us for destruction of brain cells include x-ray, positron emission, gamma radiation, radio-frequency ablation, ultrasound ablation, cryogenics, and surgery. These decisions are not left to us but rather to neurologists or radiologists. I was thinking of approaching Ralph Steele at the university and hearing what he had to say. However, I will not do this unless you agree."

Jim Hanford put on a formal face as he thought about the possibilities. His hands were wrapped around his chin, with his elbows resting on his desk. "I do not want to rush to a conclusion on this matter, and I would like to sleep on it. Right now, I cannot think of another possibility. I believe you have discovered something really big—and this baby is fraught with tangential troubles with possibilities of our death because of it. I must think about it."

"Jim, I will talk to Steele and get an EEG expert to work with me in obtaining the localization of Lee in Erick's head if possible. I can do that without telling anyone the details."

"Yes, that's good idea. I will get back to you Monday morning. Okay?"

"That will be just fine."

"Fascinating, Jacob, unbelievable!"

Jacob rose to drive home. He looked back; Jim was still shaking his head. So far, so good! Jim wasn't screaming about a fatal flaw, and that was excellent news.

Jacob knew better than to call Ralph during working hours. Ralph established many of the fundamentals of modern neurosurgery, and as a consequence, he was constantly on the move. Jacob waited until he got home to call him during the evening. They hadn't talked for some time except when they bumped into each other in the hallway at the medical school after each taught a class in adjacent rooms.

"Jacob, how are you?"

"I am doing well, Ralph. I am calling you because I have need of your services in a very unusual case of mine. I am convinced that I have two personalities residing within the same brain, and it is not a case of MPD or DID. My fellow psychiatrist is reviewing the case, and I expect his inputs Monday. I—"

"Are you sure. It already sounds strange."

"Yes, I am sure. I am calling you to locate an expert to verify this. I do not believe the typical EEG will do it. I know you are closer to these experts than me, and I was hoping that I could get a referral and good word from you."

"Have you met Dr. Wilhelm Beckmann yet?"

"No."

"Wilhelm's specialty is determining the executive center of the brain. He has developed, along with excellent help from our Mathematics Department, some wonderful multivariate analysis tools. He is on a sabbatical from the University of Austria, and he is working out of our group."

"He sounds perfect. Can you set up a meeting with him for me? I really could use his assistance."

"Sure, I'll talk to him Monday and make certain he will see you. Call my office and talk to Helen. She will see that it occurs."

Later in the week, Dr. Wilhelm Beckmann hobbled toward Jacob, who was standing in the hallway, waiting for him. Beckmann's bushy hair was disheveled and looked in need of combing. "Sorry, Dr. Gottlieb. I was down the hall, and I forgot the time. It is not like me, so I ran." His words possessed a strong German accent, the native tongue of his homeland, Austria.

Gottlieb extended his hand and said, "Don't worry about it."

"Please follow me, Dr. Gottlieb." Wilhelm walked with a decided limp from a deformed leg at birth, but he continued to stay ahead of Gottlieb to his office. "Dr. Gottlieb, how can I help you?"

Jacob told Beckmann about an unusual patient with dual personalities, and the patient didn't have DID. "I understand from Dr. Steele that you have some powerful tools available that perhaps can locate the elusive central executive of the brain based upon the Brodmann model. I need to find out if two personalities co-exist in my patient's brain, and, if so, are they separable sufficiently that one can be altered or removed?"

Wilhelm was silent for a few minutes and said, "Dr. Gottlieb, that is a very big order. Some people dispute the existence of a central executive, but I am here to tell you that I have proven that it exists."

"How did you do that?"

"Come down the hallway, and I will show you." Jacob got up and followed Beckmann down to a strange-looking room built within a room. "This is our isolation room, where I do magnetoencephalography."

Jacob sometimes had difficulty following his conversation because of the heavy accent.

"It is called MEG for short. The detectors in this device above the chair are called 'Squids.' The Squids detect the electrical current in the brain, and these signals are digitized and fed into a large Cray supercomputer. The metallic, shielded room is required to eliminate all electrical noise from the surroundings. By rotating the Squid detector around the patient's head, we can triangulate the sources of the generated signals and obtain their location."

Beckmann continued, "I believe the central executive is the control center; you may think of it as the primary computer of the brain, and it interfaces with other computers within the brain. Further, I believe it controls all the other computers. To determine this, I use an assortment of new tools. The MEG is used in conjunction with functional magnetic resonance imaging (fMRI) to identify and localize electrical activity within the brain. These experimental results are interlaced with the data from the positron-emission tomography (PET) unit down the hall.

The PET scanner tells us about oxygen consumption. When the brain is working hard in one area, the oxygen consumption increases, and we can determine this zone in three-dimensional space within the patient's head by rotating a scanner.

"If there are two distinct personality centers in the brain, I would expect to have two separable 'hot spots.' The EEG, the fourth measurement device, provides the normal demeanor information about brain activity and timing. The functional MRI consists of taking two different images of the subject, one when the subject is doing nothing and one during the requested activity. We obtain a three-dimensional image of any brain section. By subtracting the before and during images, we have another tool to determine the chemically active cells. These hot spots are color coded by our computer from dark red to bright yellow for the hottest spots. We have found good correlation between the PET and the fMRI. The MEG tests permit us to see lots of neuron activity. To date, we have found exceptional good correlation between chemical activity and neuron activity. The Cray encodes all of the digitized data and constructs 3-D activity images of the brain for each exercise. It is very complicated. We have developed incredible algorithms to do this. You can guess why it requires a supercomputer to do the analysis. That is it."

"Wow, I am impressed," said Gottlieb as he surveyed the equipment. "How can I get my patient in here to be tested, and what does it cost?"

"If we select your patient, it will cost nothing. In fact, we will pay the patient for his or her time. As you can imagine, we are very busy, but I must tell you that I am very impressed with your problem, because, if true, it taxes our system to the maximum. If there are two different personalities present, there likely are two central executive centers close together. This will challenge our system."

Jacob was amazed by the possibilities before him. This overall system was capable of detecting two separate personalities. "How do I apply for my patient, Dr. Beckmann?"

"There is a committee of three that oversees the study and selects patients. Drs. Ralph Steele, Katherine Courtney, a radiologist, and I belong to that committee. Your case sounds fascinating. I suggest that you give the three of us a briefing, and the reasons why you believe we should do it. We will meet in Dr. Steele's office next Monday evening at six p.m., and I will put you on the calendar if you like. Your presentation should be no longer than thirty minutes."

Jacob agreed immediately and walked out of the building stimulated by what he heard.

Chapter 17: The Tests

Sophia walked into Jacob's office, filled with apprehension. She was curious about what Jacob was going to say, and further, this whole matter had gone on far too long. Perhaps now there would be some sort of closure or, at least, the beginning thereof.

"Please forgive me, Sophia, for meeting in my office, but I didn't want this to appear as a treatment. This meeting is best described as a consultation. Would you join me in a cup of coffee?" Minutes later they were sipping the coffee as Jacob began.

"Sophia, I now believe Erick has a new medical problem heretofore unknown in the annals of psychiatry. He is a first. The difference lies with the fact that it is genetic in origin. The personage Lee within Erick's brain is a portion of Erick's father, who wasn't a nice person. I believe some of his personality and memory was transferred to Erick genetically, and tests must be performed to confirm this opinion. This would explain Lee's facility with the Russian language.

"What in the world are you trying to tell me, Jacob?"

"Lee has demonstrated without question that he was aware of intimate, verifiable details of Erick's father's life, events so complex and exact that Erick could never have created them in multiple lifetimes, so there can be no doubt. In fact, Erick's father was deceased when Erick was born."

"Like what facts?" barked Sophia without hesitation.

"Like a thorough knowledge of the Russian language as comprehensive as any university professor of the Russian language, and like places and things in the Soviet Union."

"I don't believe that. Prove it to me," demanded Sophia.

Jacob walked Sophia into the treatment room. While Sophia was getting herself comfortable, Jacob gathered the latest tape when Lee talked with Hunter Tripp about Russia for nearly a half hour, much of it in Russian. As the tape played for a few minutes, she watched the verbal exchange between the two men.

"Right now, Lee is speaking to a Russian expert, who teaches the Russian language here at the university. He is talking about places in Russia Lee's father had visited. Dr. Tripp was born in Russia and immigrated to this country as a child with his parents and therefore has a thorough and complete understanding of the Russian language. You can verify this by calling the university. The professor is knowledgeable of the places of which Lee speaks. Professor Tripp is not a run-of-the-mill professor. He is professor emeritus."

"I am sorry to doubt you, Jacob. How could Erick know Russian that well?"

"Erick doesn't know Russian at all, and that was the key to unlocking the elastic bubble that flexed around any diagnosis. I have confirmation that Lee's father was in Russia and spoke fluent Russian. While there, he met and married a Russian woman, Erick's birth mother. After they returned to the States, they continued to speak Russian as a family language. Erick is half Russian, and both parents speak Russian fluently. I have verified that Lee knows minute, personal details of Erick's father's life, and I have personally checked out many of these. Dr. Tripp uncovered other detailed information too. I have been out of state, verifying these points for the last few weeks; hence all my trips out of town were for that purpose. Professor Tripp, based on personal experience of living in the Soviet Union and visiting it many times as an adult, has verified other descriptions of Moscow and the workings of the Soviet economy and society in general. Further, Erick's father wasn't a nice person. Now Lee currently is in the process of taking over Erick. Lee behaves like Erick's father."

"Oh my God! Forgive me, but I just can't comprehend any of this," uttered Sophia. "I don't understand this! Jacob, I'm frightened."

After pausing, Jacob licked his lips and continued. "I am so sorry, Sophia, that it took me so long, but Erick's problem is new in the annals of psychiatry. Erick is a first, and I struggled."

Sophia was visibly shaking as she absorbed the bad news. "Poor Erick," she muttered. "How bad of a person was Erick's father?"

"He was about as bad as he could get," answered Jacob.

"Who was he, Jacob?"

"You do not want to know, Sophia."

"Why not?" she snapped.

"Because." Jacob fell silent.

Sophia raised her voice and asked again with an elevated voice, "Why not, Jacob?"

Speaking softly, Jacob said, "Because if you knew the answer, it is possible that your life would be in danger."

"You mean, someone would want to kill me?"

"Yes, that could occur."

"Then someone might want to kill you too!"

"That's correct, Sophia. If certain parties know what I know about Lee, there is a possibility that Erick and I would be executed. We cannot assess the possibility of this occurring because Erick's father lived some time ago. Maybe nothing will happen. I just don't know."

There was total silence in the room. Sophia began shaking. "Oh my God, Jacob. What have I done to you?"

Laying both hands on her shoulders and looking her directly in the eye, Jacob said, "Sophia, I did it to myself, trying to help Erick. It's my job." Sophia stood up, and simultaneously Jacob did too. They each took one step toward one another as Sophia laid her head on Jacob's shoulder. Jacob could feel her head tremble.

"Sophia, I now believe you are lucky to be alive from the time when Lee took over Erick. Knowing the potential harm Lee could inflict on society made it an easy decision to place Erick in the hospital. If both you and Erick had refused to agree to his hospitalization, I would have gone to court to do it. Lee is very, very dangerous. If I had gone to court, I perhaps would have exposed Lee's secret, and certain parties would have been aware of what I know. I could have been executed by now, so your decision actually saved my life. I am grateful."

"Jacob, is Erick doomed?"

"I am uncertain at the moment, and that is precisely why I needed to talk to you this week. There is a special diagnostic program at the medical school, and I have been asked to make a presentation on Erick's behalf Monday evening. The purpose of the meeting is to determine whether they will even accept Erick as a patient. These are only benign diagnostic tests. The doctors hope to verify my hypothesis, which is that Erick has two separate personalities operating in the same brain. I require your written approval to even talk to the oversight committee."

"What kind of testing will they do?"

"They will seek brain activity for both Erick and Lee while working a problem to see if both personalities possess the same central executive of the brain."

"What if you find this executive thing?"

"The executive center is the primary brain center. It controls other brain functions. First, we need to find it to confirm my diagnosis. Second, we need to know where it resides in Erick's brain to make any decision. We could play what-ifs for hours. These tests serve as a wonderful opportunity for us, and they could verify my diagnosis. Only one injection is required and the remainder of the tests are passive."

The conversation continued as Sophia settled down and began asking pragmatic questions regarding Erick, the testing, and test procedures. "Jacob, will Lee take control of Erick?"

"I now believe that he will."

"Then this test is very important, isn't it?"

"Yes, I cannot overstate it; it is exceedingly important. Erick's future, perhaps his existence, depends on it. This whole affair is new, so we are sailing on uncharted waters. I cannot predict the future. We do need to know what is taking place inside Erick's brain, and this is the best opportunity possible. Further, Erick won't be injured by the testing. Just remember, the technology wasn't available to us five years ago, and it is not available at most institutions in the world today either. There are only four centers in the world that can do this, and one of them is right here at our medical center. Remember, there is no assurance that they will accept Erick for the tests. All that I am asking of you is to let me make a half hour presentation to discuss the case."

Jacob left the room to return with a document for Sophia to sign. As she did, Jacob told her that this work was part of a government grant, and all costs were covered by a grant. Jacob went on to explain that Erick would be paid a small stipend for his time. She heaved a sigh and looked at Jacob, shaking her head. "Sometimes it seems that this whole thing will never end."

"There is still a very important fact that we need to discuss. As you know, Lee can tune into Erick's thinking, whereas Erick cannot reciprocate. I know, and I have tried unsuccessfully to make it happen. I don't believe Erick should be told anything about these tests at this time, so we keep as much of this secret from Lee as possible. Do you understand my thinking?"

"Yes, I do, Jacob, and thanks for all that you have done. When this is over, I want you to explain all that was involved. Promise me that!"

"Sophia, I will tell you more, but I cannot imagine endangering your life. I must keep some things secret."

Jacob had made previous agreement with Mike Garland to bring Erick to the Monday meeting with the overview committee. Jacob entered Ralph's office with Erick, Mike, and Professor Tripp. He carried his laptop computer and an attaché case. Erick was uncomfortable and uneasy with the situation, since it made him feel as if it was a freak show and he was the freak.

Jacob introduced himself to Dr. Katherine Courtney, an attractive woman in her midforties, since he had never met her before, and then he turned to introduce Erick, Professor Tripp, and Mike Garland to the assemblage.

Jacob was about to take a big gamble to convince the committee to test Erick. Following a few formalities, Jacob began. "Erick," he said, "where were you born and raised?"

"I was born in Dallas, adopted as a newborn and raised in Oklahoma."

"Have you ever been out of the United States, and do you speak any foreign language?" Gottlieb asked.

"No to both" was Erick's response.

"Now I will hypnotize Erick in front of all so we can talk to Lee. You don't mind, do you, Erick?"

Erick shook his head. Jacob purposely had Erick sit in the chair with wooden armrests. He planned to strap Lee's arms to the chair to protect all parties when the time arrived. He had Erick turn his chair around so he wasn't facing the attendees, and Jacob moved his chair around to face him. Erick couldn't view anyone other than Jacob. "For the rest of you, shut your eyes and plug up your ears. I will alert you when we can begin." After being hypnotized, Mike turned Erick's chair so that he faced the committee.

"All right," said Jacob. "Would anyone like to test Erick to see if he is hypnotized?"

Dr. Beckmann responded, "Yes, I do!" Erick eyes remained shut as Wilhelm fished through his pocket for something. Anticipating that this might happen, Gottlieb opened his attaché case and offered Wilhelm an assortment of tools including a Gordon mallet, a small sterile needle, and a few sundry items. Wilhelm grabbed the Gordon mallet and lifted Erick's leg so the foot wasn't touching the floor. With his fingers, he felt the soft spot between the patella and tibia, and launched the hammer down in the area to test for the knee reflex. Erick's foot barely moved. Then without noticed to Erick, who still had his eyes closed, he tested the reflexes in other areas. After a few minutes and a couple of sticks with the needle, Wilhelm announced he was satisfied that Erick was hypnotized.

"Erick, can you speak Russian?"

"No, Dr. Gottlieb, I cannot speak Russian."

"Does anyone wish to ask Erick anything while he is hypnotized and still Erick?" There were no questions.

"Erick, I want to talk to Lee now."

"Okay, Dr. Gottlieb."

The assemblage watched Erick as Gottlieb called for Lee. Erick's face began to twitch and distort as Lee made his appearance. He was directly facing Drs. Courtney and Beckmann as his flickering eyelids began to open in his usual squinting fashion. Although Lee's wrists were strapped, Mike moved into a close position behind him. Lee's head turned slowly as he glared at the doctors, ignoring Tripp, who was sitting closest to him. Then he shouted at the top of his voice, "What in the hell are you bastards staring at?"

Katherine lurched backward as the evil man glared directly into her eye with his jaw locked, his voice minacious. His stare contest continued until Dr. Courtney looked away. Lee leaned forward, gazing at her in a menacing manner. "You haven't answered my question, bitch." He reached toward her, but the straps held him in his chair, and he turned to Jacob, saying, "What are you doing, Doc?"

"It's only precautionary, Lee. Lee, can you speak Russian?"

"Can a fish swim?" was his answer.

Jacob then said, "Professor Tripp is professor emeritus at our university and teaches Russian." Hunter was prepared for this and handed each member of the assembly a copy of his resume.

"Okay, Professor, please talk to him in Russian." Professor Tripp began chatting with Lee, and Lee responded. The angry look on Lee's face dissipated. "Dr. Tripp is a native-born Russian who came to the United States as a youth."

Jacob turned to Hunter and asked, "What were the two of you talking about?"

"Lee wanted to know about Dr. Courtney, but I told him I had just met her and knew nothing. Then he told me she was very attractive, and he liked her body. He wanted her."

Dr. Courtney lurched backward.

"Hunter has been very helpful to me to establish the identity and idiosyncrasies of Lee. Lee knows parts of Russia that most people never have heard, even those who visit the Soviet Union on a regular basis."

Tripp then began to speak. "I am here to testify that Lee speaks exquisite Russian and is well versed in many parts of Russian cities, places, and culture that one cannot learn from books, and he certainly knows infinitely more than Erick." He also passed around his driver's license to verify that he was indeed Professor Tripp.

"Erick is a jerk," shouted Lee. Then Lee's eyes drifted from person to person, lingering on each for a few seconds, staring directly into their eyes and making each uncomfortable, before he spoke again. "And I am going to kill him!" The exactness and harshness of this terse pronouncement gave all a shiver since he felt credible to each attendee.

"Does anyone have a quick question for Lee while he is with us?" Jacob said.

Beckmann said, "Yes I do. I want to know why you want to kill Erick."

"When Erick is dead, I will take over his body and kick him out." His voice was firm and resolute, and no one doubted the sincerity of his pronouncement.

"If Erick is dead, you will be dead too," Beckmann offered.

"I am talking about his brain, stupid man.—Doc, your friends are ridiculous."

Since there was stone-cold silence in the room, Jacob turned to Lee and said, "Lee, I need to talk to Erick."

"Okay, I don't like these asses anyway. They are just a bunch of zebras. Then he laughed insidiously."

Seconds later, mild-mannered Erick opened his eyes while still under hypnosis. "How do you feel, Erick?"

"I feel fine, Doctor, but I do feel a little jumpy." Under hypnosis, Erick talked very slowly, whereas Lee spoke rapidly, another point that differentiated the two personalities.

"Erick, how long have you been speaking Russian?"

"I cannot speak Russian."

"Hunter, speak to him."

Hunter began conversing in Russian, but Erick ignored him.

"Does anyone have anything to ask Erick, who is hypnotized, while we have time? I will summarize my position in a moment."

Dr. Beckmann looked at Erick and said in his German accent, "Can you tune into Lee?"

"No, Doctor; I never have been able to do that, but I have tried. Once in a million times I have, but generally I am not able to do so, unless he lets me."

"Has Lee ever taken control of you?"

"Yes, and, when he did, he attempted to rape my wife and terrorized her with a running chainsaw when she rebuked him. He also chased her on the freeway and bumped her car when both were speeding over one hundred miles per hour, and he fought and disarmed a highway patrol officer."

"Thank you, Erick!" Then Wilhelm looked at Gottlieb for some sort of confirmation. Jacob nodded his head up and down in confirmation of Erick's answer.

"Erick, when I count to five, you will wake up and feel fine. One, two ... five." Erick yawned and smiled at the assemblage. "Erick, please go to the next room with Dr. Tripp and Mike and wait for me there." Mike unstrapped him, and the three men departed.

Jacob stood before the aghast doctors. "Committee persons, I have far more data than that, which you have seen. I hold in my hand a letter from my partner, who like me is a psychiatrist and doesn't believe Erick suffers from DID. The most plausible explanation is that much of the father's personality was transferred to Erick genetically and that both inhabit Erick's brain. Erick's birth father was a degenerate human being. I am asking this committee to approve Erick for testing for what may well be a landmark event. I hope to obtain proof that Erick and Lee possess different executive centers within Erick's brain.

"I took this dramatic opportunity for you to see firsthand the differences in the two personalities. Erick is a marketing man and can contribute to society. Lee cannot contribute. Erick's late father was a heinous person and tried to destroy society. Erick was a result of rape. Dr. Beckmann has convinced me that there is a chance to obtain definitive data from the two men in one brain that can provide a clue to why this problem exists. I have exhausted my knowledge of psychiatry to separate the two. I assure you that this is not a case of DID/MPD. Dr. Tripp's credential as professor emeritus speaks to the fact that he too believes Lee is a different person and that he speaks exquisite Russian. Further, Erick cannot speak Russian, and according to Erick, he and his wife have never studied the Russian language or been to the Soviet Union. There now are hundreds of small and large examples to verify that Lee knows details of Erick's father, who has been dead for many years. I humbly ask you to consider Erick as a candidate for testing."

Gottlieb bowed his head somewhat and said, "Please forgive my chancy experiment, but it was the most dramatic means of my short time to make my points about Erick/Lee clear. I brought along Mike Garland, a nurse at Cedar Ridge where Erick now resides, to protect us if Lee got out of control. Mike knows how to handle him and is big enough to do it. Lee claims he will escape from Cedar Ridge and become a professional assassin. Lee is that dangerous. I believe Erick is a genetic oddity. Thank you for your time."

Dr. Ralph Steele spoke. "Jacob, I understand totally your reasoning for the dramatic demonstration, and it certainly made a quick point with me. The committee will make a decision tonight after we have examined all of the pending cases. I will personally get back to you tomorrow with our decision."

On the following day, Jacob received a noontime telephone call from Ralph Steele. "Jacob, the committee has approved Erick for the next available test," Steele spouted excitedly over the phone. "You took a risk bringing Lee to the meeting. However, it was very effective, and all committee members want to help Mr. Anderson. Katherine hopes she never sees Lee again."

"Thank you, Ralph. I thought that it would be effective."

"This case certainly stimulated our interest. If this phenomenon turns out to be real, there are a number of fascinating possibilities in the new world of psychogenetics."

"Yes, Ralph, and we haven't even begun to touch the subject."

"Your accomplishment, Jacob, sounds incredible and very exciting. I wish you good luck with this study."

"Thanks, Ralph!" And then the two friends hung up.

Jacob immediately called Dr. Beckmann. Wilhelm, who was very meticulous in his work and personal life, had already arranged a time for the testing, and he further had two backup dates set. Jacob discovered that the testing required several hours, and in his situation with multiple personalities, it was perhaps twice as long. "Do we require Professor Tripp?" Jacob asked.

"Absolutely! I think we should, because Professor Tripp can engage Lee in speaking Russian. I think that is a wonderful idea."

"Wilhelm, Tripp teaches classes on Monday, Wednesday, and Friday, so he cannot be present on those days. I am free anytime. I also plan to bring along Mike Garland, who can handle Lee if he gets out of control. Okay, Wilhelm. Please give me those dates." Then, managing a smile, he thought. *It's going to happen.*

On the following Tuesday, the assemblage of Jacob, Erick, Hunter, and Mike strolled along the basement hallway of the University of Oklahoma Medical Center. As usual, Mike walked about a half step behind Erick on his right side.

Dr. Beckmann saw them and shuffled toward them. He directed them to a cramped waiting room and asked all to stay except Jacob. Mike selected the chair nearest the door as the others took seats.

The primary question the two doctors had to work out dealt with the control, where control in the medical sense was normal, and that was the conscious Erick. "Wilhelm, I have been thinking about this, and I too believe we absolutely require Erick in both the awake and hypnotized state, and then deal with Lee. We can only access Lee in the hypnotized state."

Wilhelm, staring directly into Jacob's eyes, said, "I concur, Dr. Gottlieb, and that was my major point. I believe we will find the two Ericks to be identical, but we still must prove it."

"What types of thought processes are you planning on putting him through?" inquired Gottlieb.

"There are several things we need to accomplish. We need to tax the central intelligence, and this is accomplished by using some demanding mental activities you are probably familiar with. First, Dr. Gottlieb, our three main medical devices are in different rooms, so the test aren't performed simultaneously. We must depend on the computer to interlace the test results so we can overlap the experimental questions, acoustic signals, and the EEG. That is why we require a good control condition.

You will work very hard today moving Erick from place to place. We have three different rooms for testing all here in the basement. The first test we do is the PET study. I have a nurse giving Erick an injection now, and in about fifteen minutes, the radioactive material will disperse in his bloodstream. Then we can begin. If you don't mind, I want to tell you what to say to Erick and Lee. I will be outside the room, and you will be inside. These instructions consist of activities like adding up numbers in his head. On one occasion, I will ask you to turn up the speaker so the patient can hear the music. In some cases, you will be in the room with Erick and in other cases out of the room. Sometime when you are absent, Dr. Tripp will replace you. I will communicate with you with the headphones."

"Okay, let's go." With that statement, Wilhelm and Jacob walked down the hall toward the waiting room. The nurse nodded to Beckmann as he walked by her to denote that she had already given Erick his shot of the radioactive PET agent. Jacob went to the door of the waiting room and motioned to all parties to follow Wilhelm.

The assemblage turned into the first room to gaze on a large stainless-steel-framed table with a fabric web connecting across the frame and a very complicated apparatus at the end of the table with a hole in the center. With a heavy German accent, Wilhelm said, "This is a PET machine, Erick. It will read brain activity because of the radioactive material we just gave you. Please remove your clothing and put on this gown. You can change over there behind the screen. Give your clothing to Mike and then lie on this table, facing with your head at the far end."

Minutes later, Erick handed Mike his clothing and slid onto the table. A nurse placed color-coated EEG electrodes on Erick's head, on the portions that had been shaved for that purpose, and a few others on his forehead and the base of his neck. Connectors leading from the test room to the computer network were attached to each color-coded electrode so Erick could be easily disconnected from the devices.

"Dr. Gottlieb, will you put on these earphones so I can talk to you from outside the room? When the test is underway, please remain quiet.

Do not be alarmed if you hear some sharp sounds. I am doing that for time markings for system synchronization. Okay?"

"Thanks for telling me."

Beckmann gave instructions to Jacob, and then Jacob repeated them to Erick. "Erick, it is very important that you remain very still and not move during these tests. If you cannot remain still, we will have to repeat the test." The PET scan was underway.

All went well for Erick awake and hypnotized, but Lee didn't want any part of it. It required the assertive measures from Mike to make Lee realize that being quiet was far better than what Mike had to offer. The PET scan process lasted nearly twenty minutes, whereupon the assemblage followed Dr. Beckmann to the next room with the sounds of their footsteps echoing from the walls of the sterile facility with heavy metal pipes overhead. As they exited the area, Jacob placed his hand on Mike's massive shoulder and said a simple thanks. A bad fluorescent light flickered badly overhead as the group walked down the hall toward the next room. They passed a room with humming sounds.

"What's in there?" Erick asked Beckmann.

"It is a supercomputer," remarked Beckmann. "We take all of your data digitally, and it is processed by that computer. It is not a common computer. It is the fastest one in the world. Your data will be handled by the very best computer available."

Jacob now understood what Wilhelm was doing by using the same set of questions in three different modalities. He needed sustained activity in a particular area for a certain period to collect data for the overlapping to succeed. The questions were aimed at stimulating but also maintaining that stimulation, a certain portion of the brain thereby creating the same response for all three tests; as a consequence, the data from the tests could be overlaid and compared for each subject: Erick alert, Erick hypnotized, and Lee. There were the math questions to trigger the cognitive centers, the music test to trigger the aesthetic center and the memory centers, and other questions oriented at both short-term and long-term memory. Other questions went to emotion and to reasoning and personality. The sequence of questions varied in the three modalities, but all sets of questions were asked. Besides the general questions that could be compared, the EEG and marker beeps were the time recorders.

Emotion questions were asked of each of the three personalities, and they would trigger a human response like anger, sorrow, love, and pity. When Erick was asked about his sister, Mary, he became immediately remorseful, while Lee totally ignored the name. Whereas when Lee was asked about Marina and Elsa, Lee changed his mood completely and became despondent, but Erick was impervious to the name. When Jacob asked Lee about his baby sister, tears formed in Lee's eyes as he recalled Elsa's death. The mention of the CIA brought anger to Lee, but to Erick it elicited no response whatsoever. The questions and the sequence of presenting them were the result of Dr. Wilhelm Beckmann's doctoral thesis at the University of Austria at Innsbruck. It was Beckmann who knew how to make sense from the data, and it was Beckmann Jacob depended upon.

"Here we are," Wilhelm said as he opened the door to the next room. The small room appeared in the center of the larger room as the assemblage walked into the larger room.

"Erick, you will have to stay in that smaller room and sit quietly in the plastic chair there. There is a speaker in there, and Dr. Gottlieb will talk to you using it." Mike again positioned himself near the single door outside the larger room. Two male technicians walked Erick into the small room, sitting him in the plastic chair in the middle. There was a large metal device overhead.

Erick sat as requested and felt a chill as his bare buttocks touched the cold plastic chair. The technicians started to attach EEG electrodes and then to lower a massive metallic assembly with a hole in it over Erick's head. The unit finally came to a rest slightly above Erick's shoulders. "This is the MEG assembly, and it will measure Erick's nerve impulses. Do you understand, Erick?" There was a muffled yes coming from within the unit as Erick answered. The inner walls of the room were all metallic and shiny, and all spoken words echoed in the room. "Erick, you will please sit very still in that chair and answer Dr. Gottlieb's questions as before."

Dr. Gottlieb, please give all metal objects in your possession, including your belt buckle, to Mike.

The grounded metallic walls electrically isolated the small inner room so the only detectable signals were originating in Erick's brain and heart. Jacob sat outside the small room and watched through a window. Erick sat patiently, and muffled voices came through an unusual speaker. Shortly thereafter, the overhead system began to rotate about his head, and Erick had to shut his eyes to avoid becoming nauseous. Then Erick heard the familiar voice of Dr. Gottlieb. "We are ready to begin, Erick."

The process continued with both the alert and hypnotized Erick, and all the while, the scanner rotated slowly about Erick head. The chamber was becoming cold from the heat exchange from the overhead Squids, but it was tolerable. Erick continued answering questions Gottlieb put to him.

It was now time for Lee to appear. A thin technician pushed a lever that elevated the MEG assembly so Jacob could withdraw Lee. Mike entered the room. This was no time for Lee's monkey business. As Jacob stood in front of the hypnotized Erick, he said, "Lee, I want to talk to you."

Lee dutifully arrived with squinted eyes, looked at Jacob, and took a quick peek at Mike. "You again," he mumbled.

"Mike is here to make certain you participate."

Lee looked at Mike's massive arms and quickly said, "What do you want?"

"Just like last time, we want your participation."

"What if don't want to do it?"

"Like last time, Lee, we only want to talk to you when your head is inside that overhead device."

Lee looked up to see the strange apparatus over him. "I am not certain that I want to do it."

Mike stepped forward, and his huge hand grabbed Lee's left biceps and began driving his thumbs into it while his fingers encircled the arms. Slowly Mike began to continue the pressure on one arm as Lee began to feel the pain and the unbelievable strength Mike had in his hands. "Hey, guy, that hurts!" Mike reached for the other bicep and began the same tactic as Gottlieb looked on. "Ouch, you bastard. That hurts."

There was a moment of silence from Lee. Then: "Okay. I'll do your stupid shit."

Mike released his grip immediately, and Lee issued a sigh of relief. The technician reentered the room and lowered the scanner over Lee's head as Lee was using each hand to awaken his biceps. Everyone left the room as Lee was erasing the pain.

"Lee, you may want to shut your eyes to avoid becoming dizzy and sick."

Lee agreed, and the program continued as the scanner rotated around Lee's head. Gottlieb's questions continued from outside the room. Then Hunter replaced him.

Hunter started the conversation by asking Lee in Russian whether Mike had hurt him. Lee acknowledged that he no longer hurt.

When the activity was over, Jacob reawoke Erick and moved him down the hall to the last room, the functional magnetic resonance imaging room. Beckmann nodded to his technicians as he walked down the hall. "So far so good, Dr. Gottlieb. "Only one more test to go."

They walked down to the far end of the hallway for testing with the fMRI unit. Lee had resigned himself to cooperate after seeing Mike, and testing was completed more expeditiously than earlier.

When the questions were exhausted, Beckmann looked at his technicians. "How does it look?" he asked. He got the thumbs-up sign. Testing was complete.

Jacob, Mike, and a technician reentered the room to remove Erick from the MRI scanner and to extract an alert Erick from the hypnotic state. Mike handed Erick his clothing.

"Okay, Dr. Gottlieb, Erick is through here, and now the supercomputer and my people must do their work. I will call you when it is time to meet. I am very pleased with how things have gone."

He walked up to Mike and, tilting his head back to look at him, said, "We couldn't have done it without you. Thank you so very much."

Wilhelm patted Mike on the shoulders and turned to Jacob. "It is a good thing that you brought both Dr. Tripp and Mike along. Otherwise, we would have had serious problems with Lee. I can see that. They both were wonderful." He shook Gottlieb's hand, and Jacob said his thanks as Wilhelm walked into the computer room.

In the parking lot, Hunter asked Jacob to come by his car, whereupon he handed Jacob the remaining metal components of Lee's rifle, which had been meticulously restored and blued. "Thanks, Hunter, they look like new. I expect to complete the bicycle work this weekend. I'll have you over when it's done."

Chapter 18: The Geneticist

On this Saturday morning, Jacob was ready for the final assembly of the Oswald bicycle. Jacob had earlier painted the frame of the bike and some of the refurbished parts provided by Hunter. He was a perfectionist, and the frame revealed his skill. The frame was ready for the final assembly. Although he had the trigger assembly and other small parts that weren't required for the bike assembly, final assembly would seem incomplete without them in the leather saddlebag.

Jacob took his first step in assembling the bike by hanging the frame on the bike stand. Next, he placed the rifle barrel, now newly painted exactly like the remainder of the bike frame, in the horizontal position and tightened it into place at both ends. It worked perfectly. Once mounted, one could barely see the separation at either end of the barrel, even with a magnifying glass, because of the close-tolerance machining achieved by the CIA. Little corrosion occurred at the both ends, so the barrel fit snuggly.

Jacob took great joy in every added component. Handlebars, pedals, gears, derailleurs, water bottle holder, chain, and tires found their way onto the frame. Lastly, new front and rear brakes were attached and adjusted.

With a fresh cup of coffee in his left hand, his right hand rotated the rear wheel of the bike still mounted on the bike stand. He stood back and watched the wheel spin almost forever as he sipped coffee. No one was there. He patted himself on the back. "Great job, Jacob," he said out loud. There was only one thing left to do, and that was to add the sights, special wrench, trigger assembly, pins, and tire patch kit to the saddlebag. He arranged these items on a red rag and photographed them before placing them in the saddlebag.

The garage door opened, and Jacob lugged the bike, mounted in its bike stand, out to his driveway and photographed it in full morning sun. Jimmy was passing by and noticed the new bicycle. It stopped him. "Hi, Dr. Gottlieb. Did you buy a new bike?"

"No, Jimmy, I restored an old one."

"Wow, Dr. Gottlieb, it looks new."

"Thanks, Jimmy. Could you do me a favor and photograph me holding this bike?"

Jimmy did as Jacob requested, and then Jacob asked Jimmy to take a couple of photos of him riding the bike. Jimmy complied and then continued on his morning paper delivery. Jacob said to himself. *Since I am on it, why not ride it?*

Every pedal stroke moved him faster, and a smile crossed his face. Jacob turned the corner and began riding serpentine down the street, waving to a neighbor he didn't know. He was pleased with his accomplishments. *Who would have ever believed? Thirty-plus years underwater, and look at it now. Wow—what an experience!*

Jacob called Jim after returning home. "Jim, I completed the bicycle assembly, and it looks fabulous. I rode it around the block. It's hard to believe that it's the same hunk of junk I pulled out of the lake."

"I would like to see it. Are you going to be home this morning? I'd like to drop by."

"Sure, Jim. Come by before noon. I also want you to think about something. I would like to give the bicycle to Hunter. Do you approve?"

An hour later, Jim parked in the driveway and wandered into the garage. Jacob was organizing his tools. The bike leaned against the workbench. "So, this is it," Jim said.

Jacob nodded.

"Wow Jacob! It looks like a new bike. I would like to ride it down the street too."

Jacob rolled the bike over to Jim. "Have at it! Roll up your right cuff first."

A few minutes later, Jim coasted back into the garage. "It's so quiet. This is unreal, simply unreal."

Jacob closed the garage door and began removing the rifle barrel from the frame. Then he handed it to Jim. "I see now how Lee could assemble the rifle parts into the bike frame so quickly. This is amazing."

"Regarding giving the bicycle to Hunter, I have no problem with you giving it to him provided that we remain out of any 'follow-on' activity. Hunter's earned it."

Jacob called Hunter shortly after Jim left. "This morning, I rode the Oswald bicycle around my block. It was a fantastic experience. I am done with it. Do you still want it? You can do with it as you want."

"Oh yes, Jacob. I certainly do. It will end up in our museum for sure."

"Okay, it's yours. Jim is in agreement provided that you sign a document that you will not divulge my name, my partner's name, or my patient's name and our addresses. Is that agreeable to you?"

Hunter almost shouted, "Oh, yes. I will be happy to sign it." He sounded gratified over the offer since it was placing an incredible historical gift in his hands. "Please come by my home tonight and pick it up. If you come by at seven o'clock, I'll take you to dinner."

On Tuesday of the following week, Jacob jogged down the stairs to the basement of the Stanton Young building near the Health Science Center, because his afternoon appointment was with Dr. Franklin Moseley, a geneticist in the evolution of complex traits group. He turned the corner, located room twelve, and entered. A graduate student pointed to the corner office, and Jacob meandered that direction, eyeing all the equipment and making strange sounds along the way with a lot of items rocking back and forth. Moseley, a slender, athletic-appearing fellow, saw him heading his direction and greeted him at his office door.

Jacob sat down as Moseley did likewise at his desk after closing his office door. "I know you are a busy man, Dr. Moseley, so let me get directly to the point. This matter concerns a patient in my private practice that has a second personality in his brain, and I am attempting to remove that personality named Lee. After exhaustive research, I discovered that this personality knows minute details of someone who turned out to be my patient's father. By that I mean Lee knows verifiable details of his father's life up to the point of conception but nothing thereafter.

"Most recently, I have been able to contact his mother under hypnosis in the same body, and she too is credible. She knows minute details of Lee's mother's life up to the point of conception. Perhaps the most stunning discovery was that the gibberish Lee was speaking turns out to be exquisite Russian, and the mother speaks Russian too. The mother's homeland was the Soviet Union. I enlisted professor emeritus Hunter Tripp here at the university, who teaches Russian, and he concurs that both personalities in my patient's brain speak Russian and are credible.

"I believe that I have a first. I have a man who has both the memory and much of the personality of his father and firsthand knowledge and memory of his mother locked in his brain. There is no other explanation than that it is a genetic mutation of some sort. I know that birds and mammals migrate over large distances. I now believe that instinct is learned behavior, passed on genetically by DNA and DNA switches during early embryo development. My question for you is simple. Is my patient with this suspected mutation of interest to your scientific community? I ask this because I am trying to eliminate this heinous personality from my patient's brain, and in so doing, I could destroy a valuable specimen for understanding the genome."

Moseley looked at Jacob and simply said, "Wow! There is little known about this important subject. It is of current academic curiosity. I can tell you that such a person is incredibly valuable and of extraordinary importance. There is no question about it. Your patient is one in a trillion or maybe even higher number than that. Such a person is so valuable that I couldn't even place a number on it. Zoological geneticists are examining migrating species such as whales to uncover the migratory 'DNA switch.' After all, we are doing this to understand man."

"What would you need of my patient Dr. Moseley?"

"We would of course need to verify your statement of both parents here in our lab.

"My patient, even under hypnosis, is extremely aggressive and almost impossible to handle. I happen to be associated with highly trained attendants, who know how to handle such people. My chief attendant is six foot eight and weighs about two hundred sixty pounds, a retired professional wrestler. I don't believe you or your staff can handle Lee. I should let you see some videos so you can get an idea of what you would be getting into.

May I further point out that my patient has knowledge that should not be made public. Can you work around that? After all, your tests are almost all in vitro anyway. Can you accept my word, my office partner and fellow psychiatrist, head of neurology, and the word of a professor emeritus here at the university?"

"I cannot answer that question right now, Dr. Gottlieb. That decision would have to go through the department Chairman. Please don't decide until I have an opportunity to bring it up to the chairman, Albert Whitten. I cannot overemphasize the importance of this finding. It potentially has extreme value to mankind of Nobel Prize importance."

On the following Monday, Marilyn escorted Drs. Whitten and Moseley into Gottlieb's treatment room. Jacob greeted them halfway across the room with a handshake.

"Gentlemen, please be seated there on the couch. I have selected a few videos of my treatment involving Lee. Professor Hunter Tripp of the language departments has participated in several sessions. You should feel free to contact him, particularly regarding Lee's ability to speak the Russian language. Dr. Tripp teaches the Russian language at the university. Before we begin, please understand that Erick, my patient, has never been outside the US, nor does he know any foreign language. Erick possesses a second personality within his brain named Lee. I have selected videos that reflect Lee's ability to speak Russian. You will see him in one of his difficult moods too."

Chairman Whitten cleared his throat and said, "Dr. Gottlieb, we accept your expertise and Professor Tripp's expertise as well, and while the video is certainly of interest to us, our purpose for being here is to see how we can proceed. It is true that most of our studies are in vitro but not all. It is of particular interest to discuss this element. We, of course, need to do some due diligence to verify your statements and perhaps see one such session where your patient speaks Russian. But as you can imagine, there will inevitably be circumstances where we must do more. These times cannot be foreseen. How do we get past this roadblock?"

"I do not yet know, Chairman Whitten. At the moment, this heinous personality is only contacted through hypnosis. When I show you the video, you will better understand what I am talking about. I cannot tell you how long he will be available to us because this heinous personality, Lee, is attempting to take over my patient daily. If he succeeds, Lee may become available continuously, but the patient may not!"

"I understand, Dr. Gottlieb. We have a time problem. We can only proceed with a grant from NIH, and this will take about one and a half years. Therefore, I have the following question. Can we keep the current status quo until then? There would be grant funding for you and a staff member on this project, because it seems that we cannot do it without either of you."

"Thank you, Dr. Whitten, but I have a lot to digest and a patient to be concerned about. To you, what is the importance of this project?"

"Dr. Gottlieb, I consider this remarkable discovery to be one of the most important in all of mankind. It is of Nobel Prize importance. I urge and beg you to consider what I am saying very carefully. Even if you go ahead with this elimination, we can still learn much, but to have an alert subject is mind boggling. He is the quintessential test subject and so easy to deal with when comparing him with an angry sixty-ton sperm whale. Please consider what I have said very carefully."

"Do you have any problems dealing with a patient who feels like a lab rat, which likely makes him depressed?"

"This is so new to me. I hadn't even thought about that. But off the cuff, I would believe that ninety-five percent of our activity is in vitro, so I believe we could handle it such that your patient maintains his dignity."

Then Dr. Moseley interjected, "Dr. Gottlieb, I concur totally with what Dr. Whitten just said. This is an absolutely fantastic discovery and remarkable work on your part. We can learn so much about man's embryonic development that leads to this situation. I also believe that if your patient is agreeable, he could be paid a healthy income for his time. This could eliminate the 'lab rat' effect."

"Okay, gentlemen, let's look at the video so you can see what you are getting into. You may change your minds."

After the video, all men stood. The geneticists were in awe. "Dr. Gottlieb, I now see why one requires a special person to handle your patient."

After additional conversation, Jacob said, "Thank you, gentlemen. I promise to consider what you said very carefully. Please understand, you cannot handle this patient. He could be a killer. Do remember that my Hippocratic oath requires me to place my patient first. I have to do that, but there may be ways for us to work together. I hope to eliminate the evil personality, but the DNA remains unchanged. I will get back to Dr. Moseley before I make a final decision."

Gottlieb continued. "Why not put together a series of questions for my patient that you normally ask later in the study. I will volunteer my time and the patient in both alert and hypnotize mode to answer your questions. If we do it right away, we can do it before Lee takes control of Erick. We can do this in your presence at the hospital. That maybe a start for your grant request."

"Thank you for dropping by."

Hunter, now in possession of the Oswald bicycle, wasted no time in calling for a special meeting of the John Kennedy Assassination Committee. The meeting took place at the museum in a side room. All six committee members as well as the curator of the museum, Patricia Ingle, were present. Hunter stood in front of the assemblage.

"Committee personages, I called this special meeting because I, through a party who wishes to remain anonymous, have come upon new information about the Kennedy assassination that could reshape our collective opinion. I plan to discuss the new insight and some of the evidence collected supporting new conclusions."

Edward Martindale said, "It is difficult to believe that there is new information, not in the hands of the FBI or perhaps the CIA, that is new after so many years. I remain a skeptic."

"Maybe you will change your mind," Hunter offered.

Hunter discussed Lee's version in detail, discussing the training on the new rifle at the abandoned Jett & Son Quarry up to the assassination that took place from this very building. The group was beginning to pay more attention. "With assistance from my anonymous friend, I located the quarry on August twentieth, this year 1995. I collected one unspent bullet and several casings, and I dug up nineteen bullets from the hill located behind the target area. There were armed guards there, and I almost got caught."

Hunter reached into his pocket and removed the intact bullet placed in a clear plastic bag located at the quarry. He opened his briefcase and circulated the bullet, also placed in a plastic bag, around the table. Hunter next held photomicrographs he had taken of bullets removed from the corpse and found at the site, positioned side by side. He next presented two plastic bags containing recovered casings. "In my opinion, the casings located at Jett & Son are identical to the two discovered upstairs by the FBI. Of course, these speculations should be verified by an expert."

Hunter cast his eye around the table, and all attendees appeared to be paying close attention.

Frances Martindale stated, "But we do not have the blue bicycle. Are you suggesting that we locate the bike in the lake?"

"I was just coming to that." Hunter left the group and returned, wheeling a blue bicycle. "My friend located this bicycle at the bottom of Lake Hubbard in front of the spillway and restored it. Come here and look at it." As the group arrived, Hunter lifted the rear tire off the floor and turned the pedals to show the rear wheel rotating.

"There is no rifle in there," offered Dr. Murray.

"Pick it up and scrutinize it."

Dr. Murray did and said, "I do not see how a rifle could even exist in this bike."

Hunter had assembled and disassembled the rifle into and out of the bike frame many times, so he had become adept at it. "Watch closely," he said as he began to dissemble the contributing rifle components. He emptied the saddlebag and placed those pieces on a shop rag lying on the table. He then removed the other components in front of the group and laid them on a newspaper lying on the table.

"I now have all of the rifle elements. Watch carefully as I assemble the rifle." Hunter masterfully assembled the blue rifle in front of all committee members in less than a minute. He handed the rifle to Professor Martindale, who now cradled it in his hands. "Pull the trigger. It's not loaded," prompted Tripp. I only have one bullet and it is in the bag in front of me.

Martindale did. "Wow," he said as he passed it to Dr. Thomas Mallory.

The rifle circulated around the group and ended up in Hunter's hands. He began to reassemble the rifle into the bicycle. Within a few seconds, the rifle was incorporated back into the bicycle before their eyes and became invisible.

Professor Chester had remained silent during Hunter's presentation and spoke up. "Hunter and I were witnesses to the initial dismantling of the recovered bike at his friend's home. I assure you that it didn't look like this bike." He reached into his jacket pocket and circulated his color prints. "These prints were taken during that process. It required great skill to disassemble the bike without damaging it. We poured rusty water from the tubes composing the frame. I, for one, believe everything Hunter has said. I might add that not many institutions are capable of designing such a rifle. The FBI and the CIA can do it. Two questions now remain. First, how do we authenticate the bicycle? And second, what do we do about the CIA, since they, according to Hunter, perhaps were involved?"

Following an exuberant discussion, the group decided not to address the CIA issue at that time. Rather, Hunter would contact the FBI and let them examine the bicycle, casing, bullets, and the intact bullet and perform their own ballistic tests. Hunter would become the interface person. If the FBI agreed with Hunter's conclusion, then they, the committee, had the authority to authenticate the bicycle and add it to the museum's collection. Further, a new assassination report would be written, and all committee members would become authors.

All committee members walked around, shaking their heads in astonishment.

Chapter 19: The Results

Ralph Steele's office door was open on this late afternoon, so Jacob sauntered in. Ralph was fidgeting with the back of his digital projector. After a cordial greeting, Ralph continued to try to get his computer to project on the screen in his office, muttering all the time; with a smile and a sigh of relief, the Windows logo projected on the screen. "I think I am ready for Wilhelm now," he grumbled as his disgust with computers reflected his demeanor.

Wilhelm shuffled in exactly at six p.m. and, along with him, Dr. Katherine Courtney. "Well, doctors, I think the supercomputer has done its job very well, and we have answers. Maybe not the ones you want to hear, but they are believable answers nonetheless." There was an ominous note to his words. Jacob became apprehensive, even before the meeting began.

"Dr. Gottlieb, I wanted to thank you for the magnificent manner that your team handled Lee. I frankly didn't expect good results with him when I first met him, but I believe we acquired reliable data. I am very pleased with the results. We had a number of questions that were answered, and these included brain function differences between Erick alert, Erick hypnotized, and Lee. This also gives us an opportunity for the first time to see what is happening in the brain under hypnosis. It is very exciting and certainly publishable. I also want you to remember that we are collecting three-dimensional information or locations of specific processing areas in Erick's brain. When we are done, we will be able to locate a specific volume of the brain where this event takes place."

Ralph took over the conversation to accelerate the discussion process and, to be honest, to improve communication because of Wilhelm's heavy accent slowed down the dialogue. A knock on the door terminated Steel's discussion as he got up and walked to the door. When he opened the door, Jim Hanford was standing there. "Jim, I am pleased that you could make it." Steele led Jim over to Drs. Beckmann and Courtney for the introductions.

Ralph immediately reviewed the earlier conversations as all got comfortable in their chairs. "Jim, Dr. Beckmann has been the world's leader in this trimodality brain analysis, which analysis has been made possible by the detailed algorithms developed by Wilhelm and now our team." He stopped for a moment to take a drink of water before continuing. "Our institution is the only institution outside of Europe that is doing this work, so we are indeed very fortunate to have Dr. Beckmann here with us. As you will see, we will get some clear-cut answers, and we will have some disappointments. After you see the data Wilhelm has prepared, we shall jointly discuss the Anderson case and determine whether we can come to a conclusion regarding what we have and the possible next step. Hopefully Jacob, you will not mind our doing so."

"Oh no, Ralph, I anxiously await the results, and the ensuing discussion is more than welcome and appreciated."

Ralph began, "The first order of business was to analyze Erick alert and hypnotized. As we all expect, there would be little difference expected between the two. Look at the left cortical areas of the fMRI image of the alert on the left side of the screen and hypnotized Erick on the right when Erick is listening to music he likes. Both images are exactly alike. In summary and without going through all of the data, we conclude that Erick hypnotized and Erick alert are identical."

"Then we can use the hypnotized Erick as our control?" remarked Katherine.

"Yes! There are subtle differences that interest Wilhelm but are not germane to our conversation and case history. Moreover, from a practical point of view, I have recommended that we use Erick hypnotized as the standard reference. Jacob—Jim, do either of you have trouble with that recommendation?"

Both men said they had no problems, so Ralph continued. "If there ever is a conflict in interpreting the data, then we can use both the hypnotized and alert data sets. This is very, very good news, because it provides us with twice the database to compare Erick to Lee. From this point forward for this meeting, we shall not differentiate between Erick alert or Erick hypnotized. Okay?" There was a nod of agreement between Jacob and Jim.

"Lady and gentlemen, from this point forward, you will see two images on the screen, each of the identical view of Erick's brain. The one on the left is Erick hypnotized, and the one on the right is Lee hypnotized."

Steele continued the presentation with a copious number of slides, including some in 3-D format. Then one such image was rotated. Jim Hanford was fascinated by what he had just seen and blurted out, "Hey, how did you do that?"

A smile brightened Beckmann's face. "This is what we can do with the supercomputer, but we still need to create the algorithm to do it properly. I am very pleased with our success in this area."

Jim was still studying the picture on the screen. "What is this other bright area over here?" Ralph handed him a red laser pointer, and Hanford projected the laser light to another bright spot in the dorsolateral prefrontal cortex.

"It is nice of you to observe it. We believe this area to be Lee's central executive, which is processing information. Note that it is irregularly shaped and somewhat pear shaped. This area shows up each time we give Lee a task that requires processing. Now look carefully at Erick's head. We see a similar pear-shaped volume, but please note that it is the mirror image of Lee, so that the narrow end of the two pear-shaped masses point toward one another. These are the central executives."

"On the next slide, we have superimposed the two executive centers. and all else is removed. Erick's central executive is colored yellow, and Lee's is colored red. If they are superimposed and were identical, then that volume will be colored orange." Now the audience viewed the key element of the analysis. They saw something shaped like a dog bone, which was bright yellow on the left end, dark red on the other, and vivid orange in the middle, the overlapped part. As Ralph rotated the shape by looking at it from the top of the head, it was quite symmetrical.

"What does this mean?" asked Jacob.

Ralph spoke immediately while looking at Jacob. "Unfortunately, it means that Erick's and Lee's central executive are interconnected. Although the bulk of Lee's processing is performed on the right and the bulk of Erick's thought processes are performed on the left, they are intertwined. It was our hope that Lee's central executive could be eroded, thereby completely removing Lee, but it cannot."

Jacob spoke up. "What would happen if we eroded part of Lee's central executive?"

"That is a possibility, but part of Lee's processing remains. Further, we note from the previous slide that Erick uses part of Lee's CE, and Lee uses part of Erick's CE. The risk is—"

There was silence as Ralph collected his thoughts and then resumed. "The risk is that we turn Erick into an unthinking vegetable. Gentlemen, please understand something. Dr. Beckmann is the only one in the world to uncover the CE. Therefore, there is no worldwide concordance about its existence and therefore no data whatsoever on the ramifications of its destruction. If the two were separable, then I believe there would be a reasonable chance." Jacob sighed, deeply venting his frustration over the depressing news. "Jacob, please remember that the CE serves as a supervisory control and cognitive processing. It is not that which makes Lee Lee and Erick Erick. We believe it is the central processor that shuttled information elsewhere in the brain."

Ralph continued with the slides. Slide after slide the psychiatrists saw similarities between the two personalities. The fact that Lee and Erick's data were similar wasn't surprising. After all, they were both of the same head. Finally, Jacob spoke up. "Are there any areas or zones where there is a difference between the two?"

Ralph and Wilhelm answered, "Yes" simultaneously. Then Ralph continued, "as you know, the brain has a special zone in the Broca area where emotions are processed. Let us look at that zone when Lee was dealing with thoughts of his late sister." Wilhelm, who now had control of the computer, moved ahead to this interesting slide. On the right they saw a red somewhat amorphous volume of Lee's emotions while thinking about his late sister and a comparable yellow volume of Erick thinking about his late sister." Ralph had the laser pointed at these areas as he spoke. "When I superimpose these two emotion zones, they do not coincide." Wilhelm went to the keyboard. As he played with the cursor keys, the two heads projected onto the screen started moving toward one another until there was only one skull outline.

Ralph began to speak. With a few clicks on the keyboard, the red and yellow volumes stayed the same color on the screen and remained distinct and separable. The doctors gazed at the screen intently as they visualized two colored blobs.

Katherine sputtered, "Doctors, I see separable volumes where sorrow is manifested in both personalities, and unlike the CE, they are different locations." With a few strokes on the keyboard, the volume took on three-dimensional forms, and as Wilhelm started rotating the irregularly shaped three-dimensional form in space, it was clear that the two zones never overlapped.

"What is the distance between the two closest points?" asked Gottlieb.

Wilhelm tapped at the keyboard, and a centimeter grid moved onto the screen, which he maneuvered to lay between the two areas.

"Dr. Gottlieb, the two zones appear to be no closer than six millimeters to one centimeter apart," Ralph conceded.

"Could you erode one without damaging the other?" asked Gottlieb.

"Absolutely. We work to higher accuracies in most Parkinson's disease cases."

Next, Wilhelm showed other emotions: love, anger, hatred for the case of Lee because Erick had no hatred within him, and joy. The same zone in the Broca's area was involved. This wasn't exclusive of the involvement of the CE, for it too was activated in some cases but not all. "Wilhelm," asked Jacob, "can you superimpose those four emotions into one view for each person?"

"Certainly, Dr. Gottlieb," answered Wilhelm. Then he started clicking on the keyboard, and then a new image appeared again in yellow and red on the screen. "This is sorrow and love." The images changed ever so slightly but still remained much the same. "Now I will add anger." The keystrokes continued, and when they stopped, the images changed, enlarged somewhat, filled in some of the void inner volume, and expanded in the case of Lee. But the two images were still clearly separable, although Lee's emotion center had enlarged, whereas Erick's didn't change.

"Now I will add love." Seconds later, a new image appeared on the screen as the computer collected the data from Erick's love for Sophia and Mary, and when Lee thought about his mother, Marina, and daughters. The two separable volumes filled in more and expanded a trifle but never overlapped. Dr. Steele looked at Jacob and asked, "Jacob, what does this mean to you?"

"It clearly shows a separable part of the brain in the Broca area where the two emotional centers are distinct and separable. Since Lee's social problems all pass through this area, it would appear to be a means of eradicating Lee. My concern is that we still see considerable activity within the central executive, so it is not a given that it will cure the problem. Have you seen any other major differences that we haven't seen yet?"

"No, we haven't, Jacob," Ralph answered. "Any comments, Dr. Courtney?"

"I understand the importance of what you are trying to do, but it just looks too chancy to me."

Dr. Gottlieb sat up straight in his chair, looked at Katherine, and said, "What would you say if I had evidence that Lee is a killer and wants to kill again?" Dr. Courtney sat back in her chair and shook her head without commenting.

"What do you think, Jim?"

"First, I am extremely impressed with what Wilhelm and his team have accomplished. All of the data makes sense to me. There must be a separable and existing place for Lee to reside within Erick's brain. If it were within the CE, then I believe that not only could Lee tune into Erick, which he can, but also more importantly that Erick could tune into Lee, which of course he cannot. Therefore, the concept of an emotion center is appealing, and since it is seen to exist, I can ascribe to it. However, having said that, we have no proof for any of this, and we are considering removing a portion of a man's brain based on unproven data."

Jim sat back in his chair, and since he would likely be the only naysayer, prepared himself for the onslaught likely to follow.

Jacob asked, "Ralph, how can we remove that last volume that Wilhelm showed us, and what happens to Erick if we do?"

Looking at the ceiling, Ralph responded, "There are basically seven current techniques, but only high-frequency ablation seems appropriate for us. As far as we know, no one has ever tried to destroy a specific emotion center before, so we do not know the answer. However, we do routinely destroy brain cells for certain cases of Parkinson's disease and epilepsy, so we have vast experience with limited brain cell destruction. To clarify things a bit more, all seven techniques have been employed in cancer treatment, and we can definitely draw on the published personality changes resulting from such treatment. In my opinion, it would be impossible to turn him into a vegetable. What we do know is that Erick hardly ever uses this portion of the brain. Therefore, if it were missing, it is unlikely that it would affect Erick in any way. This portion of the brain contains mainly the personality center, so I see that by removing it, we remove Lee. There is still a portion of Lee remaining in the CE and elsewhere, but the anger center has been removed, so even if Lee survives, which I doubt, he will not be hostile as he has been. It is kind of a microscopic, scaled-down frontal lobotomy."

Jim offered, "There are too many variables for success. I believe it will fail and not be worth the time and cost of doing it."

Gottlieb looked Hanford directly in the eyes. "Do you have a better way of eliminating a killer?"

There was a long pause. "No, I don't, Jacob. I wish I did."

Then Gottlieb looked directly into the eyes of Ralph and asked, "What are our chances of other negative effects like paralysis, stroke, or major personality changes to Erick?"

Ralph responded immediately. "Jacob, we cannot be certain of anything, but I ran a literature search regarding removing a portion of the brain via erosion and its effects on personality. I have copies of these papers here for you, and you must weigh them carefully. From my point of view based on many brain surgeries in this area, I haven't seen significant personality changes. Further, if we do the surgery on an awake patient, we can test the brain as we erode a portion thereof."

Jim looked at Wilhelm and waited for an opportunity to speak. "Wilhelm, what are the chances that your algorithms are incorrect and that what we are looking at is pure artifact?"

Wilhelm jerked upon hearing the question. However, it was an expected question. Still, the insinuation caused him to raise his voice in answering, "Well, Dr. Hanford, it is a logical question. I have spent hundreds of hours perfecting the software, but since it involves two or more separate modalities, I believe in the results. What it says is that there is considerable chemical, neurological, and blood flow activity in that portion of the brain simultaneously, and that can only mean one thing. The algorithms give us a picture within the brain during these activities. I believe the results."

"Okay, Ralph," asked Gottlieb, "what are the negative side effects of the electrical erosion method?"

"The major side effect is that we must tunnel through healthy brain to get to the appropriate area. Once there, is see no problem, but the tunneling damages some brain cells. There is also the possibility of hitting an artery or vein and causing a serious hemorrhage. However, we haven't shown you these data, but Wilhelm has mapped out the major blood vessels already. We shall select an entry route that avoids these vessels entirely. I also would like to point out that our probe is only 2.1 millimeters in diameter, so it wouldn't destroy many brain cells. The probe is nearly pointed and pushes cells aside as it enters rather than cutting them."

Jacob quickly summarized aloud. "We really have one approach, and that is electrical erosion."

Katherine spoke again. "How do you know where you are during the process?"

Ralph answered, "We place metallic marker at many positions on the skull of the patient. We can see these markers with CT. The CT scanner can also see the end of the probe. The CT is wired to the supercomputer too, so we have an instantaneous readout of our exact probe position. This is done routinely. I am certain that with CT guidance I can erode Lee's emotion center while not damaging Erick's. It will be a slow procedure because of the close tolerances required."

Jacob was mulling things over; he turned to Jim Hanford and asked, "What do you think, Jim?"

"I understand that we are between a rock and a hard place, but I keep feeling that we may be going too fast, and we are ahead of the technology. I am aware that Lee is getting stronger, and if we do nothing, then the prognosis for Erick is nil. On the other hand, we have very limited experience in Wilhelm's system, so I worry about making a mistake and eroding healthy brain matter."

Jacob took a drink of water before speaking. "We absolutely must look at this as experimental surgery, and Erick and his wife must be made aware of that. There are no guarantees here, and it is a best-effort scenario. We can protect the hospital and ourselves using form A2-1308. After all, we still do not know if the Andersons will be agreeable. It is my feeling that Erick will jump all over it, but his wife would have troubles authorizing it. She now is the legal guardian of Erick. I will talk to her at some length and see if she will agree if I decide to go ahead."

Then Hanford spoke up again. "What do we lose by waiting for a while?"

Jacob snapped back with a raised voice. "I am of the opinion that Lee is about ready to take over permanently. He has already tried it last week during the daytime but didn't succeed. I further believe that when he does succeed, we may never get Erick back. What do we gain? If we succeed, we gain a productive life; if the surgery fails, we have a killer in our midst. If we do nothing, we have a killer, probably permanently."

Jim countered, "Wilhelm, what do you believe would happen if we delay our decision for a while?"

Wilhelm answered, "I believe Lee's emotion center would get larger and coincide, possibly overlapping Erick's emotion center, and then we couldn't do the operation. I believe that as Lee gains more lifetime experiences, the emotion center will enlarge."

"Is it larger than Erick's now?"

"No, they are about the same size," answered Wilhelm.

Jacob leaned forward and spoke. "Doctors, I am very concerned. Lee is not just an antisocial person. Lee is a homicidal person. I cannot release Erick from the hospital for fear of Lee taking over as he has done in the past. Lee could easily kill someone. I have to cure my patient if at all possible and take a risk in doing so. I do not see many good choices here. Waiting could mean that Lee and Erick are no longer separable and therefore incurable." Jacob looked at the floor and shook his head.

Wilhelm looked directly at Jacob. "We are the only people in the world who have ever heard of an emotion center. I therefore must say that this surgery is highly speculative. It may not do any good. I do not know. Dr. Gottlieb, you have a very difficult decision to make, as does Erick's wife."

Jim asked, "If you did this, Jacob, how do you know if you have Lee or Erick?"

"That's a good question, Jim. I believe I can tell them apart via hypnosis as I have in the past."

Jacob and Jim stood up. Jacob extended his hand to both Ralph and Wilhelm.

Ralph looked at his two guests and said to Jacob, "This is in your hands now. There is nothing more that we can do or say. If you want to do it, I have a grant to cover the cost. The erosion is possible and can be done safely."

Jacob rubbed his jaw before speaking. "Wilhelm, can you provide me with a few color prints of the major items discussed here this evening? I will need these to discuss this procedure with Erick's wife."

Chapter 20: The Decision

Instead of going home after the Steele meeting, Jacob went to his office. He sat in his treatment room with Mozart playing, all lights on dim, and a cup of herbal tea. He pondered the events that had just taken place. A conundrum to be sure. He was juggling many balls: Erick, Lee, Sophia, Hunter, history, psychogenetics, the CIA, his possible assassination, and the Hippocratic oath. Suddenly, all lights went on in full brightness, startling him. His mind was considering the possible CIA efforts, and he flinched when it occurred.

"Sorry, Dr. Gottlieb," said a female voice. "I didn't mean to startle you."

Agnes walked over to him. It was the roly-poly nighttime cleaning lady. "I can go to another room."

"No. That's not necessary Agnes. I was preoccupied with a problem I have with a patient."

"Okay, Doctor." Agnes pushed her upright vacuum cleaner around the room. She always had a big smile, and this day was no different. Jacob recalled her bout with arthritis.

"How is your arthritis doing these days, Agnes?" Jacob shouted to be heard over the vacuum.

"The arthritis is doing fine, but I am not," she said with a smile. "I am done now, Doctor, so I'll get out of your hair and let you get back to your problem. Now don't let it worry you none. All you can do is your very best. I wish you good luck."

Jacob's mind went back to the juggle. *I will do my very best.*

On the following day, Jacob walked into Jim's office. The door closed behind Jacob as he leaned against it. "Jim, I really need to talk to you. I am coming down to the wire on the Anderson case."

Jim looked over his half-glasses. "Sit down, Jacob, I have been expecting you. I am sorry that I didn't get to you first. I know it is a hellish time for you."

"It's even gotten worse, Jim, at least the decision part of it. I am caught between a steamroller and the pavement. I can't win. I simply cannot win."

Jacob sipped some hot coffee, looked at the ceiling, twisted, turned, and cracked his knuckles before speaking. "This is a difficult decision to make. I have run into two additional problems with my decision-making process, and I want to talk about them."

"Fire away!"

After collecting his thoughts, Jacob began, "Earlier in the week, I visited Dr. Mosely, a geneticist here at the university. I wanted to know how important it was to leave Erick and Lee 'as is,' without surgery. Mosely believes, as I do, that Erick is one out of a billion or maybe a trillion who has inherited some of the personality and memory of both his father and mother locked up in his head at birth. When I left Mosely, he planned to discuss this phenomenon with the chairman of the Department of Zoology, Dr. Whitman.

"Mosely and Whiten dropped by yesterday. The genetics group believes Erick's mutation is of vital importance to the world and genetics. Studies are underway, trying to discover the DNA switches in whales that enable them to navigate long distances. These are exceptionally difficult and expensive studies to perform. Humans can talk, hold out their arm et cetera, and further have a studied genome. It simply makes sense to study Erick. They do not want any surgery that would alter Erick's brain, specifically in regard to Lee and Marina."

"That makes sense."

"They claim that they will accept our word, Steele's word, and Hunter's word. Therefore, they do not need to know who Lee is. However, that will change. Downstream this subject will come up again."

"Jacob, are you saying they want Lee as is, so they can study Erick genetically?"

"Exactly! These results can go a long way toward our understanding many zoological findings and improve mankind's lot. It is important publications for all of us, including you. They claim it is potentially of Noble Prize importance."

Jacob began drinking his coffee since it had cooled. "Jacob, this is mind boggling. What a terrible decision to make. You are damned if you do and damned if you don't. Good Lord, man, no one should have to make this decision. If you do the surgery, you could kiss off the Nobel Prize."

"It even gets slightly worse."

"Oh no! How can that be? What else happened?"

"Hunter has been pushing me during a phone call last night to delay the surgery until he collects more data on Marina and Lee. He was very nice about it but pointed out the historical importance of getting the Kennedy assassination correct. He wants more time with Marina in Erick's brain. He also wants to locate Marina personally to verify what we discovered last week is true. That will take time to accomplish. He needs to talk to the real Marina as soon as possible. If she is in the Soviet Union, so be it. He will travel there at his own expense. He only knows that surgery could mean losing Lee and probably Marina in Erick's head. Last, I believe that, with Erick's clinical depression, Lee can take control of Erick any time he wants. Erick may be lost anyway. I can somewhat pacify Hunter by giving him time with Marina this weekend."

"Okay, let's see if I have this correct. If you do the surgery and are successful, you lose additional facts regarding the Kennedy assassination and perhaps a small amount of genetic data. However, the genetic data is set either way, so you can't change that if it is either Erick or Lee. Right?"

"That is correct, but the ability to deal with both personalities and do cerebral testing Erick in vivo is gone. However, in vitro testing still remains."

"Okay, Jacob, now the Hippocratic oath states that you must do all possible to protect the health of your patient. Further, you believe Lee is taking over Erick, and Erick could be lost forever. If you do the surgery, then you may restore life to Erick. But there is no guarantee that surgery will work. You cannot decide. It's impossible. What in the hell are you supposed to do?" There was a pause, then Jim said, "Damn it, you can't make that decision. Is Erick more important than mankind? Can Erick tolerate being a lab rat?"

"I am still mulling over the surgery. I still have a little time, but if I decide to do it, then the decision depends on Sophia. If she says no surgery, then I cannot do it, and Hunter and Mosely will have access to Erick for a while. But the bulk of their work is one and a half years away awaiting an NIH grant.

I also do not believe that I can cure Lee, so if Lee takes over, Erick is probably doomed. I am not saying that I will not continue to try to help him. I hate to say this, but my insides are still quivering. Sounds like it's time to get drunk."

"Jacob, I am so sorry. It's simply unfair. I cannot advise you."

That night, Jacob met Sophia at Fujiyama Japanese Restaurant. Jacob felt that they had great sushi, and since Sophia had never tried sushi, it would be an interesting experience for her. Jacob ordered a bottle of warm Sake, and while they consumed it, Jacob went over the completed testing at the medical school.

"I am certainly pleased that I had both Hunter and Mike with me, because they made it work. The university scientists had to combine four different medical modalities."

Sophia asked, "What's a modality?"

"It is a medical procedure like an x-ray. There is so much data collected that they use the world's largest and fastest computers to do the bulk of the work and combine the results of the various modalities. It is a big deal. Erick had to be moved to three different rooms during the process."

"What were the results, Jacob?"

"I'll be getting copies of them shortly. We can go over them together, whether they are good, bad, or indifferent."

The sushi arrived. In between bites, Jacob asked her what she did at the real estate company.

"I'm the general manager for a large firm with three offices within the city. Real estate has started to move lately, so I have been inordinately busy. One of my jobs is to check all the calculations the salespeople create. Typically, they make mistakes. After that, I deal with the title company to make certain everything is in order. I also have to worry about team morale and that type of stuff."

"The job sounds stressful."

"It was at first, until I realized that people make mistakes, especially when finalizing a big deal. They seem to go together. Now, I let the job come to me, and when there is a lot to do, I go in a little early without the distractions of my office mates. I like it that way. I believe that I have things under control. That sounds terrific for you and a lot of responsibility too."

"There is no question about the responsibility, but I am very well organized."

"Then you must make a comfortable living."

"Yes, that's true. The owner is semiretired, so I have almost total control of personnel, and he appreciates my work. The loss of Erick's income doesn't bother me at all. Further, as GM, I established a medical insurance plan for all employees, and that comes in handy now."

Jacob patted the top of her hand and said, "I am pleased to hear that, Sophia. I have worried about it."

Sophia reciprocated by gathering his fingertips in the palm of her hand. They both stopped eating for a minute and gazed into the other's eyes. Neither spoke.

Jacob hastened over to Jim's office after work hours and sat in front of him. Jim looked up and asked, "Have you made up your mind yet?"

Jacob responded, "Yes, I have. I have decided to advise Sophia to do the surgery without pressuring her. I know how improbable success will be, but I must try. Lee told me that when he takes over, he knows exactly what he will do after escaping Cedar Ridge. Lee plans to become a hired gun—a professional assassin that goes after important people like presidents."

Jim shivered when he heard this. "Destroying Lee is really important. My job is to save Erick, and if I can destroy Lee at the same time, I have a double positive—a win-win situation. I have tried everything I know, and I haven't made a significant change in Lee or even made Erick stronger. I am at my wit's end. It seems the only chance I have is based on unproven science that at least seems credible to me. If I do nothing, I have a killer in the hospital."

Jim took a deep breath. "Jacob, I share your anguish. I am concerned. There are just too many variables. You cannot release Erick from the hospital, because you will be placing society at serious risk. Should you do the surgery? That is the question. It is a lose-lose situation for me. I know you really care about your patient. Therefore, this possible surgery may be your only chance to save Erick, and there is only a paucity of data available to make your decision. You could get lucky, and Erick's wife could say, 'No surgery.' But you still have one more chance following the surgery. You can examine both Erick and Lee under hypnosis before releasing Erick. All I can say is, good luck."

"Jim, on another subject, I have been thinking about this brain-genetic effect, and it really makes sense to me. I have concluded that there is no such thing as true instinct. Instinct is learned behavior passed on genetically. That is why infant mammals know how to suckle and geese know where and when to migrate. It is learned behavior passed on genetically because it is an attribute for survival. There is no instinct. It is learned behavior passed on genetically."

"I never thought about it before, but it sure makes sense to me."

Jacob received the color prints and written data from Wilhelm and asked Sophia to discuss the results at his home on Saturday. Sophia accepted. At exactly three p.m., Sophia drove into the driveway and parked. When she exited her car, she noticed the red 1957 Thunderbird parked next to her and walked over to it. She rubbed her hands along the side, stopping at the circular rear window. Jacob was standing there, watching her, but she did not notice him at first.

They walked toward each other to embrace in a warm, affectionate hug that persisted for minutes. Her arms were wrapped around him under his arms with her head flattened sideways against his chest. She felt so comfortable that she didn't want it to end. Tears welled in her eyes, and she blinked then away. She finally let go, blinked away a few tears, and stepped back as Jacob kissed her forehead.

"When did you get the T-Bird?" she asked.

"They just brought it to me this morning. I am planning on restoring it as my next project. The body is in exceptionally good shape, but the engine needs work." He hastily added, "But it runs."

"Oh, how neat! I hope that I will get to see it when you've completed it."

"I assure you that you will, Sophia. It will always remind me of you."

She recalled the conversation with Jacob about old collectable cars, and a warm glow passed through her body. He grabbed her hand and led her into the house via the garage door, closing the roll-up garage door.

"How do you want to proceed, Sophia?"

"Jacob, I have been thinking a lot about this, and I believe that I want to get it over with as soon as possible and then spend more time on pleasant subjects."

He led her toward the dining room table. Papers and color prints were lying there, ready for inspection.

He then went through the multi-modality test procedure implemented by Dr. Beckmann, revealing that this procedure wasn't universally accepted yet, but he believed it would be shortly. "It gives us the best possible means of understanding what is going on in Erick's head. These data give us hope to assist Erick, who now is living in a personal hell. It is the very best shot we have in understanding what is going on in Erick's head. It makes sense, but it also makes no promises. This is new and without verification from another institution. It is experimental and must be treated as such."

"Thank you for your candor. Jacob, simplify all of this for me. What does it reveal?"

Jacob explained that the brain possesses a central executive, which is the primary brain processor of brain activity. "If you think of the brain as a computer containing other computers, like one for hearing, seeing, thinking, and so forth, the central executive is the controlling computer. The central executive makes it all work together. Thus, the key questions are the following: First, does Erick/Lee possess a detectable central executive? Second, are they separable? And third, if so, is Lee's removable? These data reveal that Erick and Lee's central executive overlap, and one cannot be removed without damaging the other. Picking up the photo showing this result, Jacob pointed out the dog-bone-shaped photo with three colors. "Erick's color is yellow, and Lee's is red. The overlap is seen as orange. Since there is an orange color there, the two central executives cannot be separated. They overlap. However, there is also an emotion center. The emotion center makes Lee Lee and Erick Erick—and these zones are separable. They physically are at different locations in the brain. The two centers are separated by a minimum of six millimeters to one centimeter. Then, holding his thumb and index finger apart by one centimeter, he visually showed her the separation. Therefore, in the opinion of Dr. Ralph Steele, world-renowned neurosurgeon, Lee's is removable."

Jacob continued, "Let's summarize. Erick has overwhelming evidence of a second and separate personality who is taking over his mind. These results confirm my diagnosis. This person is an antisocial, despicable individual who is capable of heinous transgressions. I know that he must be stopped. I further believe that the best way of doing that is through brain erosion. The only possible way of removing Lee is with this surgery. Lee is beyond psychotherapy. I recommend that Erick have this surgery, but it is your decision. Further, it not without risks."

"Jacob, let's back up a minute. Your unverifiable procedures have detected a second personality. I find it—"

"Sophia, my work and your personal experiences have also shown this personality to exist. The difference is that we know where in the brain it exists."

"Okay, given that, how do you propose to do the removal?"

"Dr. Steele proposes an electrical ablation procedure."

"What's that?" asked Sophia with a disturbed voice.

"A small hole is drilled through Erick's skull, and a small surgical trocar is moved into the erosion site."

"Wait a minute. What's a trocar?"

"A surgical trocar is a small tubular device with a sharp end that can be moved into position within the brain. When in position, the trocar is replaced with a stainless-steel tubing. Wires are passed through that tubing. The end of the wire is electrically stimulated, damaging the brain tissue around it; it makes those cells incapable of functioning normally."

"How do you know where to place the probe, and where is it located in the brain?"

"These photos tell us where the emotion center is located, and the end of the probe is guided by the same supercomputer using computerized tomography, called a 'CT scan.' Metallic markers are placed on Erick's head beforehand."

Sophia's eyes grew large as an elevated response to what she had heard. She said in a raised voice, "You mean that you propose to destroy some of Erick's brain by burning it? Is that what you are telling me?"

"That is a crude way of putting it, but the answer is somewhat yes. It is more—"

"Jacob, I can't allow that," she interrupted with an alarmed voice. "It sounds barbaric."

"Sophia, it is done all the time. They use the smallest tube possible so they minimize damage to brain tissue between the erosion site and the skull. The blood vessels have already been mapped, so the safest entry possible can be determined. Dr. Steele performs this procedure routinely with patients suffering from advanced Parkinson's disease to stop the shakes and certain forms of epilepsy to arrest seizures. They do this surgical procedure routinely with minimal side effects. Risks from the surgery consists of a mild headache, but the major risk is that we are uncertain that it will work. You see, no one has ever done this before. Therefore, we cannot be certain that it will work. It could be a waste of time."

"How can you tell if it works?"

"I propose to contact Lee through hypnosis and to study Erick's behavior. If I cannot contact Lee and if Erick returns to normal, then I will say it worked. Please understand that there are no guarantees. This is the first time for this surgical eradication of an emotion center. Having said that," Jacob said, "I am hopeful that it will work. Lastly, I know of no other means of saving Erick."

"Wow" was the pretty lady's response. "That statement sounds ominous!"

"I believe that it is. Without this surgery and if Lee takes over, which he will, Erick and/or Lee could spend the rest of his life locked up in a padded room."

"What do you want me to do, Jacob?"

"Without the surgery, there is only a slim chance for Erick to defeat Lee. His nightmares continue. I want you to say yes to this experimental surgery. If successful, Erick would be home within a few days for good, and he could resume his life after a while. I will monitor him for that period, and hopefully you will provide me with feedback during that time too. I will classify this procedure as a treatment of epilepsy, so as not to encumber Erick's livelihood and his future. Further, the cost will be covered by a research grant."

"I can't make that decision. It is Erick's medical problem. I need to talk to him."

"I understand that need, Sophia, but I strongly request that this conversation not occur," Jacob said with a firm voice. "It could arouse Lee, and we could have a real mess on our hands. Remember, Lee hears and sees most of the things Erick does. If we talk to Erick about this, Lee will cause enough trouble that we may not be able to do the surgery."

"Although I am his conservator, I cannot okay experimental brain surgery without Erick's knowing and approving of it. He must know what he's getting into."

Jacob could sympathize with her position, but he also knew Lee could see this as his last opportunity to save himself. Trying to find an amenable solution, Jacob thought quickly and offered, "What if we talk to Erick and tell him the procedure will help him sleep and remove his dependency on the habit-forming Popodine. That statement is true and may not alarm Lee. I am terribly concerned about Lee. I have dealt with him many times, and he continues to be a despicable person capable of anything."

Sophia lurched in her chair.

"I am afraid that Lee will take over Erick, whereas he may not try if he believes that we are attempting to eliminate Erick's dependency on Popodine. In fact, Lee may like that thought, because it will give him easier access to Erick both day and night."

"Okay, Jacob, but I want you to be there and tell him. If he says no, surgery is off."

"I agree."

"Do you want to go see him right now? I can drive us, and we can get back here in time for dinner."

"Yes. Let's do it now. I want to put this behind me; otherwise I will fret about it for days."

Thirty minutes later, Jacob and Sophia drove into the doctor's parking lot at Cedar Ridge and entered Erick's ward. Jacob turned to Sophia and urged her to let him do all the talking. He then asked Sophia to wait inside room C3 as he went to fetch Erick.

He found Erick in the library. "Hi, Erick. Go to room C3. Sophia is in there waiting for you. I'll be there in a minute."

Erick entered the room and hugged Sophia. "What is the occasion, Sophia?" he asked in a puzzled manner.

"I'll let Dr. Gottlieb tell you, Erick. He has results from the test you went through last week."

Gottlieb walked in and asked everyone to sit down. Then he began, "Erick, we have reason to believe, from the testing we did on you, that we can halt your nightly use of Popodine and recurring nightmares. This could be a positive step in your recovery. However, it does require surgery on you."

Sophia remained quiet and looked at Erick's eyes, which were staring at Gottlieb.

"What kind of surgery, Dr. Gottlieb?" Erick said.

"It is brain surgery where we pass a very small needle to the area where the Popodine chemically reacts to numb the brain."

"Are there any side effects such as paralysis and things like that?"

"The brain surgeon has assured me that there will be none. This is very similar to Parkinson's disease treatment, where the surgeon interrupts the nerve path that creates the hand tremors. However, I must tell you that it is experimental, so there are no guarantees. It may not work."

Sophia offered, "Erick, I believe this is a good step in your recovery—no habit-forming knock-out pills at night and no bad dreams. That can only make you stronger. I believe you should consider it."

Erick looked at each person separately and, knowing his predicament, said, "Okay, Dr. Gottlieb, let's do it!"

"Great, Erick! There will be no cost to you or your insurance company. I have located a grant that will pay all expenses because your problem is unique, so the NIH grant will pick up the surgery cost and even provide you with a small amount of cash."

"That's very thoughtful, Dr. Gottlieb. Thanks!"

Sophia stood up and said, "Erick, I am not planning on staying. When Dr. Gottlieb called, I came right over here to be with you when you were making the decision.

I will have to leave too, Erick. I'll see you Tuesday." She bent over and kissed Erick softly, then walked to the door. Jacob followed her out.

Chapter 21: Sophia

"Hey, Jacob, how are the barbecued steaks doing? I am almost through with the salad, and the water for the corn on the cob is ready."

Jacob hollered, "I have another three minutes out here, Sophia, and then I'll bring in the steaks, so start the corn."

They sat in the dining room. Jacob took the opportunity to have lighted candles and soft music. Sophia continued chatter during the dinner, but the subject matter was discontinuous. She was trying hard to forget Erick's problem, and here was Prince Charming sitting opposite her. She felt warm within every time he smiled at her, and he smiled often.

After dinner, Sophia removed an ethnic Irish music CD from her purse and placed it on the rack of the CD player. She retrieved her clogging shoes, placed them on her feet, and waited for Jacob's return. When Jacob returned, the CD player changed to the Irish music with an upbeat tempo. Sophia walked over to the hardwood floor at the edge of the living room and began step dancing. The metal taps on her shoes pounding on the wood floor made a loud, rhythmic beat in perfect synchrony with the music.

Jacob turned to watch her. Her hands were straight down her sides with her palms touching her thighs. Her feet were a blur as they beat out the rhythm. Then her hands formed into a fist as the rhythm continued. The rest of her body was straight and rigid, so only the feet and legs appeared to be moving. She was good, very good.

Jacob watched her turn around in a half circle while still tapping out the beat with her back presented to him. Her hands shifted to her hips with elbows held away from the body. Then with a change in the music, Sophia's hands dropped and her palms placed facing the floor. She continued for the remainder of that song as she moved from one side of the family room to the other, head turning as required by the dance.

When it ended, an exhausted Sophia walked toward Jacob, who now applauded her efforts. "Sophia, you are really great at that—like a professional dancer."

"Thanks, Jacob," she gasped, gulping in air.

"When did you learn how to do that?"

"I started that before Erick became ill, and I have been continuing my class two nights a month. That is my escape therapy."

"You must be as good as the instructor," commented Gottlieb.

"Yes, I am almost as good as he is, but I do not know all of the steps yet."

Jacob was giving her a chance to catch her breath. "I made an apricot sorbet for our dessert and used some apricot brandy in making it. Would you like to try it?"

"Certainly, Jacob. I'll stay here and rest a little."

Jacob had started a small fire in the fireplace, and the firewood crackled as he returned with the sorbet and handed Sophia's dessert to her in a tall, tapered glass. Then he turned down the volume on the CD so they could talk. They each sat on the floor on giant pillows Jacob had retrieved from the side of the room. The sorbet was accompanied by a misty, blue tulip-shaped wine glass of Chardonnay. "This sorbet is heavenly, Jacob. Thank you!"

After the sorbet was consumed, Sophia excused herself to take a quick shower. "I'll be back in a few minutes, Jacob, wearing dry clothes."

When she returned, wearing a low-cut tailored dress, Jacob remarked, "Wow, you look stunning." Then Jacob caught a whiff of perfume that aroused his inner being. "What is that remarkable perfume?"

"It is called Misty Night. Do you like it?"

"Yes. It has a hint of flowers and a faraway aroma. I can't explain it. It's sexy."

"Good! It is supposed to be."

Jacob fetched a bed-sized, fabric-covered foam pad from the closet and threw it on the floor in front of the fire. Sophia joined him on the pad as the conversation continued. Jacob was very careful not to sound like a psychiatrist and Erick's doctor. Sophia was doing everything possible to avoid thinking of Erick or mentioning him.

Although both were contented, there was still a strong visceral attraction between them that kept them from becoming relaxed. However, they were both very comfortable with each other. "Oh, by the way," he said, "I am on call tonight. Jim is out of town, so if an emergency arrives, I may have to leave."

"Well, I hope it doesn't happen."

They lay on the pad, facing one another but not touching while continuing their personal conversation. Sophia thought, *why doesn't he touch me? After all, I am here.*

Finally, Jacob reached out and held her hand. She applied pressure with her grip. Twenty minutes later, the hand touching was still the same, but their positions changed. There were lots of laughs during that time. Sophia couldn't imagine herself doing the same thing with Erick in a hundred years.

"I must tell you, Sophia, that you are truly a lovely woman. It does my heart well to be here beside you." Sophia purred and then did something that changed the evening. She placed both hands around Jacob's face and kissed him lovingly, concupiscently. Jacob responded by kissing her back in a similar manner.

The music changed to classical romance, which fit the upcoming mood.

Jacob began to nibble on her earlobe as lust began to fill them. The flashes of light from the fireplace made her more beautiful than ever as the constantly changing light played decoratively with her face. She continued kissing him, and when Jacob moved away, she pulled him back to her lips for more passionate kisses. His lips found her smooth neckline and kissed it too as he began to explore her body.

"You have too many clothes on," she whispered and began to unbutton his shirt.

"So do you," he said while lying beside her. He reached around her back to unzip her dress. After the dress and shirt were removed, their hands began systematically to explore the other's exposed flesh.

Sophia was almost purring, hoping that time would stand still, that this moment would never end, and the phone wouldn't ring. Jacob unsnapped her bra, exposing her firm breasts. His hands explored her flesh. Her moans let him know he wasn't disappointing her. His lips moved back to her waiting oral cavity.

Sophia began to massage his back, feeling the tightened muscles. Then inexplicably, she began to touch his side softly with the tips of her fingernails. Gooseflesh formed on the skin, and she took delight in feeling it. Her hands moved up to his face and caressed it lovingly, and then she placed a warm, sexy kiss on his open mouth. They yearned for each other.

Now each lay on the pad with the flickering firelight illuminating their near-naked bodies. The music of Debussy played, and neither noticed it directly; it sounded right. Everything was right. Sophia crawled back to the cradle of his arm and torso, and nuzzled his chest with her teeth. Jacob found new areas to explore. His free hand caressed her smooth skin. The process continued until the clothing vanished. Minutes later, it happened—the burst of energy as the two became one, followed by fulfillment, contentment, and then... silence.

A short while later, Sophia began to chuckle and said, "I got lucky— the phone didn't ring." That was no sooner said when the phone rang, and Jacob staggered awkwardly to the phone.

There was a dialogue, and Jacob returned to her side. "Do you have to go?" she asked.

"No, it is all handled now." He brought a large comforter with him and laid it over Sophia; then he crawled under it with her.

Sophia began kissing him again. "Jacob, I never knew that this experience could be so wonderful—I never knew."

"It was equally wonderful for me too. What are we going to do tomorrow?" he asked.

"Let's ad lib, just ad lib."

On Monday morning when Sophia awoke alone in bed, Jacob was downstairs, eating breakfast. She took a quick shower and headed to the aroma of fresh brewed coffee. Jacob handed her a cup of coffee as she entered the kitchen. "I have to leave now, Sophia. Thank you for sharing the most memorable weekend of my life. I loved every minute of it, and that includes our ad lib Sunday."

"Me too, Jacob—me too." Sophia knew that if the surgery was successful, she was stuck with Erick. She couldn't leave him in that situation whether she loved him or not. This weekend with Jacob would likely be their last time together, and therefore his departure for work made the moment very difficult.

Sophia wanted to say something profound that would stay with Jacob forever, even *I love you,* but a lump in her throat kept her from speaking, even if the words were present in her head. Instead, she walked up to Jacob and kissed him lovingly with tears trickling down her cheeks and onto his face. When Jacob stepped back to leave, Sophia observed tears in his eyes too, and she felt certain that this time together meant as much to him.

She walked to the front door with him, squeezing his arm so tightly that her grasp wrinkled his pressed shirt sleeve. He turned and gave her a last kiss, then walked out to his car. She stood there, leaning against the door and watched him drive away. Tears rolled down her cheeks. Her new love was out of her life, but she did have a wonderful memory that would last a lifetime. Then she thought, *Remember this weekend always; it never gets any better than this.*

The drive to work wasn't without great guilt for Jacob. He knew better than to step between a husband and wife, but he had allowed it to happen. He now had to pay the price. He believed that if the surgery was successful, Sophia would be obligated to stay with Erick. He didn't want that. He had placed himself in an awkward situation of hoping the surgery was successful and that to the contrary it would fail. *Don't think that Jacob.* His obligation was to his patient first. He was in a quandary he had created, and his stomach churned. He couldn't control his feelings for Sophia. He had never felt that way about any women before. His torment followed him to work and throughout the day.

Chapter 22: The Escape

Mike and Erick stepped out of the elevator and walked directly to the fifth-floor nurses' station. Erick was told that his room was 524 and that he should put on only the hospital gown and socks, and return to this station. Mike and Erick left and headed to room 524 diagonally opposite the elevator. When they arrived in the room, a folded gown lay on the bed. Mike handed it to Erick and walked back near the door as he waited for Erick to change. Erick did so and handed his clothes to Mike, who dutifully placed them in the closet. Erick was now garbed in only a thin wraparound blue gown with an opening on the backside and hospital socks. He was bald headed after Mike shaved his head before departing to the hospital.

The two men walked back to the nurses' station. Gottlieb was waiting there for Erick. Gottlieb explained the surgery procedure. "Because of hypnosis, you will not feel any pain whatsoever. Do you understand?"

Jacob walked through the double doors as an orderly named Joe walked out. Joe looked at Erick's wristband and said to Mike, "I'll take him now."

Circumstances changed when Erick and Joe were walking down the hallway on the other side of the double doors and making polite talk as they neared the scrub room with no one in view. Joe heard some arguing from Erick and looked at Erick, who was making strange faces.

Joe heard him speak fiendishly. "Get out of here, Erick, or I'll kill you!"

"No, I won't let you."

"I'm in charge now!"

Joe turned and watched as the transformation took place. Lee suddenly grabbed Joe's left wrist, twisted it, and with his hand on Joe's neck slammed Joe's head into the steel door jamb. Joe fell to the floor like a sack of beans, unconscious.

Lee opened the door and dragged Joe into the room, closing the door behind him. He turned and ran out the double doors. He stood there for a moment and saw Mike waiting for the elevator, with his back to him, so he scampered down the women's ward hallway, out of view of Mike while looking for the stairs. When he couldn't locate them, he slipped into a patient's room.

A woman lay sleeping in her bed, and the second bed was unoccupied. Lee noticed a brown wig laying on the dresser, so he grabbed it along with a few hairpins and rubber bands; he returned to the empty bed. He crawled into bed and slipped the wig on letting it hang above the covers. He placed his back to the door, pulling up the covers, pretending to sleep, and listening intently.

Joe, with blood running down his face, struggled to his feet, staggered into the scrub room where doctors were scrubbing, and yelled, "He got away!"

"Who got away?" asked Steele."

"Anderson! He knocked me down and got away."

"Oh my God!" Gottlieb uttered. "Lee is loose." He shouted at the Joe, "Go get big Mike before he leaves the hospital. Hurry!"

Joe staggered out the doors to the elevator, shouting Mike's name. Mike was not there. Joe raced to the stairs.

Jacob turned to Ralph and said, "That was Lee, and he is dangerous and loose. How do we shut down this floor and keep Lee up here until we locate him?"

Steele ran out to the nurses' station and began barking orders. Jacob arrived there with Ralph, saying, "We are looking for a Caucasian male, about thirty-five years, with a shaved head, and he is wearing a hospital gown."

Steele hollered, "Get out the alarm for him. Do not let him leave this floor or the hospital under any circumstances. Call the police and tell them that a mentally unstable patient has gotten away, and we have an emergency."

The nurse started the procedure by first calling the front lobby and the guard down there. She described the man and told him to lockdown all downstair doors. In teams of two, all employees on the floor started a methodical search of every room. A team arrived in Lee's room and noticed two sleeping patients. One nurse looked under the beds and behind the drapes, and the other went to the lavatory. They quickly departed, and Lee gave a deep sigh of relief. He thought about returning to his room to retrieve his clothes. He would have to wait before escaping. There were too many employees in the hallways.

Lee thought, *Mike likely left the hospital, so no one will think about my clothing.* He continued to pretend to be asleep.

Jacob was talking to Ralph at the nurses' station and noticed Joe and Mike were walking toward him. Joe looked at Gottlieb and said, "I got Mike! This's all my fault. You warned me. I wasn't paying att—"

"Let's find Lee," Jacob said, "I mean Anderson. It's my fault. I'm sorry."

Mike said, "I have his clothes here, so he is still wearing his blue gown unless he has stolen someone's clothes."

Steele turned to the nurse, who spoke first.

"Dr. Steele, the police are on the way and will be here momentarily. All first-floor doors are locked, so no one can get in or out without assistance."

Gottlieb turned to Joe. "Go down to the lobby, wait for the police, give them the description of Anderson, and tell them what happened. Tell them Anderson is unarmed but may have stolen something from the hospital. He is dangerous, but they should capture him and bring him to surgery on the fifth floor. Do not shoot him! We will be waiting here. We will begin another search and work our way downstairs."

Lee could hear sirens from his bed near the window. He had to get out of there. He took the rubber bands and turned the wig into one with a long ponytail. Then he crept to the door and peered up and down the hall. When the hallway was clear, he headed toward the nurses' station, which was situated at the intersection of the two long hallways.

He peeked around the corner and saw Mike and Gottlieb talking. He needed to get by them to locate his clothes. Further, he assumed that the police would arrive momentarily. When Jacob and Mike entered the double doors into surgery, Lee walked to room 524, looking for his clothes. Only his shoes remained.

He slipped into the adjacent room. The male occupant was preoccupied with the television and didn't notice him. He located some clothes, which were too large, but the pants had a belt. He donned them and darted across the hall to the stairs.

Having arrived at the fourth floor unseen, Lee started down the stairs to the third floor, still buttoning his oversized shirt, when he heard male voices. He looked over the railing two floors below him and saw the blue coats of police officers, who were jogging up the stairs.

He pivoted and returned to the fourth-floor hallway. He headed to the end of the hallway without being seen. When he entered the room, he heard voices and looked around the corner, but no one was there. The source of the voices was the television. He walked over to the windows and peered out. He tried opening one, but it was sealed shut.

Lee crept over to the door to peer down the hall; one male and two female nurses were approaching him, about five rooms away. He returned to the window where he could see the area below near the front entrance. Six police cars and two motorcycles were parked near the sidewalk. A large, dark-blue and white, rectangular canvas canopy extended thirty feet in front of the door to protect patients and visitors when entering or leaving the hospital from the weather. It was a chance for him to escape.

In examining escape possibilities, Lee noticed outside the concrete building that there was a ledge extending over to the canopy. If he could manage to work his way along the four-inch-wide ledge to above the canopy, he could jump and let the canvas canopy break his fall.

He would have to break the window, but the sound of breaking glass would surely alarm the search crew. He could muffle the sound by closing the door. Lee crept over to the door and slowly closed it. Then he increased the volume of the television and returned to the window. A police officer was talking on his car radio. He certainly would hear the breaking glass, so he had to wait.

Two minutes later, the officer walked under the canopy. Lee gave him a minute to reenter the building, then picked up a metal chair and smashed it against the window, breaking the glass. Using the back of the chair as a glass breaker, Lee passed it along the side of the window, freeing the frame of most glass splinters to gain access to the narrow ledge. He kicked the glass pieces with his shoes against the wall under the drapes to hide them and closed the drapes. He returned to the television and decreased the volume, then again opened the door ever so slowly, leaving it half open to obscure him as he made his way back to the window.

Lee exited through the window, stepping on the ledge with his toes pointed away from one another and his hands and chest flattened against the side of the building; he inched toward the building entrance. Each step was dangerous on the narrow ledge as the wind whipped his baggy clothing. One gust caught the wig and sent it spiraling earthward.

His purchase was only a shoe width. He moved deliberately. Progress was slow. Acrophobia bothered him, so he kept his eyes straight ahead, staring at a small wall that jutted out about six feet to his left. Fortunately, the ledge followed the wall, so there was a good chance of him making the right-angle corner without being seen. His center of gravity wasn't where he wanted, so he placed his feet on the outermost portion of the ledge and leaned into the building. *If only I could get around the corner.*

He inched forward as fear consumed him. His toes tingled. The wind tugged.

He finally reached the wall protruding outward to his left and felt queasy. It was emotionally impossible for him to step across an abyss to make the ninety-degree corner. The overhang of his heels from the ledge made him feel unstable since he had two orthogonal walls to touch. His center of gravity always seemed to pull him over the edge. His left calf began to cramp.

This is not a good idea. He couldn't do it; he had to get back to the broken window. He began his return, but now his legs screamed at him to get out of there, and his head was oriented in the wrong direction. Gravity pulled at him, especially when he glanced down to the ground some fifty feet below.

Meanwhile, the three nurses entered the waiting room and saw nothing unusual. They didn't notice a drape moving from the wind and entering through the broken window. They too were on alert, and when one turned to exit the room, a shoe fractured a broken piece of glass, which had bounced almost to the door when Lee fractured the window. Her heightened attention caused her to stop and examine her shoe.

"Broken glass," she said to the other two nurses, who had already exited the room but returned. She called the male nurse and pointed to the broken glass in the sole of her shoe. He went to the left side of the window and stepped on many broken pieces of glass before arriving. He pulled open the drape a small amount to peek out and saw the broken-out window. Looking out the missing window, he observed Lee trying to make his escape, facing away from him.

He returned the drape to the way it had been and asked the two female nurses to call the fifth-floor nurses' station and inform them that the patient was out on the ledge on the fourth floor west wing. The male nurse departed, running down the stairs seeking the police.

When the call came in, Jacob was there by the phone. The nurse hurriedly told him Anderson had been seen on the fourth floor on a narrow ledge outside the building. Jacob sprinted to the stairs and descended them four steps at a time, holding the railing, with Mike following. He darted from the stairs. The head nurse saw him and pointed to the end of the hall. Jacob, now breathing hard, hurried in that direction with Mike behind him.

The nurse who remained behind walked over to Jacob and whispered, "He is trying to get back to the room now. There is a corner out there he couldn't get around. He has not seen us and doesn't know we are here. His head is facing the opposite direction."

Jacob held his finger to his lips to get everyone quiet and peeked around the drape.

Lee tried to turn his head to face the broken window, but he couldn't manage it. Still struggling with acrophobia, he felt that when he tipped his head back to rotate it, he would fall. He had no recourse but to return without looking. His body ached from the stress he had undergone, and his fingers became numb. He inched his way back toward the room on cramping legs.

"Mike, I believe you should be the one to catch him when he reenters the room. If we need to talk to Lee, let me do the talking. You stand by the right side of the window, and I will try to watch from the left side of the drapes." Jacob turned to the nurses and held a finger across his lips. One nurse went out of the room to warn those getting close with a finger in front of her lips; she pointed to the room.

Lee continued to inch his way back to the window, now only two feet away. A gust of wind nearly dislodged him, and although his toes tingled from the event, he regained his balance and crept closer. His shoe cracked a broken piece of glass, so he judged he was now almost in reach of the window. The door to the room was open, and temporary low pressure sucked a drape out through the window. It snapped a little in the wind, startling Lee.

Lee wanted to hold something stable to steady himself, but he couldn't see anything. Even a drape would work. He could only hear it snapping. He inched his return. The drape was now outside the window. Lee stretched out to grab the window frame. His fingers touched the aluminum frame, but his fingers were now too numb to determine whether he had a secure grasp. He began to pull himself into the room when his hand slipped.

Lee lost his balance and fell.

Mike, as quick as a cobra, grabbed Lee's right wrist with only his right hand. Lee felt a pronounced jerk as his fall was halted by Mike's one-handed grab, which nearly pulled Mike out of the window. Now dangling outside of the fourth-floor window, Lee heard a pronounced scream from above. Down below, a pedestrian walking to the entrance looked up when he heard the screams. He stared in disbelief seeing a man dangling above.

Mike hollered in pain. When he fell to his knees, the combined forces caused him to fall forward, and a large triangular chunk of razor-sharp glass, still affixed to the window frame, drove into his abdomen, cutting his abdominal muscles. Gottlieb rushed over to Mike and wrapped his arms around his chest, placing his feet against the wall. All of Mike from the waist upward was outside the window, and the combined weight pulling him outward. Only Lees strong thighs and cut abdominal muscles kept him from following Lee.

Mike tried to straighten and pull Lee in, but in so doing, he drove the broken glass deeper into his abdomen.

Blood squirted against the wall.

Gottlieb held Mike mightily to keep him in the room. A heavyset nurse came over and grabbed Mike's shoulders.

Mike screamed in pain.

Lee continued dangling and cussing as Mike with both strong arms began to lift Lee back to the window. Tears flowed freely from his eyes, pain writhing through his abdomen. Slowly Mike straightened his body and began to pull Lee into the room. Jacob had a grasp of Lee's underarms, and while he pulled him upward; blood flowed down the wall.

Just then a puffing police officer ran into the room to witness Mike in action. Lee managed to get his left hand on Mike's wrist. Mike continued to reel Lee in by straightening his knees and uncoiling his mighty body.

With a final flurry, Lee entered the room, landing on top of Mike and Gottlieb. Mike cried out in pain again, with the triangular broken piece of broken glass buried within him and blood running onto the floor.

The officer quickly rolled Lee over so he was facedown and cuffed his wrists behind his back.

Mike rolled over onto his back, moaning while blood oozed through his shirt from his belly. He called to Gottlieb, "I have broken glass inside me."

The room was chaotic as the officer was on his communicator, and nurses shouted orders. Within minutes, an orderly brought two gurneys into the room as Gottlieb barked orders to get Mike to the Emergency Room immediately.

Lee was still swearing in Russian as the police officer and orderly picked him up and laid him on the second gurney. Lee glared while lying on his cuffed wrists.

"Doctor," said the officer, "we have orders to stay with this man until discharged, and that includes the surgery."

"That's fine, officer," offered Gottlieb. "We do not want to go through this again. We are taking him up to the fifth floor now, and we will begin surgery shortly. I will sedate him when we get there."

Lee lay on the gurney, glaring alternately at both the officer and Jacob. His tongue remained silent.

Chapter 23: Brain Surgery

An orderly wheeled Lee into surgery as Drs. Steele, Beckmann, and Chapman were already scrubbing. The orderly left the room, but the officer stayed. Shortly thereafter, a nurse appeared, examined Lee's wristband, withdrew a filled hypodermic syringe, and injected it into Lee's rump. She turned to the officer and said, "This tranquilizer will calm him down in a few minutes."

Lee now changed his position on the gurney and began to relax.

Ten minutes later, a very calm Lee lay on his side in surgery as Dr. Steele walked in, scrubbed and ready for surgery. Dr. Beckmann had already placed the metal markers on Lee's head. Steele spoke, "Okay, officer, you may uncuff him now. You may stay here if you like, but you will have to scrub and wear a lead-lined coat or watch in the next room through that leaded window over there."

The officer noticed that the only door out of the room was near the window. "I'll watch, Doctor! Thank you."

"Officer, you do not have to worry about him running away now, so just relax."

"Jacob, it is time to hypnotize Lee." Steele announced.

Gottlieb went over to a very upset Lee, who believed he was now incapable of being hypnotized. "Lee, it is time to hypnotize you."

"Like hell."

"It's for your own good so that you will feel no pain. That is the primary reason for it."

"What do you mean by pain?"

"The surgeons must drill a hole in your skull and then pass a probe deep into your brain. You will feel every bit of this excruciating pain as he pushes the probe into the brain, tearing brain cells. You will not be able to move. Your head and body will be tied down. It will be a hundred times more pain than the worst headache of your life. You will not be able to do anything except deal with the pain as best as possible and scream. If I hypnotize you, you will feel no pain whatsoever and still remain aware of what is going on."

Lee remained quiet so Jacob took that as consent and began. Three minutes later, he had finished hypnotizing Lee and informed him that he would feel no pain and asked to speak to Erick. "You don't need him," Lee said.

Thinking fast, Jacob said, "Oh, but I do, because if he feels pain, you will too, so I have to say the same thing to him." Lee consented, and Jacob greeted Erick for the first time that day. He informed Erick of the proceedings and that he would feel no pain whatsoever. Erick understood and then consented to Lee's return. "Okay, Lee—remember, you will hear sounds, but you will not feel any pain. You will remain alert throughout the surgery." Lee indicated that he understood, so Jacob stepped away from the operating table and headed out of the room.

Lee was placed on a special table, which was part of the CT scanner system, whereby they could do their surgery and see the results almost instantaneously. Both surgeons wore heavy, lead-lined coats as they maneuvered Lee under the scanner. The table contained a circular steel ring with four flathead, plastic bolts in it. Steele carefully positioned Lee's head inside the ring and then brought the bolts into contact with Lee's skull. The ring was firmly attached to the table so when the bolts were tightened, Lee's head was securely affixed. Lee's wrists, elbows, waist, knees, and feet were then fastened to the table, and then a nurse placed three more straps around the chest and abdomen. Lee was now prevented from any head movement and other body movements. All he could move were his jaw, fingers, and toes.

Ralph Steele now placed additional metallic markers on Lee's head as Wilhelm walked into the surgery and sat at the computer about ten feet from Lee. He too had scrubbed and was wearing sterile operating room attire and a lead-lined coat. His computer terminal and keyboard were placed within a thin, sterile plastic bag. Wilhelm could operate the keyboard through the bag. Within seconds, he had the CT at the ready position and had the images collected from two weeks earlier on the monitor. Then he said, "Dr. Steele, I am ready."

Ralph had a speaker set up outside the room so Jacob could hear what he was saying. "Okay, Jacob, here is where we are. We are in the calibration stage. We must get Erick's head precisely located under the scanner so his head position will conform to the CT images collected a few weeks ago. It could take Wilhelm and me about twenty minutes before his position is perfect. Then I will have to drill the hole through the skull." Lee blinked. "Following that, we need you to access Lee. Okay?"

Jacob nodded. He wasn't looking forward to the twenty minutes of wearing a lead-lined coat anyway, so he was pleased to remain outside the surgery room.

Time passed as Wilhelm, Chapman, and Ralph continued to reposition Lee's head in miniscule amounts. Lee remained motionless during this period.

Fifteen minutes later, Steele said, "Okay, Jacob, we are ready for you. It is now up to you to get Lee to respond."

Jacob entered the room after donning the heavy leaded vest, manipulated over his torso by Helen, and new sterile gloves, a mask, and a cap.

Jacob began to communicate with Lee. Lee was in a sleepy, almost incoherent state. Jacob talked quietly to Lee because other conversations were taking place between the two surgeons. "Lee, this is Dr. Gottlieb. Do you hear me?"

"Yes, I hear you, Doc."

"Did you feel the drill?"

"No, Doc!"

"We are going to move the probe into place, and you will feel nothing. Do you understand?"

"Yes, Doc."

Jacob nodded to Ralph, and the trocar moved inward about two centimeters. "Do you see the tip, Wilhelm?"

"Yes, Dr. Steele."

"Wilhelm, I see no blood—we are ready for the electrode. It is time to replace the trocar with a stainless-steel tubing."

Dr. Chapman removed the tubing from its sterile wrap and handed it to Steele. Then the long wire was threaded through to the end of the tubing and connected to the electrical power supply placed on a roll-up cart. "I will advance the tubing into place. Dr. Beckmann, tell me when you see it."

The doctors stepped back, and the CT snapped more x-rays. "I see it, Dr. Steele. You are in perfect position to begin."

Ralph stepped over to Jacob and whispered to him, "I want you to keep Lee talking about anything."

"Okay, Ralph," Jacob whispered back. "Lee, this is Dr. Gottlieb again. Do you feel any pain?"

"No Doc, none."

"Good! We now need you to do some tasks for us. I want you to move your left index finger." Lee was finally in a compliant mood, and the left index finger flexed. Jacob nodded to Ralph, and Ralph turned on the power supply. Then he tested it, and a barely audible zapping sound was heard. Jacob began his conversation with Lee, and Ralph Steele started the erosion procedure. "Lee, what was your sister's name?"

"Her name was Elsa," he said in a monotone voice.

Infrequently, Jacob switched to Erick to assure him all was well, but he quickly returned to Lee, keeping him in dialogue. The process continued for nearly twenty minutes. Jacob began to hear and see a difference in Lee. "What do you feel, Lee?"

"I feel lightheaded, Doc. It is getting hard to think. I cannot focus."

"Lee, what is the name of your sister?"

"Her n ... a ... m ... e is El ... sa." The slow conversation between Jacob and Lee continued.

"Dr. Steele, advance two millimeters and rotate counterclockwise slowly about 45 degrees." The CT snapped another image.

"Okay, I am starting now." The conversation between the two doctors continued with frequent interruptions by the CT. Simultaneously, the conversation between Lee and Jacob continued.

"Doc, I cannot see. I am blind," Lee said, speaking very slowly.

"Open your eyes, Lee. You are fine. We are not near the optic center."

"Doc, I can see now, but I cannot think. My head seems fuzzy. I do not know what is happening to me. Where am I?"

"You are in surgery in a local hospital."

"Oh!"

"Okay, Wilhelm, take a CT image and inform me where to move next."

The CT buzzed a little. Beckmann said, "You are almost there. We need to go inward a last three millimeters and then rotate from two o'clock to five o'clock."

"I am beginning now."

"Doc, I'm feeeeeeel … ing v … e … ry funny. I a … m float … ing. I c … a … n … n … o … t th … ink at all." Lee's conversation was drawn out and very slow. Lee's voice was higher pitched than normal and very faint. Then they heard the last of Lee when he said, "I a … m fe … e … ling f … u … n!" Then silence.

"Lee, Lee, can you hear me?" asked Gottlieb, but there was no answer. "Lee, if you can hear me, move your finger." There was no finger motion.

"Ralph, I cannot connect with Lee."

"Jacob, we are done here. Try communicating with Erick while I finish up here."

"Erick, I know you are there. Speak to me!" There was total silence from Erick as Gottlieb waited. Jacob tried again and again, but there was no response from Erick either.

Wilhelm spoke. "Dr. Steele, the erosion is complete now."

"Very good, Wilhelm. I will irrigate and close." As Jacob continued to make contact with Erick, Ralph withdrew the tools of the surgery, irrigated the wound, and vacuumed out the debris. Then Dr. Chapman began stitching the scalp.

"I am through now, Jacob. I am going to unclamp Erick's head. Since he is so relaxed, I need you to hold his head in position until I get the equipment out of the way." Although he didn't say anything, Jacob became concerned as he held Erick's head at the jaws. His inability to reach Erick bothered him. The braces were removed, and the nurse untied the remaining ties and clamps. She then brought in the gurney and said, "Dr. Gottlieb, you will have to revive him in the recovery room so we can prepare for the next surgery."

Jacob followed the gurney. He hadn't expected this, nor did he want it to occur. Once in the recovery room, Jacob looked at Erick. Erick's eyes were open, which was unusual for Erick. Jacob's stomach churned as he wondered what to do next. This had never happened to him before. He pulled up a chair and rotated Erick's head so it was facing him. "Erick, Erick, can you hear me?" Again, there was total silence as Erick appeared in a dreamworld and not in a hypnotic state.

For the next ten minutes, Jacob continued to try reaching Erick without any sign or signal whatsoever. Then he wondered, *What if I am dealing with Lee and he is incapable of transferring me to Erick?* "Lee or Erick, at the count of three, you will awake and feel good. One, you are beginning to wake up. Two, you are almost awake. And three—"

Erick's eyes fluttered a little, and he stared at Gottlieb. His mouth twitched as if he were trying to speak. Then nothing happened. Again, he moved his mouth, and he spoke softly. "How did I do?"

"You were terrific, Erick. I believe Lee is gone for good. You are in the recovery room, and the surgery is now complete. This is a big day for you, Erick. How do you feel?"

"Right now, I feel no pain, but I do feel a little light-headed."

"Do you have a headache?"

"No, I just feel light-headed."

"Try to get some sleep, Erick; I will get Dr. Steele and go tell Sophia."

Jacob waited patiently for Steele. When Steele walked in, he asked. "How is Erick, Jacob?"

"He seems to be just fine. He did say that he felt light-headed. Other than that, he seems fine."

"That is to be expected."

Steele reached down and shook Erick's shoulder. Erick opened his eyes. "Erick, I am Dr. Steele, your neurosurgeon. How are you feeling?"

"Okay," said Erick. "I remember meeting you before the testing."

"Oh, that's right, Erick. I wanted to let you know that the red marks around your head will go away in a couple of days, so do not worry about them." Steele withdrew his rubber reflex hammer and tapped Erick a few places on his body. "Erick, you are looking very good, but do not get out of bed and follow the nurse's orders. Do you understand?"

"Yes, I understand."

On Saturday near noon, Gottlieb walked into Erick's room. Sophia was seated near him after the police officer had checked her for weapons. Erick was already dressed in the new clothing Sophia had purchased for him, and his smile lit up the room. "I cannot believe this day is finally here. Imagine, I'm going home."

Jacob looked at Sophia and smiled, saying, "Good morning, Sophia." Sophia looked away and did not answer.

"That's certainly the case, Erick." There was a pause. "Sophia, would you please leave the room for a while? I must examine Erick one last time under hypnosis. I will come and get you when I have completed my examination."

Sophia exited the room and walked down the long hallway to the waiting room.

"Okay, Erick, I need to hypnotize you one more time before you go home." Erick sat on the edge of the bed, and Gottlieb brought him into that altered state of consciousness.

After talking to Erick in that state, Jacob said, "Lee, I want to talk to you." There was no response, so Gottlieb became forceful. "Lee, I know that you are there—speak to me." Gottlieb tried every trick in the book with no reaction from Erick's eyes, mouth, or other parts of his anatomy.

A smile crossed Jacob's face as he brought Erick back to awareness. Erick arrived quickly. "Erick, did you hear me asking for Lee?"

"Yes, I did, but I didn't sense his presence as in the past."

"Thank you, Erick. On the count of three, you will wake up feeling as good as before. One, two, three!"

Erick smiled. "How did I do?"

"Wonderful, Erick, wonderful!"

Gottlieb walked to the door and turned toward Erick. "Erick, it will be a few minutes before you can leave. I have to sign a few dismissal papers." Hunter was standing at the door.

Jacob walked out of the room and asked Hunter to join Erick for a short while. Jacob stuck his head back in the room and said, "Erick, it appears that a friend has come to visit you. Talk to him while I am filling out your paperwork."

Erick looked up as Hunter Tripp walked into the room.

"Hi, Erick. Congratulations. I heard that you are going home, so I came over to wish you well."

"Thanks, Doc. Yeah, it looks like it in a few minutes."

Jacob was sitting outside beside the officer listening intently when he heard Erick say, "Doc." Erick never said "Doc"; only Lee did. He tapped the police officer, and they both stood.

Then Hunter, unexpectedly addressing Erick in Russian, said, "What's the first thing you will do?"

Erick answered in Russian, "I am planning on driving Erick's car around and enjoying my freedom." Then Lee realized his blunder and sprang to the door to be met by Jacob and the officer.

Jacob lowered his shoulder and drove him to the floor, with the officer lying on top of Lee too. Lee cursed them in Russian and tried to throw punches.

"Okay, officer, let's roll him over onto his stomach."

Lee thrashed and fought against them. They managed to get him facedown with Hunter's help too by keeping the legs together and off of the floor to prevent a purchase. Within seconds, a nurse rushed in with a prepared tranquilizer and injected the struggling Lee in his buttocks through his pants. A few minutes later, Lee lay quietly on the floor.

"Officer, a special crew will arrive shortly and return Mr. Anderson to the Cedar Ridge Hospital. They handle people like this all the time. Plus, he is tranquilized. You do not need to go with them."

"Thanks, Doctor. I'll head back to the office when they arrive."

"Thank you for your help, Officer Martin."

"Hunter, you saved me again. Thank you for coming over as requested. I appreciate it, and Sophia does too, although she doesn't know it yet. It now appears that Lee will be around for a long while. Further, you will not need me to talk to him in the future, but Marina, like Erick, may be gone forever."

Jacob patted Hunter on the back, turned, and headed down the hallway to see Sophia. He entered the waiting room. Sophia stared at the wall, her head in another world oblivious of Jacob's presence.

"Hi," said Jacob.

She looked up with a jerk and managed a smile. Jacob imagined the inner torment she was going through. He was uncertain whether what he was about to tell her was good or bad news.

Sophia stood up, and Jacob pulled her down onto the chair again; he sat next to her. Holding her hand, he tried to speak, and nothing happened. Sophia doled out a quizzical gaze.

Then Jacob almost whispered, "Sophia, Erick is not going home with you."

"He's—he's not?" she murmured.

"No, Sophia. Erick is returning to Cedar Ridge Hospital. That wasn't Erick. That was Lee in the room, pretending to be Erick. He is on his way back to Cedar Ridge right now."

Then Jacob almost whispered, "I have very bad news for you. Erick is gone, probably forever. I failed you, and I am so sorry. Dr. Hanford was correct. There were too many variables. I tried, but I failed the ultimate test of saving your husband and my patient. I failed!"

Jacob looked at the floor. Sophia placed both hands beside his face and rotated his head until their eyes met.

Sophia stood up and pulled him to his feet. Then, using both hands, she pulled him close, and they embraced. She wrapped her left hand behind his head and the other around his back. Their foreheads touched. Then she said softly while still touching, "Thank you for trying so hard."

Then holding his hand against her ribs, she said, "Come on, Jacob, there is nothing more we can do here. We have a new set of circumstances. Let's go; we'll just ad lib!"

Acknowledgments

This novel was stimulated by the writings of Michael Crichton, specifically *Jurassic Park*. Dr. Crichton had a fantastic ability to start with established scientific facts, add his creative concepts, weave these into a fictional 'fact,' and then create a credible story line.

This novel uses established facts and interlaces them with the author's ideas, which are entirely fantasy. The views expressed herein are my own. I alone am responsible for whatever factual errors might exist in this manuscript.

9 781664 151246